THE TWICE-WANTED WITCH

By Katie Hallahan

THE MCKENNA ELLERBECK SERIES

The Twice-Sold Soul
The Twice-Wanted Witch

THE TWICE-WANTED WITCH

THE McKENNA ELLERBECK SERIES: BOOK 2

KATIE HALLAHAN

orbitbooks.net

orbitworks.net

Copyright © 2026 by Katie Hallahan

Cover design by Alexia E. Pereira
Cover illustration by Elizabeth Peiró
Cover copyright © 2026 by Hachette Book Group, Inc.
Author photograph by Katie Hallahan

Orbit
Hachette Book Group
1290 Avenue of the Americas
New York, NY 10104
orbitbooks.net
orbitworks.net

First Edition: January 2026

Orbit is an imprint of Hachette Book Group.
The Orbit name and logo are registered trademarks of Little, Brown Book Group Limited.

The publisher is not responsible for websites (or their content) that are not owned by the publisher.

The Hachette Speakers Bureau provides a wide range of authors for speaking events. To find out more, go to hachettespeakersbureau.com or email HachetteSpeakers@hbgusa.com.

Orbit books may be purchased in bulk for business, educational, or promotional use. For information, please contact your local bookseller or the Hachette Book Group Special Markets Department at special.markets@hbgusa.com.

Library of Congress Cataloging-in-Publication Data
Names: Hallahan, Katie author
Title: The twice-wanted witch / Katie Hallahan.
Description: First edition. | New York, NY : Orbit, 2025. | Series: The Mckenna Ellerbeck series ; book 2
Identifiers: LCCN 2025027569 | ISBN 9780316580212 trade paperback | ISBN 9780316580205 ebook
Subjects: LCGFT: Witch fiction | Fantasy fiction | Romance fiction | Novels | Fiction
Classification: LCC PS3608.A548247 T86 2025
LC record available at https://lccn.loc.gov/2025027569

ISBNs: 9780316580205 (ebook), 9780316580212 (print on demand)

For Mom and Dad

*For showing me what unending love and
unhesitating support look like*

For never once not believing in me and my dreams

*. . . And for never being anywhere near as
complicated as McKenna's parents!*

SUPERNATURAL FAMILIES OF ARCADIA COMMONS

Witches

*denotes Witches Council member

Bellerieve: Water magic, blue-green
- Jefferson Bellerieve (deceased), m. Abigail "Abby" Zichenko Bellerieve (generalist)
  - Dorian Bellerieve
  - Brooke Bellerieve Luppino (cousin/adopted daughter), m. Lucca Luppino

Blackwood: Plant magic, green
- Hilary Blackwood, m. Steve Sands Blackwood (mental magic) (deceased)
  - Aspen Blackwood, m. Marjorie Decatur Blackwood (herbalist)
    - Ash Blackwood
    - Rose Blackwood

Ellerbeck/Younger: Summoning/binding magic, gold
- Wendy Younger Ellerbeck, m./d. John Ellerbeck (mundane)
    - McKenna Ellerbeck★
    - Cameron Ellerbeck
- Louisa Younger, m. Alice Howard Younger (generalist)

Harwell: Mental magic, silver
- Karen Harwell Phillips, m. Tobias Phillips (luck magic) (deceased)
- Douglas Harwell★, m. Helen Jackson Harwell (empathy magic)
    - Jacqueline "Jackie" Harwell (deceased)
    - Thomas "Tom" Harwell

Lemaire: Portal magic, blue
- Laurent Lemaire★, m. Marie-Jeanne Renaudin (deceased)
    - Armand Lemaire, m. Claudia Brunet (illusion magic)
        - Sebastien "Bastien" Lemaire
        - Celine Lemaire
        - Adrienne "Adri" Lemaire
    - Andre Lemaire
    - Aurelien Lemaire
    - Adele Lemaire★

O'Brien: Fire magic, red
- George O'Brien★, m. Hailey Bell O'Brien (generalist)
    - Danielle O'Brien
    - Trent O'Brien

Perez: Dream magic, white
- Sofia Perez*, m. Emilio Navarro Perez (enchantment) (deceased)
  - Mateo Perez
  - Mariposa "Mari" Perez (deceased)

Phillips: Luck magic, copper
- Tobias Phillips (deceased), m. Karen Harwell Phillips (mental magic)
  - Simon Phillips
  - Winnie Phillips
  - Natalie Phillips
  - Hugo Phillips

Werewolves

Luppino
- Giovanni "Gio" Luppino, m. Mariella Quintos Luppino (human)
  - Lucca Luppino (alpha werewolf), m. Brooke Bellerieve Luppino (water magic)
  - Leonora "Leo" Luppino Pallas (human), m. Alexander "Alex" Pallas (deceased)
    - Griffin Pallas
  - Teodore "Teddy" Luppino (werewolf)

Other pack members

Christopher "Chris" Miller
Elle Bankston
Parker Carlisle

Fae

Trevan Stonehill (satyr)
Pip (dryad)
Preston Chang (half Fae, leanan sidhe)
Astrid Bramble (half Fae, cait sidhe)

Demons

Remiel "Remi" Blake, Archdemon of Desire and Madness
Forneus, Archdemon of Desire (deceased)
Saranthiel, Archdemon of Madness (deceased)

THE TWICE-WANTED WITCH

Chapter 1
Happy Solstice

It was snowing inside the library.

The perfect light snowfall sprinkled down from the ceiling, flakes glittering in the lantern-style lights in the Arcadia Commons branch of the Uncommon Collection. It had always been, to me, one of the most magical places in town. Gleaming hardwood floors, long tables with marble inlays, lantern-style sconces on the walls and fancy chandeliers above, all lit by magic. And, of course, shelves upon shelves of magical texts. The fact that it was connected to branches in other locations via permanent portals just made it all the more extraordinary; the dedication to shared knowledge and open access for everyone, across borders and distances, represented everything a supernatural community should be.

Tonight, the sense of warmth and magic and inclusion was at its peak. The illusory snow drifting down, each tiny flake holding just a whisper of winter cold, dissipating without any real damp or lasting chill, added to the cozy aesthetic that made the event feel so cheerful and welcoming. All the charming parts of the winter season and none of its drawbacks.

The charm was only amplified by the horrible conditions outside. The drive over had been slightly treacherous, and the hurried walk from the parking lot to the door had left me thinking I should've worn boots instead of heels. But I had kind of a lot riding on looking the part at this Solstice Ball—my first major event back in Arcadia Commons in ten years, where I, McKenna Ellerbeck, was not only actually invited but a guest of honor, and where I had no plans to end the night with a demon battle (fingers crossed). It wasn't every day the prodigal pariah returned *and* got promoted to the Witches Council to boot.

To that end, my best friend and my plus-one for the evening, Leo Pallas, had insisted on dress shopping earlier that week, so we were both wearing "dresses that slayed." Though she wasn't herself supernatural in any way, being from a family of werewolves put her in the know. So, with her in a knee-length, bright-red, lace-and-velvet cocktail dress and me in a long, metallic gold gown with a slit up one side, very little back, and only slightly more front, we were both plenty chilly after our brief stint outside.

"Hair and makeup check!" Leo said after we handed off our coats at the door. "You're good. Me?"

"Not a hair out of place," I confirmed. "The green really complements the dress, by the way. Very festive choice." Leo's dark hair, currently chin length, had highlights whose color changed monthly.

"Gotta keep it current. Shall we?"

"We shall." We hooked arms and entered the enchantingly enchanted ballroom. "Thanks again for coming with me. I get why my mom and Cam weren't so into it, but it's nice to not be on my own here."

"Anytime—you know I'm here for Team Mickey. Also, always down for a reason to get out of the house for adult company and a break from single-mom-dom. The fancy dresses and free drinks don't hurt, either," Leo said. As awesome as her four-year-old son Griffin was, and as much as I was enjoying getting to be Aunt Mickey, he was still a four-year-old and had all the manic energy that comes with that age. "Wow, they go all out for this, huh?"

I gazed at the glimmering snowflakes in the air and smiled. "They sure do."

"I haven't been to something this fancy and flush with magic since Cam's prom," Leo remarked.

"How have I not yet seen pictures of that?" I asked. "It's still weird you dated my little brother, but I absolutely deserve to see his awkward prom photos!"

Leo shrugged. "He probably burned his copies, but my mom's got them somewhere. Ask her next time you're over." She grinned, nudging me with her elbow. "Speaking of, there's *your* prom date. And he even wore the same tux!"

Sure enough, Bastien Lemaire was here, wearing a sharply tailored tuxedo and chatting with a group of local witches. Somewhere inside, eighteen-year-old McKenna's heart stuttered when she saw how much more handsome he'd become. On the outside, I cleared my throat. "No cummerbund this time," I noticed.

"Yeah, he traded it in for biceps," Leo said, prompting a laugh from me. "Knew you'd noticed."

"You have successfully proven I'm not blind. Drinks?"

"Drinks. Did you also notice you match?" she asked. I steered us toward one of the bars set up along the edges of the room.

"Match?"

"Yeah, his vest has a gold tone, like your dress. Not matchy-matchy, just enough to look nice next to it."

I glanced back over—she was right, his vest had a subdued gilded pattern, along with his lapels. "Leo, are you trying to tell me to hit on my grieving ex?"

"Maaaybe. Two proseccos, please," she ordered.

"That is a *terrible* idea."

"Why, because of the whole his-wife-was—"

"Yes, because of the whole his-*fiancée*-recently-died thing," I interrupted before she could possibly say more than the college-age witch working the bar should hear. Officially, Mariposa Perez had died in the sudden ballroom collapse at their wedding *before* the ceremony had taken place.

The bartender gave us a strange look but wisely just kept pouring and handed us the glasses.

"Thanks!" I passed him a big tip, taking the glass, and we walked a few steps away. "Watch what you're saying!" I hissed in a whisper. The truth was far worse: After marrying him to gain access to his portal magic, "Mari" had revealed herself to be Saranthiel, the Archdemon of Madness. With a whole lot of help and by tearing down most of Arcadia Commons' anti-demon barrier, I'd killed Saranthiel and granted her crown to my other ex, Remi Blake. Remi had already been the Arch-demon of Desire, and I hadn't seen a lot of her since basically forcing her to take on a second crown.

"I wasn't gonna say what *really* happened," Leo replied, giving me a look.

"Sorry, I'm . . . let's just say it's been made clear I'm not supposed to go talking about that night in public," I explained.

"Is that so." She rested a hand on one hip. "Was it just Laurent or the whole Council giving that order?"

I huffed. "Is there any difference? But yeah, the whole Council. Zipping up the truth and stashing it away like always."

"Mm-hm. And you're sure you still want to join up?" she asked.

"I can't change them from the outside. This way, I've at least got a chance," I replied, then glanced at her. "Right?"

"If anyone can, I believe you can, Mickey. Even if it's just 'cause you're too damn stubborn not to." She grinned and clinked her glass to mine. "To bringing down the system from the inside."

"Something like that. Cheers!"

Truthfully, I'd been asking myself that question a lot lately, ever since Laurent had offered me a seat on the Council. More so since I'd finally said yes. The witches of Arcadia Commons were very much made up of the haves and the have-nots, and they tended to take charge when it came to running things in town. Events like this were open to all supernaturals, one reason I'd always loved them when I was younger . . . but looking around the room now, I saw that this one was definitely witch-centric. Remi, the only demon who was technically invited, was not exactly welcome, and it looked like she'd chosen not to attend. At least, I didn't see her go-to male or female forms among the attendees. Lucca and his wolfpack weren't attending on account of Lucca's wife, Brooke, having been explicitly uninvited since she'd been Saranthiel's thrall, and only a handful of Fae, part Fae, and the mundane but in the know were present. Of the witches, the more powerful families and those of the Council members were a strong presence, while the rest—the lower-powered adepts and the bottom-of-the-pecking-order generalists, formerly known as hedgewitches—made up a smaller portion of the attendees.

I sighed. *A party that's supposed to be for everyone, and it's actually for the privileged witches after all.* And I was about to be one of the people who planned it.

"McKenna! Leo! You two look fabulous!" Preston Chang, half-Fae event planner and former classmate, gushed as he saw us. His green tuxedo jacket kept on going into a flared skirt, showing off his dancer's legs. "How have we still not properly caught up since you came back?" he asked me as we hugged in greeting.

"I've been a little busy getting myself declared not dead. Turns out that involves a lot of paperwork. And fees," I replied. "But it's great to see you. How are you?"

"Fantastic. Living as my authentic self and getting paid to throw parties with other people's money. It doesn't get any better." Preston had come out as trans after high school, in the years I'd been away. Half leanan sidhe, he had his Fae mother's penchant for the arts but without the drawbacks. While a leanan sidhe inspired artists like a muse, they also tended to slowly sap the life force of their lovers. His mother didn't stay with anyone too long, and so he'd been raised by his human father and stepmother. "Speaking of, what do you think? The stacks clean up pretty nice, huh?"

"They do. I mean, my biased opinion is this place is always lovely, but this is something else," I agreed. "Your doing?"

Preston preened. "But of course, and thank you. The special effects are courtesy of some up-and-coming witches who enchanted the chandeliers."

"Knocked it outta the park, Preston," Leo said, while I wrapped my head around that. "So, you've got all your toes dipped into the society pages around here, what's the latest on everyone? I'm locked in mom-land, and we've established Mickey's woefully behind the times. We are desperately in need of an update."

Preston grinned wolflike and leaned in. "Well, *the* biggest news is still Arcadia's own Red Wedding, but what else… Rose Blackwood supposedly has a Fae boyfriend, but she came stag to this, as did her sibling, Ash. Danielle O'Brien called off her engagement and her hair and is currently backpacking through Europe. Natalie Phillips and Isabella Martinez are both single and here to mingle, and Tom Harwell has been making eyes at Hugo Phillips all night, whenever he's not making them at a cocktail glass, that is. Jury's out on whether Hugo's interested or not."

Leo and I exchanged a look. Tom had a bad habit of overindulging. "Where's Tom now?" she asked.

"Getting a refill." Preston nodded at a drink station not far from us.

"Right. I'll go—" I started to say.

"No, you stay here, I've got this one. I could use some water before my next round anyway," Leo said. She tossed back the rest of her drink and headed over to Tom.

"You know he's got it bad for your brother, right?" Preston asked me.

"I'm pretty sure everyone *but* Cameron has figured that out, despite them being best friends and roommates. But I'm also pretty sure Cam's a hundred percent straight and as clueless as that implies. Which I'm also *also* pretty sure Tom is fully aware of."

"Crushing on a straight, the queer rite of passage," Preston said with a rueful smile.

"I'll drink to that," I chuckled, and we did.

"I know you're only newly back in town, but I've been hearing rumors and catching some vibes from you and your two exes," Preston said. "Anything going on there?"

"No, absolutely not. Strictly just friends with both of them." Granted, I had fallen into bed with Remi when I first came back to town, but I'd put a halt to that after learning she'd kept my mother's illness from me. "And aware there are more than two people in the world available for me to date."

"Sure, but you could do a lot worse. Have you *seen* Bastien in that tux?" Preston growled.

"I'd say you should go flirt with him, then, but speaking of a hundred percent straight..."

"More's the pity." A string quartet started playing a coyly sophisticated cover of a pop song. "Look, he might be in mourning and all, but it'd be criminal if you didn't at least dance with him. The boy could use a pick-me-up, and it could only increase your social standing. Which, no offense, you could use."

I arched a brow at him. Fae liked games, and Preston's game of choice was social hierarchy. "Offense slightly taken. What do you mean?"

"I mean that, as the event planner, I may have been privy to certain information being announced tonight," Preston said in a conspiratorial tone.

"Privy to or stole a look at?"

Preston shrugged enigmatically. "Does it matter? You're about to take a big step up, McKenna, and you're going to need more friends in that social sphere if you don't want to get eaten alive. By my count, that number is hovering between zero and one. Dance with Bastien and you'll be starting out on the right foot."

He had a point, but that didn't mean it sat right. "I'm not going to use Bastien for the sake of social climbing."

"And you won't be! He could use a real friend, and if there happens to be a fringe benefit to being there for him, that just makes it a win-win. Come on, you really think he's enjoying being circled like a piece of meat?"

I followed his nod to where Bastien was chatting with a group that did include many of the single, young witches in attendance: the Blackwood siblings, Natalie Phillips, and Isabella Martinez. Isabella I'd briefly seen at the wedding— she had been one of Mari's bridesmaids and oldest friends, from an earth magic family. I remembered her from our high school days, one of the quieter and nicer members of Mari's posse. Probably the only one who had never taken up Mari's favorite nickname for me: "hedgebitch."

Surrounded as he was, Bastien's pleasant, polite society mask was firmly in place—the guise of social nicety that he wore at events such as these. All while the elder Blackwoods and Mrs. Phillips lingered nearby, watching the interactions with clear anticipation. "Seven hells, what is this, *Bridgerton*?"

"No, he's much more of a Darcy."

I snorted, finishing my drink and handing over my empty glass. "All right, I'm going. But only for his sake!"

Preston grinned. "Whatever you need to tell yourself. Go get 'im, tiger!"

I had only seen Bastien a few times since his disastrous wedding almost two months ago, all of them brief and tense with unsaid things. His life had been turned completely upside down, and most of it was my fault; I didn't want to insert myself. The last real conversation we'd had, if you could call it that, had been him making me promise, in the middle of fighting Saranthiel, not to disappear again.

"McKenna," he said when he saw me approach. He seemed to be pleasantly surprised, but his smile was more practiced than natural. "It's good to see you. Happy Solstice."

"You, too," I replied, smiling at him. "Happy Solstice, everyone. Rose, Ash, Natalie, Isabella, it's nice to see you all again." They gave some polite greetings, but I turned back to Bastien. "Sorry to interrupt, Bastien, but you *did* promise me a dance."

He quickly caught on. "Yes, of course! I did. If you'll all excuse me," he said to the others, and took my arm. Out on the dance floor, one of his hands settled at my waist, the other taking my hand. Bastien was tall, but with heels on, I was only a few inches shorter. "Thanks for that."

"You're welcome. Figured you wouldn't mind getting away from the vultures."

He smiled stiffly. "I think they mean well, but it's hard not to notice a distinct pattern in the people who keep coming up to chat."

"Apparently the collective witches of Arcadia Commons have never heard the term *too soon*," I replied, and caught the way his eyes tightened. "Sorry. How *are* you doing?"

"All right. The hotel could be better, it's unusually quiet for this time of year," he said, despite that my question hadn't been about his job. "We lost a number of reservations due to the construction. We've had to run some discounts to fill the rooms. Louis—my general manager—kept things running smoothly while I was on leave, and the renovations at this point are practically running themselves. I only need to check in when there's something to sign off on." He shrugged. "What about you?"

"A proud new member of the gig economy," I replied. "Bartending at the Veil and Horn and Delivery Door driver."

"Should I offer congratulations or condolences?"

"Congratudolences works." He chuckled, the mask falling a little, and I smiled back.

"Congratudolences it is. Sounds like you're keeping busy."

"I am, but gotta make ends meet." *Plus I'm about to start an unpaid third job with your grandfather . . .* "Mom still doesn't have a job, but I don't want to rush her."

"I can imagine. How is Wendy? I'd rather hoped she might come tonight." Bastien had stayed friendly with my mom in my ten-year absence, visiting her often while she was in the Harwell Institute.

"She and Cam didn't feel comfortable with this particular crowd. But she's doing good overall," I said. "She's going to look for work after the New Year, should be more openings then. Once she does, I can cut back my hours at the bar. How about your family?"

"Doing well. Adrienne graduates in May, and Celine's in New York following her acting dreams," Bastien detailed. "My parents are still in Hyannis. They invited me to come stay with them, but the last thing I want at this point is to feel run out of town on top of everything else," he admitted, the mask of small talk slipping further.

"Good. This place would be lesser for it if you did." I smiled and squeezed the hand that held mine.

His storm-blue eyes brightened more this time, holding on mine as he squeezed back. "Thanks. It's nice knowing some-one thinks that."

"C'mon, I'm not the only one," I replied.

"I suppose. Still, it's nice hearing it. It's—" He took a long breath in, looking at me. "—it's nice having you here, too, McKenna." His hand pressed at my waist, drawing me closer. His fingers just barely brushed my back where the dress dipped low, sending a shiver over my skin. One of the good ones. I felt like a teenager at a school dance again, right down to the same dance partner. The illusory snowflakes swirled around us, twinkling in the lights, but there was no chill, only warmth.

"Thanks." I finally found my voice again. "I'm glad I'm here, too."

For a moment we just danced, naturally moving in time

with each other. I belatedly noticed he'd started leading me in a waltz and that my feet were matching his before the rest of me had caught up. When he saw I had, he smiled—*actually* smiled, this time—and spun me under his arm, catching me again with his arm around my back, holding me close. I felt the room shrinking to just the two of us and wondered how soon was too soon to want to kiss your ex whose dead wife was an Archdemon that you'd killed.

But the song ended, and there was some light applause as the quartet announced they were taking a short break, ending the moment before it went any further. Probably for the best. We went over to grab a drink, reuniting with Leo, Preston, and Tom. The five of us fell into chatting about anything and everything. Leo showed off videos of Griffin and his preschool class singing an adorably terrible rendition of "Jingle Bells," and Preston pointed out some minutiae in the library decor and gave us the latest gossip on various other people from our academy days. Tom, who taught at the academy now, regaled us with stories of some of his students' antics. And, perhaps proving Preston's theory about social standing correct, a few others dropped in and out of our circle as well, including the society singles who'd been eyeing Bastien earlier.

It was going about as perfectly as possible, and then Laurent Lemaire stepped up to the microphone.

"Happy Solstice, everyone." His gravelly voice crackled over the speakers. "Welcome and thank you for attending. And thank you as always to the Uncommon Collection for hosting us. The reading room looks lovely, doesn't it?" There was a smattering of applause; next to me, Preston pouted about not being mentioned by name. "I won't take up too much of your time," he said, before going on for a good five minutes about our community and how unique and special our town was. I couldn't help but notice, however, how much he talked about the witches specifically.

"This would mean a lot more if it felt like he ever actually looked out for the community as a whole," I muttered to the others. "The wolves, the Fae, the not-elite families."

"Same old Laurent," Leo replied.

"Let's keep being the change we want to see in the world, then. Our day's coming. Isn't that right, McKenna?" Preston said, with a wink at me.

Bastien looked at him quizzically, but Laurent finally got to the part everyone had been waiting for.

"Finally, as you know, after the passing of Tobias Phillips, may he rest in peace"—there was a murmur of shared sentiment through the room—"the Council was left with an empty seat. After much discussion, we are pleased to extend an invitation to one of Arcadia Commons' most promising young people, who will no doubt bring new perspective to the position as well as considerable talent."

I noticed Bastien straightening up next to me, tugging his suit jacket into place, and with dread began to realize why. *Oh, no. He doesn't know. How does he not know? Didn't Laurent tell him?* "Bastien—" I started to say.

"Please join me in congratulating McKenna Ellerbeck, the newest member of the Arcadia Commons Witches Council!"

Every eye in the room turned to me. You could've heard the flutter of a pixie's wings in the silent shock that followed.

But no one was more surprised than the man standing next to me. Bastien's blue eyes were wide, stunned...*hurt.*

I suddenly knew how Remi had felt when I'd learned what she had kept from me.

Then Preston and Leo, bless their souls, started to clap, and the rest of the room disjointedly followed suit. Bastien was one of the last to join, but as he did, I saw the polite mask slam firmly back in place. I was caught between acknowledging the rest of the community gathered here, even if they were only a small slice of the witches I now represented, and explaining myself to Bastien.

Leo nudged my arm and spoke between her teeth, holding a smile for show. "Now is when you wave to the people, Mickey!"

With one last look of apology, I put on a smile for the room, waving and nodding my thanks. There was a bit of ceremony to follow, including a short ritual of me pledging to protect the people of our town and all witchkind and signing the Council grimoire. The book was mostly symbolic; more of an enchanted logbook and not a true grimoire like the ones some witch families had.

Afterward, Laurent bade everyone enjoy the rest of the evening, and a small crowd of other witches came over to congratulate me in person. I made my hellos and thank-yous and so forth, but my eyes kept scanning for Bastien over everyone's head. Finally, I spotted him heading down the spiral staircase that led here from the mundane town library downstairs. "Excuse me," I said hastily to the person in front of me, and hurried after him. He was out the doors to the parking lot by the time I caught up. The blast of winter wind and very real snowflakes hit me as soon as I stepped outside, coatless and nearly bare to the elements.

"Bastien, wait!" I called out. "I'm sorry. I didn't know he hadn't told you."

He turned slowly to look at me, jaw clenched but shaking with anger. "'Didn't know'...it doesn't matter, McKenna. *You* didn't tell me."

"I...I know. I should have, I just...with everything I already screwed up for you, I didn't want to have to tell you more bad news."

He shook his head, scoffing. "More bad news? Please. When have you ever told me bad news?"

I looked at him in confusion. "Are you kidding? When have I *not*?"

"Never." Cold anger flashed in his blue eyes. "Not once have you had the courage to tell me yourself. Not even when you killed my best friend."

The words hit like a fist. "I...Bastien...you know I didn't..."

"No, it wasn't your choice, not your doing. I know that. But you still didn't tell me. For *ten years* you didn't tell me, McKenna. You ran away, you told *Remi*, got *her* help, and then let her string me along pretending to be you for weeks—"

"I didn't know she did that, I never asked her to!"

"Of course not. But you still didn't tell me yourself. Not then, not even when you came back."

"Hey, I told you when I came back," I pointed out angrily.

"Because Remi forced your hand! Even she knew you had to come clean before you were willing to admit it!" Bastien roared back at me, throwing his hands into the air. "Seven hells, the only reason you ever told me about Forneus was because I found you out for myself first!"

Snow swirled as the wind blew, biting and cold. I hugged my arms around me, wishing I had my coat, shivering and stammering and trying to think of a reply, but I had none. He turned away, running his hands through his hair, ruffling its neatness.

"I used to think you were brave, McKenna. Brave for facing down Archdemons, owning up to your choices and their consequences. Even brave for just putting up with the judgment of those around you. For standing up to the Council when you were only in high school. I thought...I thought the world of you for it." He turned back to face me, and despite the kind words, I knew the blow was coming next. "But you're not. You're a coward. You might be good at cleaning up your messes, but you still just can't help making them, can you? And you don't do messes by halves, oh, no. When you make them, the goddamn order of things has to come crumbling down and bury everyone around you!"

"I—"

"*I married a demon, McKenna!*" Bastien's furious face was inches from mine before I even saw him move, the storm of his eyes alight with anger. "I opened up to her, I fell in *love* with her, I *married* her! And if you had just had the courage to think about me, to think about anyone else, for five seconds and tell me the truth, it never would've happened!"

Winter cold turned my tears to ice, their sting stabbing at the corners of my eyes before they fell, frozen rivers down my cheeks. My hand clenched against my lips to hold in the sob that shook me. "How...how can I make this right, Bastien?" I pleaded, shivering as the snow swirled around us.

Bastien didn't meet my eyes this time. "You can't. Just stay away from me."

Chapter 2
Blood in the Water

Four months later

"You're late!" Cameron called out from the beach.

"You *just* texted me, and I had three deliveries to finish first." I grabbed my demon-hunting bag from the car and jogged over the sand to join my brother. The sun was low in the sky, painting it in beautiful shades of blue, orange, and pink. If only we were here to take in the sunset. "Where's everyone else?"

"Beats me. No reply from Remi or anyone in the pack." He was bent over, hands on his knees as he caught his breath, his pants damp with ocean spray. "Which sucks, cause there are three of these things and they're walking squid horror shows."

"Again? Spring really brings out the marine demons around here." Three days ago, two creepy mer-abominations with fish tails and pincers instead of legs had tried to come ashore, and last week giant spider crabs with sharp spines and shark-like mouths had terrorized the beach near Remi's condo.

"Gimme your knife? One of them stole mine."

"Yeah, sure." I pulled my athame, a ritual knife, from my bag and handed it to him, keeping my eyes on the water. We were standing on a small stretch of private beach sandwiched between two jetties that belonged to the Bellerieve Bayside Bed & Breakfast. It was owned and operated by Abby Bellerieve, adoptive mother and distant cousin to my estranged friend Brooke. The Bellerieves were water witches but fell on the low-powered, hedgewitch end of things. Waves lapped at the beach, normal as anything, until I saw a tentacle pop up a few feet back from the water's edge. "Where's Abby?"

"On the porch, holding an illusion over the beach." I glanced over—sure enough, Abby sat cross-legged and in a focused state, making sure our activities went unnoticed. "Where's Codex?"

"Coming, hang on." I closed my eyes and sent out a pulse of magic, which confirmed both that there were three demons in the water in front of us and the location of the family grimoire, in my room in my house across town. When I tugged on the thread that was the book, the air shifted as it appeared in my hands: leather-bound, with uneven, hand-cut pages edged in gold. The power it contained and represented welcomed my touch, sending a ripple over my skin, my magic stirring in response. I laid my hand on the handprint on the cover, and it opened up, gold light flaring over the page and settling into black ink that wrote itself.

Hello, McKenna. What are we doing today?

I smiled. "Hello, Codex. We're banishing three tentacle demons."

And erasing their memory of getting past the barrier, I assume?

"As usual, yeah." Arcadia Commons and its rare leyline crossroads had been protected by a powerful anti-demon barrier. It had, unbeknownst to us, been powered by slowly draining the magic of my family for centuries. Six months ago, I'd put a huge dent in it when I used it to kill Saranthiel. Ever since, smaller demons had been able to slip in unhindered. We weren't interested in advertising this, or the fact that the barrier was drained a little more every time my family cast something, so we made sure to take the memory of it away from all the demons we banished now.

"Ready to rock, Codex?" Cameron asked, taking the book.

Cameron is casting? The letters might as well have had a frowning emoji next to them.

"Yes, deal with it. I'm playing defense."

Fifteen minutes later, I could confirm that tentacle demons were my new least favorite demons, especially the one currently latched onto my leg, trying to drag me into the Atlantic Ocean.

"Cameron! A banishment anytime now would be great!" I yelled at my brother, kicking at the tentacle grasping my ankle. Surprisingly strong grip for something half-rotted; all demons manifesting in our world had to cobble together some kind of flesh-based body for themselves if they wanted to stay. Pulling together a patchwork of decaying parts was the easiest option.

"Working on it!" Cameron yelled from farther up the beach, where he was drawing a ritual circle to banish the demons. "It would help if this book didn't play favorites, you know!"

"Codex, stop being—ahh!" Another yank pulled me into the surf. The damn thing was long, strong, and keeping its bulk hidden in the water, making it hard for me to target it with any spells. A blast of force at the tentacle grabbing me might do it, but it also might break my ankle, and, unlike me, this thing had seven limbs to spare. "Knife, knife, give me the damn knife!"

"Shit!" Cameron sprinted down the sand, tossing my athame, both of us steadying the throw with unspoken magic. My hand closed around my old friend and I brought it down on the tentacle, thick ichor oozing out. A scream bubbled up from the waves as it released me, and Cameron helped me get up and away from the thing. "You okay?"

"I'll live. But if we don't get those things onshore and in range, that spell's for nothing," I said. "And I'm so not playing bait again. Your turn." Keeping the athame and grabbing the book from him, I hustled back up the beach.

"You know, we never got tentacle demons before you got back," Cameron called over his shoulder.

"That's me, diversifying the Arcadia Commons tourism industry!" The demons were gross, sure, but honestly? Hands-on magic, working with my brother, helping out a non-elite witch family? This was probably my favorite job, even if it didn't pay.

I flipped open the grimoire. "C'mon, Codex, give me the rune to banish these d-bags."

The grimoire acquiesced, showing me the final banishing rune for the ritual circle Cameron had drawn in the sand. We'd opted for a spot a safe distance from the demons but still in range of the waterline, in sand that was wet and packed enough to hold the lines etched by knifepoint. "Almost done!"

Very apt that you are forgetting the rune for forgetting, Codex wrote, sketching the rune in question on the page. A glance confirmed that Cam's circle didn't have it already.

"It would help if you hadn't held it back from him," I said as I worked.

He didn't ask or notice.

"Do not have time for your attitude right now." I snapped the book closed and dropped it into Cameron's bag on the sand. After wiping the athame's blade clean on my wet pants, I pricked my fingertip, adding a drop of blood to fuel the spell. Our family's magic lived in our blood, and we needed it to power rituals like this. The circle in the sand flared with golden light. "Ready to roll, Cam! Where are the—oh, shit!"

Cameron was now the one being dragged into the ocean, only he was being grabbed by multiple tentacles, one of them over his mouth. I sprinted down the sand, throwing several blasts of force at the water, accuracy be damned. *"Repello!"*

One must've hit, as a single tentacle let go of him and something roared in the water again. I started slashing at the remaining ones, freeing up his mouth and hands first so he could cast with me. "Really wish you hadn't lost your knife right now!"

"Really wish your ex or the wolves had shown up to help!" he fired back, throwing more blasts into the ocean. "This is *not* a job for two squishy witches!"

"Fuck, you're right—Abby!"

Abby looked up from her calm, cross-legged perch on the porch. "What's—oh! Oh, no!" She scrambled to her feet. "Why didn't you snap me out of it sooner?"

"We could use some water witch action!" I yelled, and then

yelped as one of them grabbed my ponytail and hauled me headfirst toward the water. "Ow, ow, fuck, *help!*"

I reached back, grabbing my hair to lessen the vicious, needlelike pain all over my scalp, kicking and screaming until a wave sloshed over my face and left me choking on salt water as I was pulled under entirely. Sound dropped off, screams becoming distant, muffled things. Salt water stung my eyes, the cut on my finger, and a new scratch on my calf from a shell or rock I'd been dragged over on the way in. Water rushed into my mouth and down my throat mid-cough. I couldn't breathe, but I couldn't stop trying. The world heaved and spun, the tentacle my only tether. Another grabbed my shoulder, and a third wrapped around the hand I was holding my hair with. My knife was gone, lost in the struggle. I twisted and saw the sharp-beaked maw of the demon rushing at me.

Out of air, out of options, and out of time, my instincts took over. My blood was in the water, which meant my magic was, too. I pulled on the barrier magic and it answered, rushing to fill the water around me with the golden light of my magic. Then, with nothing more than an act of will, I sent it slamming into the demon, pouring in through its mouth, its skin, until the thing was glowing from within. I felt every mote of magic latch onto the demon that lurked inside the fleshy shell. With strength fueled by desperation and anger, I tore it apart. The thing's body exploded, blood and viscera blooming in the water. The slippery shadow that was the demon's true form in this world was caught in the net of the golden strands of my magic. The pulse of its power was clear as day to me despite the murky water, and I brought it close enough that it slid along my skin, touching, tempting, begging to be let in.

My mind flashed back to Bastien's wedding. To Saranthiel after I killed her, her power acting exactly like this, and the knowledge that I could claim it if I wanted to was as clear now as it had been then.

The consequences of that, however, were still both unclear and unwanted.

I shoved the shadow away and, noticing again how my lungs burned for air, tried to swim upward. The thing's heavy tentacle was still caught on my ponytail and my hand, however, weighing me down. Twisting, I grabbed the tentacle and slashed with my other hand, wordlessly directing my magic to cut it loose, then finally kicked up and out of the water. I gasped for air as I broke the surface, coughing and sputtering. The waves heaved around me, much bigger than before, and I saw Abby on the shoreline, her bright–blue-green magic rocking the water to and fro.

I flailed onto the shore, riding one of the waves. Cameron grabbed me before I could collapse. "I thought you were a goner! Are you okay?"

"Been better," I said between coughs. "But they're down one body."

"Nice. Can you cast?"

I panted heavily but nodded, getting my feet under me. "Yeah…yeah. Where're we at?"

"Abby'll throw them on the beach with a wave and then we banish 'em."

"Good plan. Great plan. Excited to be a part of it." I spat

seawater onto the sand and pushed my soaking-wet hair back from my face. "Let's do this."

Cam and I got back up to the ritual circle, still activated and aglow with unspent magic. "Ready, Abby!"

Abby nodded, teeth bared with concentration. "One... two...three!" With each number she pushed the water backward and forward again, gaining momentum and height. On "three," the water sucked back several feet from the beach, creating a whitecap several feet tall that crashed with concussive force onto the sand, dumping two rancid and writhing tentacled masses a few feet from us. They were both damaged from the fight, but far from incapacitated, and they immediately began scrambling back toward the safety of the water.

I grabbed Cameron's hand, my other aimed at the demons along with his, and as one we chanted, "*Ego daemones abicio!*" The runes flared brightly, the magic circling once before shooting off through our hands and blasting apart the demons' bodies, splattering the beach and all three of us with viscera. Two shadowy wisps rose up from the remains, and I pulled back the third that I felt trying to escape through the water. Once all three were together, we banished them back to the Pit.

I collapsed onto the sand. "Fuck me. Let's never do that without backup again," I said, wiping my face and trying to get the grotesque stuff off my clothes, only managing to smear it around.

"No kidding. I could sleep for a week right now," Cameron agreed, bent forward, hands on his knees. "Can't believe we still have to work the bar tonight."

Abby approached, panting as well. She was only lightly splattered, having not been as close to the explosion of rotting sea creatures. "Are you all right? I'm so sorry. I had no idea those things were that strong."

"I'm just glad we took care of them before one of your guests got grabbed by one," I said. "And hopefully none of them saw the big finale there."

"I doubt it. I've only got two rooms full right now, and I told them both the beach was closed while we dealt with a jellyfish problem," Abby said. "Thank you again for coming so quickly. I'll grab some towels and clothes for you from the gift shop. And a first aid kit."

"Water bottles, too, please?" Cameron requested.

Abby nodded. "If you want to rinse off, there's a showerhead over there," she added, pointing to one on the side of the house, presumably for guests to wash off the sand and seawater before going back inside.

I went first, washing myself off fully clothed—everything I had on was already soaked and stained, after all. While I did, Cameron scuffed out the ritual circle with his foot, gathered the spell implements, and recovered my athame from a tangle of seaweed. "You called down some barrier power, didn't you?"

I scrubbed at my shirt, trying to scrape off the gunk. "It was that or drown or get eaten. Honestly, I barely thought about it, I just did it."

"I'm not judging. But someone's gonna notice, sooner or later," he pointed out. "On both sides of the line."

"From how tough those three were, I think the other side is *already* noticing," I sighed. We had hoped to keep the weakening barrier a secret for as long as possible, but six months after the major blow I'd dealt it, the demons getting through were coming in stronger and more frequently.

"Yeah, well, we knew that was coming eventually," Cam said. He knew as well as I did that it was more complicated than that.

I ran my hands through my hair to rinse it more thoroughly. "I don't love that we're getting so many marine attacks lately, either. I'm starting to wonder if they're—what the hell?" My hands reached the ends and slipped off into the air far too soon. "What happened to my hair?!"

Cameron looked over and gaped. "Uh...some of it's... kinda gone?"

"Gone? Gone how, what do you mean, gone?" I stepped out from under the water and tried to bring the ends, which *should* have hung down to my shoulder blades, around to look at them but ended up awkwardly twisted around trying to see them and failing.

Abby reappeared. "I've got the towels and...oh, dear, what happened?"

"I don't know! I had it in a ponytail before...oh, no." I suddenly remembered haphazardly cutting loose the tentacle holding me while underwater. And now, sure enough, several inches were missing from one side. Cameron started laughing. "It's not funny! Ugh, stupid tentacle demons!"

"Sorry, sorry, it's just—I mean, it's a little funny!" Cameron said.

"I'm so sorry, McKenna," Abby said, offering me a towel. I grabbed that and started drying off my very uneven hair while Cameron took his turn rinsing off. "It's not too bad,

I'm sure you can get it evened out without losing much more length."

"Better your hair than your head," Cameron said, failing to contain his smirk. I made an annoyed face at him.

"Sit down, I can at least bandage your leg," Abby offered. She had just cast a mild healing spell to stop the bleeding when bells started chiming over the town.

"It's already six? Shit, I have to go. Thanks, Abby." I grabbed the clean clothes and ran to my car, casting a quick-dry spell so I wouldn't be sopping wet when I got in, and floored it to my next destination.

———————•———————

"Nice of you to join us, Miss Ellerbeck." Laurent Lemaire's voice scraped over the greeting as I hurried into the stately living room of his mansion, miraculously only nine minutes late. Only then did he turn his head to see me, eyes boggling at the state I was in. "What in the seven hells happened to you?"

All the other Council members stared at me, offering varying responses of shock or disgust. Mostly disgust.

Adele Lemaire wrinkled her perfect nose and covered her face with a cloth napkin. "And *why* do you smell like low tide?" Laurent Lemaire's youngest daughter was in her forties, the next-youngest person here after me, and had all the family trademarks: perfect golden hair, perfect icy blue eyes, an immaculate designer wardrobe, and a perfectly perfected fake smile. I'd had to kill two Archdemons and save the town to earn my spot here. All she'd had to do was be born.

Not that the Council knew I'd killed two of them. As far as everyone but myself and Remi was concerned, I'd killed one as a teen with a one-of-a-kind magic sword and then helped hamstring the second so Remi could strike the killing blow and claim her mantle of power.

"Not to mention dressed like a tourist," added Hilary Blackwood, caught between frowning and snickering at my clothes. Hilary was a well-dressed brunette in her late sixties but looked younger. Her family specialized in plant magic and owned several garden stores and flower shops in the North Shore area.

Both women had made unfortunately accurate observations: I was fully decked out in Bayside Bed & Breakfast gear—oversize T-shirt, zip-up hoodie, terry cloth shorts with *Beach BUM* written across my backside—my wrecked hair under a baseball hat to hide the damage as much as possible, and there was no pretending I didn't reek. I was never dressed up to snuff for this crowd, all of whom were at least upper middle class, but this was especially undignified, even for me. At this point, I just desperately hoped no one figured out I had no underwear on whatsoever.

"And injured!" Dr. Douglas Harwell exclaimed. He was one of the few good eggs on the Council, in my opinion. He got up from the couch and came over to check my leg. "May I?"

"Yeah, of course. Thank you. There were some demons down the coast. Cameron and I took care of them, but they were . . . feisty," I explained.

He held a hand over my injury, and a pale-red pulse of magic lit up his palm. Moments later, the mild pain of the cut was gone, as if it had never been there. The Harwells specialized in mental magic, and Douglas himself ran a mental health facility the next town over, but being a doctor by trade had made him good with healing spells of all kinds. One of his ancestors had probably married someone who specialized in physical healing. Still, I always felt a little guilty accepting his help, considering I'd unwittingly killed his daughter, Jackie, ten years ago. Saranthiel had manipulated me, driving me temporarily insane and making me hallucinate to trick me into killing Jackie and turning her body into a human host body. I still didn't understand how Douglas didn't hate me for it.

"If everyone's quite done fawning over her, let's finally get down to business, now that we're all here." The stern admonishment came from Sofia Perez, perched daintily on the edge of a couch cushion, her graying dark-brown hair swept up into a graceful twist. She didn't look at me as she spoke, but this was no surprise. I'd been on the Council a little more than four months, and she had yet to look at or address me directly even once. Considering she blamed me for her daughter Mari's death, I was just relieved she hadn't come after me with murder charges in a mundane or magical court.

Not that I'd had anything to do with Mari's *actual* murder. If it even *was* a murder. Mari had died cliff diving five years ago, and Saranthiel had seized the opportunity to assume Mari's identity and infiltrate Arcadia Commons' witch society undetected in that host body I'd made for her. Brooke Luppino, the only person present for the cliff diving, swore up and down that Mari's death had been an actual accident. Given that Brooke had also been Saranthiel's thrall and loved her like a best friend, however, her account wasn't exactly the most trustworthy or reliable.

As for Sofia, I'd been shocked that she hadn't protested my joining the Council. It was entirely possible some of my nightmares were courtesy of her oneiromancy—dream magic—but I had plenty of genuine fodder for those, too. Still, I never planned to bring it up. Grief is a strange and illogical beast, after all. I could hardly fault her mild act of retribution on the person easiest to blame.

Douglas gave me a sympathetic look and returned to one of the plush chairs. I chose to remain standing. Every good seat in the posh living room was already taken, of course, leaving only a single, wood-backed chair in the corner, which was not only uncomfortable but well away from the circle of discussion. Perfect for becoming invisible. Most of them would've liked me better that way, or just plain absent.

Suffice to say joining the Council had not exactly been the clear path to changing how the elite witch families treated the supernatural community that I'd hoped. I hadn't expected it to be easy, but the faux-polite disdain I'd gotten from most of them and the way they wove their words, made their decisions, and pursued their own interests made it impossible for me to gain any headway. Only Douglas Harwell and George O'Brien—fire witch, editor of the local paper, and my mom's former employer—treated me like an actual peer and listened to my ideas with any real interest. Unfortunately, they also held little sway with the others.

So, despite that I was still tired from the fight and would be on my feet for the rest of the night, I remained standing. No one offered me a seat, either, but given how I smelled, I didn't blame them.

Besides, the shorts had something of a wide leg opening and, again, I *really* didn't want to risk anyone discovering I was going commando.

"Indeed, now that Miss Ellerbeck has finally joined us, we can get to the reason for this emergency meeting." Laurent Lemaire's voice scraped over the greeting like gravel. "Perhaps next time you can schedule your extracurricular activities so they won't interfere with your Council responsibilities."

I threw my hands up. "There was less than an hour's notice for this meeting, and I can't exactly schedule for surprise demon incursions. I was lucky I could deal with that in between jobs as it is. But I'm here, my voice will be heard and my vote be counted, et cetera, et cetera," I said, quoting some of the flowery, archaic language of the Council's charter.

Cameron's message had come right on the heels of the emergency Council meeting being called. I had a shift at the Veil and Horn after this, too. Not, of course, that anyone here ever lifted a finger to help deal with the demons. Since I was skilled at banishing demons and the weakened barrier had been deemed my problem (aka my fault), the demons were also filed under "my responsibility."

"What exactly *is* this meeting for, anyway? You're playing this a bit close to the chest, Laurent," George observed, adjusting his glasses. Balding and the exact picture of "dad bod," he was more practical and less of a rich snob than the rest. He, Sofia, and I were the only ones not related to anyone else here, even distantly. Although Sofia had technically been an in-law to the Lemaires for all of a half hour last October.

"The short notice was unavoidable," Laurent said, checking his watch. "Certain developments were required before it could be brought before the rest of you." He and Sofia exchanged a look that I didn't like at all.

"Bringing *what* before the rest of us?" George pressed.

As he spoke, I felt a prickling sensation under my skin, in my veins. I glanced out the window at the view of the bay. *Twice in one night, really?* Sometimes when demons came in past the barrier, prickles like this were my early-warning system. The Lemaire estate had strong wards, but we weren't all that far from the water's edge and the limits of the barrier. Sighing to myself at another incursion so soon, I made a mental note to message the others. Hopefully Lucca or Remi would reply this time.

"Sorry I'm late, Grandfather," said a familiar voice behind me. One I hadn't heard since the Winter Solstice Ball. Judging by the brief, emotionless look Bastien Lemaire gave me as he saw me, he wasn't any happier to see me now than he had been then.

Although he *was* clearly startled by my tourist-caught-in-a-windstorm aesthetic, the overall indignity of which I was suddenly that much more aware.

The former golden boy of the Lemaire family was dressed to impress as usual, though wherever he'd been since skipping town after the Ball, it had left him dressing more on the business casual side than he used to. His gray slacks and button-down shirt were well tailored and wrinkle-free, but he'd skipped the tie and suit coat and even had his sleeves rolled up. His hair had grown out a little, long enough to have some waves styled back away from his face, and he was tan—or, at least, as tan as someone in his fair-skinned family could get. Formerly clean-shaven as a rule, dark-blond stubble now highlighted his jawline. Carefully manicured stubble, granted. The thin gray metal eyeglass frames he wore over his blue-gray eyes were the same ones he'd worn last fall.

"Couldn't be helped, I'm sure. Come in, have a seat." Laurent welcomed his grandson. He even made a quick gesture that parted two of the couches and dragged the wood-backed chair forward for him. *Seriously?* The old man either didn't see or ignored my scowl.

"That's all right, I'll stand, thank you," Bastien replied. He made a gesture toward the chair, looking at me. "The seat's yours, if you'd like."

It sounded like a perfectly polite offer, if you didn't know any better. Which I did. "No thanks, I'm good," I said, flicking my eyes back to Laurent.

"While it's good to see you, Bastien, could one of you let us know what this is all about?" Douglas asked.

"Earlier today, Brooke Luppino gave birth to her child," Laurent informed us.

What? Why didn't I hear from them? Or Leo? I glanced at my phone, as if some phantom message would suddenly appear. Nothing. *And how the hell does Laurent know this?*

"Reports are that there were no complications, both mother and daughter are healthy. As such, Sofia, I believe it's time to put your petition before the Council."

Oh, no. This couldn't be good.

Sofia's glare could've cut glass. "Good. Then I formally accuse Brooke Luppino of murder, treason, and conspiracy. The Perez family petitions this Council to put her before tribunal and, if she is found guilty, deliver a sentence of severing."

That caused a stir.

"*Murder?* Sofia, come now—"

"Why are we just hearing this?"

"Severing?"

"Long overdue, if you ask me."

Severing was the official term for stripping a witch of their magic permanently. It was the highest punishment the Council could carry out, rarely requested and more rarely used. I'd gone through a trial as a teen when my being a thrall to Forneus had been discovered, but I'd avoided severing on account of having helped kill him. The last witch to be severed was my mother, almost six years ago. Repeated exposure to Saranthiel had led to her developing schizophrenia and eventually to my brother developing it as well. When it progressed to the point where my mom tried to burn down the town forest, it had become a significant safety concern, and the Council had severed her before she was committed to the Harwell Institute. While both her and Cameron's minds had since been completely healed through favors Remi owed me, Mom's magic was gone for good.

I stared at Bastien, but his face was unreadable, his society mask solidly in place. What did he have to do with all of this? Surely he didn't support it. He'd seen what my mother went through, had visited her regularly. He'd even been the one to tell me what had happened to her and taken me to see her. His lack of reaction told me he'd known this was coming for Brooke, and coming now, tonight.

But why was he here?

Laurent finally raised his hands and his voice. "Quiet! One at a time, we'll answer your questions and put the matter to a vote. Hilary, you first."

"Why hasn't this been brought up before now?" Hilary asked. "I'm not surprised, or against it. Sofia deserves justice for her daughter. But why keep it from us?"

"Sofia brought her desires to me after the Solstice Ball, once our quorum of seven was complete again. But Brooke's pregnancy was deemed a reason to delay. The spells involved in a tribunal are harsh, and we saw no reason to endanger the child," Laurent replied. Having been put through them myself as a teen, I could attest to that.

"We still could have been told," Douglas said, sounding quite stung by this. "We *should* have been told."

"It was my decision and my right as her accuser to wait. I asked Laurent to respect my family's wishes," Sofia replied.

"Your family wasn't the only one hurt by that demon, Sofia," Douglas chastised her.

She turned her unforgiving gaze to him. "You know you have our sympathies, Douglas. But if your family wished to pursue justice via the Council, you've had ample time to do so. Since you haven't, nor has anyone else, my family is not waiting any longer. I certainly hope you'll vote to support my petition."

Douglas leaned back on the couch, letting out a breath and looking bereft. He would've been well within his rights to demand this trial for me or Brooke. He wasn't a vengeful man, but I didn't expect he would get in Sofia's way, either.

"Shall we put it to a vote, then?" Laurent suggested.

"Wait." I spoke up. "Why is Bastien here?"

"I've been wondering that myself. Is he part of your petition, Sofia?" George asked.

"Not as such," Sofia replied. "First, let's vote. Then I'll explain."

The dread creeping up my spine was almost as bad as when I detected a demon. Something was up, and I knew I was not going to like it. Her answer mollified the others, though.

"All in fav—"

"Wait!" I interrupted a second time, earning myself a few displeased looks. "Sorry, but—if Sofia's the one bringing the petition, why does she still get to vote on it? She can't be a judge and the prosecution at the same time."

Adele answered me this time. "Once we've voted to try Brooke, Sofia will name a proxy for her vote at the trial. Any Council member directly involved in a trial does the same."

"If the vote passes, you mean," I said.

Adele gave me a patronizing smile that didn't reach her eyes in the slightest. "Sure."

"If there's nothing else…" Laurent paused, looking at me; I shook my head. "All in favor of bringing Brooke Luppino to trial for the crimes of murder, treason, and conspiracy?"

Laurent, Sofia, Hilary, and Adele all raised their hands without hesitation. Douglas hesitated, looking at his lap for a long moment before raising his as well.

George exchanged a look with me before raising his as well. "If nothing else, we all need to know the truth."

They had the majority of votes they needed to try Brooke, no matter what I did now. In the end, it would take seven unanimous votes to confirm the sentence and seven witches to execute the severing. Brooke and I were still finding our footing with one another since the truth had come out last fall, but the idea of doing this to her, to anyone, made me ill. But being the odd witch out on a matter as big as this worried me, as well; would Sofia come for me next? Being on the Council didn't protect me from that. I'd avoided that magicless fate once. I had no desire to test my luck on that measure again.

In the end, I supposed that George was right—we needed to know the truth, once and for all. I raised my hand.

Laurent nodded. "The ayes have it. Sofia, who will speak for your family?"

"The Perez family has chosen Sebastien Lemaire as our advocate," Sofia said.

"What?" I blurted out. "You're serious?"

Bastien regarded me coolly. "Very."

So that's what he was doing here. Waiting to do to someone else what had been done to my mother, his friend. I stared at him in disbelief.

"Bastien…this isn't you," I said.

His eyes were unflinching. "All due respect to an esteemed member of the Council," he said, his words like knives, "it's been a long time since you knew me." He turned to address the rest of the Council with a cool, polite turning of the mouth that might be called a smile, were it not wielded for such a cause. "I'm honored to represent the Perez family before the Council in this matter."

Adele practically exuded pride at her nephew's words. I, on the other hand, felt as terrible as I smelled.

"Very well. We'll reach out to the Luppinos tomorrow morning to inform them and inquire if they wish to select an advocate," Laurent said, "as well as to finalize a date within the next week for the trial."

"Next week? Why? Brooke just had a baby, she's not going anywhere," I said.

"Severing trials are considered urgent by nature, heard and decided within seven days," Adele replied in a condescendingly "helpful" tone. "Or did you forget how fast your own happened?"

"I remember, thanks," I said. "Considering I was there and you weren't. But it's already been months since Sofia brought it up to Laurent."

"That was before we voted on it," Laurent said.

The extent of their careful planning started sinking in. "But...she *just* had a *baby*."

Sofia lifted her chin. "And now she'll pay for taking mine from me."

A heavy silence sat in the room, and no one would look at me. Not even Douglas or George, and I knew they'd both known what was being voted on far better than I.

I tried to look at Bastien, tried to read him. "You know what this did to my mom," I reminded him. There was a flicker of emotion, his society mask cracking for just an instant. But it wasn't regret I saw; it was anger, cold and just barely held in. The same look he'd given me at the Solstice Ball.

"With that in mind, we should all review the procedure for—" Laurent started to say.

"I'll tell Brooke," I said, interrupting for the third time that night. "Tomorrow morning, I'd like to be the one to tell her."

Laurent regarded me. "As the senior member of the Council, that falls under my responsibility, given the severity of the matter."

"Fine. Then I'd like to be there when you do," I said. "When are you going?"

Laurent Lemaire looked at me with strained patience. "First thing. Eight a.m.," he finally replied.

"Okay, then. I'll see you at eight." I turned and headed for the door. I had no desire to deal with this any longer.

"Miss Ellerbeck, this meeting isn't over," Laurent called after me.

"Text me the highlights or tell me tomorrow. I have to get to work," I called over my shoulder, and let the door slam shut behind me.

Chapter 3
The Life of the Party

"You're late." Trevan Stonehill didn't even look up from his cocktail mixing as I joined him behind the bar at the Veil and Horn.

"So people keep telling me." I grabbed the eyedropper next to the register, distilling two drops into each eye. The elixir would let me see through Fae glamours during my shift. "Tentacle demons, Council meeting, and trust me, you would not have wanted me here without a shower first," I told him. French braiding my hair with several bobby pins to hide the damage had taken time, too.

"A shower?" His lips quirked in a grin. "Must've been one hell of a meeting. Did it end in a bloodbath or an orgy?"

"Ew! Gross. Please do not *ever* make me picture Laurent in that context!" I half laughed and half gagged. "Neither, but for the record I'd prefer the bloodbath. The shower was because of the tentacle demons. Which I was *fighting*!" I added before he could imply otherwise.

"That all sounds very on-brand."

"I'll stay late to make up the time. Or skip my break, whatever."

"Breaks are a legal requirement. Stay late to cover it," Trevan replied. Working for a Fae meant my employment contract counted as a Promise, and the terms were interpreted *very* literally. "Get some Guinness for those two." He nodded his horned head at some patrons.

"Aren't I on the back bar today?" I asked as I started pouring.

Trevan strained two martinis from a shaker. "You were, but Cameron got here on time, and he claimed it."

"What? Dammit, it's supposed to be his turn for 'Who's doing shots?'"

Trevan shrugged. "Looks like it's yours. Next time, don't be late!" He picked up the two martinis and clip-clopped over to the other end of the bar to deliver them. With the eye drops in, I clearly saw Trevan's true Fae nature as a satyr, as well as that of Pip, the very tall, bark-skinned, green-haired dryad working the front with me, and some of the patrons as well. The Friday happy hour and dinner crowd was finishing up and transitioning into the ones here to party and bring on the weekend. Not too many other Fae so far, but I smiled as I noticed the pixies in the rafters were already getting rowdy with a tiny multicolored rave.

With an envious glance toward the back room, where the stage and the other bar were, I got to work. On the drive over, I'd sent Lucca and Brooke a message of congratulations on the birth and a brief warning about some Council business coming their way soon. I'd thought about giving a more specific warning, but I didn't want to send them into a panic before tomorrow morning. They had a newborn to focus on right now. Despite a few odd looks and curious inquiries about the sucker marks on my arm (they'd been covered by my sweatshirt earlier, so Douglas hadn't seen or healed them), the night was going smoothly until—

"*Wooohooo!*" A woman's voice crowed over the crowd.

Please don't say it, please don't say it . . .

"Who's doing shots?!"

Pip patted my shoulder as she suddenly found she desperately needed to be at the other end of the bar. "All yours, McKenna."

With a heavy sigh, I trudged over to the woman calling for shots and put on my best helpful-bartender smile. "Hi, Mom."

The Wendy Ellerbeck comeback tour made regular stops at the Veil and Horn. "There wasn't even a *gay* bar in Arcadia before, never mind a Fae bar!" she had declared when she learned about the place. Every weekend, and sometimes weeknights, she popped in, made friends with twenty-somethings often younger than both her children, and partied until closing or until she made a French exit with one of said twenty-somethings, whichever came first.

"Ixnay on the m-word, you know the rules!" she chastised. "And a round of Redheaded Sluts, we're celebrating the new look." My mom tossed her hair. What had been graying dark-brown hair had transformed into a bright crayon red. It was a jarring change, though it did match her yellow top nicely.

In the decade I'd spent running from demons, my mother had changed both greatly and not at all. Beyond the standard passing of time, her illness had taken a deep toll on her physically as well as mentally. She'd had a lot to recover even after Remi healed her mind. Gray hairs were only one of the signs of her ordeal, and the others were harder to hide—lines in the skin where there had been none, loss of muscle tone, a certain amount of tiredness. In the six months since we'd been living together in our old house, she'd thrown herself into regaining what she'd lost—new clothes, new diet, new workout regime. She'd come a long way from those first few fragile weeks. Her brush with death and severe mental illness had left her eager to live and live hard.

And what midlife crisis would be complete without dressing young and partying with even younger arm candy?

"Who's 'we'?" I asked.

"Me and my girl here." A young woman who looked vaguely familiar caught up to her. She had a round face, brown skin, a stud in her nose, and a short bob of tight rose-gold-colored curls.

I lined up two shot glasses. "I'm only covering your drink, you know. And only the first round, we agreed."

Mom pouted. "Oh, c'mon, McKenna, at least take care of Gretch's shot, too? She just graduated!"

I weighed whether it was easier to just cover both or continue to argue with her, and opted for the first. "Fine. But *only* this round."

"Thanks, hon! You're a peach. So, the hair! I decided it was time to switch it up, what do you think?" she asked me.

"Looks great. Did you do it yourself?" I asked mildly while mixing up the drinks.

"Gretchen's handiwork. She's working on her own line! And

you can't even tell it's enchanted," Wendy stage-whispered, throwing a wink and a smile at her drinking buddy.

Gretchen, apparently, beamed at the praise. "It looks so good on you, Wends!"

"You did all this?" I asked Gretchen, gesturing at the both of them and honestly impressed.

Gretchen smiled. "Yep! I did Wendy's today at your house—oh, but I promise, the bathroom looks totally fine," she assured me.

"I told her about that time you turned it purple trying to magic your hair," Mom said, both of them looking very amused. "Don't worry, Gretch sticks with potions, and they're super easy to clean up."

"Right…good to know." It shouldn't matter that Mom had told that story to this stranger, but it still felt weird.

My mom peered at me. "Speaking of hair, did you do something different to yours?"

Instead of answering, I turned to her stylist friend. "Gretchen…Grothmann? Your mom teaches chemistry and potions at the academy, right?"

"Yes, and please do *not* tell me you're one of the people who called her 'Grossmann,'" Gretchen said, rolling her eyes. Mrs. Grothmann had been a harsh grader, and there was *always* a foul stench from her classroom. "You know the real reason the room smelled was because the students kept screwing up the potions, right?"

"Huh. No, I didn't call her that, and now that you mention it, that does make a lot more sense," I admitted. "Her hair looks great, by the way. Yours, too. Nice job."

This appeased her and she smiled again. "In that case, nice to meet you. And thanks! When I launch this line, Grothmann's finally gonna be a name associated with something that looks *and* smells nice for once."

"You're gonna nail it, Gretch," my mom said confidently.

Gretchen beamed, slinging an arm around her. "Helps that I've got such a gorgeous model!"

Just as I was starting to wonder if maybe I could get Gretchen to fix my hair at a discount, Trevan reappeared. "Wendy!"

My mom smiled and threw open her arms to embrace him. "Trev! How's my favorite horny bartender?" she asked with a saucy wink, prompting a laugh from him. She brewed her own glamour drops at home, having fully embraced the magicless art of being a kitchen witch since her recovery. Probably aided by Grothmann the Younger here, now that I thought about it.

"Good, good. Finally went for the red, eh? You look stunning," Trevan replied. *"Finally"? Am I the last to know everything in this town?*

"Well, obviously you think so," my mom teased, reaching up to playfully ruffle his natural red hair.

Seven hells, Mom, do you have to flirt with my boss? I focused on pouring out the shots. "Nonsense. You're a credit to the color, and we're lucky to have you, and that's just facts," Trevan replied. "Nice to see you ladies again. Having a good time?"

"Getting ready to," Mom replied, grinning at the others. "Have some drinks, hit the dance floor, make some new friends, right, Gretch?"

"Here you go!" I interrupted, pushing two full shot glasses at them. As much as I didn't love running into my mother's conquests in the kitchen in the morning, literally anyone would be better than my boss.

"Thanks, sweetie!" Mom plucked hers up. "Cheers! The night is young and so are we!" With a laugh and a *"Woo!"* they tossed down the shots. The Redheaded Sluts were followed by a round of tequila shots—Mom dragged two young men over to serve as salt licks and lime wedge holders for them—before they settled in with seltzers and headed to the back room to dance.

Not my place to judge, I reminded myself as I got back to my other customers. My mom deserved as many easy days and wild nights as she wanted. She'd effectively lost ten years of her life to demonic wild goose chases and demon-induced mental illness. She'd lost her daughter, her mind, and her magic. I'd been able to give her back the first two of those, but we were both keenly aware that nothing and no one could give her back the third.

Didn't mean I wanted a front-row seat to said wild nights, however.

It turned out I wasn't done serving familiar faces yet. No sooner had Mom's entourage drifted away from the bar than a perfect parting of the crowd opened up between me and my ex, the world's only double Archdemon, Remiel Blake.

Wearing a little black dress with a peekaboo halter-style top that was too fancy for this bar and too racy for my don't-sleep-with-your-ex-again intentions, Remi accessorized with her trademark smirk as she approached. Her dark hair was in an angled bob today, her lips painted wet and red, and her eyes dark brown with a hint of very real and flickering flames.

"Hello, McKe—" she greeted me, resting an elbow on the bar in front of me.

"Where the hell were you tonight?" I demanded.

She blinked, taken aback. "I…was I supposed to be somewhere?"

"Yes! Have you not checked your phone? Cameron and I had to banish three demons by ourselves and I nearly drowned in the process!" I showed her the sucker marks on my arm.

She stood up straighter, the flirtatiousness replaced with concern, her dark eyes scanning me for other injuries. "What? Where? When? Are you okay?"

"I've been better. At the Bellerieve B and B. The pack didn't show up, either," I grumbled.

Her hands darted out to my arm, her fingers tracing the red suction marks there. "And what was their excuse?"

"Probably that Brooke had her baby today." Her gentle touch, always enticingly warm, sent prickles along my skin, far too reminiscent of our past. One that I'd firmly closed the door on…even if moments like this had me peeking through the keyhole. I pulled back my arm, grabbing a glass to dry off as an excuse. Better not to touch hot things, lest you get burned.

"I'm sorry, McKenna. I've been otherwise occupied, I haven't looked at my phone in…a while. Actually, I'm not sure where I left it, now that I think about it." She frowned in thought but brightened as she went on. "But speaking of, that's why I'm here. There's a friend I'd like you to meet who's going to help me keep everything more sorted."

I looked at her with wary curiosity. "Friend?"

"Yes, she should—ah! There she is."

She waved someone over and angled to make room for a young woman who stepped up to the bar straight out of some 1950s *Playboy* spread of sexy secretaries. The very picture of an ingenue begging to be preyed upon, she had dark-blond hair in a high ponytail with the ends curled, cat-eye glasses perched on her button nose, a fitted blouse buttoned to the top, and a pencil skirt that hugged her hips.

Even through the crowded bar, my nose pricked at the scent of sulfur, but more than that, it was the creeping sensation that shot through my veins like lightning that confirmed it: This was a demon. Walking around in my town, in my bar, passing as a human, and *that* was fucking terrifying.

I kept my eyes on her as I put down the glass slowly, ready to grab the athame that was tucked in my boot. I tried not to bring my extracurricular activities to work, but if I had to banish a demon right here and now, so be it.

"You don't need to go for the knife, McKenna," Remi cautioned, seeing my intent. "This is my new assistant. Dara, this is McKenna Ellerbeck. Arcadia Commons' own knight protector."

Long ago, Remi had gifted me a necklace with a black knight chess piece—"Because you're no one's pawn, darling, and we all know you don't need a white one." It had become not just a symbol of our relationship but, for me, a personal talisman of sorts. I hadn't worn it in a while, despite that I was doing more demon fighting than ever. Somehow, I didn't come away from that or much else feeling very knightlike.

Dara cutely nudged her glasses up her nose, smiling brightly at me. "It's an honor, McKenna, I've heard so much about you!" She reached out her hand. I did not return the gesture. I made a point of not touching demons I didn't know.

My gaze was still locked on the target that was Dara. "Remi. Explain why I'm looking at a demon that can pass as human. *Now.*"

"It's an illusion, crafted by yours truly, that's all," Remi explained. "Like I did for you, remember? Once she officially swore herself into my service, I made one for her. It'll make hanging around here much easier."

"And beneath that illusion? Am I going to be wiping ichor off the seats, or is this 'friend' of yours somehow here in her own flesh?"

Remi finally started looking a little less than certain. "Ah... which one makes you less mad?"

"Neither." *What the* fuck *was she thinking?!*

"If I may?" Dara interjected. "My own flesh, but it's not Remi's doing. I was already in this world before finding her."

I arched an eyebrow. "Explain."

"A few months back, you may remember, there was a portal...?" Dara prompted.

I remembered all right. At Bastien's would-be wedding, his would-be bride had revealed her true nature when, upon gaining his portal magic in the ceremony, she had ripped open a portal directly into the Pit and marched an army of minions into our world. They would've been but the first of many if my friends and I hadn't rallied to beat them back and Saranthiel hadn't died.

Apparently, in all the commotion, we'd missed one.

"And it took you six months to find Remi here? How interesting. What exactly did you get up to in the meantime?" I asked. Cam and I had been wondering how and why demons kept sneaking in—with increasing regularity—since we wiped the memories of any we banished and Remi swore to secrecy any minions in her service.

"Not hanging around populated areas, if that's what you're asking," Dara said. "Unlike some demons, I've got a sense of self-preservation, and the writing on the wall was very clear after that night: Don't cross an Ellerbeck. Or a werewolf, or Remiel."

Remi added, "We've talked at length, McKenna. Dara hasn't been spreading any word or any rumors around demonkind. And like I said, she's now sworn into my service."

That wasn't terribly reassuring, but it at least meant that if Dara tried anything, Remi could and would deal with her on a cosmic level. I scanned her accessories and saw she was wearing a necklace tucked under her shirt—the illusion was probably attached to that. "Uh-huh. Yet I can't help but notice how vague that answer was, so, again, what were you doing since then, and when did you get back into town?"

"This isn't really the place for that conversation," Remi pointed out. "But for your second question, I brought her back here earlier tonight."

Dara smiled and nodded. "Yes! Remi took me to see the

highlights on our way here. Arcadia Commons is a lovely town. So adorable and quaint."

Explains the barrier flare-up earlier. And why Remi didn't respond to our texts. Hmph. "Otherwise occupied." I turned a stern look on my ex. "Remi, what happened to giving me a heads-up when you're having guests?"

"It's been a busy day, and I don't recall needing your permission," Remi replied.

"I didn't say 'permission,' I said 'a heads-up.' Which, for friends like *this*, you might want to consider. For *their* safety."

"Mm-hm. Say, is Trevan still hiding the bubbly in the fridge back there?" she asked, changing the subject. "I'd like to toast properly to Dara's first day."

I found some single-serving bottles of prosecco in the back of the fridge. As I poured them out, I eyed Remi's new assistant with distrust, and Remi herself with concern.

This wasn't the first time something had slipped her mind lately. She'd shown up late for other demon incursions, gone to the wrong place, neglected to cash a rent check for weeks at a time. Nothing major until now, and I knew she was busy. Being a double Archdemon meant more minions to manage and enemies to dodge. Having an assistant made sense—what must *that* job posting have looked like?—but missing my messages tonight, losing her phone, not telling me she was bringing an in-the-flesh demon into town until it was said and done? Not for the first time, I wondered what mixing the mantles of Madness and Desire was doing to her. There'd never been an Archdemon with two mantles at once before, and mixing Madness with any of them seemed like a bad idea on paper. Not that I'd had a lot of options at the time, and crowning Remi had seemed the least bad idea available. Still, I'd promised not to freak out and hold it against Remi that she'd do what she needed to manage things, considering both of those mantles being hers was my fault. I supposed the least I could do now was give Dara here a chance.

"Two proseccos, enjoy," I said, pushing the glasses toward them. "Welcome to Arcadia Commons, Dara."

She beamed at me, a smile that even seemed genuine. "Aren't you sweet! Thank you, McKenna."

"And if you get out of line, your ass is going back to the bad place," I added with my own saccharine grin.

Dara had the decency to look nervous, whether or not she truly felt it. "Right, ah, noted. Truly, though, I'm thrilled to be here. I know this town means a lot to Remi, and to you, and I know it's going to be special to me, too." *Okay . . . maybe she won't be so bad. Clearly can't be trusted, but maybe not a* problem *at least . . .*

"To the beginning of a beautiful partnership," Remi toasted, lifting her glass.

"The beginning? Remi, please, like we haven't been partners before," Dara said, with a smooth, suggestive smile.

Never mind. I hated her and I wanted her stupid pretty face gone.

"You two are old friends, then?" I asked. Super casual.

Remi nodded. "We go way back, but I hadn't seen Dara in . . . what is it, decades? Centuries?"

"Somewhere around there," Dara said, sipping daintily. "Oh, this is quite good!"

It wasn't. The Veil and Horn was an Irish bar, gastropub at best, and we did not carry fancy wines of any sort, sparkling or not.

"Thanks." I forced a smile. "So, why didn't you come out to support Remi when she took over for Forneus?"

"It was a…chaotic time. You know how messy leadership transitions in the workplace can be. And I was sworn to Saranthiel at the time," Dara said. "But I'm glad to be here to help support her now."

"And I'm glad to have you," Remi replied. *Have her how, exactly?…Okay, calm down, McKenna, she's your ex and you've been pretty clear she's going to stay that way. Who she wants to hook up with is her business, not yours.* This particular brand of non-judgment was starting to become a theme tonight.

While Remi would've been happy to help me scratch any itch with or without strings attached, she'd respected my decision to not revisit that aspect of our relationship. Not since one hot night when I first returned, anyway. Since then, I had been plenty busy readjusting to life in Arcadia—I was too busy to date anyone, much less my ex who was literally complicated on a metaphysical level.

One thing that made everything less complicated? Keeping it at arm's length. I opened my mouth to excuse myself and step away, but then my mom appeared from the crowd with two empty glasses in hand.

"Two more cosmos, please!" she ordered loudly. Sighing, I took the empties and got to work mixing the next batch while she turned her tipsy gaze on Remi. "Well, well, well, Remi Blake. Fancy seeing you here."

"Wendy, always a pleasure," Remi greeted her genially. "Love the hair, it suits you."

"Mm-hm." My mom looked at Dara, eyes narrowing.

"Who's the side piece?"

"More like an executive assistant. This is Dara," Remi introduced.

"Wonderful to meet you, Wendy," Dara said with another enthusiastic smile, extending a ready hand.

Mom glanced at it but did not take it. I smiled to myself. *Like mother, like daughter.*

"Assistant, huh? Assisting with what, your pants?"

I nearly dropped the bottle of vodka, torn between embarrassment and laughter.

Remi was mildly surprised but shrugged. "I won't say I'd never mix business and pleasure, but in this case, Dara's just an old friend who's recently joined the team."

"You sure she knows that?"

Dara appeared flustered, pushing her glasses up on her nose. "Yes, yes, she knows that—I mean, *I* know that."

"Good, 'cause trust me, whatever candle you're holding for her isn't gonna come anywhere *near* the candle she's holding for McKenna," my mom said, gesturing at me.

This time I did drop the lime wedge in my hand, my whole face heating up. "Mom!"

"Ixnay!" Mom chastised.

Even Remi was a little thrown by that comment. "Wendy, that's—"

"What? Like everyone and their mom—ha!—doesn't know that's true! Pip knows I'm right, right, Pip?" she called out to my coworker as she walked past.

"She's not wrong," Pip said, not pausing in her stride at all.

"Pip!" I protested.

"Trev knows it, too. Where'd he go—hey, Trev!" My mom got a knee on the barstool to lift herself over the crowd, cupped her hands at her mouth, and yelled to my boss at the far end of the bar.

"Mom, get down!" I put down the shaker, reaching for her.

She dodged my grab. "TREV! True or false, Remi's got it bad for my girl here?"

"True, and get off the stool, Wendy!" Trevan yelled from elsewhere in the crowd.

"*Mother!*" I got a hold of her arm as she came back down, laughing and wobbly, before she fell off the stool entirely. "That's enough. Stop it."

"Oh, pfft, so someone loves you! Nothing to be ashamed of," my mom said, waving a hand at me. "Terrible idea to date her, of course, but that's beside the point."

Remi glared this time. "Is it now."

Dara was looking about as uncomfortable as me at this point. "Maybe we should go, Remi…"

"Do what you gotta do, girl, but trust me, even if she's with you, she's still thinking of her!" Mom declared, gesturing sloppily at me again, this time knocking over the shaker, splashing cosmo all over me. Her face fell into a perfect *oops* expression before she burst into laughter.

Gretchen finally arrived. "Wendy, what's going on?"

"Nothing, nothing, McKenna just—ha ha, just had a little accident!" Wendy laughed.

Dripping with booze, with yet another person laughing at me, I felt the burn of embarrassment snap into anger. "Get out."

Seeing my face, Mom's laughter lessened, and she tried to wave it off. "Oh, come on, McKenna, it was an accident."

"Get. Out."

"That's not neces—"

"*Get out!*" I screamed. All conversation near us stopped dead. Mom finally stopped laughing. "You are a drunk mess and an embarrassment, *Mother*. Now get the hell out of this bar before I get someone to escort you." I pointed to the door.

Gretchen gently took one of her arms. "Come on, Wendy," she said softly.

"...Yeah. Fine. I know when I'm not wanted." With one last glare at me, Mom lifted her chin and let herself be led away. Gretchen looked back at me and mouthed, "Sorry" as they made their way to the door. The tension didn't break, I didn't move, until the door had closed behind them, and the sound whooshed back into the room.

Pip appeared with a washcloth. "I got this, go clean up," she said, wiping down the counter. I stormed my way to the bathroom, tears pricking at my eyes for a dozen different reasons.

I was splashing water on my face when Remi walked in. Naturally, as if by magic, the bathroom was empty apart from the two of us. My eyes met hers in the mirror as she walked over.

"It's beginning to occur to me that bringing Dara here tonight may have been a mistake," Remi said.

"You think?"

"My apologies for that."

I sighed. "You don't need to apologize for my mom getting hammered and making a scene. That's all on her. Or possibly me, I suppose, since I keep letting her have the first round for free." I dabbed at my face with some paper towels. "But that particular perk is now officially revoked." Tossing the paper in the bin, I turned to her. "But yeah, some warning about Dara would've been appreciated."

"I see that now, yes." Remi stepped closer, eyes flickering from within.

"Are you sure you can trust her?" I asked.

"I trust her enough. But I'm more concerned about you right now. Are you all right?"

"Unpleasantly damp, for the second time tonight, but yeah, I'm fine."

"Mm-hm. And whatever is it that happened to your hair?" she asked, gesturing at where some strands had come loose from the braid.

"Don't want to talk about it." Tucking them behind my ear, I grabbed some more towels to dry my shirt, still sticky with cosmo, but it was going to take more than that. After a quick mental debate, I said, "Let me know if anyone's coming in," and pulled the wet T-shirt off over my head.

I could feel Remi's eyes drink me in even as I turned around to run water over the shirt. "I can do one better than that." She went back to place a hand on the door, and I felt the pulse of power she pushed into it. "Everyone will be compelled to skip this bathroom and use the one in the back room for a few minutes."

I snorted. "Don't tell Trevan you did that."

"I don't plan to. But back to you, there's clearly more than your mother on your mind," Remi said. After a pause, she added, "About what she said..."

"It's not that," I quickly assured her. "It's been a long night and that was just the shitty cherry on top. Sorry she went off on you like that, though."

Remi's shoulders rippled, a lithe shrug, her heels click-clacking on the floor as she took a few steps. "Unexpected, perhaps, but it's nothing untrue. I'm not ashamed of how I feel."

I met her eyes in the mirror again for a moment before dropping my gaze down to my T-shirt and starting to wring it out.

"But I know you prefer not to be reminded." Click. Clack. "And I don't like being used to embarrass you."

"*You* didn't embarrass me." I twisted the shirt, water running down into the sink. "All night, all anyone's done is want shit from me and then laugh at or belittle me for it. My brother, the Council, now my hot mess of a mother joins in, using our feelings for her own amusement!" I tossed the shirt into the basin of the sink, leaning with both hands on the edge of it, filled with the invigorating and irritating rush that was self-righteous frustration.

Click. Clack. " 'Our feelings'?"

I felt the heat of her behind me before I looked up. Remi always did run hot. Her ambient warmth felt good on my skin. Her flickering eyes met mine in the mirror again.

She lifted a hand, tracing it down my arm, leaving trails of tingling warmth that chased away the reasons I'd kept her at a distance. My mind filled in all the details of her dress as her fingers found mine on the edge of the sink, her brows lifting in a question. An invitation.

Bad idea, bad . . . oh, fuck it.

Resolve shattered, and I spun around and kissed her. Remi pulled me against her, wonderfully warm, as her lips parted. Her fingers curled against my back, nails lightly scratching as her mouth trailed down my neck, pleasure lighting up my nerves. I leaned my head back, my hands tracing her curves through the dress, reveling in feeling *good* for once. *How does she do this, how does this always feel so right?* The thought fled as she undid my bra and her mouth dipped to my chest, leaving me moaning.

"We . . . shouldn't . . . Trevan's gonna be pissed . . ." I tried to say, a tiny shred of good sense reminding me I was still on the clock.

"Shh. Let someone else take care of you for once," Remi whispered, placing a finger to my lips. I caught it in my teeth and felt her smile against my skin before she dragged it down my front to the button on my jeans. Deftly undoing it, she slid the material off my hips and crouched even lower. I gripped the edge of the sink behind me as she delivered on that promise.

Everything else faded from my brain, and nothing was left but the feel of her, her fingers, her tongue, nothing, nothing, until it burst outward into everything.

"Remi!"

Chapter 4
Advocate for the Accused

The persistent ringing of the doorbell rudely interrupted my attempt to catch a few more minutes of sleep. It was barely 7:30 a.m. when I wrapped a bathrobe around me and made my way downstairs, apparently the only one home this morning.

Pulling it open, I was quite surprised to see Laurent and Bastien Lemaire on my front step, both fully dressed in suits and ready to go. "...Bastien? Laurent?"

Both appraised my appearance and quite clearly found me lacking. "Miss Ellerbeck," Laurent greeted me.

"Morning, McKenna," Bastien said. His neutral expression slipped into a befuddled one as he stared at my head. "...What happened to your hair?"

Right. That was still a thing. I tucked it behind my ears. "Demons. What're you doing here?"

"You requested to be present when we spoke with Mrs. Luppino," Laurent reminded me.

"Yeah, but you said eight. I figured you meant we'd meet there. I wasn't expecting you this early. Or at my house."

"Eight is when we intend to arrive there, but we'll do so as a group to properly represent the Council's unanimity on this matter," Laurent said.

"You might've mentioned that before literally right now."

"You said to text you, so I did," Bastien said. "May we come in?"

"Uh…yeah. Come on in. I mean, you're not vampires, right?" I joked lamely. I held the door for them as I pulled out my phone to check my texts. Sure enough, there it was, sent by Bastien while I'd been at work last night.

Grandfather and I will be at your house at 7:30 tomorrow morning.

"So that's what it takes to get him to unblock my number," I muttered.

I had a few other unread texts from the night before. After Remi and I collected ourselves and I dried my shirt with a spell, Trevan told me to clock out early since I had been seen being "openly hostile to customers." I was to make up the time Sunday night doing inventory, which meant no tips. Lucky me.

Other texts included:

Cameron: *Wtf happened with u and mom??* (Definitely not answering over text.)

Mom: *won't be home tonight* (Big shocker.)

Remi: *Lovely to see you, all of you, tonight. Sweet dreams.;)* (Seven hells, I really did that, didn't I?)

And finally Leo, sent even earlier this morning: *Call me when you can! Not urgent, but it's good news.* (Probably about the baby, but either way, it would also have to wait.)

The two Lemaires were chatting quietly in the foyer. Bastien had been here before, but not in many years, and if Laurent had ever visited my family's house, it hadn't been in my lifetime. It was unimpressive compared with the Lemaire mansion on the water, but once you left their tax bracket, it was a nice house. A spacious colonial, it wasn't the original house on the lot, but the exterior had kept much of the same style when it was rebuilt some decades ago. The foyer was wide, with the staircase in the center of the house leading to the second floor. The rest of the first floor was a large living room on the other side of the stairs, and the kitchen and dining area in the back. A sliding glass door there led to the backyard, which had a covered porch and a pool.

I brought them to the kitchen and flicked on the coffeemaker, glad I was in the habit of prepping it before bed. "Either of you want a cup?"

"No, thank you," Laurent replied.

"Sure. Bastien, how about you? Coffee?" I asked, reminded of the very first time Bastien Lemaire had come to my house.

"Coffee?" I hoisted the half-full pot.

Bastien looked at me skeptically. "At this hour? It's after dinner."

I shrugged. "Yeah, and? Archdemons aren't going to plot their own demise. So, coffee? Yes or no?"

"Sure. Thank you," Bastien replied.

I pulled down two mugs. "Help yourself when it's done, I'll be back in a few minutes."

Retreating to my room, I dug out something to wear that would be on the level of what the two of them were wearing, cursing that I hadn't checked my messages sooner. I usually set my phone to Do Not Disturb while I was working, and after being told to leave, I hadn't even wanted to look at it. I'd had quite enough of dealing with people for the day and known I had an early morning coming up. Nightmares and anxiety both had me tossing all night, however, and now I didn't even have time to fix my hair before diving right back into it. At least I'd showered the night before.

The coffee was done by the time I returned, my hair braided and pinned back, dressed in a black skirt and short-sleeved blouse. I grabbed the pot only to see that Bastien had poured a mug for me. I caught him glancing at me and nodded my thanks; he gave me a nod of acknowledgement in return. After a welcome sip of the smooth, dark brew, I addressed the two of them. "Anything else I need to know before we see Brooke?"

"I'll do most of the talking, laying out the charges and the potential sentence," Laurent said. "Bastien is present on behalf of the Perez family, and Mrs. Luppino can let us know if she's chosen an advocate or will be speaking on her own behalf."

"Right, I remember the process," I said. "Are there many witches working as advocates in Arcadia Commons these days?" When my trial had come up, there hadn't been any in town to go to, plus the Council had brought the trial very quickly, so finding someone outside of town wasn't possible. I'd taken an interest in becoming an advocate after that, but going on the run for a decade had thrown that ambition off track. There weren't any formal requirements to acting as someone's advocate, beyond being a part of the witch community and the town. The more you knew about the tenets by which witches were expected to act, the better. But that was tricky in and of itself, because much like with pirate code, they were more like guidelines.

"No one of note, since the need is rare," Laurent said. "This is only the third trial in Arcadia Commons of this severity in the last twenty years." We all left unsaid that two of those had been for people in my family.

"But there are other reasons people need advocates: budget decisions for the academy, especially the scholarships for boarding students, business permits, residency requests," I pointed out. "Just since I've been on the Council, we've heard and turned down three new families who wanted to move to Arcadia on the grounds that it risked too much exposure."

While Arcadia Commons was a notable center of supernatural activity on the East Coast, the majority of the town's residents were unaware of this. Whenever a new witch wanted to move here, they had to seek approval from the Council. In theory, more supernatural beings meant a greater risk of exposure. We'd had a lot of luck in that regard, and mundanes tended to create excuses for the seemingly unexplainable even when they did encounter it. Still, we weren't so far removed from Salem or its famous trials to not be cautious. The Council couldn't control the Fae or werewolf populations, but we could control the number of witches. Living here had its perks, beyond just the anti-demon barrier: Witches who lived in town matriculated at the academy for significantly less than it cost out-of-towners.

"A valid reason that keeps us all safe," Laurent replied.

"And the fact that all three families were generalists?" I asked.

Laurent didn't bother responding, but Bastien set down his coffee mug. "Grandfather, weren't you saying not long ago Arcadia could use some new blood?"

"It could, but only—"

"So help me, if you say 'only the right kind,'" I cut in, giving him a dark look.

He continued, giving me a level look. "Only when the *timing* is right. This town's seen enough upheaval lately. No need to add to it just now." On this note, he gave both Bastien and me a judgmental look. On the one hand, we had been involved in said upheaval. But on the other hand, fuck him. "It's time we left. Finish your drinks."

Bastien poured out at least half a mug of coffee in the sink while I chugged the rest of mine. "Let's roll."

Laurent gestured, and a crisp blue circle appeared in my kitchen, opening a portal to an empty hospital room. While I disliked plenty of things about Laurent, I had to admire his skill with magic. He was a master-level witch, able to cast most spells without runes, rituals, or even words, including ones outside of his family's specialty. I could cast a handful of spells without words, but not nearly enough to qualify as more than an adept.

Not counting doing whatever it is I do to demons without speaking, I thought, remembering how I'd pulled apart that tentacle demon last night.

"After you," Bastien prompted.

I shook off the thoughts. "Right. Keep your hands and arms inside the portal." I glanced his way, hoping to see even just a hint of amusement at the old joke we would make about portal travel, but got nothing for it. Sighing to myself, still unsure what to make of this version of Bastien, I stepped through the portal.

We signed in at the front desk and made our way to the maternity ward—unlike the Harwell Institute, the local hospital was not run by witches, and we still needed to abide by hospital policies. I was able to convince Laurent to let me go in first by myself, and he grudgingly agreed when I pointed out werewolves don't do well with surprises, much less threats. Armed with an offering from the gift store, I made my way to their room, pausing to peer through the glass panel before knocking.

Brooke's blond hair was a warm golden halo in the morning sunshine, turning her into almost a modern Madonna holding her newborn baby to her breast to nurse. Lucca sat at the foot of the bed, the sun highlighting his olive-toned skin and dark hair as he gazed upon his wife and child adoringly. Brooke gasped and looked up at him, smiling brilliantly. "She did it! She latched on!"

"Yes! I knew you could do it, babe. And Josie! You're a superbaby already, not even a day old and totally nailing it," Lucca said, beaming with pride.

It was so idyllic, I hesitated to interrupt. I didn't want to. They'd come so far and through so much to be here in this moment. Lucca had wanted to be a dad pretty much his whole life, and Brooke had always been eager to have a new family after losing hers to a hurricane when she was twelve. Abandoned and alone in the aftermath of the storm, the sole survivor of the New Orleans Bellerieves, she had become Saranthiel's thrall out of her desperation to survive. The Archdemon's manipulations over the years had twisted her idea of what love was. Lucca's steadfast loyalty had, no doubt, been what gave her the courage to rebel even the slightest bit against Saranthiel in the end, and to do what she could to warn the rest of us.

It hadn't been much. But when you were bound like she had been, like I had been, every inch of ground gained was a battle waged, every decision that was your own was a victory.

Her personal hell was over. She was free and clear. And now I was here to punish her for it.

Lucca looked over, nose twitching. "McKenna? Hey, come in!" He came over and hugged me as I entered.

"Hey, guys. Congratulations," I said, returning the hug. "She's beautiful."

"Thank you! She is, she's *perfect*," Brooke agreed, smiling at the suckling baby. "Josephine Lorelei Luppino."

"Josie for short," Lucca added. "Do you want to hold her?"

"Uh, she looks kinda busy," I said.

"Yeah, I mean after that," Lucca said.

"Um...maybe." I hadn't been around many newborns in my life. Plus, I wasn't exactly here to celebrate anyway, but I did hand him the gift bag. "Here, this is for her. It's not much, just a onesie from the gift shop, but I didn't want to come empty-handed. Especially since, well…I'm here about the thing I texted you about."

"Thanks—oh. Yeah." Lucca's mood darkened as he took the bag and set it down. "We were gonna get in touch after they release us tomorrow. Kinda shitty timing."

"Lucca! Language!" Brooke chastised.

"Oh, sorry. Crappy timing."

"Better." Brooke smiled, but I could start to see how tired she was under the new-mom glow. "We weren't exactly shocked, but yeah, it would've been nice to get some more recovery time in first."

"I don't think the timing is a coincidence," I said. "I'm pretty sure Sofia was waiting until you had the baby just to make it that much worse for you. These things are taxing at best and potentially traumatic."

Brooke's brow furrowed. "Traumatic? Oh, right. That truth circle thing, I remember you said that was difficult. But it's not like I'm planning to lie."

Time to rip the bandage off. "It's not just a truth circle thing, Brooke."

"What do you mean? What is it, then?" Brooke asked, her fatigue showing when her smile faded. Perhaps sensing her distress, baby Josie began crying.

Lucca swooped in to gently lift his daughter, who was comically tiny in his arms, throwing a cloth over his shoulder and gently patting her back. Her cries settled into whimpers. Brooke had only just covered her chest when the door opened again and Bastien and Laurent entered the room.

Lucca glowered—an impressive feat while burping a baby. "What are you doing here?" he growled at Laurent.

"I'm here to inform you, Brooke Luppino, that by unanimous vote of the Witches Council of Arcadia Commons, you've been accused of the murder of Mariposa Perez, treason against witches, and conspiracy. Your trial will take place within the next seven days. If you are found guilty of any of these crimes, your magic will be severed," Laurent informed her, with no cushioning or preamble of any kind.

"Seven days?" Brooke gasped. "But … I just had a baby!"

"Unanimous vote?" Lucca echoed, turning his glower on me.

"I was outvoted no matter what, I didn't want them to find an excuse to cut me out of the whole trial at that point," I replied.

He snorted. "Yeah, wouldn't want to get in the way of your career aspirations."

"That's not it at all!"

"And why is Bastien here? He's not on the Council," Lucca asked.

Bastien stepped forward. "I'm here because I'm acting as the advocate for the Perez family."

Brooke flinched and looked away. Lucca growled again, his eyes taking on a lupine shade of golden-yellow. "Dude, you were—" but his words were interrupted by baby Josie starting to cry again and him wrinkling his nose. "She needs to be changed. Did this really have to happen right freaking now?"

"I'll get her," Brooke said, easing out of the bed carefully. She was wearing a pajama set with little baby animals on it, the top of which could easily be pulled down for nursing, and she moved slowly as she took the baby and brought her to a changing table in the room.

After carefully handing over Josie, Lucca tensed again. His eyes weren't yellow anymore, but I doubted his scary side was very far away. "You're helping them do this? You're our friend! You were in our freaking wedding!"

Bastien lifted his chin to coolly meet Lucca's gaze—which could be dangerous when dealing with an alpha werewolf, even one in human form. "And you were in mine. I believe you remember how that turned out."

"For what it's worth, Bastien isn't the one who petitioned for this, Lucca. Sofia did," I said.

"Yeah, and you only voted for it, so I guess everyone gets to be a bad guy today," Lucca snapped back. He focused on Laurent. "I get it, you want your pound of flesh, but seriously, this can't even wait a month? It's not like we're going anywhere."

"Severing trials are an urgent matter. Mrs. Perez delayed because your wife was pregnant. That's no longer the case, and so the Council is moving ahead with what is, frankly, a long-overdue matter," Laurent replied.

Josie began bawling, the sharp, loud cries cutting through Laurent's words, but the man remained unmoved. Brooke made gentle shushing noises, trying to calm her while still trying to get her changed. Lucca hovered between dealing with Laurent and helping his wife, visibly stressed by the two factors. I was on the verge of stepping in and helping her myself, even though I knew almost nothing about diaper changes, but then Lucca growled and made his choice. Turning his back to us, he chose Brooke—of course he did—grabbing a diaper and some other supplies.

I glanced uneasily at Bastien. He remained stoic for the most part, but I saw his brow crease at the baby's cries, his eyes flick between the new mother and the child.

"Do you have an advocate to represent you to the Council in this matter?" Laurent continued, as though none of this were going on.

"What do you think?" Lucca snapped, not looking at him. Josie was still wailing. "I've got this, go ahead," he said more gently to his wife.

Brooke faced us, her mouth tight with stress as Josie continued crying. "I don't have an advocate. I…no one would take the case." Her gaze dropped as she softly confessed this, her mouth starting to tremble in a way I knew was a prelude to tears.

They said they weren't surprised…of course they would've asked around, even if they didn't think it was this serious. And of course no one would take it up. An accusation like that, with Brooke very much known to have been a thrall? Losing a trial like this against a justifiably angry Council would be a black mark on anyone's advocate record, if they even thought she had a chance to begin with.

Laurent nodded once. "Yes, I thought that might be the case. Bastien will be in touch with the details, in that case. Are there any questions at this time?"

"Um…" Brooke looked at Bastien, tears welling up. "N-no. We'll…we'll see you at the trial."

"This trial is for witches only. Your husband is not

permitted to attend." Laurent's face was without sympathy as he dropped that one on her.

Brooke's green eyes widened in distress. "What? I can't—I have to go in there alone?"

Lucca growled, whipping around, eyes golden, hackles raised. "Like hell, Laurent. I'm going with her and you can't stop me."

"Witch trials are witch matters, Mr. Luppino. And you are not a witch," Laurent reminded him. "We discipline our people as we see fit, the same as you do with yours."

"Not letting me accompany my wife when you're trying to sever her magic is bullshit and you know it," Lucca growled. "You just want her in there alone. She's my wife, that makes her part of my pack, meaning this *is* werewolf business."

"Please, Mr. Luppino. No need to get aggressive."

"When I start getting aggressive, you'll know," Lucca said in a dangerous voice.

Laurent's expression changed then. Almost unnoticeably, but I'd spent more time than most studying the careful micro-expressions of the Lemaires, and his in particular the last few months. It was the smallest change in the corner of his mouth, matched by the smallest glint in his stony gaze. He was *glad* this was happening.

And if everything else about this, from Sofia's predatory timing right down to the crying baby and the tears on Brooke's exhausted face, hadn't been enough, that certainly was.

"Actually, Laurent, she *does* have an advocate," I said, stepping between him and the Luppinos. "Me."

The elder Lemaire's more familiar look of displeasure appeared. Personally, it was my favorite. I just loved the way his eyes narrowed at the corners and his whole face frowned without frowning. "What?"

"You heard me. I'm an adept, I'm familiar with witch law, I'm a resident of Arcadia Commons. I will be representing Brooke Luppino in this matter. That is"—I turned to Brooke—"if you'll have me?"

Brooke blinked wide, tear-filled eyes at me. "You want to? After...after everything...?"

"After what she did to you?" Bastien blurted out, baffled, his neutral façade falling entirely. *The Tin Man still has a heart after all. Good to know.*

My knot of trauma was far from undone, but I wasn't about to let Laurent Lemaire bully her for what she'd gone through. Or, apparently, try to manipulate Lucca into some kind of charter violation. "I do."

"Th-then yes! Yes, please. Thank you," Brooke said, nodding vigorously.

I turned back to the Lemaires. Laurent still looked displeased; Bastien still looked confused, but he was trying to piece his façade back together.

"Very well." Laurent's voice grated. "Bastien, you'll communicate with Miss Ellerbeck on any and all matters related to this trial, and vice versa. As well, you understand you'll be forfeiting your own vote on the matter, Miss Ellerbeck?"

"I do. I'll name a proxy," I said. "If there's nothing else, then I'm going to have to ask you to leave so I can talk to my client."

"And *neither* of you is allowed back in here," Lucca added in a dark, threatening voice. "Or we'll find out if a witch can be a werewolf, too." Supernatural beings were singular in nature. A witch couldn't become a werewolf, a werewolf couldn't gain access to magic, neither could become Fae, and so forth. It was yet another reason my ability to interact with demonic power was unusual and worrisome. But Lucca's subtext was clear—if Laurent came near his family again, Lucca would readily take a bite out of him.

Laurent grunted acknowledgement and turned to leave. Bastien lingered, his unsettled gaze drifting between Brooke, Lucca, and me, and landing on me.

"What are you doing?" Bastien asked me, but the look in his storm-blue eyes asked a different question: *Why?* It slid through the cracks in his mask, the ones I finally realized were there. His cold, neutral front, it really *was* just that. I wasn't sure what held it together, or why he wore it. His grandfather's presence was one thing, but taking it so far as to be trying to get Brooke severed? Why indeed?

Because I wished someone had done it for me. Because severing was cruel. Because I couldn't stand seeing Laurent Lemaire bully people more vulnerable than him. Because I felt I owed it to her, and I'd hurt enough people through inaction in the past. Because I knew how it felt to be in the position she'd been in.

"I know I can't make everything right," I said, "but I can at least try to keep this from going wrong."

For a moment, something in him softened. But then his grandfather called, "Bastien, we're leaving," and he hardened again.

"Coming, Grandfather."

I waited for the door to close behind them before turning back to Brooke and Lucca. Brooke was finally getting Josie to quiet down, holding her against her shoulder and gently rocking her, while Lucca was doing some box breathing by the window.

"I'm sorry, guys. I didn't think this was going to turn into . . . *that*," I said.

"You seriously thought that was gonna go *well*?" Lucca asked over his shoulder.

"No, that would've been naive, but I hoped it would be a little more civil at least," I replied. "Is Josie okay?"

Brooke nodded, smiling softly at the baby. "Yeah. She's asleep now," she replied. Very carefully, she set the newborn down in the small plastic crib in the room, bending down to lightly kiss her forehead as she did so. "Thank you for your offer, McKenna. But if you want to back out, that's okay."

"I'm not backing out unless you tell me to. Although, to be honest, I'd still argue with you about it, because you need someone to help you out with this," I told her. "Sofia doing this the second she could get away with it is shitty to start with, but you can't tell me you're in a good place to try and handle it on your own."

"Unfortunately," Brooke agreed. "Speaking of which, I need to sit down."

Lucca came over to help get her settled back into the bed. "Why does she need an advocate at all? This isn't an actual legal trial, you're not a lawyer," he said. "Besides, they'll just do that circle of truth they did to you and that's that, right? They'll know she didn't kill Mari."

"There's that, yeah, but having all the facts doesn't mean you have the truth. What happened with…with me and Jackie is proof enough of that," I said, uneasy at mentioning it aloud. "It's not just Mari's death they're bringing up, either. Conspiring with a demon, treason against the witch community at large? Those are going to be a lot easier to show, and either one could mean severing."

"They didn't when you did it," Lucca pointed out gruffly.

"Barely. The truth circle proved I didn't know what I was getting into—which, yes, I know you didn't at first, Brooke, but you were a thrall much longer than I was, and the circle also proved that when I did realize, I tried to get out of it. The fact I was the one to kill Forneus and that Remi was more or less on our side after also helped," I explained. "Believe me, I'm sure they've all regretted it since."

"So why aren't they trying to sever you now?" Lucca asked.

"I honestly keep half expecting it," I said, sighing. "I think the only ones who have the grounds to do so are the Harwells, and they are exceptionally understanding and forgiving."

Brooke smiled. "That, and I'm sure they know if they tried anything, Remi would raise absolute hell to stop them. You're the only thing standing between her and them."

I shifted uncomfortably. "That's not true."

"Please! You're totally her anchor." Brooke yawned, then frowned, gaze distant. "You're a better one than I ever was."

Saranthiel's death, for me, had been a triumph. The moment I'd finally taken my life back, messy though it may be. For most people, however, it had been a tragedy. The Perez family and Bastien and others had lost Mari, and even worse, they'd lost her five years before they knew it. They mourned the loss of their daughter, friend, and would-be wife.

Brooke was mourning, too, but she was the only one who mourned Saranthiel. Saranthiel had insinuated herself into Brooke's life as thoroughly as any abuser. She'd been Brooke's best friend and protector, practically her family. She'd also controlled almost every aspect of Brooke's life since she was twelve, convincing Brooke there was no one else who loved her, that Brooke owed her everything for saving her life, that she was the only one Brooke could rely on, to the point that Brooke's sense of right and wrong itself had been badly skewed.

Lucca brought a chair over to the bedside so he could hold her hand. I didn't know how he'd gotten through learning the truth and not left her. I didn't doubt it had been hard for them both, but here he was, still by her side. That love and undying loyalty were why Brooke hadn't been entirely corrupted by her former master.

"How do you…how are you doing?" I asked her.

"Hm? Oh, well, kind of exhausted, honestly, and sore in places I didn't think you could be, but she's worth every bit of it," Brooke said, smiling fondly at the sleeping Josie.

"I'm sure, but I actually meant about Saranthiel," I clarified.

"Oh! I…" Brooke glanced at Lucca, who just nodded. "It's…it's hard. I know how awful she was, I do, but I…I still *miss* her. It's wrong, I know. After everything she did to me, and you and Jackie and Mari, but…" She shrugged.

"I…I don't know that it's wrong. Fucked up—" They both gave me a look. "She's asleep! And I don't think she can process words like that yet anyway."

"Consider it practice," Lucca suggested.

"Not for me it isn't," I assured him. Kids were great, but I'd never been terribly inclined toward having my own.

"I meant for being around her," Lucca said. "We're not doing Leo's 'whatever, they're just words' thing."

I shrugged. "Okay, sure. What was I saying...right, yeah, I don't know if it's wrong, really, just messed up."

"Is it, though?" Brooke said. "She was awful and abusive and—"

"And an evil murderous psychopathic megalomaniacal demon?" I prompted.

Brooke cleared her throat. "Yes, that. But she also saved my life. She was also my friend."

"Only so she could use you—"

"I know, McKenna!" Brooke interrupted. "I know. Look, I don't want to argue about her. I'm too tired. But there's still a space in my life that's empty now, and I'm...learning how to grow around it. I can't—I *don't* love her anymore, but I can love the things I've learned about myself. Good and bad."

The indignant fire in me faded in the face of that. "Well... sounds like someone's been in therapy," I joked weakly.

Brooke smiled. "I have. *We* have, actually." She squeezed Lucca's hand. "It's been really helpful."

"So I hear." I saw her about to make the obvious suggestion, so I hurried to the next order of business. "We can do this later, but I am going to ask you what happened at the cliffs in detail. And probably a number of other things. If you're up for it, we should do some memory reconstruction spells on the cliff and the beach where Mari and Saranthiel swapped. I'll see if Tom can help."

Brooke nodded, gaze falling again. "Sure. Give me a few days, at least?"

"Of course. Meanwhile, I need to do some research. And talk with Bastien, apparently."

"Yeah, good luck with that," Lucca said dubiously.

"I'll need it. I'll be in touch, and congrats again on Josie. She's beautiful," I said.

"Thank you. And…it's good to see you, McKenna," Brooke said with a hopeful smile. "I'm sorry we didn't tell you ourselves she was born. We didn't really tell anyone outside our family and the pack."

"They were all guarding around the hospital last night," Lucca added. "Sorry we couldn't help with the demons."

The phantom sensation of the tentacle wrapped around my arm flared up, but there was no need to get into that story with them. "Cam and I managed. And I get it, I'm on the Council, you didn't want them—us—to know just yet. You were right to worry. I don't know how Laurent found out so quickly."

"Dude's probably got spies all over this town," Lucca said. "Chris is on top of things for now until we get home." Chris Miller, another friend since high school, had been Lucca's second-in-command as long as he'd been the alpha of the pack.

"It wouldn't shock me," I agreed. "And noted, hopefully we don't get another—" But even as I spoke, I felt that creeping sensation in my blood that meant something had crossed the barrier. While the hospital was farther from the water, it wasn't far from the inland edge of the town and the barrier. "I had to say it. Feels like something just got through, I'll text

Chris and check on the town line on my way home. You two just focus on the baby."

It wasn't until I'd signed out and messaged Chris that I remembered that I hadn't driven here but come through the portal with the Lemaires. I could call a rideshare, but it was likely this advocate thing was going to eat into my wages this week as it was, and I did not feel like suffering the local bus line schedule. I could also ask Remi, but I wanted to avoid the conversation about last night for a little longer. A portal home shouldn't be too hard; the room the Lemaires and I had entered through had a few spell supplies stashed.

But to my surprise, when I finally located the room, I found Bastien and a portal waiting for me.

Bastien was leaning against the end of the hospital bed, so lost in thought he didn't notice me at first, and for a moment I saw him plain. The blue light of the portal a few feet away limned his face and tinted his hair. The suit jacket was gone, and his sleeves were rolled up over his lean forearms. He stared at one hand, at something that glinted as he slowly turned it between his fingers. His other hand rested at his chin in thought, thumb idly stroking his bottom lip.

From the seat next to him in the auditorium, I grabbed Bastien's hand as his thumb stroked his lip, kissing it. "Kiss for your thoughts?"

"Isn't it supposed to be a penny?" he asked in a whisper. The speaker onstage went on about the secret degree programs available for supernaturals at Brown.

"You have enough pennies."

He tried to stifle his own smile so as not to give us away. "I was thinking, what if we both went to Brown?"

My heart jumped happily at the suggestion. "What about your whole Harvard family legacy?"

Bastien shrugged and glanced sidelong at me, telling me without a word how much he'd rather be kissing me than listening to more of this lecture. My pulse sped as he tugged my hand back to his mouth. He ran my thumb along his lip this time, before placing a slow, gentle kiss on it that sent sparks up my arm. "I've had enough of my family's plans. I want to make my own. With you. Toi et moi."

You and me.

"Bastien?"

My interruption was more like a reset button. He stood up, face resolutely neutral once again. The shiny object disappeared into his pocket. "McKenna."

"What are you still doing here?" I asked, quietly closing the door behind me.

"I realized we'd stranded you," Bastien said, gesturing at the portal. Blue light lined a semitranslucent door that looked a little like the one to my house. Unlike his grandfather's open-air blue circles, Bastien's portals tended to have doors.

"Oh." The polite gesture felt oddly deflating. "Well, thanks. I'll just..." I walked toward the portal door.

"Wait," Bastien said just before I got there. I looked over my shoulder, catching a whisper of some kind of conflict in his face, a quick and silent war between formality, anger, and... something else. Finally, he schooled his features and continued in a formal tone. "You'll want to make use of the advocate archives at the Uncommon Collection. Grandfather's sent word for us both to have access to them. They include records of past severing trials as well as what spells will be used in the course of the trial. You'll need to—"

"—sign items out and they need to stay in the library. I know, Bastien. I used to work there, remember?" I reminded him.

"Right. Of course."

I couldn't think of what else to say, though it felt like something should be said. Something to clear the air between us because it very much was not. But what could I say? He'd been clear at the Solstice Ball.

"How . . . how can I make this right, Bastien?"

"You can't. Just stay away from me."

After a sufficient pause I nodded. "Okay, awkward silence achieved. Thanks for the portal." I reached for the door again.

"Tomorrow."

"Huh?" I turned back around.

Bastien cleared his throat. "I mean—I'd like to speak with you tomorrow."

"You . . . *want* to talk to me?" *What the hell?* "About what? The trial?"

"Yes." Somehow it felt like there was more to it, but he didn't elaborate. "Come to my house. At eleven. I'll send you the address."

"I know where your house is, Bastien."

"I don't mean my family's house. I mean *my* house," Bastien clarified. "It's on the southern edge of town."

"Oh." I had been aware that Bastien and Mari had a home of their own but had never been to it, for obvious reasons.

"So? Will you come?"

Would I? He'd told me to stay away, in no uncertain terms. He'd been cold since showing up last night, and he was actively trying to get Brooke severed. He was, in short, acting like a Lemaire.

I met his gaze, and stoic as he was, there was a crack in his mask. Maybe he still hated me . . . but maybe not. Maybe there was something to be saved here after all. There was only one way to find out.

"I'll be there."

Chapter 5
The Secret Life of
Bastien Lemaire

The rest of my Saturday was spent buried in the advocate archives at the Uncommon Collection, reading up on old severing trials and their outcomes. They didn't happen often, maybe one every ten or fifteen years. The fact that three had happened in the last twenty years, including this one, was very unusual. Before that, the last one had been a few years before I was born, for someone named Curtis Craig, for the nebulous charge of "endangering witchkind." Oddly, there was another entry after that, but the text detailing it had been blacked out. Maybe someone had changed their mind between the petition and the trial itself.

While I briefly spotted my mom at the Veil and Horn that night, she kept her distance. Which was just fine by me, especially since it was a particularly horny crowd that night. She wasn't home when I finally got in, but Cameron and I got an obligatory text to assure us she was alive and well and that was that.

Until the next morning.

My search for the shears I knew we had somewhere in the house—I'd been too absorbed with research and then work to even out my hair yet—was interrupted by the doorbell being rung repeatedly and aggressively. "Calm down, I'm coming!" I jogged down the stairs and opened it. "...Mom?"

"There you are! I was starting to think I'd have to break into my own house," Mom said, digging around in her purse with the hand that wasn't on the doorbell. She was dressed in what must be last night's clothes, and it was profoundly unfair that her unwashed hair looked better than mine.

"The spare is in the garage, you know. What happened to your keys?" I asked.

She shrugged carelessly, giving up on looking for them as she came in. "Eaten by this bag or somewhere between the bar and...I wanna say Liam? Liam's place." She looked me up and down. "You're dressed early. I thought you weren't working till later?"

"You know my work schedule?" I closed the door.

"Of course I do. How else would I throw my wild parties when you're working nights?" Mom joked sarcastically. She set her purse down on the table just inside the door. "Coffee?"

"There's a pot on."

"Good." Dumping her heels next to the door, she beelined for the coffee. I followed, wanting another cup myself.

"So...we should talk about the other night," she said. I looked at her warily. "I know, I know, you've got some sarcastic, indignant quip lined up, and I thought of a few myself, but..." She sighed, pausing with the fridge door open. "Well, I was talking with Gretchen about the whole situation...where did I put that creamer?"

I filled my mug and frowned. "You talked to her about it? About us?"

"There it is!" She emerged with the French vanilla–flavored creamer. "One, like you don't talk to your friends about us? And two, I didn't mean you and me, I meant you and Remi."

I nearly spat out my sip. "What?" I sputtered. "Okay, one, that's my business, not yours or anyone else's, and two, there's nothing to talk about!"

Mom raised an eyebrow at me as she mixed her coffee. "Uh-huh. Don't think I didn't notice there were two mugs in this sink yesterday. You hooked up with her again, didn't you?"

"Mom!" My face flamed at the not-inaccurate accusation. "That's—she's—I repeat, it's none of your business, okay? And you made it very clear what you think of her the other night."

"I'm not so sure I did. She's a demon, sweetie! Not to mention our landlord."

I threw up my hands. "She's always been a demon! Why does that matter more now than when I was a teenager?"

"Because she's an *Arch*demon now—twice over!" Mom exclaimed. "That's a little more dangerous than she used to be. And don't think I *didn't* have some serious concerns back then, either."

"Then you should've said something then instead of waiting until I was an adult," I countered.

"Just because you're an adult doesn't mean you can't make some catastrophic mistakes in love, McKenna."

"Yeah, I guess you'd know, wouldn't you?" I sniped. "Talk to Dad lately?"

As soon as the words left my mouth, I knew I'd gone too far. My mom looked like I'd slapped her, and the creeping numbness of wishing I could leave my body spread through me. "Mom, I…"

"Believe it or not, McKenna, sometimes I actually am trying to spare you repeating my mistakes," she said. Coffee in hand, she left the kitchen without another word. Her steps thudded up the stairs, followed by the click of her bedroom door closing firmly.

I slumped onto the counter, head in my hands, knowing exactly how shitty I'd just been. My dad had left us when I was twelve, without a word or so much as a cent of alimony or child support. I never knew why, but Mom later told me he'd repeatedly cheated on her. While it had been awful at the time, it was probably the best thing that had ever happened to us. My mom was so much happier with him gone, and eventually, Cameron and I were, too. Truly, the Ellerbecks were living proof that what didn't kill you made you stronger, many traumatic times over.

On the other hand, I felt justifiably irritated that she was trying to dole out advice about my relationships. As if I didn't know how complicated they already were. Hell, I still hadn't replied to Remi's text. I'd been too busy to think about it, much less actually reply.

Definitely that and not me avoiding anything.

Besides, I had a different but still-complicated relationship to a different but still-complicated ex to navigate today. Remi could wait.

Speaking of, I was out of time to attempt a haircut before meeting Bastien. After braiding and pinning my hair once again, I hustled out the door.

Like his family's historical mansion, Bastien's house was on the water, though away from public view. At the start of the private drive that led to it was a FOR SALE sign, suggesting it wouldn't be his much longer. He must have bought it with Mari, so I wasn't surprised he didn't want to remain in it. But where would he go next? He'd been out of town for months, after all—had he found some other town he'd rather start over in? Even though I hadn't seen him until two days ago, it felt wrong to think of him leaving Arcadia Commons forever.

At the end of the drive was a deceptively modest-looking home. It had that faded, gray, natural wood siding with white trim that beach homes often do, making it feel smaller and more quaint than it was. But the cottage hideaway aesthetic did not hide the sleek, expensive blue Audi parked outside, the inviting porch that ran along the side of the house and wrapped around to the back, or the hot tub with an ocean view. The only thing missing was a forty-foot schooner; probably that was docked at a yacht club.

I rang the doorbell, but there was no answer. Another ring...still nothing. I tried to peer through the windows alongside the door, but the glass was textured and impossible to get a good look through.

"Bastien?" I called out, knocking loudly.

Still no answer. *Maybe he's in the shower? Or on the beach?*

I walked around the wraparound porch to the back of the house, the side facing the beach. I felt a bit of relief seeing that there was indeed a boardwalk leading to the shore.

Then I heard the crunch of glass under my shoe.

A handful of glass was scattered across the back porch: the remains of a sliding door that had exploded inward.

"Seven hells—Bastien!" I yelled, carefully but quickly stepping inside.

There was no answer as I scanned the living room, stepping over the worst of the glass. Something had come in through the door and with great force, no doubt about that, but what and why and *where was Bastien?*

The room was large, high ceilinged and open concept, with the kitchen to one side past a half wall. The chaotic remains of a ritual were on the wood floor between the fireplace and the couch: smudged chalk circle on the ground, broken lowball glass, melted and snuffed candles, and, strangest of all, the coffee table was toppled on the ground and sliced in half at an angle, with no sign of the other half. *What the seven hells were you doing, Bast?*

Athame in hand and a spell ready on my lips, I quickly dashed through the rest of the house, checking each room. I even pricked my finger to be extra certain when feeling out if there were any demons inside; nothing pinged back at me, no sulfur stung my nose, though I did feel the traces of demonic power having been used here. However, my search turned up no other obvious signs of Bastien, a burglar, or a demon. I went around the outside of the house as well but likewise found nothing. I called his phone, only to find it on the desk in his home office. His keys hung by the door. The beds had not been slept in. There was no note excusing his absence, and I had no missed messages, either.

When I returned to the living room, the breeze off the ocean carried the salty air and soft crashing of the waves through the shattered door. The wind chilled my arms, sure as the winter breeze had four months ago. Bastien had disappeared from my life then, but this felt so much worse. Then it had been my fault, a direct result of my behavior. There had been a reason and I had known he was still around, just not present in my life. But now? Now I had no clear cause to point to, no assurance he was otherwise okay, every reason to assume he wasn't but nothing I could do about it. The room felt like it was spinning as my breaths came rapid and shallow. I stumbled to the couch, grabbing a pillow to hug and bending over, eyes closed.

I'll figure this out... I'll find him... he has to be somewhere, I'll find him, I'll find him...

Fuck me. This is exactly what I did to him, isn't it? To everyone?

The realization did not help.

"Fuck, fuck, fuck..." I clumsily pulled out my phone and called Leo.

She picked up quickly, at least. "Hey! What's up?" Leo answered.

"Bastien's missing and I'm having a panic attack," I said in a rush.

"What? Whoa—okay, breathe. Whatever's happening, we'll figure it out," Leo replied, going right into a soothing tone. "Just breathe, okay? In for four... out for six..."

This is why Leo is my best friend. I could hear the alarm in her voice, but she didn't linger on that and went right into helping me. There were a lot of other reasons, too, of course, but since I was the type to have a lot of crises, it helped that she was so good in one.

After a few minutes of slow, deep breathing, she finally asked for details. "What happened, exactly? Where are you?"

"I'm at Bastien's house—his house, on the south side, not the Lemaire mansion. He asked me to meet him here. But there's no sign of him, and something or someone broke in through the sliding glass door," I told her.

"Okay, yeah, that's a big yikes. When's the last time you talked to him?"

"Yesterday morning, at the hospital. Before I left, he asked me to meet him here today. Said he wanted to talk about the trial," I told her.

"The one where he's trying to take my sister-in-law's magic away?" Leo griped.

"Leo..."

She sighed. "Right, I know, not the time. Okay, is there any sign of who broke in? Or when? Maybe he wasn't home when it happened."

"Nothing yet. There's a ritual circle on the floor, but it's too smudged to make out much. And for some reason half of the coffee table is missing."

"C'mon, the day McKenna Ellerbeck can't ID a rune at fifty feet is the day I turn into a werewolf," Leo encouraged me; sure enough, I laughed. "That's better. Take a close look, I'm sure you can get something out of it."

"Thank you, personal cheerleader. I'll give it a go." I made my way over to the table and the circle.

"You know it. Also, say that again about the table?"

"It's weird. It's like it was cut clean in half, the wood and the metal, but there's no sign of the other half. Who steals half a coffee table?"

"Beats me."

I crouched down next to the circle and put my phone on speaker while I looked at it more closely. "Okay. The circle. There are candles. Knocked over, but in puddles of wax. They must've been burning awhile before they got knocked down. There's a broken glass here—" I picked up the base and sniffed. "Smells like bourbon. Looks like that spilled and washed off some of the lines. The rest looks like it's been walked on…" I tried to pick out even a single specific rune from what was left and noticed the streak marks of the chalk all went in one direction. "Make that walked on and wiped away. Someone tried to get rid of this on purpose."

"Hm. But was it Bastien or whoever broke in?" Leo asked.

"Exactly. There's one here that might have been a binding rune, but it doesn't quite look right. Can't tell if that's because it's smudged or not."

"Can your grimoire help?"

"Cam's got it right now, but I can get a picture to compare later." I snapped a few, getting the circle, the table, and the broken glass documented. As I started to stand, light glinted off a gold ring on the couch cushion. "Huh. There's a ring on the couch. Gold band, one—oh."

"Oh what?"

I'd seen it up close once before, glittering on the hand of Saranthiel posing as Mariposa Perez. "It's Mari's engagement ring. But it's missing a diamond." Bastien had it made using two heirloom diamonds, from both of their grandmothers. The gold band was smooth, with tiny diamonds along the front of it leading up to what had once been two large, lovely, round-cut diamonds. Except one setting was empty now.

"Who steals one diamond instead of just taking the whole ring?" Leo asked.

"Half a ring and half a coffee table. This burglar has a very weird MO," I replied. I pocketed the ring for now. "If I find half a bottle of bourbon, this guy's officially the Half-Off Bandit."

Leo snickered. "Good, you're snarking. You must be feeling better."

"Thanks to you, yeah," I said. "And panicking isn't going to help."

"True. Not that it's not warranted, I mean, some shit clearly went down over there," Leo replied. "That's why you need backup." A car horn honked outside, and when I went to the front door, I saw Leo getting out of her car, phone in hand and grinning at me. I hung up and went out, hugging her tightly.

"I'm super glad to see you, but also, what the heck are you doing here?" I asked when I pulled back. "And how'd you get here so fast?"

"Helping you find our friend," Leo replied simply. "And I just dropped Griff at his gymnastics lesson, it's not far from here. Now, if you're about to say this is a witch problem—"

"I wasn't, but—"

"—then I will show you exactly how many hidden object mystery games I've played." She brandished her phone at me. "And if you're going to say 'What about Griffin?' I will tell you my dad already said he'd pick him up and watch him for a while, so no mom-guilting me, either!"

"I would never. And I'm not turning down help, especially yours. Although I'm dubious about how applicable your 'experience' is going to be," I said, chuckling as we headed inside.

"You say that now, but when you run into a shredded paper puzzle, you'll be eating those words!"

I knew Leo was elevating the joviality for my sake, or maybe both our sakes, but that didn't mean I wasn't grateful for it. Just having her there made me feel more grounded, especially on the heels of the panic attack.

After we looked over the living room again, we stepped into the kitchen, which was remarkably clean and tidy.

"Looks like a lot of the dishes have already been packed up and moved out. Any idea where he's moving to?" Leo asked, going through the cabinets.

"Nope. If you'll remember, he hasn't spoken to me since the Solstice Ball up until Friday night," I replied. "Coffeepot is full, but not hot, and I don't see any used mugs."

"Is it on a timer?"

"Hm…yep, set for seven a.m. So he's been gone since before then."

Leo pointed back toward the smudged circle. "Bourbon in the glass, right? Probably having a nightcap when he was doing all this."

"Good point. But that means he's been missing since last night," I said, rubbing at the scar on my left hand.

"Doesn't mean that happened last night," Leo replied, pointing to the shattered glass. "No spiraling without hard evidence. C'mon, let's check the other rooms. Bedrooms always have good secrets, right?" She gestured at the first door off the living room.

"I guess so. You've been here before?"

"Housewarming party last year. It's so screwed up to know that wasn't really Mari," Leo reflected. "She was so *believable*. I showed her pictures of Griffin, she asked about him, said how sorry she was about Alex. She even…fuck."

"What?" I turned back at the bedroom door.

"Just realizing yet another clever little concealment. She 'confided' in me that she'd found out she couldn't have kids. Went the whole nine yards, put on this sad–but–strong front and everything," Leo said, anger growing as she went on. "And sure, she couldn't, but it's because she was a demon. I doubt she even cared! It just…it feels like this awful mockery. Like I got played for having empathy. There are people who can't and genuinely want to, but to her it was just another way to play human, another way to twist the truth to sell the bigger lie."

Another little lie, another manipulation in a long line of them. Bastien's anger at the Solstice Ball echoed in my mind yet again. Leo was upset over just one instance of Saranthiel's gaslighting; he'd endured so much more and so much worse. *Because I couldn't just tell the truth about what happened.*

"You've got that face."

"Huh?" I looked up. "What face?"

"The face that says, *I'm blaming myself for something that isn't my fault.*"

"Except that it *is* my fault," I replied, pushing the door open and going in. "If I'd told someone—"

"Then we still wouldn't have known who she was. Maybe it wouldn't have been Mari, sure, but that just means she would've been someone else. Or she would've made you do a lot worse," Leo insisted. She turned me to face her, her hands on my shoulders. "Repeat after me: Bad people being bad people is not my fault."

"I'm not saying it is, but she never would've had the chance—"

Leo made a buzzer sound. "Incorrect, please try again! Bad people…?"

I sighed. "Bad people being bad people isn't my fault," I dutifully repeated.

She grinned; it was contagious. "There you go! Now ten more times, out loud, while we search this place."

This is why Leo is my best friend.

With affirmations in the air, we searched. I'd only briefly looked in the other rooms before to check for Bastien or a home invader, and the master bedroom had looked as untouched then as it did now. The king-size bed was neatly made and had not been slept in. A clock sat on one of the nightstands, but the drawers for both were empty. In fact, *empty* described a lot of this room—the dresser only held spare sheets, and the walk-in closet was entirely empty. A TV was mounted on the wall opposite the bed, but the remote didn't have any batteries in it. The master bathroom, too, was weirdly spotless—no drying towels, no toothbrush, nothing. That touch of demonic power was absent from this room as well.

"Is it just me, or does it look like no one lives here?" I finally said, coming out of the bathroom.

"Yeah, I'm pretty sure no one does," Leo confirmed, closing yet another empty drawer.

"I know he's been out of town, but he was here at least the last few nights," I said. "Or so I thought. I mean, the coffee-maker didn't set itself."

"No, he's living here, just not *here*-here," Leo said. "I did pretty much the same thing after Alex died."

I gave her a quizzical look. "What do you mean? He's… sad Saranthiel is gone?"

"Not Saranthiel. *Mari*." Leo looked at me. "This is me making an educated guess, but it's not just that she lied to him and used him, McKenna. It's also that she convinced him, and everyone else, that she *loved* him. And he really did fall in love with her. The person he loved, that he thought loved him, is dead and gone now, too."

"…Oh." I looked around the room again, remembering what Brooke had said at the hospital, about that empty space in her life where her friend had been, even if her "friend" had been a lie. It had still been real for her, and it had been real for Bastien, too. *"I opened up to her, I fell in love with her, I married her!"* Guilt wanted to rush back in, but I was fresh off the affirmations, so it was easier to hold it at arm's length. For now.

"I guess I kind of forget that part. I know it's there, I know it was real, but…I wasn't here when she was pretending. I never knew her as Mari, and the Mari I knew…not that I wanted anything like that to happen to her. But the last I knew her, she was still queen of the mean girls."

"I get it. But yeah, for the rest of us…well. It's probably why he's selling the house. I moved out of the apartment Alex and I had as soon as I could. I hated being there without him," Leo said. "Well, that and living at home so my parents could help with Griffin was a lot easier and more affordable."

"Do you ever think about moving back to the city?" I asked. Leo and her husband had lived outside Boston when they were married, before he died of cancer two years ago.

"Sometimes. I miss parts of it, miss the friends we had there. Getting them to visit up here is a lot harder. But right now, Arcadia still feels like the right place for us to be," she replied, and threw an arm around my shoulders. "In other words, don't worry, you're not getting rid of me anytime soon."

I smiled and gave her a one-armed hug. "Good to know. Thanks again for coming out here."

"Anytime. I mean, c'mon, we've got ten years of mischief and misadventures to catch up on, right? I gotta jump on these chances when I get them," Leo joked.

We moved to the rooms across the hall—a home office and a guest room that were connected by a shared bathroom. It was quickly apparent that these were the rooms Bastien was using: The guest room had a queen-size bed that, while made, showed signs of recent use. The TV remote sat in the middle of the bed; maybe tossed there, maybe forgotten while Bastien was falling asleep. An open closet held some neatly hung shirts and suits. At the bottom, the dress shoes were lined up, while the casual boat shoes and a pair of sandals were askew. The nightstand had a hardcover book on it, bookmark poking out from somewhere in the middle. A mostly empty water glass was next to it, and an empty glasses case. Bastien had been wearing them at the hospital, and wherever he was now, looked like he still was. A TV was mounted to the wall opposite the bed in here, too, though this one sat above a bureau with a few drawers cracked but not fully open.

The neatness was very Bastien, as were the small, controlled clusters of clutter. It lacked any personal photos, but between his selling it and, I imagine, his stripping out reminders of Mari, that made sense. Even so, the room still felt more like it was *his*. The scent of him, the feel of him, his presence was anchored here more than in any other room so far. It wasn't hard to see him reading the book in the chair by the window or watching TV in bed or selecting which expensive suit to wear in the morning.

It would've been comforting if the traces of demonic power hadn't sunk into the room in exactly the same way. It tingled under my skin, prickling my veins not unlike whenever I visited Remi's condo—while she didn't set off my demon-sense, she frequently had minions dropping by who did. Once again, however, there was no sulfur scent, and that was a hallmark of demons. Even the other night in a crowded bar I'd picked up on it from Dara, despite her being under one of Remi's illusions. But not here.

Here, the power had soaked in. But the demon scent had not.

How?

"Okay, two things. One, this is much more lived-in than for someone who just got back into town two days ago," I observed as we took the room in.

"Definitely," Leo agreed. "You notice what else is missing, though? Boxes."

"Huh. You're right," I realized. "Not even flat ones for packing later. Maybe they're in a closet somewhere or something."

"Maybe. If I had to bet, Mari's stuff probably got moved out a while ago by her family. But all *his* stuff is still here."

"Mari's family!" I exclaimed. "Of course. *That's* why the ring is missing a diamond. They took it back."

"Oh, good catch! But I kind of doubt they took half the coffee table, too," Leo said. She pulled out her phone, tapping on the screen. "I wonder…huh. This place has been on the market for a few months now. At an actually affordable price, too, so…why hasn't it sold yet?"

"Let's put a pin in that for later," I suggested. "Because two, this place is *covered* in demonic power, but I'm not sure that any actual demons have been here."

"Is that possible?" Leo asked.

"Possible, but rare. If you had an item with demonic power in it that you were using often, it could happen. That's how Bastien picked up on the aura around the illusion Remi gave me last fall," I explained, investigating the room further. "Or maybe if the house had a frequent demon visitor, just not recently enough to stink the place up. But neither of those things makes sense for Bastien." Even in the wake of losing his best friend and his girlfriend when I fled town and Jackie died, he didn't make a deal with Remi. I couldn't see a scenario in which he would do that now.

"Yeah, I think he and my brother are tied for least likely to hang out with demons willingly or take favors from them in this town," Leo agreed.

"No kidding. Remi's the only demon he could hope to deal with safely, and I don't see that happening," I said. "And I'm pretty sure she'd tell me if he'd tried."

Leo gave me a look. "You sure about that? Wouldn't making a deal, you know, include a promise of her keeping it quiet?"

"Well…yes, but…I'm sure she'd at least hint at it or… something…" My brow furrowed.

"You've got 'but' face."

"But…she also made no mention of her new assistant that she brought to the bar the other night, either," I admitted. Leo gave me a quizzical look, and I explained about Dara, which led to explaining about the scene my mother made, which led to confessing about our little tryst in the ladies' room.

"Okay, that is a *lot* to unpack!" Leo said when I was done. "First question, though, does any of it explain why your hair is all weird and uneven?"

"Ugh, no, that's from the squid demon that almost drowned me before work that night." I stepped into the bathroom to see my braid was failing me again. Unlike the master bathroom, this one looked recently used—towel on the back of the door, dental hygiene products, and so forth.

Leo followed. "You *almost drowned*? Why am I just hearing about all of this now?"

"I've been kinda busy since it happened!"

"No kidding. No wonder you hooked up with Remi."

I glanced at her in the mirror. "Come again?"

She smirked. "Isn't that what you did?"

I snorted with laughter, definitely blushed, and threw a hand towel at her. "Couldn't help it! But seriously, hear me out: You almost die, Bastien shows up without warning, the Council has their shitty severing vote, Remi surprises you with her hottie new right-hand demon, also with no warning, and then your mom deeply embarrasses you at work. All in one night. After a night like that, who wouldn't want some uncomplicated sex?"

My face was still flushed as I finished fixing the braid. "... Yeah, I can't really argue. It was definitely nice to just... be brainless for a bit and feel good about something."

Leo hopped up to sit on the bathroom counter, which was large enough for that with room to spare. "And now you're back to thinking about how she showed up with this Dara demon and what else isn't she telling you?"

"Bingo." I slid in the last pin and sighed. "I promised Remi I wouldn't judge her for taking Saranthiel's mantle, especially since I kind of pushed it on her. But I'd be lying if I said I wasn't worried."

"You wouldn't be you if you weren't, Mickey." She pulled open a drawer under her legs. "And honestly, even at her best, Remi *is* a little sketchy."

"Yeah, but it's usually the kind of sketchy that's a good thing."

"Then find out what's up if you think it's going in the other direction."

"That's all? You don't think it was a bad idea to hook up with her?" I asked, my mom's admonishment from that morning coming to mind.

"I think you're both adults and if you want to hook up, go for it. Just know who you're getting in bed with." She nudged the items in the drawer around. "Q-tips, headache medicine, Band-Aids . . . nothing weird in here. Office?"

"Office." Not that I'd expected her to judge me, but it was a relief when she didn't all the same.

The office was the same size as the guest room, and though the relaxed beach house vibe was present, it was more obviously modern in its furnishings and decor. The L-shaped desk was large, but there was still room for a facing chair, a loveseat, and a coffee table, not to mention the filing cabinet. A closet door was partially open, but at a glance looked empty. Despite that he was clearly using the room, decorations were still sparse and impersonal. The most notable one was a large square artwork over the couch, nice enough, but even that looked like he'd probably lifted it from the Grand's decoration storeroom. The sensation of demonic power was present here, too, as thick as it had been in the bedroom.

On the desk was a laptop, a second monitor, a pile of paperwork, his cell phone, pens, and a printer. A partially empty bottle of bourbon sat on the desk as well. The paperwork turned out to be entirely related to hotel business, and the drawers largely held office supplies, plus some personal documents, but nothing that explained his absence. If anything, it was the opposite, considering his passport was still in one of them.

"Aha!" Leo exclaimed, making me jump. She stood up with the trash bin held triumphantly in both hands. "Jackpot!"

"What is it?" I looked up.

"Shredded paper puzzle, baby!" She held it out—sure enough, in the bin were thin strips of shredded paper. I couldn't help but laugh.

"I officially stand corrected. Your puzzle game experience is valid and invaluable."

"Damn right it is! Is there tape in any of those drawers? I think it's just one or two pages, I bet I can put it back together pretty quick." I retrieved a roll and handed it to her.

"Here's hoping it's not just another business bank account statement," I said. "All right, filing cabinet, let's see what you've got…"

I pulled the top drawer open; inside was his personal stash of ritual and spellwork equipment. Candles, salted chalk, a few crystals, a knife, some corked potions, copies of spells that had probably come from his family's grimoire. Nothing out of the ordinary for a witch; a little sparse, even, but there were several candles still in the living room to explain that. Closing the drawer, I went to open the second one, but it was locked.

Leo glanced up. "Can't you magic that open?"

"Maybe. Depends if he's thought of that or not. *Revela.*" The spell revealed that, sure enough, the drawer wasn't just locked with a key but with magic as well. "No, he's locked this down pretty tight. There's a spell that's probably bound to the actual key. The drawer's reinforced magically, too. Anything I might try to brute-force it open would probably destroy whatever's inside along with it. I *might* be able to

105

counter it, but that would take hours. This is really intricate work."

"In other words, it probably has exactly what we're looking for, so naturally we can't get into it."

"Bingo. And he probably has the key on him if it's that important, since we haven't seen one anywhere around here. I'll take another look around just in case."

I went back through every drawer in the house in search of a key but came up with nothing. Returning to the office, I slumped onto the couch, where Leo was sitting as she reconstructed the paper. "I'm only about halfway there, but this looks like one of your binding ritual circles."

She had a few sections pieced back together, though not consecutive ones. "Those are definitely runes, but I don't quite recognize them. What was he working on? And why?"

"Any luck with the key?"

"Nothing!" I said, frustrated. "I know it's gonna be a small key, so it'd be easy to miss, but there's hardly any clutter in this place. If it was in any of the drawers, I would've seen it."

"Take a breath and think about it. There's got to be some kind of hiding spot around here," Leo said, taping another strip of paper.

I rubbed my temples. She was right. Something that important, he wouldn't want to risk it being tied to only a single key. But he wouldn't make the spare easy to find, either. *If I were Bastien, where would I hide it? C'mon, think, where'd he hide stuff in his dorm?*

Eleven years ago

I flopped backward on Bastien's dorm room bed. "Why does Grothmann's midterm have to have both a practical *and* a written component? It's not even the final!"

"You know, if you'd been in class and fully paying attention on a regular basis this semester, you wouldn't be so stressed about the written now," Bastien pointed out coolly from his desk chair.

"Not fair. I was retrieving a one-of-a-kind sword from a mystically sealed cavern that was only accessible once every hundred years so I could kill an Archdemon and reclaim my soul. That should *absolutely* be worth an exemption."

"Yes, but did you use *chemistry* to do it?" Bastien's smile was slight, but the corner of his lips turned up just enough to belie his serious tone.

I laughed, propping myself back up on my elbows. "I should've said I did. Explained the literally one-of-a-kind blacksmithing ritual."

He smiled again, shaking his head. "Somehow I doubt it would've helped. You're lucky you got an extension on the written at all."

"I know, I know. It's just…this week has kind of been hell." I sat up, resting my elbows on my knees. "How has it only been a week? It feels like a month."

"And yet it feels like a day." The haunted quality in his voice and his eyes matched mine, and I knew we were both reliving the night of my demonic former patron's demise. We'd all almost died; Chris Miller had lost his leg, only surviving thanks to werewolf healing and Brooke's magic. Of course, unlike mine, Bastien's week had not then also included his having a breakdown over his girlfriend inheriting said patron's power, breaking up with her in the middle of a days-long panic attack, enduring an intense interrogation under a truth spell by the Council, and just barely being allowed to return to the academy with his magic intact. Not that his trauma was any less valid than mine. It wasn't a competition, certainly not one I wanted to be in. If anything, knowing my friends knew how I felt was a comfort.

After all of that, a chemistry exam should've been nothing. Somehow, after all of that, a chemistry exam was my absolute worst nightmare.

My breath came out shaky, and then Bastien's hand was on my back, pleasantly cool as it moved gently up and down. "It's going to be okay, McKenna. You'll get through this test, I promise." His voice, too, was a cool, calm breeze over the turbulent sea within me. I sniffed and only then realized tears were slipping down my cheeks.

"Oh—geez. Sorry. I didn't mean to...I'm sorry," I stammered. He handed me a tissue.

"You don't have to apologize," he assured me. There was a gentleness there I hadn't expected but had begun to realize was central to who he was. Yes, he was disciplined, he followed the rules and frowned upon breaking them, and yes, he'd made me promise to come clean to the Council once Forneus was dealt with. I would have followed through on it, too, but the bombastic near-fuckup that was our last stand against Forneus had drawn plenty of attention all on its own.

Truthfully, I was grateful. Without Bastien being there, we would've failed utterly. My friends would be dead, my brother would be dead, maybe even Remi would be dead, and I'd still be enslaved to a psychopath.

"Thanks," I replied, wiping my eyes. "And thanks for helping me study. Even if my brain is a traumatized hot mess incapable of learning right now."

"Well…maybe I can help with that, too." He opened a desk drawer, pulling out a bottle of perfectly mundane headache medicine.

"Thanks, but I don't really think that's gonna…whoa." I trailed off when he opened it, revealing a few rolled joints. I laughed in disbelief. "I'm sorry, is Bastien Lemaire, *the* Bastien Lemaire, Arcadia Commons' golden boy, class president, captain of the sailing team, valedictorian hopeful, sharing his *personal weed stash* with me right now?"

That hint of cheek was back in his smile. "You think all of that doesn't come with any pressure? This helps sometimes. Do you want one or not?"

"Oh, I absolutely do."

He pulled one out and went over to the end of the bed nearest the window, cracking it open so we could blow the smoke outside. I shuffled down next to him as he lit one up and took a deep breath in before passing it to me; I did the same. For a few minutes, we sat in silence, shoulder to shoulder, passing the joint back and forth.

I started giggling.

Bastien snorted and looked at me. "What are you laughing at?"

"You!" I got out between giggles. "You're, like, one of the most powerful witches at this school, you could probably pull off hiding just about anything in here, and your big contraband is totally normal *weed*? In a totally normal pill bottle?"

He started snickering halfway through my explanation, and by the end of it we were both tearing up. "It's the best place to put it! No one at a magic school gives a shit about mundane headache medicine!"

"Of course they don't! They can just cast a spell for a headache!"

"Exactly, it's perfect!" he exclaimed.

"Oh, my god, Lemaire. I thought you were such a stiff," I laughed, falling back on the bed again. "But you're really a dork!" He laughed and hit me with a pillow, which kicked off a pillow-and-magic battle until we called a truce and had to spell his pillows back together while still giggling like idiots.

I got an A on the test.

———————————•———————————

I jumped up from the couch and ran back to the bathroom, startling Leo, and yanked open the drawer she had poked through earlier. "McKenna?"

One bottle was the same brand he'd kept in his dorm room, and sure enough, when I shook it, something in there clanked in a very un-pill-like way.

Pulling it out and twisting off the top, I saw the bottle contained some vape cartridges—old times made modern—and, more importantly, a small silver key. Exactly the kind that would fit an office filing cabinet.

Grinning in victory, I went back to the office. "Found it!"

"Way to go, Sherlock," Leo said, giving me a thumbs up.

"Let's see what you're hiding, Bast…" I slid it into the lock and the wards slid away. I felt another tiny tingle of demonic power in the air as the drawer opened.

A simple leather folio lay inside, bound shut by a wrap-around strap. Pulling it out, I half expected it to be warded as well, but it opened without any fuss. Inside was a small stack of loose-leaf pages with sketches of runes and ritual circles, like the one Leo was patching up. Some were experimental, with things crossed out and rewritten. The ones on top looked recent, more complete, drawn with a more certain hand. But still in configurations I'd never seen before. Which meant one thing.

"Bastien's creating spells," I murmured. "And they definitely have something to do with demons."

"I know that's obviously got to be possible somehow, but I'm also guessing from your voice that it's not exactly common," Leo said.

"Essentially. These…I don't recognize all of these, but they look like binding and banishing runes. Except it doesn't make any sense to use them together. If you're going to banish a demon, why also bind it? That's just making it more complicated for no reason."

Leo cleared her throat. "Let's say, for fun, that you explain that to me like I'm not a witch who got an A-plus in Rituals 101 or whatever?"

"Right. Sorry. Okay, so—spells take magic. The more complicated the spell, the more magic you need for it, and witches have different levels of magical strength," I began.

"Right, that's the whole generalist/adept/master thing?"

"Yeah. So when you don't have the magical strength, or don't want to totally rely on it, we've got ways to make spells easier. We use spell words, group casting, stored magic, making potions or enchanted objects, tapping into a leyline, there are a lot of options for boosting power. But if you want to boost complexity, then you want to use runes and ritual circles," I explained. "First, you've got your runes—they can be anything, really, but the more the caster believes in what the symbol represents, the easier it is to use."

"Believes in? Like clap-if-you-believe-in-fairies?"

"Sort of? It's not a perfect word, but…with magic, belief in a thing gives it strength. Kind of like how words, or fears, have power because we assign it to them. Like *fuck* is bad word because we all just kind of agreed it is."

"Hey, *fuck*'s a great word," Leo replied, grinning. "But okay, I think I follow you."

"Anyway, magic ability isn't entirely about confidence, but it helps. The more you believe what you're doing is something you *can* do, the better you are at it. Same with words and runes. The old tried-and-true symbols are great because they've got a lot of history, and it's easy to believe in those. They kind of come preloaded with symbolism, and if you're casting with more than one witch, it's easy for everyone to get behind that."

"With you so far. Where's the complexity part come in?"

"It's not a perfect one-to-one, but for purposes of this example, think of it as one rune equals one spell. If I want a spell that can do more than one thing, that takes more power, and it's more complex. A ritual circle combines those runes so that the spells are cast at the same time. When Cam or I banish a demon from Arcadia, we use a circle so we can banish it and wipe its memory of how it got in here at the same time. Plus, if we've got multiple targets, we can catch them all in one go."

Leo nodded. "Cast one big spell instead of several little spells, save time and some effort."

"Exactly. Making a new rune *and* a new ritual is tough because you're doing a lot of things at once, which require your absolute belief in all of them. This"—I held up the top sheet of spellwork—"is doing all of that, and doing it in a way that makes no sense. A binding is tied to a physical vessel. But a banishment expels a demon from our world, and therefore from their physical vessel. You'd only bind something if it was going to stick around, and you wouldn't bind something you're going to banish at the same time you bind it. It's making the spell more complicated for no reason."

Leo was studying the paper now. "That's not the only thing. If Bastien's binding and banishing demons, he's doing it with some other demon-binding expert," she said. "There's a second set of handwriting here."

"What?" I jerked the sheet back to look at it. Sure enough, unfamiliar writing was on the page, offering suggestions and tweaks to the spell.

Demons and bindings and banishments. All the things my family magic was centered around.

And he'd chosen to go to some other witch for help.

"Bastien Lemaire, what in the seven hells are you doing?"

No one answered me, of course. But that is when a pair of pitch-black tentacles grabbed me from behind and threw me against the wall.

Chapter 6
Nothing but the Truth

I collided with the wall so hard the plaster cracked and crumbled under me. Something crashed, someone screamed, my head spun, the world wobbled around me. The thing holding me was entirely black, in a way that seemed to suck at the light in the room. Its body was an unsettling combination of arachnid and cephalopod and the size of a full-grown human, easily coming eye to eye with me when standing on one of its many pairs of legs. Some of the limbs were rigid and sturdy enough for standing, but others were more flexible and tentacle-like. *Why did it have to be more tentacles?*

This thing was also *really* freaking strong. It pinned me to the wall, more plaster dust showering me as its tentacles secured my hands and feet and covered my mouth, preventing me from casting. I struggled all the same, wriggling against its superior strength, panic spreading as it came to hover in front of me.

"Let her go!" Leo screamed, bashing something against its back. It was jostled, but barely, and its hold on me didn't even waver. The oblong, eyeless head, made of seamless darkness, pivoted toward Leo, a crack opening in it to reveal rows of recurved teeth and four nasty, glinting fangs. It slammed Leo with another tentacle, flinging her backward into the filing cabinet. It toppled to the ground under her, spilling the witchy contents of the top drawer on the floor.

Spell…I need…a spell…nghh… but my head was still swimming from my being thrown into the wall. I couldn't move, I couldn't cast—*what fucking good am I?! Stupid tentacled motherfucker—ah, shit, this is gonna suck.*

With all the mandibular fortitude I could muster, I sank my teeth into the tentacle covering my mouth. The thick skin gave way, and I gagged on an oily ichor that tasted of dirt, salt, and raw meat. Its head whipped back toward me with a hiss. Before I could try anything else, however, it opened that fault line of fangs again, roared, and sank them into my upper arm. Fire exploded in my veins as I screamed again. *Fuck, fuck, fuck, I'm gonna die, Leo's gonna die. Does demon antivenin even exist? How the fuck did I not sense this thing!* There was no smell of sulfur and no cobbled-together flesh—this thing was here in its own body. But even when I'd actively looked for demons, there had been nothing, not so much as a ripple or a tingle in my blood. I was a living, breathing demon alarm system, but somehow this thing had hidden itself from me completely. *How?*

Not that it mattered right now. The damage done, its face sealed up seamlessly once more. "*Witch,*" it hissed without opening its mouth again. "*Where?*" To my surprise, the tentacle across my mouth peeled away.

Free of the pressure holding it up, my head lolled for a

moment and I spat out a mouthful of demon blood. *A spell, fire a spell at it, do it*, I told myself, but I couldn't keep my focus enough just yet. "Right...here," I gasped, panting.

It hissed in anger. "*Not you, demon's witch! Where is the male?*"

"Wha...Bastien?" I asked, finally getting my head up. Blood trickled down my arm where it had bitten me. "Like I'd tell you."

At least, I meant to say that. What I said instead was, "I don't know. Probably got kidnapped by one of your buddies, as far as I can tell. Or maybe lounging at his family's mansion across town." The words tumbled out of my mouth without any hesitation, leaving me slack-jawed. "Wh...what did you do to me?"

"*Truth.*" The bastard was smiling, I swear.

"Oh, shit," I groaned. "Okay, well, you should know something else, then." The demon cocked its head at me. "I'm not a portal mage. I don't need my hands and feet to cast. I just need blood. *Repello!*"

The blast of power threw the thing off me and into the opposite wall with another crack of plaster. As I'd cast it with no particular focus point, it shoved me farther into the wall I was already pinned against, bruising my back and spine, before I slumped down onto the couch and then the floor. *Get up, get up, banish this thing!* I grabbed the edge of the coffee table, trying to do so. The demon was far faster, though, already back on its feet—so to speak. It went to lunge—and got a face full of potion as Leo smashed a glass tube onto it.

"Suck on that, you wannabe Cthulhu!" she yelled. Its flesh sizzled and it screamed, opening its mouth this time and darting at her with teeth and fangs bared. But Leo was ready for it, stabbing at its mouth with the knife from Bastien's spell supplies. The demon roared again, pulling back. Leo circled to my side, knife held out toward it the whole time. "Now would be a great time to banish this thing, Mickey!"

"Working on it," I grunted. I was on my knees, holding myself up on the coffee table and forcing my thoughts into cohesion. I held out a hand toward it—hands weren't required for my casting, but they *were* useful for directing it when available. "I don't know what you are or how you snuck up on me, but I am banishing you right back where you came from!" I frowned. This truth venom was making me far more literal than usual. "*Ego daemones abicio!*"

A blast of golden magic slammed into it. It staggered back slightly from the force of it...and *smiled* at me as absolutely nothing happened. "Seven hells..." I gasped.

"*Secrets, secrets!*" it hissed with a creepy giggle. Two tentacles lashed out, shoving both of us off our feet again and toppling the coffee table on top of us. This time, rather than press the attack, it snapped out a third limb and snatched up the folio before bursting out of the room into the hallway.

"Are you okay?" I asked Leo, who was more pinned by the table than I was.

"I'm fine, go, don't let it get away!"

Assured for now, I ran to follow it, but vertigo from my head wound hampered me. Cursing aloud, I set my hands to my head and chanted a healing spell to address the concussion. My senses sharpened up, the headache subsiding, but by the time I reached the living room, it was gone.

There was no open door or window—the quickest way out was the shattered glass door. The one that, I realized, must be how it got in here. I dashed for it, only to have the thing surprise me yet again when it swung down from just above the door and shoved me backward into the living room. My left ankle twisted under me as I went down, erupting in pain so intense it stole the very sound of my scream. The demon slipped back outside, thumping over the roof before it was gone. I lay there, useless and lost to the pain in my ankle. Even if I could get to my feet right now, what the hell could I do against that thing? It had several limbs and considerable physical prowess on me, on top of being undetectable and unbanishable by my magic.

The cherry on top? "That thing is here in the flesh—its *own* flesh, straight from the Pit, which should be impossible, but—*why* am I talking out loud?" I interrupted myself. "This venom had better wear off soon. *Fuck*, this hurts!"

Every movement or slightest pressure on my left ankle set off a lightning bolt of pain that made my brain go white. I didn't think it was broken, but like hell could I imagine putting any weight on it.

"Seven *hells*, I'm never gonna judge someone for saying, 'Go on without me' after twisting their ankle in a movie ever again," I panted, then called out down the hall. "Leo! Are you okay?" I sure hoped so, because it was all I could do to cling to the couch and try in vain to breathe through the pain.

"Bruised as fuck, but yeah. How're you?" Leo said, walking gingerly out of the office.

"Twisted my ankle, it hurts like a bitch. That thing got

away—oh, shit, I think it might be headed for the Lemaire mansion," I groaned.

Leo crouched down with a grunt, holding her side, and checked out my ankle. "Put a pin in that, we're not exactly in any shape to help. I'll go find some ice packs."

"I can at least text them," I said, but my back pocket was empty. "Or not. My phone must've fallen out when it was throwing me around."

"They'll be fine, they can just portal the thing back to the Pit," Leo said, digging in Bastien's freezer.

"They can't portal to other dimensions, only within this one," I explained. "But Laurent could send it into space if he wanted. I saw him do it to a hellhound once. At least, I think he did, I never really asked."

"Oh, good, that's not terrifying to know or anything," Leo replied. She limped back over and handed me a bag of frozen peas, holding a rectangular freezer block to her side. "Here." She sat on the couch behind me. "What *was* that thing?"

Even the slight weight of the bag made my ankle throb with pain, but I arranged the peas around it anyway. "No idea. I've never seen a demon like that before. I saw some squidlike ones the other night, but those were the standard slapped-together-from-dead-flesh types, nothing like that thing."

"You said it was here in its own flesh?"

I nodded. "Yeah. Which should be impossible; the barrier's not *that* weak yet. Remi's new-old friend Dara is only here in *her* own body because she crawled out of Saranthiel's portal and then ran off and kept a low profile until recently. That thing might've done the same, but it didn't look like any of

Saranthiel's other minions. And truth venom was not in her wheelhouse."

Leo cocked her head at me. "Is that why you're being so chatty for someone in so much pain?"

I grimaced. "Lack of inner monologue is apparently a side effect. At least it didn't bite both of us. Not that I think you're keeping any deep dark secrets from me! Or that I'm pro-lying, I just mean—"

Leo gave a tired chuckle. "I get it, no worries. But for your sake, I hope it wears off soon."

"Same. Not that I'm constantly fibbing, but I'd rather not be a font of unfiltered blunt honesty. Can you imagine if I had to deal with my mom like this? Gah, please change the subject before I say how fed up I am and how guilty I feel about it and—"

"Right! We got attacked, what does that tell us?"

It worked, thank goodness. "That we're not the only ones looking for Bastien."

"Bingo. Whoever or whatever that thing works for doesn't know where he is, either."

"But they seriously want to. Question is, who is that, and if they don't have him, where the hell *is* he?"

"Can't you do a spell to try and figure that out?"

I smacked my forehead. "I can't believe I didn't try that yet. Yeah, I just need something of his to do it—something either personal or biological. Problem is, he's pretty much stripped this place of the personal, and, like most witches, he's careful with the biological." I thought for a moment. "That folio might've worked, but the demon grabbed it."

"Could they use it to track him?"

"Maybe. Only a witch could use it for a spell. If they're capable of tracking by scent, it might work. But if they were, it would've done that already instead of lurking around here. But why steal a spell it can't cast and that isn't going to tell it where he is? So…what the hell did it want that for?"

Leo drummed her fingers on the couch cushion in thought. "What about the key? The one that opened the locked drawer? That seems kinda personal."

I considered it and nodded. "Might work. Can you bring it out here? And bring my bag over? I can cast a scrying spell from here without having to get up."

Leo grunted again as she got up to fetch the requested items. I used my chalk to draw a small circle on the floor next to me and cast a scrying spell by placing the key on top of a small hand mirror among my supplies. The magic consumed the key, and I could feel the resonance—Leo had been spot-on, this was a personal enough item to him. It had been protecting something that he valued deeply. I felt a twinge of guilt that it was now gone, but the drawer was already open and its contents gone. The material-turned-magic sank into the surface of the mirror, and we both watched and waited for an image to appear to show us where he was now.

The mirror showed us nothing. Not even our reflections, not until I felt the magic fade a few moments later.

"I'm gonna guess that's bad?" Leo said.

"Probably," I confirmed, brow furrowed. "Something's blocking him from being found. When my wards are activated, it would do the same if you tried to find me." I gestured with my tattooed wrists.

"So he's blocking us from finding him? Or someone else is blocking him from being found?"

"One of the two. And there's no way to know which it is. Dammit."

Leo puffed out a sigh. "I think it might be time to call the Lemaires."

"Yeah, any longer and they'll find a way to say this is my fault, too—oh, shit."

Leo gave me a look. "Much as I'd love to see how you bend over backward to make this your fault, seriously, McKenna?"

"I'm not! 'Oh, shit' because your brother and Brooke got home last night, right?" I asked; Leo nodded. "Yeah. The two people who right now would *most* benefit from Bastien going AWOL, with me being a close third. We know the wolves didn't do this, and I didn't do this, but brute-force entry isn't going to look good to the rest of the Council, and neither is a witch who can't be found when I kinda perfected that trick for ten years straight."

"But we both just saw what happened! And hell, you can't *stop* telling the truth right now!" Leo protested.

"I know, but I don't want to make things worse for Brooke and I don't want to waste time explaining this shit to the rest of them," I replied.

"And what about the demon that just probably hightailed it to their mansion? That's not proof enough?"

"Proof that even *I* can't detect. Hell, knowing Sofia, she'd accuse me of being in league with it and sending it after them on purpose," I said. "Assuming Bastien isn't at the mansion, that thing seems more likely to lurk until it finds him, or bring that folio back to its master, whoever that is. I don't think any of them are in danger right now. Not that a good scare wouldn't do them some good," I couldn't help adding, then winced. "Sorry. No, I don't mean that—okay, maybe I do, a little, but I'm not—ugh, this is annoying!"

Leo smirked a little. "I get what you mean. And unfortunately, you make some good points. Okay, what do we do now, then?"

"First, we get my ankle and your ribs healed up so we can both move. Then I get the grimoire from Cam and find out what that thing is," I said.

Healing magic wasn't my forte. I'd been in enough scrapes in the last few months fighting demons, however, that I knew the ritual spell to help by heart. First I took care of my ankle, gritting my teeth through the painful process wherein I could feel the ligaments warping and twisting to get closer to where they should be. It was still tender, but I could walk on it, and Leo found a compression bandage in the bathroom for me. Next I got to work on her injury, which luckily was just a nasty bruise and not a cracked rib. Magically, I was feeling pretty spent, but when someone knocked on the front door, it didn't stop me from getting ready to throw a spell at them.

"Down, girl! Demons aren't gonna knock, remember?" Leo said.

"Sorry," I replied. "Who is it?"

Leo cautiously leaned over to look through the beveled glass windows of the door from a distance. "Do we know anyone with bright-red hair?"

I looked as well. "Mom?" I blurted aloud.

Sure enough, as she knocked again, we could hear her calling out. "Bastien? It's Wendy."

"What the hell is she doing here?" I hissed in a whisper, but Leo just shook her head, likewise out of ideas.

"Bastien? I can see you over there. Sorry I'm late!" she called, trying to look in.

"We cannot let her in here!" I whispered to Leo.

"She already saw us."

"She doesn't know it's us!"

"She will when she comes around the porch and sees the door," Leo pointed out.

I chewed my lip and faced the shattered door. "Not if she doesn't see it." Golden light gathered at my fingertips as I summoned my magic, forming an image in my mind of what the door, porch, and living room *should* look like. "*Damnum abscondere,*" I cast, sending my spell to literally hide the damage.

Except I didn't. I *couldn't.* I started to say the words but they stuck in my throat.

"Mickey? Nothing happened. And you look like you just ate a bug," Leo observed.

"This stupid truth venom won't even let me cast an illusion over something!" I hissed.

The lock on the door clicked open.

"Hope you don't mind that I let myself in—" my mother started to say before her eyes landed on the two of us. "...McKenna? Leo? What are you doing here?"

"We're—wait, you have a *key* to Bastien's house?" I blurted out as I spied the key in her hand.

"Of course I don't! This is the spare," Mom replied.

"You know where he keeps his *spare key*?" I said.

"Are you bleeding?" She stepped in, seeing my bloody, torn shirt where the demon bit me and then seeing the mess in the living room a beat later. "What the seven hells happened in here?"

"A demon attacked us while we were looking for Bastien, who's missing, and it injected me with truth venom," I said, unable to help but answer truthfully and in great detail. "And no, I'm not bleeding anymore."

"A *what* while you were *what*?" Mom exclaimed. "Are you—no, never mind, I can see you're not okay."

"I've been better. What are you doing here, Mom?" I replied.

"I'm meeting Bastien. What do you mean you're looking for him? Is *he* okay?" my mom asked.

"We don't really know. Probably not. Meeting him for what?" I asked.

"For lunch, but can we please focus on what the hell's going on in here?" Lunch? Were they lunch friends? I knew they were friends, or at least friendly, but as far as I knew, she hadn't seen him since he left town months ago, either. Then she adjusted the yellow scarf she was wearing around her neck, fastened with a pin that looked like the Sun card from the Tarot deck. Classic Wendy Ellerbeck lie detection— fiddling with accessories. She was hiding something.

Leo, however, spoke up before I could ask what. "McKenna was supposed to meet him here earlier and found the door smashed in. I came over to help her look around, and then we got attacked. We're okay, but we don't know where he is." All true—lying would've been hard for either of us given my condition—while dodging the nitty-gritty details she didn't need to know.

"This would be the demon that injected you with truth venom?" Mom asked.

"Yeah. I don't know what kind of demon it was, never seen it before," I said.

"I've never heard of one that could do something like that, either. You didn't banish it?"

"Tried to. It didn't work."

Mom's eyes went about as wide as mine had. "That's not possible."

"And yet!"

"Are you sure you did the spell right? Maybe you missed."

I gritted my teeth. "I've known that spell by heart since I was a teenager and I use it multiple times a week. I cast it *right*, it didn't *miss*, it just didn't *work*."

"Then how—"

"I don't know! I didn't sense it, I couldn't banish it, it jumped us, kicked our asses, and vamoosed with whatever spell Bastien's been working on!" I snapped, belatedly realizing my slipup. "Shit."

"Spell? What spell?"

Leo jumped in. "We don't know. The demon ran off with the copies."

A light bulb went off. "Oh! No, it didn't!" I turned to Leo and at the same time we both exclaimed, "Shredded paper puzzle!" Leo darted off to the office to get it.

"How much more aren't you telling me?" my mom asked when we were alone.

"I don't know how one quantifies that sort of thing," I replied, managing to avoid spilling it all outright. "How much are *you* not telling *me*?"

Her lips pressed together, but once again, Leo inadvertently came to the rescue.

"McKenna, Wendy, you're gonna want to see this," Leo called from the office.

"What now?" I grumbled, and carefully walked over to join her, my mom at my side. Her hands hovered, and I could see her about to ask, so I got there first. "I don't need help, my ankle's just sore. I twisted it."

Her hands lowered. "If you say so. Tell me about this demon, then. What did it look like?"

"Big, entirely black, like a creepy squid–spider hybrid," I described. "Really fast, really strong."

"Basically, like that," Leo said as we rounded the doorway into the room. Panic shot through me and I threw a hand out to fire off a spell, but no new demons awaited us. Leo pointed instead at the ground, where, among the mess of furniture, desk papers, and crumbling plaster, was a full–on conspiracy board.

The large square artwork that had been hanging above the couch had fallen in the fight and flipped over in the process. It now sat on the floor, revealing a hidden cork board inlay on the back, covered in handwritten notes and sketches. All it needed was a little string and some surreptitiously taken surveillance photos.

"Bastien…what the hell have you been doing?" I murmured aloud, stunned. I pulled it up onto the now wobbly coffee table, and the three of us gathered around to look at it. Among the pinned items was a drawing of the demon that had attacked us, but my attention was taken up by ones that were far more alarming.

Across the top were eight Post-its, all bearing Bastien's neat handwriting, and the other items were organized roughly into columns beneath them. Three of the Post-its had words written on them: *Desire, Madness, Rage.* Four others only had question marks, and one had an actual question: *Are there more?*

"These are Archdemons. He's…he's been tracking information on Archdemons," I realized. *Desire* and *Madness* were next to each other, with the names *Forneus* and *Saranthiel*, respectively, written and crossed out, and *Remiel* written in to replace them both. The others did not have associated names, but the notes below each did expand on things like known types of minions, abilities, and sightings.

"But why?" Leo asked as she took it all in.

There was only one reason.

"To kill them." But it wasn't me who said it—it was my mother.

She was right. And I would know—I'd had a notebook that looked just like this after I fled Arcadia Commons ten years ago. I would've gone in for a proper murderboard, but my lack of secure housing made a notebook far more practical.

When I left home, I hadn't planned to be gone indefinitely. I'd planned to take a breath, lead the Archdemon after me away from my loved ones, and figure out how to kill it. Step one was finding out more about who was after me. I knew it dealt in madness, what it looked like, and the rune for its true name. I thought that would be enough to learn more, to find a way to kill, contain, or block it more permanently. It wasn't.

Standard witchcraft books and resources offered plenty of information on the dangers of demons, the natures of the lesser ones, signs of possession, and simple wards, while warning the reader of the dangers of summoning one. Even mundane mythology had plenty of that information, warnings included. If you dug a little deeper, into the shadier sources, like the ones that lived in the restricted section of the Uncommon Collection, they had a little more to offer: a few names, a few rituals, a few accounts of witnesses or practitioners from the darker corners of magic. Of course, that information was largely only written down if an Archdemon wanted it to be, as I'd learned the hard way. As a teen discovering the information that led me to summoning Forneus, I'd thought I was so clever and sneaky, when all I'd truly done was walk right into a trap.

I suspected then, and still did, that the Uncommon Collection had an even *more* restricted section, but that was well out of my reach while I was actively running from hellhounds through Europe. Weeks became months, I got my ward tattoos and sought out less legitimate sources of information, but while the well wasn't dry, it was damn close. Demons kept a tight lid on information that could lead to their demise, using my magic to summon one would only hasten my own, and I had been neither willing nor able to look for thralls who might betray me.

Eventually, I'd had to accept that what I was after didn't exist, not in that secret collection or anywhere else. There was nothing more I could learn, there was no way to take out this enemy, no way to end the threat it posed. I burned the notebook the night it became clear to me that I was never going home.

Much of the information on this board was the same as what I had learned in those early years. *And he did it in a few months. Well—to be fair, he has money to throw at the problem and isn't being hunted.* I paused, thinking of the demon who'd attacked us. *Or is he?*

"How do you know that he was trying to kill Archdemons?" I asked my mother, putting aside my musing.

Her mouth worked over an answer for several seconds before she gave me one. "I didn't get committed and severed for letting my lawn get overgrown, you know."

Even with truth venom loosening my tongue, I didn't know what to say to that. Mom rarely brought up being severed, and *never* talked about her time suffering from demon–induced schizophrenia. I knew she'd become obsessed with the idea that demons had taken me from her and that they were inside the town. She'd been half-right on one and entirely right on the other, but Saranthiel's madness had slowly made her lose her sanity until she almost burned down the town forest and even Cam was unable to protect her.

It made sense that before that, she'd also learned as much about Archdemons as she could. Like mother, like daughter.

Her mouth pressed into an uncomfortable line as the silence stretched between us, then she gestured sharply at the board. "Come on. Let's see how well our boy did."

"Considering he's been doing this for, what, four months, maybe five? Pretty good. There's one Archdemon I know of that he's missing, but it's damned hard to find," I said, looking it over. "I never found the last three, but he's right that there are at least seven."

Mom nodded. "Seven Archdemons for seven hells."

Leo plucked up the sketch of our attacker. It was done in black ink on a paper with an Arcadia Commons Grand letterhead. "*Geheimnissucher.*" She pronounced the German word carefully.

"'Secret…sucker'?" I logicked out. I knew some German from living in Germany for a short time, though this particular combination of words I'd never heard before.

"Close. 'Secret-seeker.' He translated it on here," Leo said, pointing to the paper. "Ring any bells for either of you?"

We both shook our heads. "Check the grimoire," Mom suggested.

"I can't, Cam has it right now."

Leo read more from the page. "'Secret-seeker. Truth venom bite'—sure, now he tells us—'strong, fast, sneaky. Seeks people with secrets and gains strength from hearing them.'"

Great. I was probably lucky it hadn't interrogated me further, given all the secrets I was sitting on. "Explains the venom and the interrogation. Anything about dealing with the venom?"

"'Counteracting requires a willing confession,'" Leo read. "Sounds like you're gonna need to drop a big reveal."

I searched for things neither of them knew. "Okay…I hid from hellhounds in the London Underground once," I tried.

"Do you feel any different?" Leo asked.

"No."

"Okay, try telling me you do."

I tried but couldn't make the words come out. "No. Dammit. Okay, something bigger…my magic blew a hole in a café wall another time I was fighting them. I ran away before anyone could see me and get me arrested because I couldn't pay for it and I didn't want to end up in any news articles or on TV."

"Do you like my hair red?" Mom asked.

"It's a nice color, but you're trying too hard," I blurted out, then winced. "Sorry."

Mom looked annoyed but shrugged. "About what I thought you'd say."

"Okay, I…oh! I dated a brother and sister in Edinburgh by accident. No, not at the same time."

Leo laughed. "Okay, I have *got* to hear more about that story."

Mom smirked as well. "Same here. Say, have you hooked up with Remi lately?"

"Yes, two nights ago at the bar. Fuck!"

"I knew it!" Mom crowed.

My face was hot with embarrassment. This was bad. Bad in a way I knew I wasn't fully grasping right now, but…my secrets were secret for a reason. And I'd already dealt with a good number of them being forced into the open under duress last fall. "Okay, that's enough of the *True Confessions of McKenna Ellerbeck* show."

My mom lifted an eyebrow at me. "Come on, surely you can think of something bigger than that you could tell us."

Like that I almost became an Archdemon? That I'm the one who actually killed Saranthiel? That I'm glad I'm home but I also might kind of hate my life right now? Whoa. That was new. *Did* I hate my life right now? It felt true—maybe I couldn't even lie to myself right now—but it wasn't something I had time to unpack.

"Can, yes. But would you be happy about being forced to confess something you didn't want to?" I replied instead. "People keep secrets for a reason."

"Good to know the lengths you'll go to to keep them," my mom replied, rolling her eyes.

"There's a difference between being willingly honest and being forced to speak the absolute truth," I pointed out, annoyed at her for the second time today. "And you're lying about why you came here, so you really don't have the moral high ground here."

"Okay, time-out!" Leo interrupted before my mom could clap back to that one. She made a T with her hands in between us. "Before this turns into World War Ellerbeck, can we please focus on the bigger problem here? Bastien's still missing. I don't know about you two, but I'm thinking this murderboard might be why."

Mom and I agreed to drop it with one of those silent exchanges that dated back to my teenage years. I let out a breath, trying to release my irritation with it. "It's possible. Maybe he poked the wrong hornet's nest finding all this out, and out came the demonic yellowjackets." The image made me suddenly glad we'd only had to tangle with the secret-seeker. "But that demon didn't know where he was, either. I think it broke in after he was gone."

"It was pinned in a blank column, so we don't know who it works for," Leo noted. "What's the other Archdemon you know about?"

"Fear."

Mom nodded. "That's the only other one I know, too."

Leo got a pen and filled in the name on the board. "That seeker's MO was not very fearlike."

"It wasn't, no. Two of these are Remi, and we know it wasn't her—"

"Do we?" Mom asked.

"Can we not? It's not her, and honestly, she's going to be our best bet for getting more information. So on this board, that only leaves Rage," I continued. "That thing also wasn't very rage-y, though."

We all stared at the board, trying to will answers from it that weren't coming.

Leo clapped her hands together. "Maybe if I finish taping together that shredded paper, it'll be a clue. You two see if you can figure out anything else from this."

The house was quiet for a few minutes, aside from the sound of Leo taping things and the distant hush of waves and wind coming in from the broken door. Mom and I looked over the board; I took some photos with my phone while she checked her watch several times, but epiphanies remained in short supply. "Starting to think this is a bust. I either need the grimoire or to talk to Remi," I finally said.

Mom's brow furrowed. "Why did you come here?" she asked. "You never said, and I know you and Bastien haven't spoken in a while."

I wanted to dodge it, or cushion it, but that wasn't an option. "He asked me to meet him here this morning."

"He did? You've been in touch?" She seemed surprised.

"Yes. No. Sort of. Only since he showed up at the Council meeting the other night," I found myself saying.

Mom snorted. "What, is he gunning for your spot directly now? Oh, don't give me that look. We all know the next spot was going to be his before Laurent decided to teach him a lesson. So why was he there?"

I sighed. "He was there because…because the Council is trying Brooke for Mari's murder now that she's had her baby. Sofia Perez wants her severed. And Bastien is the Perez family's advocate."

A whole series of micro-expressions flitted over my mom's face—shock, anger, hurt, fear, incredulity—before she landed on indignant confusion. "What…that…no, he…he would've said…no. No, Bastien would never try to get someone severed."

"Not even Brooke?" I replied. "I'm not sure he wouldn't, Mom. I want to think he doesn't really want this, either, but whatever else he's thinking, and doing"—I gestured at the murderboard—"he's definitely angry."

"I get it, but he's not vindictive! Come on, you know him, you know he isn't."

"Do I? I've been out of his life for ten years. I don't know that I know him at all at this point."

"But he would've said something," Mom protested.

It was the second time she'd said it. "Meaning *you've* been in touch with him."

Mom sighed. "Now and then, yes. I knew he came back to town recently."

"How long has he been here? How long have you known?"

"A week, and I found out a day or so after he came back. He came by the house when you weren't home," she told me.

"Of course he did." I ran a hand over my face. "You know, most people would get weirded out by their mom being so chummy with their ex. Especially when their mom likes younger men," I snapped, the words once again out before I could stop them.

"McKenna!" my mom exclaimed. "I would never do anything like that with him!"

My face was red, but somehow I couldn't help pushing. "Then why are you keeping this from me? Why is he coming to our house when I'm not home? Why are you secretly meeting him at his house?" I didn't think she was sleeping with him, not really—Solomon's bones, she better not be—but I was frustrated. I wanted answers from *someone* about *something*, and my mom was being especially irritating right now, on top of having been so for the last several months.

My mother's jaw set and she glared at me angrily. "First of all, Bastien is practically like a nephew to me. And even if he weren't that and your ex-boyfriend, he's much too smart and considerate to be my type."

Just like that, my ire deflated. "Mom, do you...think you don't deserve those things?"

"So, let's set aside the notion that I would ever cross that line, or even want to. Or that he would, for that matter. Got it?" she continued, ignoring my question. Awkwardly,

I nodded. "Good." She brushed her hair back from her face, looking elsewhere. "Second…he invited me to a support group."

Once again, I was taken aback by her answer. "Support group? For what?"

"Demonic abuse survivors, covenless witches…that sort of thing," she said.

I blinked, exchanging a look with Leo, who had paused in her taping to watch all this. "Those exist?"

"So it would seem. I didn't want to, I don't know…blow up his spot? Or mine," Mom said, sniffing. "He's been going to one and thought it would be helpful for me. Gave me a few days to think it over, said when he'd be portaling to it from here if I wanted to come with him. Even gave me a portal stone in case I wanted to go on my own." She pulled a glowing white moonstone from her pocket, about the size of a quarter. Portal stones were powerful enchanted items, rare for most witches to ever even see, but the Lemaires used them often. Each stone was keyed to a specific compass spell, a ritual circle that could be drawn anywhere. When activated, the stone opened a portal to the location of the compass and could be later used to return to the place of origin. The compass was often set up like most ritual circles, on the ground or floor somewhere. The Arcadia Commons Grand had a portal room with one, and portal stones were available for certain esteemed guests. But the compass could also be made portable by placing the spell on another stone or other small item.

"Wait a second. You knew he was talking with other people who've been hurt by demons, they're meeting right now, you've got a round-trip ticket to join them, and you didn't mention this until *now*?" Leo said. "Wendy. Not cool!"

"It's not a demon-hunting club," my mom replied. "He said it was just like any other support group, but one where we could actually be open about what happened to us. No using other words to hide it."

A support group for demonic abuse survivors. It made perfect sense he'd go to one. That he'd tell my mom about it was actually very kind of him. Honestly, she could use an outlet that wasn't the bar and the latest young, dumb, inconsiderate himbo the early-to-mid-twenties crowd had to offer. I was... I was glad. I was glad for him that he'd found something that helped.

A small voice in my head couldn't help but ask, though: *Why didn't he tell me, too?*

"I should've said something when we found the board. I was already thinking about it, I guess I just...wanted to respect his privacy about the matter," Mom was saying while my thoughts spiraled.

"Fair in normal circumstances, which these are not. Okay, obviously that's gonna be our next stop, then," Leo decided, laying another piece of tape down. "And just in time, this reconstruction is finished! Any of this mean anything to you, Mickey?"

I went over to take the paper from her, glad for something else to focus on. "Nice work. Similar to the other one. Same runes trying to bind *and* banish."

"Bind *and* banish? That's a waste of magic," Mom commented.

"Exactly what I said. No second set of handwriting on this one, though." My eyes flicked to a corner where something was lightly scratched out. Squinting, I could just make out the words: *toi et moi.*

My heart thudded. My thoughts swirled again. *Was he going to show this to me?*

"Mickey? What is it?" Leo asked.

"It's—just something he wrote here. Something we…we used to say to each other. It's not part of the spell," I said, my face warm, managing to find a way to answer honestly enough. Last thing I needed was to discuss romantic callbacks that were a decade out of date. "Um. The rest of this looks pretty similar, he took that other person's notes into account, and…and fucking *what?*"

My eyes fell on an area that had been blank in the previous version. That one had not had any runes relating directly to the target's identity, be they general or specific. This one, however, had filled it in. With a rune that was etched into my mind with blood and tears alike, a rune I would never forget. "That's Saranthiel's rune."

They both uttered disbelief and came to look at it. "But she's dead," Leo said.

"Extremely dead! This—salt and chalk, this whole ritual doesn't make sense!" I looked at my mother. "Did he say anything about this to you?"

"No, nothing."

I folded up the paper. "We can analyze this later. That meeting must start soon, and it's our best lead," I said. "Maybe he's there. And if not, maybe someone else will know something. You two ready?"

"You know I love a group field trip," Leo said, grinning. "And my dad's good for at least another hour or so of watching Griffin."

"It's where I was headed anyway." My mom held up the stone between her fingers—enchanted objects could be made to work for anyone, witch or not. She spoke the activation words: "The road goes ever on and on."

A shimmering, door-shaped portal appeared, limned in blue and gold. This one was circular, like a hobbit door. I couldn't help a small smile. *"There and back again." Bast, you're such a dork.*

"Okay, everyone," I said, reaching for the door, "let's go get some therapy."

Chapter 7
A Safe Space

The thing about Bastien's portals is that you can't see the other side. He's got a thing about doors, for whatever reason, and whether he does it consciously or unconsciously, his portals almost always have them. Maybe because it's handy for visualization, maybe because he's always certain where his portals lead, I don't know. For some reason, opening this one was especially unnerving. Maybe because his fate was uncertain, maybe because I didn't exactly know what I was walking into. Maybe because my nerves and emotions were pretty raw, I was unable to be anything but truthful, and the people on the other side might expect me to share my feelings. Whatever the case, I braced myself for the worst, the words for my standard attack spell on my lips and ready to go, just in case we somehow walked directly into a nest of hungry secret-seeker demons or something along those lines. Actually, maybe that would've been better than a support group...

I did not, however, expect to step into a store room full

of role-playing games, board games, and sets of polyhedral dice.

"Where the hell are we?" Leo asked, baffled. "Are you sure that thing worked?"

"It had to, it can only go to one place," my mom said. "Though I am wondering if he gave me the wrong one."

"Is this…a gaming shop?" I asked, peering at a selection of Dungeons & Dragons books on a shelf that declared themselves to be 5th Edition. "I know Bastien likes chess and all, but this seems…a little different from his taste."

"No, you're right. He likes games well enough, but this is a little beyond what he's into," Mom agreed. "Though the decor makes for perfect camouflage for the circle."

On the hard cement floor, someone—maybe Bastien—had painted a ritual circle with the compass spell for the stone. This might be a storage room, but anyone coming in was sure to see it, and Mom was right, it did match the ambience. We were alone in here, but muffled voices carried through the curtain that had been pulled across the only doorway out.

"Even if they are trouble, this is our only lead. We're going out there," I replied, reaching for the curtain. Before I got there, however, it was yanked aside, revealing a stout young woman with deep-brown skin and curly dark-brown hair that hugged her chin, with softly pointed half-Fae ears peeking out. She was wearing a black T-shirt with a logo of a multisided die inside a pentagram and the words *Bedlam Books & Games* curved above it, and a name tag that said *Brun*. She gave us a skeptical once-over. "You here for the meeting?"

"Yes, we are," my mom replied. "We got a little held up, did we miss it?"

"Nope." Brun pushed the curtain open wider for us. "You've still got time to grab some coffee and snacks." She gestured to where about a dozen people were gathered across the room.

Bastien's golden-blond head was not among them. Dammit.

The rest of the room, which was on a windowless basement level, was lined with shelves featuring board games and role-playing games of all kinds, most of which I'd never heard of. One entire unit was dedicated to colorful sets of dice ranging from standard black-and-white plastic sets to playful sets in bright colors and patterns to fancy ones made from wood, metal, or even different crystals. The wall behind the table bearing coffee and donuts had action figures on it, but not the ones you'd find in toy stores. These, instead, were from various popular TV shows and movies, some of which I didn't recognize, some of which had been off the air since I was a kid. I chuckled when I saw a fortieth-anniversary Stormy action figure from the Rainbow Brite line. Stormy was Cameron's roommate Tom's preferred nickname for me.

"I didn't even know half of these existed," I remarked, pouring myself a cup.

"Nostalgia makes a lot of bank these days," Leo said. "Ooh, they've got Faith from the 'Bad Girls' episode."

"Girls, we're not here to shop," Mom reminded us.

"I'm not entirely sure *what* we're here to do. Is this a support group or a gaming club?" I replied.

"Support groups meet in a lot of places you might not expect," Leo said. "Churches or town buildings often, but sometimes stores let them use the space. Alex went to some veterans' groups, and he was in a cancer support group after his diagnosis." She rubbed the dog tags she wore around her neck next to a man's wedding ring. They had belonged to Alex Pallas, her late husband and Griffin's dad.

I rubbed her shoulder consolingly. Never getting to meet Alex and missing so many huge moments in Leo's life were among my biggest regrets about having been gone for ten years.

"Wendy! Wendy Younger, is that you?"

We all turned to see a handsome middle-aged man looking at my mother with surprise and delight. After a startled moment, my mother smiled and waved at him, and he began making his way toward us.

Still smiling, my mom tilted her head slightly toward me and spoke quietly without changing her expression. "Spill your coffee."

"What?"

"Spill your coffee on the floor, now." Though her smile was wide and sparkling, her eyes belied some hidden fear. It was not a look she often had, and it shook me enough that I did as she asked, accidentally-on-purpose knocking my cup to the floor between us.

"Sorry!" I exclaimed. It was true enough that the venom didn't prevent me from saying it.

"Oh, that's okay! Here, let me help," Mom offered. We both grabbed napkins and knelt to clean it up.

"What's going on?" Leo asked, helping to wipe up the spill.

Mom ignored the question and spoke directly to me. "Lock up your magic, call yourself Kendra, and don't call me Mom."

Her voice was unnaturally flat, with an absence of emotion that spoke to wild ones being tightly controlled. A feeling I was very experienced with.

"That's going to be complicated with this whole truth venom thing," I pointed out, keeping my volume low to match hers.

"You're smart, you'll figure it out. Just do it. Please."

I don't know what about this man had her spooked. Mom had requested I not call her that at the bar ages ago, claiming it made her "feel and look old." I resented being made part of her midlife crisis as she flirted her way to free drinks and other things and partied with people younger than me and Cameron, all while not getting a job and letting me pay for everything at the house. But this, whatever it was, was clearly different. I exchanged a look with Leo, who seemed likewise confused and suspicious.

"Fine. But we are talking about this later." I wiped up the last of the puddle.

She lifted her eyes to meet mine, exhaled, and nodded. "I will. After. For now, follow my lead."

I nodded back. "Okay." I grabbed the napkins and brought them to a bin a few feet away. As I tossed them in, I crossed my wrists, lining up the runes on them, and whispered, *"Claude."*

One second my magic was there, the next it was gone, an invisible and essential piece of me gone numb and my senses all felt duller for it. The world somehow became dimmer, less vibrant, and I felt heavier. Vulnerable. It had been months since I'd done this, so long that I didn't even realize how used to having my magic unlocked and free I had become. Had I really lived like this for nearly ten years?

By the time I turned back, the man had reached us and

was embracing my mom in what looked like a warm greeting between old friends. He had used her maiden name when calling out to her earlier, so it had clearly been a while.

The shock in Mom's eyes was gone now; she looked entirely happy to see this person. "Cyrus! It's been forever! What are you doing here?" They pulled apart, but for a moment his hands lingered at her waist, and hers on his shoulders.

"Picking at scars, as always," Cyrus replied, and Mom laughed softly. "What about you?"

"A friend invited me. He thought it might be good for me, I guess," Mom admitted.

Cyrus's brow creased with concern. "Oh…oh, I'm sorry to hear that, Wendy. But whatever's happened, I am glad you're here. This is a good group. And selfishly, it's wonderful to see you again." He clasped her hand in his, smiling kindly. "You look like it was yesterday."

"Charming as ever, Cyrus," she said. There was a softness to her expression once again, a genuine affection that only sparked more questions in me. I cleared my throat to remind her she hadn't arrived solo. "Right! Sorry, let me introduce you. Girls, this is Cyrus. He's an old friend of mine. And these are Leo and Kendra, new friends of mine." A bubble of laughter accompanied the wordplay.

Cyrus turned to us at last, shaking both our hands with a warm, firm grip. He was tall, well built, with handsome brown eyes and silver streaks in his dark hair and beard. His hair was slightly grown out, brushed over his expressive brow in a way that embraced the signs of age gracefully. His smile was wide, bringing out a set of crow's-feet around his eyes. "A pleasure to meet you," he said, taking each of us in and shifting to a look of concern in my direction. "You're bleeding!"

Crap. I'd forgotten about the blood that still spotted my sleeve from the demon attack. "Oh—I'm fine. That's from earlier, it's healed up now."

"Are you sure? We have a first aid kit. Or at least a clean T-shirt, the store has plenty, so long as you don't mind geek culture jokes," he offered.

"T-shirt" meant short sleeves, which meant the tattoos on my wrists would be visible, and given my mom's subterfuge, I didn't think that would be a good idea. "No, I'm all set, but thanks," I replied.

Cyrus nodded. "All right, then. If you don't mind my asking, what happened?"

Once again, the truth was compelled out of me. "A demon attacked me," I blurted out.

His expression became concerned again, and he lifted his hands as though he might rest them on my shoulders to comfort me. I shifted away slightly and saw him notice, and instead he clasped his hands together. "I'm sorry to hear that, Kendra. But I can assure you, this is a safe space. Emotionally, physically, and magically; the store is warded against demons. None of them will be able to find or follow you here."

What the hell did we portal into? Although...considering the last few days? It was kind of comforting to know. We were definitely outside Arcadia Commons and its constant, if imperfect, anti-demon barrier. I'd been in two demon fights in the last forty-eight hours, with scars to show for both. I was not eager to make it a hat trick. And Cyrus's concern and comfort both seemed genuine, even if getting touchy-feely with strangers wasn't my thing. "Thank you," I said. "So, do you run this group?" I busied myself getting another coffee and a donut.

"In a manner of speaking. I help organize it and facilitate the meetings, but it's hardly mine," Cyrus said. His watch trilled, and he tapped it to silence it. "You'll see, we're about to start. Please, take a seat."

Cyrus walked to the front of the room, inasmuch as there was one, calling out, "Let's get started, everyone!" The folding chairs were arranged in a loose circle, with space made for a group member who was in a wheelchair and a few extras in case of latecomers.

Mom sat down roughly across the circle from Cyrus; someone we didn't know was on one side of her. She looked at us expectantly, gesturing to the two chairs next to her. The meaning was clear: *Come, sit.*

I stared at her: *What?*

She patted the chair: *Sit!*

I subtly shook my head, incredulous: *We're not here for the meeting, we're here for information!*

Mom gave me a stern look. *Don't be ridiculous. Sit.*

I gestured at the telltale bloodstain on my sleeve. *I can't lie, and you want me to do therapy?*

Mom raised an eyebrow. *Do you even hear yourself right now?*

I pointed at her. *It was* your *idea!*

She rolled her eyes, and I was about to throw up my hands and walk away, but Leo grabbed my arm, semigently dragging me toward the chairs. "Pretty sure I followed all that, and let's all agree we'll help cover for you. We're not gonna get any new leads until this meeting is over either way."

I sighed. "Fine. But don't expect me to say anything."

"It will probably be for the best if you don't," Mom agreed.

I made a point of taking the chair farther away from her. With a sigh of her own, Leo sat between us.

"Welcome, everyone. I'm so glad you could all join us today," Cyrus said, greeting the group, smiling and making nonaggressive eye contact with everyone in turn. "And glad to see some new faces here, as well! For those of you who are new, welcome to our cabal of the covenless." *Cabal of the covenless? Is that a serious statement or a joke?*

The stiff metal chair felt even more uncomfortable with the eyes of everyone else on us. I sipped my coffee and looked noncommittally in Cyrus's direction as he went about an affirmation or something. I tried to picture Bastien here, both in this store and in this group. It was easy and difficult at once.

He could fit in anywhere, despite the privileges that would have made it easy for him to hold himself above and apart from most. In spite of the power and wealth he came from, though, Bastien was genial, genuine, intelligent, and respectful. He hadn't become class president by accident, and for all that my brother sarcastically called him Mr. Mayor, Bastien could've run for any office and won handily on charisma alone. Coming here, listening to stories of others who had been hurt, commiserating and sympathizing? Yeah. I could see it.

It was the idea of him speaking to them of his own pain that tripped me up. He could hide it so well. Had he yelled? Cried? Spoken plainly with his society mask on? Or had he been largely silent, letting the experience happen around him without engaging with it?

No, McKenna, that's what you're *doing. What you* keep *doing.* I was chastising myself, but I could almost hear it in Bastien's voice, shot through with the same bitter anger he'd had at the Solstice Ball.

Yeah, well, you're the one who decided to invite my mom here and not me, I argued with the blond phantom of my own guilt.

Did it ever occur to you that maybe this meeting is what I wanted to talk to you about this morning?

Shit. Well, *now* it did. As the affirmations wrapped up, I tuned in. I might not intend to share anything, but I could listen.

"Remember," Cyrus was saying, "this is a safe space for whatever you're feeling, whatever you've gone through, even whatever you've done. We come together here because we cannot go elsewhere. We share our stories that we might reclaim our lives and our power, because we've all learned the hard way that no one's going to do it for us." *Okay, yeah, that one hits a little close to home.* "Does anyone have anything to share to start us off?"

"I'll go." A man named Karam, a little older than me, spoke of having been a thrall to a demon I realized had to have been Saranthiel—of how the last few years were a blur, of things he couldn't remember doing, until suddenly six months ago his mind cleared, his spirit lightened, and he realized he'd somehow become free.

"It's been…it's been real fucking hard ever since, but… gods, it's good, y'know? I feel like life is mine again. I even got a job. Part-time grocery store stocking, but it's something, and…" He had to pause to steady himself. "I don't know what happened, and I don't want to. It's probably pretty fucked up. I'm just focusing on getting back to some kind of normal. There's a lot I won't ever get back. That's on me. But it's a start."

The group clapped for him. I didn't. I couldn't. I was shaking inside, trembling like I was walking an unraveling rope bridge over an abyss, unable to fully take in what I was hearing. I'd killed Saranthiel, but... other than Brooke, I hadn't given much thought to whatever other thralls I'd freed by doing so. Never mind the ones I'd freed by killing Forneus years ago.

"What about your reparations?" asked Brun. "Those families? Did you make it up to them?"

Karam shifted in his chair. "It's... I'm working on it. I have to get myself back on solid ground first, you know? And some of them... I don't even know what I did, exactly. I can't remember." *Just like I couldn't remember what I did to Jackie...* "I'd ask, I would, but a lotta people, you know, they don't really want to hear from me..."

His interrogator crossed her arms, not looking away. "So no."

"Brun," Cyrus gently chastised her. "No projecting or judging. We've talked about this. Remember, this group is about healing from things we've done as much as things done to us."

Brun exhaled forcefully, uncrossing her arms. "Sorry, Karam."

Karam nodded. "It's okay. I get it. Have you heard anything from Melanie?" The name caused a ripple of recognition in the group, especially when Brun nodded.

"Yeah. She came by the store this week," she said. "Still trying to make excuses. She says she's sorry, but then she just launches into the usual BS: She made a Bargain, she had no choice, she had no control, blah blah blah." Brun rolled her eyes. "But she still did those things. She chose that over me. She could've said *something*."

"It's harder than it sounds." I almost didn't realize I'd spoken until all eyes landed on me.

Cyrus smiled and gestured for me to go on when I froze up. "Please, Kendra. Share your thoughts."

"Um . . ." *Where's a surprise demon attack when you really need one?* The uneven feet of the metal chair clunked as I shifted. Seven hells, what I wouldn't give to be able to lie right now. "It's . . . well. It's just that it's not easy. The telling-people part, sometimes the terms are very specific and you—the person who made the deal, I mean—literally can't. I'm not saying they can't do anything, but it *can* be that hard."

Brun eyed me sourly. "Then what's her excuse now? It's a pretty shit apology."

"It . . . it is, yeah. But . . . look, no one likes admitting they fucked up," I replied. "Especially to a hostile audience. It means facing the truth. What you did, who you hurt, and no more dodging or explaining or trying to place the blame somewhere else, even if it *isn't* entirely your fault. Accepting that you did these things, that the blame's all on you, that there's no undoing them, maybe no coming back from them, either? Yeah. Yeah, it's pretty fucking hard." I paused, feeling out of breath, but the words, the truth, weren't done flowing out of me yet. "And if you're lucky enough to be out from under the Archdemon and the bad decisions that landed you there, all that means is the only one stopping you from apologizing, from making reparations, is you." I let out a breath.

Bastien's anger loomed large in my mind: *Just stay away from me.* "By the time you get there, the words *I'm sorry* aren't enough. They never will be, and you know that. So what do you do? Start with those? Or just stay away, because there's nothing you can ever do to make up for it anyway?" I spread my hands. "You tell me."

Brun stared at me for a long moment. "Were you a thrall? Or did you just get stabbed in the back by one?"

Talk about picking at scars. My eyes fled hers. "Both."

There was some murmuring once again, folks looking at me anew. No doubt they didn't see many of us in here, much less two at once.

"Sounds like you've been through quite a lot," Cyrus said sympathetically. "Would you like to talk about it?"

"No." His phrasing left me a way out of saying more, thankfully. I felt his gaze on me, his and everyone else's, and wished I could escape. His dark eyes lingered, looking like he might ask a follow-up question, but he didn't get the chance.

"I'd like to share, actually." Attention shifted to my mother, Cyrus's first among them, as she spoke up. Her hands fidgeted in her lap before she stilled them. "I spent the last five years in a mental institution. Demons basically drove me mad. One of them took…took something from me, and I tried so hard to get it back that I…I lost myself…I lost everything."

My eyes fixed on the coffee cup in my hand, my teeth biting into my lip again, the nails of my other hand clenched and digging into my palm.

"I'm better now, health-wise, but I…I have no idea who I am anymore," Mom confessed, with a sound that was half laugh, half cry. "The friends my shitty ex-husband didn't cut me off from stayed away when I started losing my mind. Most people think I moved away for five years for family reasons, and it's not like I can tell them otherwise. My license is revoked, and I've been unemployed for about six years, my credit is shot, my bank account is empty. Everyone looks at me like I'm either pitiful, having a midlife crisis, or like I might snap again any second now, and I can't even tell them they're wrong!" She threw her hands up in an almost comical shrug. "Because I might be sane now, but…I can remember *not* being sane. I can remember being *so* certain about everything, about the things I saw, or heard, that I know weren't there. Maybe the worst part is that…that sometimes I miss them." Tears slipped down her face now; she tried to wipe a few away before giving up and letting them go. "Or maybe the worst part is that…my magic is gone. Forever. Our Council severed me."

A few sharp gasps followed that; some of the attendees muttered a few choice words for Councils and severings. By now, my eyes, too, were riveted on her.

Mom continued. "I understand why. Not like I can say they made the wrong call, I mean, I tried to burn down a forest, right? I'd have severed me, too!" She tried to play it off with dark humor again, but it didn't work this time. A sob shook her frame, a sob she held in, letting it rattle her inside instead of releasing it where it could do less damage. "No, the actual worst thing is…is knowing that I used to be a *really* good mom. Wasn't perfect, sure, but I was good, I really was. And now I'm just…a real shit mom. My kids can't stand me, and honestly, I don't blame them. I kind of hate me, too."

Her shaky breaths, her failing attempts to say more, echoed in the room, or maybe just in my ears. Cyrus suddenly crossed the circle, on his knees before her and gently taking one of her hands in both of his.

But I couldn't move. Bracketed to the chair by the weight of my guilt and all my fuckups, the harm I'd done to my mom, to everyone in my life, when I'd chosen to run away. One move and it would crush me. One breath and it would surely be my last, as surely as when I'd been dragged under the waves two nights before.

Leo turned to me with a wide-eyed expression somewhere between *What do we do?* and *Why the hell are you just sitting there?* But what could I do? What could I say? My mom had specifically asked me not to acknowledge who we were to each other. I had to . . .

. . . *to do as I'm told? When have I ever let* that *stop me?*

Once. Bastien told me to leave him alone. And, I finally realized, fully bowing to that request had been a mistake. He'd needed space, sure, but I'd let him disappear from my life, and look where that had gotten us.

The thought loosened the invisible grip that moored me to my chair. I got up and went to her, taking her free hand. Her red-rimmed hazel eyes met mine. "Your children don't hate you, Wendy. They love you. You taught them to be strong and loyal and loving. Because you're all those things."

Mom pulled me into the hug with one arm, holding me close and crying onto my messy hair.

Chapter 8
Old Boyfriends

A half hour later, stress sugaring mode had taken over completely. With a second donut in one hand and sweetened coffee in the other (which I desperately wished was one of Rocket Café's cookies 'n' cream lattes), I watched my mother and the man who had rushed across the room to comfort her chat quietly by a display of miniature plastic fantasy creatures. Who was this guy? Why did she want me to lie about who I was? To lock up my magic and use my pseudonym? I'd fought hard against myself and outside forces alike to reclaim my name, my magic, and my family—I did not like going back to hiding them again.

Leo returned from a bathroom trip to stand next to me. "So. Ex-boyfriend, right?"

"Has to be. But not one I've ever heard of," I said. "And he's got to be from before she met my dad."

"You think Bastien knew? Is that why he invited her to this?"

I frowned, thinking. "No...no, I don't think so. Cyrus was clearly surprised to see her. I think Bastien invited her here just for the support group part of it."

Coming here clearly *had* been something my mom needed. As she and Cyrus talked, her smile was lighter than it had been in a long time. Truth be told, my tangled feelings toward her had shifted since our moment earlier, too.

I've got you to thank for that, Bastien...wherever you are. He'd visited her regularly in the mental institution while I was on the run, and now, even with her mind restored and me back home, even though he and I weren't speaking, he was still her friend, still looking out for her.

It mystified me, sometimes, how some people always managed to both know the right thing to do and also follow through on doing it. I admired them; I envied them; and in a world where people like me made choices that got others killed and made my mom think I hated her, I was incredibly grateful they existed. That he existed.

"Do you think Bastien was going to tell me about this?" I asked Leo, turning to her.

Leo thought about it. "Maybe. There was only, what, an hour between when he asked you to be at his place and when your mom came? Either way, though, seems like it worked out. You two definitely had a moment there."

"We did. But one moment doesn't fix everything." I wanted to think Mom's confession and my response *could* be the start of a better path for us. I meant what I'd said: I didn't hate her. I never had, no matter how frustrated I'd been. But as soon as the meeting wrapped up, Mom and Cyrus had sequestered themselves over in their corner. Maybe she wanted to flirt while she still could, maybe talking to me was too much to tackle right now. I could relate to that, at least.

So that would have to wait. In the meantime, our first priority remained: find Bastien.

"Since she's busy flirting, let's ask around about Bastien." I turned to look at the other group members, who were milling about, chatting in groups. "Let's start with Brun. She works here, he's got the IP address of her portal circle, she must know him."

We got a lucky break for once, as the half-Fae woman was refilling her coffee cup by herself. "Hi. Brun, right?" I said, approaching her.

She brusquely scanned me with suspicion of her own. She'd been looking at me in a less-than-friendly way since learning I used to be a thrall. "That's me. What do you want?"

Yikes. "We're looking for a friend of ours, he's part of this group—"

"I'll stop you there. These meetings are *anonymous*, okay? As in, we don't gossip about who may or may not be attending or the stuff they're dealing with," Brun informed me bluntly.

"I'm not asking for gossip, I'm—"

"The answer's no, *thrall.*"

Oh, that was *it.* "*Former* thrall," I corrected her, glaring.

"Just 'cause your demon died and got you off the hook doesn't make you any less responsible."

"That is *not*—" But my retort stuck in my throat. I couldn't tell her how I'd gotten out of it; that information was kept close and for good reason.

On the upside, any and all compulsion to tell the truth, the whole truth, and nothing but was gone. On the one hand, thank all stars and spells; on the other hand, yikes, telling my mom I didn't hate her counted as a major confession? I inwardly cringed, shoving that away to unpack later.

Leo stepped in. "Hey, you wanna slow your roll and quit harassing my friend? You're not the only one who's been through some shit here.'

"Yeah, I'm really sure she—" Brun started, but Leo wasn't done.

"And two," Leo cut in, "if you would stop interrupting, you'd know we're looking for Bastien. He's missing and we're worried about him. Do you know anything that might help?"

Brun's demeanor shifted at hearing this, open hostility becoming concern. "Wait, seriously? When did he go missing?"

"Sometime last night," Leo said. "He said he'd be at this meeting, gave us a stone so we could get here, too. We hoped we'd see him, but…" She gestured at the room, where he very much was not.

Brun spread her hands. "Last time I saw him was a few days ago. He met with me and Cyrus to plan for today's meeting. He mentioned bringing a friend. I didn't realize he meant more than one."

"He helps plan these?" I asked.

She gave a short nod. "Yeah. He…well, like I said, I don't gossip about people in the group, even if he did invite you here. But yeah, he's been helping out. He's the one who set up the portal circle for us." She jerked her thumb toward the storage area we'd come in through.

I'd suspected he might have, but confirmation was something else. "You didn't have one at all before?"

Brun shook her head. "Nope. He enchanted the portal stones so everyone could use them to get to and from here, too. Even the ones without magic. He's good people."

It meshed with the Bastien I knew he was deep down. Coming here for his own healing and finding a way to make everyone else's lives better. "Yeah, he is."

"But I don't know where he is now. Sorry," Brun concluded.

"Thanks. Is there anyone else here who might know?" Leo asked.

"Cyrus is your best bet," Brun said. The man was still talking with my mother, his hand on her upper arm, his thumb rubbing as if to soothe her. Brun gave them a gruff look. "But he looks pretty busy getting to know your other friend right now."

"That he does," I agreed. "Thanks, Brun." She grunted an acknowledgement and left.

Leo's brow furrowed. "Why didn't you tell her you helped kill those Archdemons?" she asked quietly.

I tossed out my empty coffee cup. "Because it's need-to-know information, and no one here needs to know. Also, the truth venom has finally worn off. Let's go see what my mom's old beau knows."

I studied Cyrus more as we crossed the room to them, trying to divine what he was to my mom and what he wanted from her. He was attractive, in that handsome older guy way; I'm sure he had been handsome when he was younger, too. Mom met my dad just after college when she moved back to Arcadia Commons, and they got married when she was twenty-four. Cyrus had used her maiden name, so he had to be from her high school or college days. I knew the names of most witch families in town, but she hadn't told us his last name, and with my magic locked up, I couldn't take a look at his aura to tell if he was a witch.

They had to have parted on good terms, given the greeting they'd had. Not to mention the way he was looking at my mother now, smiling at her, eyes crinkling at the corners, half in love, half in awe. Like they were somewhere much brighter than a demon abuse survivor support group in the basement of a gaming store, of all places.

I couldn't remember my dad *ever* looking at my mom like that. Despite the tears she'd so recently shed, my mom was smiling at Cyrus that way, too. She looked…*happy*. For the first time since I'd come back.

But then…why did she ask me to lie and lock up my magic? Why did she look so afraid when she asked? What is she hiding, and from who?

"Those two have a major one-that-got-away vibe," I whispered to Leo.

She nodded. "Do we think that's a good thing or a bad thing?"

"Jury's still out."

Mom spotted us. "Girls! There you are. Sorry, Cyrus and I were just reminiscing on our misspent youth." She shared another private-joke smile with him.

"Though I get the feeling Wendy's sense of adventure hasn't dulled any since then," Cyrus replied before looking at Leo and me. "Thank you both so much for participating today. For being there for Wendy and for sharing some of your story, too." This last part was directed at me in particular. "I hope someday you'll feel ready to tell us more, Kendra."

"Yeah, don't hold your breath. So how do you two know each other?" I asked, determined to get answers this time.

"Well...we used to date. Before I met my ex-husband, back when I was in high school," Mom replied.

"When *you* were in high school?" I echoed, raising a brow at her. "He wasn't?"

Cyrus chuckled and my mom blushed. *Blushed.* "I may have been the slightly older man. Only slightly!"

My eyebrow was quite nearly in my hairline by then. "Isn't that interesting." *Note to self for the next time she gives me shit about Remi!* "What happened?"

"Oh, you know how it goes. I moved away for college and that was more or less it," my mom said. "Cyrus moved out of town, and...now here we are."

"Indeed we all are," I replied. I had about a million follow-up questions, naturally, but that was going to have to wait. "I hate to break up the nostalgia, Cyrus, but we were hoping you could help us. We actually came here looking for someone."

"Our friend, Bastien," Leo said. "He's the one who told us about the group and invited us, but he's been missing since last night, we think. We hoped he'd be here, but, obviously, no luck with that."

Cyrus's brow furrowed. "Missing? I was expecting him today, especially since he mentioned bringing a friend who'd been severed with him. He only mentioned one, though, I'm not sure which of you he meant...?"

Right. With my wards up, my aura looked as magicless as

Mom's. "He meant Wendy," I said, rubbing my wrist through my sleeve. "Leo and I were last-minute add-ons. Wasn't sure this was my kind of thing."

"Glad you changed your mind," Cyrus said.

I smiled dryly. "Not so sure I have yet."

"Cyrus meets with another, smaller group of severed witches as well," Mom explained.

I cocked an eyebrow at him. "Oh? Are you one yourself?"

"No. I nearly was, though," he said.

Leo and I were both surprised. "What happened?" Leo asked.

"It's a long story, but suffice to say I did not see eye to eye with my local Council on some things." My esteem for him instantly rose.

"Now *that* I can relate to," I replied.

Cyrus grinned at me, a far less practiced expression than I'd seen from him yet. "Always nice to meet a fellow rebel. The Councils as a whole are well past their expiration date, in my opinion. Severing is just one example," he went on, building up steam. "It's barbaric, outdated, and causes far more harm than good. As though there aren't other measures they could take when it's actually necessary."

"That's what I've been saying!" After all the Council's insistence on it, it was good to hear someone agree with me.

"I still can't believe that they did that to you, Wendy." His jaw tightened, one hand clenching into a fist. Mom laid her hand on his shoulder.

"Don't get worked up on my account. I appreciate it, but it's done. There's no sense in anyone else getting in trouble over it now." Mom said it to him, but I could swear her words were for me, too.

"Just because something is done doesn't mean it's over," Cyrus said, reaching up to take her hand in his, the fire in his eyes flickering from anger to something else entirely. Something that seemed to echo in my mother as her gaze locked with his.

I cleared my throat before those two forgot they had an audience. "Anyway, we really need to get back to looking for Bastien."

"Maybe we missed something back at his place," Leo said. "Let's do another pass."

"They're right, we should. But it's been...really good to see you again, Cyrus," Mom told him. "Let me get your number before we go?"

"I wouldn't dream of letting you leave without it. But might I come with you? If he's missing, I'd like to help, and an extra set of eyes and hands can't hurt, right?" Cyrus offered, looking at all of us.

Mom turned to us. "It *could* help."

Leo looked on the fence. "That's true, but...what do you think?" she asked me.

I didn't love continuing to hide myself, or a further delay to having a straight talk with my mom. But at this point, we needed whatever help we could get to find Bastien, and I wasn't against getting to know more about this guy who had Mom over the moon at the same time. "Welcome aboard Lemaire Airways, Cyrus," I said, a joke I'd often made with Bastien. "Keep your extremities inside the portal at all times."

———————— • ————————

"This is the house Bastien's been so keen to get rid of?" Cyrus said, taking in the cozy but well-appointed beach home with a low whistle. "I know his reasons, but it's hard to argue with that view. Ipswich Bay! It's been too long." His gaze softened as he took in the stretch of beach and ocean below.

"Technically not the bay, that's on the north side of town and we're south, but yeah, it is a nice view," I said. Just six months ago, I'd stood in the Grand and looked out at the Atlantic from the American side for the first time in ten years, letting memories wash over me like the waves below. It was easy to find the beauty and the nostalgia in the whitecaps, the docks and jetties reaching out like fingers into the blue. "How long since you were last here?" I asked.

"Almost thirty years now," Cyrus replied, stroking his beard.

"Wow. And I thought ten was a long time."

"Oh? Back from a recent sabbatical yourself?"

"Something like that. What kept you away?"

His mouth pressed into a line. "It was clear I wasn't welcome anymore. And you?"

My right hand rubbed over my left, thumb smoothing over the scar in the center of the palm, and I thanked whatever gods there were that I could lie again. "I wanted to travel."

Cyrus pulled his eyes from the waves to look at me and gave a wry smile. "I like your version better, I'll have to steal that one."

I grinned despite being caught out. "I suppose I can share."

He chuckled, and I could see what my mom might see in him. I'd be inclined to like him more if not for how shady she was acting. Why try to hide me? What was I missing?

"Right, enough nostalgia. Why don't you show me what you've found?" Cyrus suggested.

"I got here this morning…" I started walking him through things. *Seven hells, has it only been since this morning?* My stomach growled, reminding me I'd consumed all of a few cups of coffee, a granola bar, and two donuts today. What I wouldn't give for one of the Veil and Horn's veggie burgers right now.

As if on cue, my phone buzzed with not just a text but a call from Trevan himself. I excused myself and stepped into Bastien's office, closing the door and answering. "Hey, Trev—"

"Get over here, *right now*," Trevan growled, his Irish brogue coming through stronger than usual.

"Is everything okay? Is Cam okay?" I asked in alarm, praying no one else I cared about was in trouble. The list was long enough as it was.

"Cameron's just fine, so's everyone else, but *you've* got a mess to clean up in the bathroom. And yes, it needs to be *you*."

"In the bathroom? Cam's covering my shift, whatever it is, he can deal with it. I'm in the middle of something here."

"Cameron didn't mystically fuck up my bathroom. You did and you know damn well what I mean."

He couldn't mean—oh, shit, is this about me and Remi? "'Mystically fuck up'? What are you talking about?"

"Easier for you to see it than for me to explain it."

I rolled my eyes. "Whatever it is will have to wait, I can't—"

"You can, or you're fired," Trevan cut in, effectively shutting me up. "Now get over here." He hung up before I could protest.

I stared at the phone in my hand. Fired? For what, hooking

up in the bathroom? Not exactly the best employee behavior, I know, but hardly something I would expect Trevan to fire me for, especially this far after the fact. And I had no idea what this "mystical" business was all about.

What I *did* know, however, was that I couldn't afford to lose that job. I was already out a chunk of money this weekend as it was. "Dammit!"

Mom poked her head in. "Did you find something?"

"No." I pocketed the phone. "But if I don't go take care of something at the Veil and Horn, right now, I'm going to lose my job."

"What? Why?"

"I'm not even sure, but Trevan's pissed about something, and we both know I can't afford to get fired."

"Whatever it is, he's clearly overreacting," Mom said, waving a hand. "He won't fire you, just talk to—"

"Mom!" I exclaimed, cutting her off. Her eyes went wide and she shushed me, throwing a fearful glance over her shoulder. It only stoked my annoyance further, though I did lower my volume. "I get that money is, for some reason, not something you give a shit about, but I actually need to keep paying our bills. And I don't know why you want me lying to your old boyfriend, but when I come back, I'm coming back as myself."

"It's...it's complicated, sweetie," Mom said, fingers twining uneasily.

"Then uncomplicate it." I stormed out past her. "I need to go take care of something. I'll be back as soon as I can. Keep me posted if you find anything, okay?" I announced to Cyrus and Leo.

"What's going on?" Leo asked.

I yanked the door open. "Apparently, I need to go see a satyr about a bathroom."

———————•———————

The boiling pot of irritation and stress was not helped when I went into the bar and saw Remi, whose text I still had not answered, was also here. "Seven hells," I muttered as I approached the bar.

Remi was wearing his male form today, that of a dark-haired metro-styled man who looked similar enough to his female form that Remi passed them off as cousins who happened to have the same name. His hair was slightly grown out, a longish look that was currently popular, and he was wearing expensive-looking slacks along with a casual patterned button-down. The way the pants sat low on his hips and the rolled sleeves of the shirt showing off his leanly muscled arms drew my eye almost instantly, just in case I'd needed a personal reminder I was still bi. The smirk on his face being both amusing and annoying when he caught me doing it, on the other hand, was a personal reminder I still didn't know where I wanted things to stand with him.

Trevan was at the bar as well, not even wearing a glamour to hide his horns, pointed ears, and goatlike eyes. It was then I noticed the bar was otherwise empty right now. Though the hours between lunch and dinner were slow sometimes, empty was outright strange. There weren't any pixies zipping around the rafters, nor were there other employees around.

I slowed my steps. "Uh…what's going on?"

"Go ahead in there and you tell me," Trevan replied, pointing at the bathroom in question.

I exchanged a look with Remi, who shrugged and started to get up, but Trevan stopped him with his other hand. "Separately, this time."

"All right, all right, I'll wait my turn," Remi replied, sitting back down.

I pushed the door to the women's room open, at this point preparing myself for anything from a pile of bodies to a graffiti-tagged nightmare, but it was completely normal. It was clean: There weren't even scraps of paper on the floor or random water drops on the mirrors. What was Trevan so pissed off about? I wondered as I walked to the far end of the sinks, my hand trailing on the edge of the ceramic I'd gripped the other night when Remi—

Ohh. A wave of pure lust shot through me, and I clung to the sink's edge again to steady myself. My skin was flushed and warm, blood pumping through me, a carnal need to be touched, kissed, and other very direct verbs vibrating down to my core. Memories of that night jumped to the forefront of my mind and demanded to be repeated, strong enough to make me groan.

"Let go of the sink!" Trevan yelled from outside.

My eyes snapped open at the interruption to the fantasies taking over my mind. In the mirror I saw the wild, wanton look in my eyes, and that my free hand was already sliding down into my pants.

"*Now,* McKenna!" Trevan interrupted again. I gritted my

teeth and with great effort pulled away from the sink, stumbling back against a stall door, panting. After a minute, I walked back out into the bar. I took the glass of water my boss had already left out for me, letting the icy liquid cool me down quite literally.

I set it back down half-empty. "Okay. I, uh, I think I see the problem."

Trevan gave a caprine snort. "Yep. You two turned the ladies' room into a sex-charged hot spot, and I had to close early because not one, not two, but *seven* different people were going at it in there during lunch."

"At the same time?" I blurted.

Remi smirked. "Good for them."

Trevan ignored both of us. "I nearly made a fool of myself trying to figure it out. Finally had Cameron take a look, and he confirmed he could see *your* magic and *your* power tangled up in there by the sink," he said, pointing to each of us in turn.

"Fuck." I buried my face in my hands.

"Find a more creative expletive, I've been hearing that one a *lot* today," Trevan grumbled.

The heat of embarrassment crept over me, but I looked up at Trevan again. "I swear I have no idea why this is happening. We didn't—I didn't—no spells were cast, is what I'm trying to say!"

Remi raised his hand, looking abashed. "This, ah, this might be my fault, actually."

Trevan and I both turned to him. "Explain, please?" I asked.

"It's . . . possible that my control got a little loose," Remi said, a little too casually. "I was . . . distracted."

I arched a dubious eyebrow at him. "You've been distracted before, and *that* never happened."

"I don't particularly give my goat's arse what the cause is, I just want it fixed, as soon as possible," Trevan grunted. "Whatever that happens to require. This place is empty. I'm giving you an hour."

The sentence very clearly had a silent second half, but I had to ask. "What happens after an hour?"

"We find out who's still got a job and who owes me for the money I'll lose if we have to keep this place closed any longer than that." With one last goatlike huff, Trevan stomped out the front door, flipping the sign to CLOSED and letting it slam behind him.

Remi watched him go. "Hope he remembers to put his glamour up, or he's going to have even more problems."

I rounded on Remi. "What the hell happened? How and why did we create an orgasm sink?"

Remi turned his smirk on me. "I'm fairly certain you know the how, but I'm happy to remind you if not," he flirted. "We've got an hour, that's more than enough time to deal with this issue with plenty left over."

A flush of heat went through me again; my body still remembered quite well, all the more with the hot spot's reminder. "We need to fix this *now*, Remi. I have somewhere else to be."

His smirk fell, replaced by a look of confusion and curiosity. "Oh? Where's that?"

There might be reasons to not tell Remi—as much as I hated to admit it, a tiny part of me suspected that he might have something to do with everything going on—but with our leads waning and additional demon involvement more likely all the time, they didn't matter much. "Bastien is missing. There's a good chance demons might've kidnapped him, but I don't know who or why or where they've taken him. Or if...or what condition he's in."

He sat up straight. "Tell me everything."

I did. Everything from what happened at the Council meeting to finding Bastien missing that morning, the demon attack, the support group, all of it. By the end of it, we each had a half-empty whiskey in front of us and I was showing Remi a picture of the sketch Bastien had made of the secret-seeker.

"Not one I'm familiar with, but I'll find out who it answers to," he said, stroking his chin.

"You don't recognize it at all?" I asked, surprised.

"Just because we're all demons doesn't mean we all know each other," he pointed out. "Plus some of us, as you've experienced, are more secretive than others. There are some Archdemons who've gone so quiet I sometimes wonder if they even still exist."

My brows went up. "Seriously? I could never find info on all of them, but like you said, secretive. I chalked that up to that they kept their names and natures away from being written down on purpose."

"That, too, yes. But we owe each other no loyalty unless we've bargained for it, and even those alliances are fleeting, so there's little communication between camps, so to speak."

I frowned into my glass. "But you knew Dara before she swore herself to you, and she worked for Saranthiel before."

"She did, and Forneus before that, for a time, that's how I met her. Before Forneus, she worked for another Archdemon," Remi recounted.

"So her loyalty is very flexible. Gee, that makes me feel much better about her being around," I griped.

"She had her reasons, but she *is* sworn to me now. I trust her, why can't you?" Remi asked.

"Literally everything you just said."

"Our morality might be malleable, but being sworn to an Archdemon is as serious for a minion as it is for a thrall. Anyway, my point is, the one before Forneus? That one's been silent for a very long time. So silent that its own minions weren't sure what the deal was. Its thralls didn't lose their power, so it wasn't dead, but they eventually died, and no new Bargains were being made. The minions started losing power, too, and while their master might not be dead, it seemed to at least be compromised. Most of them moved on to serve new Archdemons," Remi recounted. "Some are still waiting faithfully, I suppose."

It was both fascinating and chilling to hear. You didn't study demonology as much as I had without becoming deeply interested in the subject, and this was a story I'd never heard before. At the same time, it was a peek inside what Remi's life as a demon minion had been like. I knew he'd served Forneus for a few centuries at least. At some point, he'd somehow gotten his hands on a host body—using a spell that it was almost certain some ancestor of mine had cast. But his memory of it was hazy, and while my grimoire had the spell, it didn't have any details about prior uses of that spell. What was certain was that Forneus had been the one who was supposed to get that body, and when he didn't, he threw Remi in demon jail for at least a hundred years before letting him out to keep an eye on me, the promising teenage thrall who Forneus secretly knew could make host bodies. A decision that did not work out well for Forneus, in the end.

"Did you ever work for another Archdemon?" I asked. It hadn't occurred to me until now that Remi might have.

He shook his head. "No, I was Forneus's from the start, whenever that was."

The origin of demons was also unclear. Thralls who died still bound by Bargains became demon minions. But there were demons like Remi who had simply always been, as far as anyone knew.

"Hm. This Archdemon, has anyone ever found out what happened to it?" I stood, finishing my whiskey and starting toward the problematic ladies' room.

"Nope. But the thing is, that one was the Archdemon of Secrets. It may just be leaning very hard into its nature for all anyone knows," Remi said, finishing his whiskey as well. "Or lulling everyone into a false sense of security. Or something else entirely. Are you using the facilities, or are we switching gears?"

"I need to get back to finding Bastien, and I definitely can't lose this job. We can talk while we figure this out."

"Very well."

The bathroom was as innocuous as when I'd entered before,

but now I knew to be wary of that last sink. "Speaking of talking and figuring things out," Remi said, leaning in next to my ear; in his male form, he was just slightly taller than me. His breath tickled my ear, sending a pleasant prickle down my spine, despite my not wanting to be in the mood. "You never answered my text."

I stepped away. "Yesterday and this morning kind of got away from me."

"Mm-hm. But here we are."

I chanted a spell to let me look at the traces of magic; sure enough, I saw golden threads of mine inosculated with the tendrils of shadow that slid about the edge of the sink. The shadow came in two shades, however, one black, one more of a deep red, reflecting the two aspects of Remi's power, Madness and Desire. "This is pretty tangled, all right. And both of your mantles are mixed up in there. Guess that explains why the Saturday crowd was so handsy."

"Mm, I do so like when your eyes light up like that. You flexing your power, very attractive," he purred.

I glowered, dismissing the spell and with it the golden light on my eyes. "Could you please focus? You aren't even touching the sink, so there's really no excuse."

"What, I can't just be turned on by you in general?" Remi replied, then sighed at the look I gave him. "Fine, fine. Let's take a look." His eyes flickered with an inner flame as he reached for his own power. "Ooh. Very tangled indeed. But I think this should be fairly easy. I pull on my power, you pull on your magic, and there we have it. Ready?" He lifted his hand over the edge of the sink.

"What're you doing?"

"If we're going to pull back on the power we've left here, we are going to need to touch it," Remi replied. "And yes, it will need to be at the same time so we can untangle them. How did you plan on doing it?"

"Guess I was hoping we could do it one at a time," I replied. I'd known that wasn't likely, but it also would've been less awkward.

Remi sighed again, putting a hand on his hip. "Okay then, let's morning-after this shit."

"What?"

"You regret what happened."

I flushed again, this time at being put on the spot. "I don't! I...ugh. I don't know." I ran a hand through my hair, forgetting that half of it was pinned up, and cursed as I fouled up the entire haphazard hairstyle. "Dammit." I turned to the mirror, pulling out pins so I could redo it.

"You don't know. Meaning...?" he prompted, watching me in the mirror.

"Meaning I don't know!" I exclaimed. "Meaning I was having a shitty night and it felt good to feel good."

"I certainly don't regret making you feel good," Remi said. He leaned against the sink next to me.

"I know you don't. But I know what my mom said about how you feel and what I sort of said about how I feel and..." I finger-combed the short side of my hair back up and started repinning it.

"How *do* you feel?"

"I don't know!" I spun to face him, throwing my hands

in the air in frustration. "I don't know! I barely have time to feel anything lately!" Slumping forward, I leaned on the sink and—*oh, no.*

"McKenna—" Remi shifted, reaching for my hand before I could warn him, and suddenly we were both touching the hot spot, and each other.

Heat rushed through me, prickling every nerve along the way with an undeniable desire, a *need*, to be touched. Remi's hand tightened on mine, fingers interlacing suggestively, locking our hands to the ceramic, while his other arm snaked around my waist and pulled me against him, hard. His hand slipped under my shirt, fingertips dragging along the small of my back. I was already breathing heavily as I looked up at him, my hips pressing against his, a whimper escaping my throat. I saw his dark, flickering eyes for a second before he was kissing me, open-mouthed and intense. My tongue tangled against his, my spare hand in his hair as I kissed him back.

After minutes, hours, who knew, Remi's lips left mine and started down my throat. "Say what you will, darling," he panted, suckling at a tender spot, "but you can't deny we do good work together."

I tipped my head back, groaning at the new tingles he was setting off across my skin. "Almost annoyingly so," I panted. "Nngh. Fuck. We need to untangle this thing. And don't call me darling."

"Must we, really," Remi murmured, his lips down to my collarbone, his hand coming around to start undoing my shirt.

"We...really...must," I replied. Not that it stopped me from grabbing his ass. "This isn't us."

"On the contrary, this is *precisely* us." His hand slid inside my shirt, cupping my breast, *oh, goddamn.*

"This is…Friday-night us. Not-thinking-just-feeling us," I replied, groping at the hardness straining against his pants now.

"I still fail to see the problem with that," Remi replied, groaning at my ministrations and pressing into my hand. "And I daresay you're sending some *very* mixed signals on your opinions right now."

My eyes squeezed shut. *He's not wrong. I am. But I'm not… oh, fuck, that's his tongue, yes, yes…can't we just…do this first?*

It would be easy. It had been easy two nights ago. A blissful island of easy in the sea of difficulty that was my life. A place where there were no demands, where I could just be. But I knew, deep down…*This isn't what I want. This isn't what I need.* My heart throbbed, telling me that wasn't right, either. *Okay, maybe it is. Maybe. But not right now and not like this.*

Eyes open.

"Remi. Stop."

He stopped. His lips ghosted over my collarbone as he pulled away.

Ragged inhales and exhales punctuated the stillness that followed.

"I have to admit, this might be easier if you told me it was an exercise in edging," Remi said after several moments.

A light laugh left me, all I could afford, barely balanced on the edge of my own desire as I was. "If that's what you need to hear, sure."

"McKenna." His voice was still a thrill-inducing whisper across my ear. "Tell me what *you* need."

I need to not *want you to bend me over this sink right now.* I focused on breathing slowly in and out for a minute before replying aloud.

"I need you to remove your power from this sink while I remove mine." Direct, simple, clear. "Can you do that?"

Remi closed his eyes, taking his own deep breath, and nodded. "I can do that."

"Good. Let's begin."

I kept my eyes open as I stared down at our clasped hands, calling my magic forth to let me see the tangled mess once again. Everything was so close to the surface now I didn't even need words.

The tangle was worse, larger, and more active now thanks to our little make-out session. The mass of magic and power writhed together, reacting to each other, my golden threads sliding through Remi's twin sets of shadow in a way that was highly suggestive, especially with our hands still resting in the midst of it. I followed the thread that was still connected to me directly into the jumble, trying to tease out the rest and reclaim it bit by bit. Whenever I pulled on mine, however, Remi's stubbornly came with it. "You need to pull yours back, too," I reminded him.

"I'm *trying.*" A glance up confirmed that he looked as strained as he sounded. "It doesn't . . . *want* to."

"It's your power, don't *you* tell *it* what to do?" I asked pointedly.

"Most of the time, yes, but in not-so-shocking news, it seems to want to keep having a little magic orgy with yours," Remi replied. He let out an exasperated breath that was half a groan. "I can't help but notice yours is being just as clingy."

"…Yeah. It is."

"Are we quite certain this won't resolve itself if we bang this out real quick and try again?" he asked, his voice husky. To his credit, he kept his eyes off mine and didn't make any moves to reinitiate intimate contact.

"We already made it worse just by getting to second base, I'm fairly confident sex isn't going to help," I replied, but the lusty vibes were getting to me, too. *Deep breaths, focus, I am not a hormone-driven teenager!* "Okay. We can't untangle it right now, maybe we can at least move it. Throw it into something else and get it out of this bathroom so Trevan doesn't fire me."

"That sounds as doable as you are right now, my dear." He cleared his throat. "Sorry. Do you happen to have a suitable receptacle?"

The contents of my bag raced through my mind. I hadn't exactly prepared to create an enchanted object, and some materials were much better than others. Spell components weren't great—candles and salt-chalk were better for creating spells than holding them. Really, a gemstone would be ideal, more so if it were one prepared for such a thing, but I didn't have…oh, wait. Yes, I did.

"Hang on." I dug in my bag with my free hand and produced the ring I'd found in Bastien's place. The remaining diamond glinted in the light, perfect for this purpose. "This should do."

Remi laughed in a tight, nervous manner. "Gosh, McKenna, this is a bit sudden. Take a demon to dinner first, won't you?"

"Ha ha. It's for storing this…clusterfuck."

He snorted. "Appropriate name. And why do you have an engagement ring in the first place?"

"Bastien's place. It was Mari's." That seemed to sober the Archdemon.

"I see. And why is the *toi* missing its *moi*?" he asked.

I did a double take. "What'd you say?"

"*Toi et moi*. That's the style, the two gems set together like that?" He nodded at the ring. "I recall Mari saying it was made from stones from both their families. I assume the Perez family took theirs back."

"Since when do you know so much about ring settings?" I asked, mind still reeling.

Remi rolled his eyes. "You wouldn't believe how many people's deepest desire is for a highly specific engagement ring."

Toi et moi. Bastien's words, a lifetime ago. Bastien's note on the shredded paper. Had that been about Mari, then, and not me? Had our thing become theirs? My gut twisted as though this were some kind of betrayal, even though I knew I had no right to feel that way.

Deal with it later, I told myself. "We only need the one gem for this, so—I'll hold the ring, we move the clusterfuck into the diamond, and I'll bind it there."

"One orgasm ring, coming up," Remi quipped.

I snorted in amusement, then focused on coaxing my magic into the gem.

"*Magiam transfer*."

Now that we were moving the tangle of magic and power together instead of trying to separate them, they went easily.

However, it seemed this gem was spoken for—I detected it was already holding magic within it. Weird that I hadn't noticed that before. "Hang on a sec. I need to empty it first."

Examining the stone more closely, I saw it contained raw magic rather than a specific spell. Nothing more than stored magic, bright blue in color. Lemaire magic. Probably Bastien's, given where I'd found it. What did he need to store magic for? He was an adept in his own right. Yet more questions for the deal-with-it-later pile. I was about to murmur a spell to claim the magic, but then I noticed a tinge of demonic power in it. "Remi, I said wait."

"I am."

"Then why is there demonic power in here with Bastien's magic already?" I said. "It's starting to tangle more, the last thing we need is to add portal magic into this. Get yours out."

Remi frowned in concentration. "I can't. It's not mine."

"What?" My eyes went from Remi to the various magics in my hands. Around our joined hands, my golden threads and Remi's two-toned shadows twined and writhed, more tied together by the moment, but still distinct. In the ring in my other hand, the bright Caribbean blue of Bastien's magic was edged with a deep, dark-blue shadow, forbidding as the deepest depths of the ocean. They were joined, undeniably part of the same magic, integrated in a way that even the clusterfuck hadn't achieved.

"Bastien's magic. It's . . . it's *demonic*."

Chapter 9
Tainted Magic

"His magic is *what* now?" Remi asked, stunned.

"There's demonic power in here," I said. "But that's…that shouldn't be possible. Not for him."

"Oh? And should it be for someone else?" Remi asked, giving me a loaded look.

"Um. No comment."

"Uh-huh. Clearly we have some things to discuss, but in the meantime, can you empty that ring out or what?"

"Don't suppose you've got anything else on you with a gemstone?" I asked.

He shook his head. "Not on me, and I don't want to pop off to the condo while we're midtransfer here. I could ask Dara to bring something, but that will take more time than we have."

Good. I didn't want to involve her anyway. But that left me only one option: take the stored magic, and all the baggage that came with it, into me.

It had been a long, long time since I'd willingly let a

demon's power into me. When I'd briefly been Saranthiel's thrall six months ago, there'd been no real time for her power to settle in me before I killed her. But Forneus, on the other hand…he might have reconnected my family to our stolen magic, but he'd also given me a portion of his power, as happens with any thrall, and I wasn't proud of how I'd used it. Because he'd been the Archdemon of Desire, the sliver of his power that I'd had let me gain insight on my peers, on the things they desired, and I'd used that to my advantage. Plenty of teenage girls might go through a period of realizing they can manipulate people, but I was doing it with a distinct advantage. It was so much easier to get bullies to back down when you suddenly knew the things they wanted, especially when those wants were unspoken. It made pushing their buttons and getting them to back off much easier. I'd still held back a lot, something Remi found baffling and intriguing, and something Forneus found irritating. He wanted me further under his thumb, after all. When I refused to comply, he forced the matter…

———————————•———————————

Eleven years ago

Fairy lights illuminated the dance floor on the *Siren Queen* as she slowly looped around Ipswich Bay, a cacophony of teen voices hollering pop songs echoing off the water as she went. The Homecoming Harbor Cruise was a seniors-only event, one we all looked forward to, the unofficial kickoff to our final year at Arcadia Commons Academy. A time to start making memories of our last hurrah, taking pictures with friends and high school sweethearts. Remi and I had picked out our dresses together—hers black with red stitching, mine red with a black pattern of roses—excited for a night away from the drama that had become dealing with Forneus of late. A night to just be together and pretend we were normal teenagers doing normal-teenager things.

I guess hiding in the bathroom during a school dance and vomiting into a toilet, praying to not be caught, was sort of a normal-teenager thing to do, but it sure as hell hadn't been on my list. I wasn't even drunk or, hell, secretly pregnant. I was just a disobedient thrall.

Seduce the werewolf had been Forneus's order, direct into my mind while I was getting ready earlier that night. He couldn't pass the barrier, but he could always reach me.

What? No! Lucca is with Brooke, I'd replied.

You young people break up all the time. Get him to leave her for you.

I'd frowned before continuing to do my makeup for the dance. *No. I'm not doing that to two of my best friends. I don't like Lucca like that, and you can't force me to do anything I don't want to. We've been through this.*

The communication ceased just long enough that I thought the discussion was over. Then my phone lit up with a text from Remi, who was suddenly unable to come to the dance on account of "new orders from the home office." In other words, Forneus was taking her away from me as punishment. We'd never explicitly informed him we were together, but obviously, he knew.

That isn't going to change my answer. I knew he was still listening.

Enjoy your three-hour tour was his only reply. Stupidly, I thought that was the end of it.

The real end of it was when I became horribly seasick shortly after we left the dock. Forneus couldn't force me do anything, but he sure as hell could make me sorry I'd said no.

Slumped on the bathroom floor in the captain's quarters—luckily, I'd been able to magic open the lock on the door so I could endure my punishment in peace—I panted and wiped at my face with a damp paper towel. Two decks up, my classmates jumped and hollered along to a pop song. I slowly pulled myself up and turned the faucet on again, my hands shaking as I tried to cup them under the water. But I'd barely collected any when my stomach heaved and I flung myself to the toilet once again.

That's probably why I didn't hear anyone approach until I was done retching and someone behind me said, "McKenna?"

I spun around to see Bastien Lemaire standing just outside the bathroom in a pair of fancy wrinkle-resistant gray slacks, a deep-blue button-down that complemented his eyes, and a silver-patterned tie.

"Crap," I muttered.

"Are you okay?" He crouched down.

"'M fine, I'm fine," I said, pulling away. "'S not great in here, you should…stay back." Sheesh, hair held back by the class president at the school dance? No thanks, that was not on my high school bucket list.

"What happened?"

"Bad...ocean. Food. Seasick, poisoning. Don't eat the shrimp," I babbled, flailing to form both a sentence and an excuse.

"Uh-huh..." He frowned, brows pinching together behind his glasses, and then dug in his pocket. He pulled out a tin of strong breath mints. "Want one?"

My mouth was five kinds of terrible right now. "Yes, please." I popped one in, leaning back against the wall just inside the bathroom door. "Thanks."

Bastien sat down as well, leaning against the wall outside the bathroom and on the other side. We could see each other through the doorway, but he didn't say anything as I basked in the minor relief of the breath mint. The song changed above us, slowing down into a recognizable love song.

I gestured vaguely upward. "Shouldn't you be up there? Dancing with...someone?"

Bastien shook his head. "No. I don't have a date tonight."

"You don't? I thought you and Jackie were a thing."

"We get that a lot, but we're just friends. She's here with Darren Whitglass."

"Right, right, the aeromancer," I nodded, remembering seeing them together now.

"What about you? Where's Remi?" he asked.

"Personal emergency," I said, complete with air quotes. It wasn't her fault she couldn't be here, but that didn't mean I had to like it.

I could feel him peering at me. "Not one you're happy about?" I shrugged and didn't elaborate. "I could get your other friends. I saw Lucca and Brooke earlier."

My friends, the ones who had no idea about my Bargain, much less that I'd been told to come between them? I could picture the two of them now, dancing together to the love song, gazing at each other, blissfully unaware of and unaffected by the predicament I'd gotten myself into. *Maybe if I just, like, danced with Lucca or something, that would be enough to make this stop...* I could practically hear Remi agreeing with me. *"Dance with him. I'll keep Brooke busy, she's clearly bicurious. Everyone has fun and no one hugs the toilet all night!"*

I considered it and instantly hated myself for it. "No, please don't—mm!" My stomach lurched on me again, and I barely made it to the toilet in time. My hair fell around my face, I didn't have time to try to save it this time—but then I felt Bastien's hands pull it back for me. *Guess I'm checking that off the list after all.*

A few minutes later, he handed me a freshly damp paper towel. "Thanks," I said, dabbing at my face and neck again. "...What *are* you doing down here, anyway?"

"Ah...truth?" he asked. I nodded. "I was dating someone this summer. A girl from town, non-witch. Her name was Chelsea. I knew it couldn't last, but I kept putting it off. She knew this was coming up. Finally asked if I was going to ask her, and..."

"And you broke up with her?" I asked.

He nodded. "Yes. So I'm not exactly in a party mood."

"Was it because she's not a witch?"

Bastien nodded again. "My grandfather was constantly in my ear about how it couldn't go anywhere all summer." He popped another mint in his mouth, offering me the tin as well. "I think I broke it off half just to get him to stop reminding me."

I frowned as I took another mint. "That sucks. You should date whoever you want, magic or no."

"It'd be nice, but he's not wrong."

"Doesn't mean he's right, either," I pointed out.

Bastien half smiled. "No, no, it doesn't."

I smiled back. I'd known Bastien a long time; we'd both been in the academy since middle school, and though we'd been classmates, acquaintances, and academic rivals at times, we'd never quite been friends. Until this past year, my magic hadn't held a candle to his.

"Can I ask you something?" he asked.

I chuckled and gestured around us. "I think we're past asking permission to ask questions."

"Why are you really sick?"

I swallowed the lump in my throat. "I told you—"

"I've seen you sailing in the bay dozens of times, I know you don't get seasick. I know the shrimp upstairs is fine. You don't smell like you're drunk. You don't feel like you've got a fever. You're dating a girl, so you're unlikely to be pregnant, and no one here could've hexed you because the boat is warded against that," Bastien listed, his tone confident though not accusatory.

"I . . ." I sucked in a breath. "I can't tell you."

"Hm." He looked at me. "And if I cast something to settle your stomach? Would it work?"

"It might . . ." I was pretty sure Forneus could overpower a simple charm spell like that, but to be fair, I hadn't tried it myself. "It couldn't hurt, at least."

"And if I do, would you tell me what's going on?" he asked.

I arched my eyebrow at him. "Are you blackmailing me into telling you?"

"No! Of course not." He looked genuinely scandalized at the suggestion. "I was just wondering. Here, give me your hand."

He leaned forward, kneeling in his fancy slacks on the bathroom floor, and took my hand in one of his, turning my palm to face up. His own hand was comfortingly cool as it cradled mine. With his other hand, his fingers lightly traced a rune on my palm. My hand twitched at the sensation, and I laughed a little. "That tickles."

He grinned. "Well, try to hold it in, okay? It won't work if you keep moving."

I nodded, letting out a breath, trying to still my nerves. His fingers moved again, the light touch gone and a stronger, more certain pressure replacing it. It set off a spark that ran under my skin and had nothing to do with magic. My breath caught, and I found my fingers curling up, brushing his palm in return. My eyes found his as he quietly chanted, "*Va bien sur les vagues.*"

A voice in my head: *This one will do. Dance with him, flirt with him, and I'll give you a reprieve.*

Forneus let me feel a moment of blessed relief before threatening to send me back into sickness. I caved. *Okay. I'll do it.* At least it didn't involve stealing Bastien away from anyone.

The wave of relief came over me fully. My stomach settled, and I felt ravenously hungry and thirsty. Bastien helped me stand; I rinsed my mouth, sucked on another mint, and began to fix my makeup to be less of a hot mess.

"Thank you so much," I said. "You'll have to teach me that spell sometime."

"Sure. I can fix some of this for you, if you want," he offered, gesturing to my very tousled hair.

"You can?"

He shrugged. "I have two little sisters. I can do a decent braid."

Huh. Curious, I handed him the small comb that was in my purse. "Sure. You're . . . surprising."

"Thanks, I think." He smiled and started to gently brush out the tangles. "So are you."

I smiled at him in the mirror and found my next question to be more genuine than I'd anticipated. "Do you want to dance with me?"

———————————•———————————

Now

"McKenna, I hate to rush you and all, but this is getting *quite* uncomfortable," Remi said, snapping my wandering mind back to the here and now.

"Right. Sorry. Just . . . one does not lightly invite in demonic power," I replied.

"Believe me, I know," Remi said. His spare hand cupped my cheek; the contact sent a pleasant wave of sensation across my face, and my eyes strayed to his lips as he spoke. "But you can do this, my black knight. You're stronger than any demon."

The reminder of his unwavering belief, as much as the lust

of our accidental creation, made me surge up to kiss Remi again, my mouth opening to his as he pulled me to him. For just a moment, I reveled in it, the warmth of his hands and his lips, the knowledge of how he felt about me, that he never stopped wanting me, and wondered if the truth was that part of me never stopped, either. With Remi, there was always a challenge, always a give and take, always some degree of risk—but if I was being honest, didn't I love a challenge and a little risk?

Now was not the time to contemplate it, however. I let the thoughts pass and beckoned Bastien's magic into me. It hit with a wallop, setting my hands and feet tingling, prickling with a new kind of magic, a sense of the air around me and world around me that hadn't been there before.

"Push, *now*," I murmured urgently against Remi's lips. He did so in more ways than one. His hips ground against mine as we both pushed our tangled power into the diamond in my hand. The supernatural buzz of lust began to fade, though we'd built up quite enough of our own by now. Still, our kisses ebbed, losing their enhanced urgency and fervor, though Remi kept grabbing for just one more until I finally, slowly pulled away, catching my breath.

He didn't close the gap, though he did nuzzle my cheek, my ear, whispering, "Why not?"

"I think Trevan would be a little put out if we caused the same problem we just fixed all over again," I said breathlessly.

"There's always my place," Remi offered. He could tele-port us both there in an instant; for that matter, with Bastien's magic, I probably could, too.

"I need to find Bastien," I replied, as Remi's hands gripped my hips.

"He's not invited," he grumbled. "And you're avoiding the question. Why *not*, McKenna?"

Why not indeed? When I'd first come home, things had heated up quickly with Remi. Learning he'd hidden my mother being severed and institutionalized from me had ended that as swiftly as it had rekindled. Since then...well, for one, I'd been too damn busy to date, and he had, too, what with being a double Archdemon. Something that, judging by this little hot-spot issue, had not exactly been going smoothly.

There was something more, though, but it was something even I couldn't put my finger on yet.

"Do you need to hear me say it? I will. Whatever you want this to be, I'm happy to give you," Remi whispered, his lips just grazing my ear this time. I inhaled sharply at the chill that the touch, the unspoken promise, sent through me.

I knew the words he was dancing around. I knew it was quite possible that I still felt that way, too.

And for some reason or another, *that* scared me more than anything else I'd been dealing with this week.

"I need to find Bastien," I repeated, this time stepping away and putting an actual physical distance between us. After being pressed against Remi's warmth for so long, I felt a chill of a different sort now. I turned away, grabbing a paper towel to wrap the ring in before slipping it back into my bag. "Something bad's going on. Or maybe it already did, but all the clues are pointing toward him being in trouble with a demon. The sooner I find him, the better. Especially now."

I lifted my hand—Lemaire magic concentrated itself in the extremities—as I felt out the tainted magic that was now there.

Remi sighed and looked down. "Very well. If I can be of assistance, I'm sure we can negotiate something."

Because that's how it had to be with Remi: transactional. "Let's let Trevan know he doesn't get to fire me today, and then we'll talk."

———————————————•———————————————

Once Trevan was satisfied, he let me grab a veggie burger and bottle of water to go as he got the place ready for the dinner crowd. I ate it on a bench outside; Remi joined me, lounging at the opposite end of the bench.

"Where to now, then?" he asked.

"I'm thinking." I took a bite, trying to put together any kind of lead.

"While you're thinking, then, tell me, whose magic is capable of combining with demonic power and why is it you?" I shot him a look; he just smiled expectantly. "You can finish eating first if you like. I've been waiting on this one for a while, a few more minutes is fine."

I swallowed, chasing the food with some water. "A while?"

"Certain things about your fight with Saranthiel don't add up. I saw you stop her power and throw it back at her at one point. Which may have been a spell, but frankly, the fact that *you* could choose what happened to her mantle of power when she was dead was the real giveaway."

"Guess it was a little naive to hope that might've fallen under some kind of to-the-victor-go-the-spoils clause, huh?" I set the to-go container down next to me on the bench.

"But very *charmingly* naive."

"Please don't patronize me."

He held up his hands. "Apologies. Now then, what's the deal?"

I took a deep breath and began. "Since I got back last fall, demonic power has acted weird around me. In a way it doesn't around my mom or Cameron."

"Your summonings, bindings, and demon detections have always been stronger than theirs," Remi pointed out.

"It's not just that." My hands gripped the edges of the bench.

"Does it have to do with the barrier? You did pull a fairly unprecedented amount of power from it to kill Saranthiel."

I shook my head, my eyes squinting into the late-April sky, where the invisible barrier still surrounded the town. "No. This was going on before I did that. It's been like…like I could use it just as easily as I use my own, the way I tried to against Saranthiel," I tried to explain, turning my gaze his way. "Like it was mine. Like I could claim it, if I wanted to."

Remi sat up straighter. "…Are you saying what I think you're saying?"

"If you think I'm saying that I could have claimed Saranthiel's power after I killed her, then…yeah, I am." A steadily growing lump took hold in my throat as my fingers drummed on the edge of the bench.

Remi slumped back, taking this in. "…Well. That really puts that whole 'demon's witch' thing into a new perspective."

"Yeah." I cleared my throat; the lump remained. "Don't suppose you're sitting on any deep demon lore that would explain that, huh?"

Remi slowly shook his head. "I can't say that I am. As far as I know, it's always been that demons have power, human witches have magic. If you were still a thrall, *maybe*, but you'd be limited to power that belonged to your master at most. And only what they gave you, at that."

"This started before my short stint with her. And it's still happening. That tangle of our powers on the sink? They weren't even fully integrated, but you felt how hard it was to untangle them. And the other night…" My hand strayed to the half of my hair that was still unevenly cut and pinned back.

Remi moved closer, frowning. "You said you nearly drowned, but that's not all, is it?"

"No. One of them dragged me underwater and…it just *happened*. I was drowning, panicking, and I pulled it apart. I reached for its power and I just yanked the damn thing out of the body it was in." My throat tightened, feeling the phantom choke of seawater, the ease with which the shadowy core of the demon had come to me, leaving its rotting body nothing but a vacant deadweight. "I had to cut the tentacles to get loose."

"Hence the half haircut." Remi's fingers brushed the short ends. "I did wonder about that. What did you do with the demon?"

"Let it go. It got caught by the banishing spell we did when I got out of the water," I said. "The idea of actually taking that kind of power…no offense, but it disgusts me. I literally feel like I'll be sick if I do."

"None taken, considering what my predecessor would do when you pushed back," Remi replied. "Are you doing all right with what you took in from that ring?"

"So far…" I paused, closing my eyes and feeling out the magic in me. Bastien's was very distinct from mine, and the way it felt was a wholly new experience. My magic lives in my blood; when I feel it, it's everywhere, coursing through me, something deep and essential. When it's warded off, therefore, everything feels dulled by comparison.

Lemaire magic, though, was all about the hands and feet, and when I reached for it, I felt like I could start wall-crawling. Every sensation along my hands was enhanced. The rough wood of the bench when I gripped it, the way the breeze lightly brushed over the backs of my knuckles. None of this in a way that was overwhelming, just enhanced. My feet felt horribly confined in the sneakers I was wearing, and Bastien's ease with dancing and the piano suddenly made perfect sense.

But there was something more. Something almost familiar. A tingle in the air, an almost electric frisson along my fingers, a promise of more that I could almost touch, if I just reached out to it. It reminded me of the sensation that had gone through me when I'd touched demonic power before, the promises it whispered to me, the thrill I knew would shoot through my veins and fill me up. With Bastien's magic, that promise was realized, and the lure of finding out what that meant was very real.

"I'm not sure what'll happen if I use it. It's as much his magic as not."

"Makes sense." Remi was silent for a moment, his face a bit more guarded than usual. "Does your family know?"

"No. Leo and some of the pack were there the first time it happened, but none of them really knew what it was or what that meant. I try to avoid it, but it's possible Cam's noticed. He hasn't said anything if he has. And talking about magic with my mom is...complicated." Her words at the support group echoed in my mind.

"Aren't they the ones most likely to help you figure this out?" Remi asked. "*Especially* your mom?"

"Yeah, I know," I said, slumping back on the bench. "But things are hard enough at home without dragging this into it." Seeing him arching an eyebrow at me, I whacked him with one hand. "Hey, that's *my* thing."

"You weren't using it, someone had to," Remi chuckled. "Seriously, though."

"I know, I know. But my situation doesn't apply to Bastien, and his is the mystery I need to solve right now," I reemphasized.

"Mm-hm. So that you can go on ignoring your own for just a *little* bit longer?" Remi replied. I gave him a look, but he only smirked. "Maybe we can help each other out. Before we do, though, one question."

"Shoot."

"This strangeness with your magic, does that have anything to do with why you haven't worn your knight necklace lately?" he asked. "I don't think I've seen it on you since the night you killed Saranthiel."

My hand strayed to my chest, where it would've sat had I

been wearing it. *Was* that why? "I…don't know. It doesn't really fit, I guess." I shrugged, uncertain and unexpectedly uncomfortable with the question.

"In what way?" he asked, voice soft and curious.

"In…" I let out a breath, forming up my thoughts. "The black knight is the outsider. The one who's not welcome. I don't want to not be welcome in my own home. Hometown."

"Mm-hm." Remi looked thoughtful, but didn't offer insight into what those thoughts might be. Meanwhile, I felt a little like I'd missed a question on a test I hadn't known I'd be taking. "Fair enough. How about this: I help you solve the mystery of the missing Lemaire, and then we solve your little mystery next. Maybe even figure out what spot on the board you're occupying these days."

The trouble with demons: It always had to be a negotiation. "And what do you get out of that?"

"Information I suspect will prove to be both interesting and valuable," Remi replied.

That didn't sit so well. "Bastien's secrets aren't mine to share."

"Since his disappearance is yours to solve, he'll just have to accept that as a consequence of being rescued," Remi countered. "Now. Do we have a deal?"

To my credit, I paused to consider it first. But Remi had resources well beyond mine, and if this was a demon problem, chances were that would come in handy.

I shook his hand and felt the just-a-little-too-hot and slightly off-putting sensation of his power sealing the agreement. "Deal."

Remi's grin broadened. "Excellent! Okay, Sherlock, what's our next lead?"

I finished my burger and nodded at the apartment building next door, where my brother lived. It made for an easy work commute for him. "First, I need to get Codex back from Cameron. Possibly have him examine the stored magic, too. And what I said about my magic stays between us," I added. Remi mimed zipping his lips closed. "Good. Let's get to Cam before he has to go back to wor—"

A crash and a scream loud enough to be heard from my brother's second-floor apartment cut me off. I was on my feet and halfway to the building before Remi grabbed my hand and *bamf*ed us to outside his door. Remi rubbed his nose when we got there. "Dammit. I forgot how good his wards are."

Scrambling to get out the spare key Cam had given me, I unlocked the door and threw it open. "Cameron! Are you—"

"On the arm!"

"It's on my leg!"

"No, the arm of the couch, there's one on the arm of the couch!"

"Repello!"

I ducked as something went flying past me, smacking into the wall with a *splat!* It left a trail of black ichor as it slid to the floor. "Cameron, what the—"

Cameron and Gretchen Grothmann were on his couch, soaking wet, fending off a small army of foot-tall bipedal squid demons, one of whom was indeed clinging to his leg.

"—what the fuck?"

Chapter 10
Potion Problems

Gretchen spotted me first. "Oh, McKenna! Could you give us a hand?"

"What the hell happened?" I exclaimed.

A pair of the tiny squid demons raced by. "Close the door! Don't let them out!" Cameron yelled.

Remi's grin was more feral than usual and his eyes were fiery. "Oh, they're not going anywhere." The two tiny demons saw him, skidded to a stop, and ran back into the apartment. Remi tried to give chase but bumped up against the wards again. "Ugh. Could you please?"

"No!" Cameron answered without even looking over. "There are enough demons in here already—*repello!*" He finally got the one on his leg off and threw it to the ground.

I stomp-kicked another one back toward the center of the living room, where a chalk circle was drawn on the floor. "Get them all in the circle and we can banish them."

"McKenna, get my bandolier!" Gretchen called out.

I did a double take. "Your *what*?"

"It's on the chair, it has my potions!"

I spun the armchair nearest the door, dislodging one squidling, though another clung to it. Sure enough, there was a bandolier with at least a dozen potion bottles tucked into it.

"Third from the bottom, spray top, use that on them!" she instructed.

Wondering how my life had become horny magical hot spots and potion bandoliers, I grabbed the bottle and sprayed it at the squidling on the chair. It screeched and clutched at its face, falling onto the floor. I kicked it into the circle and tossed the bottle into Gretchen's outstretched hands. She unleashed it on the squidlings climbing up the couch like a spray bottle on unruly cats, and between the three of us, we rounded the squidlings into the circle.

I grabbed Cameron's hand to cast the banishment with him. *"Ego daemones abicio!"* With a flare of golden light, they were gone, banished back to whatever corner of the Pit they came out of.

"Just when I thought you were getting boring, little Eller-beck, here you are, having wet T-shirt contests and hosting a demon battle royal in your apartment," Remi remarked, leaning against the doorframe.

"Neither of those things is right," Cameron said.

"Maybe not, but for the record, I would totally win that contest," Gretchen said with confidence.

Remi's eyes glinted. "You certainly would, my dear."

Gretchen grinned. "But speaking of, can I borrow a shirt?"

"Yeah, I'll grab you one. Can you guys start getting the glass?" Cam asked as he went into his room.

Turning to finally get a good look at the living room, I saw that there was a broken aquarium on the coffee table—probably where all the water soaking the two of them, the couch, and the floor had come from.

"What in the world were you doing?" I asked, retrieving a brush and dust pan.

"Trying to make the beaches of Arcadia Commons demon-free for the summer," Gretchen said, helping me collect the glass. "He told me you've had a lot of sea-based demons lately, and I had some ideas for some anti-demon potions that might work. Thought we might be able to come up with something to treat the water around here without harming humans or the regular sea life." She frowned at a large shard of glass. "Better than last time, but it still needs some work."

"Last time?" I echoed. "How long have you been working on this? Actually, how long have you been hanging out? First you're my mom's drinking buddy, now you're Cameron's lab partner, too?"

"Mom came first, but those are related," Cameron said, coming back. He tossed a shirt to Gretchen, who ducked into the kitchen to change.

"I can't wait to hear this," Remi commented.

Cameron gave him a brief glare before continuing. "Gretch was hanging with Mom at the bar, and I kinda recognized her from school—"

"I was a freshman when he was a senior," Gretchen called out.

"—so I asked her if she could keep an eye on Mom. Y'know, just make sure she didn't overdo it, watch out for any sketchy dudes, call me if things were going bad, that kinda thing," Cameron went on.

"Aww, Cam. That was sweet of you," I said, touched but not terribly surprised. My brother could be gruff, but he was sweet under all that, and he'd been looking out for Mom for a long time now. "Also smart, since she acts like a freaking teenager."

"Yeah, she can be a handful!" Gretchen agreed, returning in a faded Veil and Horn T-shirt.

Remi made a noise. "Cameron! Is that really the nicest shirt you could offer this lovely young woman?"

"That's the most comfortable shirt I have that's clean!" Cameron retorted.

Gretchen waved a hand. "I'm fine, and it *is* comfy. But thanks for the compliment."

"*Anyway*, from there, Gretch and I got to talking—"

Remi waggled his eyebrows. "And one thing led to another?"

Gretchen laughed; Cameron glared. "Would you stop interrupting?"

"I'm bored out here! If you'd just let me in . . ." Remi hinted.

"Not. Gonna. Happen. Turns out, Gretchen's dad's side were monster hunters, and her mom's side are alchemists, so she's had a lot of good ideas for demon hunting," Cameron finally finished.

"Explains the anti-demon potions," I said, looking back over at Gretchen. "Why the bandolier, though? You haven't been out demon hunting on your own, right?"

"No. Not yet, at least. This is actually from a steampunk cosplay," Gretchen admitted. "But it is really handy for easy access to the potions when I need them. So long as I'm wearing it, anyway."

"Huh. Well, wouldn't be the first time a witch hid in plain sight with a costume. What were you guys doing that all this happened?" I asked, gesturing at the coffee table.

"The idea was to make a sort of demon pesticide-slash-water barrier by combining alchemy and binding magic," Gretchen explained, picking up a very wet piece of paper. "We needed to test it, though, so we got the aquarium and Cam summoned in some squid demons, but, well…"

"I summoned a few too many and the aquarium broke," he said. "Managed to shield us from the glass, but not the water."

The mental image of the aquarium rapidly filling with so many squidlings that it exploded, unleashing gallons of water and the demons themselves, jumped to mind and I couldn't help it. I burst out laughing.

"Glad you find this amusing," Cam grumbled.

"Less amusement, more pressure release, Cam," Remi commented from the door.

Cam gave him a look. "What's that supposed to mean?

"Is this one of those everything's-so-fucked-you-have-to-laugh things, or everything's-so-absurd?" Gretchen asked.

"The…the first one," I said between laughs, wiping my eyes. "It has been a *day*."

"It's only, like, two p.m.," Cameron pointed out.

I leaned against the wall with a half laugh, half groan. "Fuck me, it is."

"What is going on? And why are you two here?" Cameron demanded.

I waved a hand for Remi to explain while I collected myself. "Specifically, we're here because we heard a crash and a scream from outside. We just finished fixing Trevan's bathroom," Remi said.

"Thanks for *that*, speaking of."

"For the dose of afternoon delight? You're welcome," Remi said, with a Cheshire grin.

An annoyed noise escaped my brother. "How, how do you even?" he asked me, gesturing at my ex. All I could do was shrug while coming down from the giggles.

"I could venture a few guesses…" Remi started to say, a twinkle in his eye.

That dispelled the rest of the mirth. "Don't *you* even!" I cut in. "Okay. Sorry, Cam, I'm really not laughing at you, I swear. Is this why you've been itching to get so much Codex time lately? Why didn't you say something?"

"I wanted to wait till we had something that worked. And it seemed like you had enough on your plate lately," Cameron said, shrugging and looking aside. There was a certain nonchalance to his answer that made me wonder if there was more to it—like, say, spending time alone with Gretchen—but I didn't push it.

Cameron and I had a never-spoken agreement to not inquire about each other's love lives. Mine was messy when it existed at all and far too storied in local supernatural circles as it was, and all I knew about his was that he and Leo had dated for a year or so after I disappeared, and it ended badly. Cameron's roommate and best friend, Tom Harwell, seemed to think Cam was still in love with Leo, but then again, Tom was also essentially secretly in love with Cam, who was in return either clueless or very good at acting like that. In conclusion, we were all idiots when it came to love and relationships.

Whether this thing with Gretchen was friendship or something more, though, it was nice to see him making new connections. Cameron had hardened in the decade that I'd been gone. Once he'd been friendly and openly sweet, but he'd been through a *lot*: losing me, his volatile relationship with Leo, my mother's decline, losing our childhood home, and losing most of his friends. Not to mention the psychosis that fighting Saranthiel had inflicted upon him. Who wouldn't lose their soft side after going through all that? He hadn't trusted anyone other than Tom by the time I came back, and he'd single-handedly fought demons for years, with no one believing him that they were even there. After months of working together, both at the bar and against the demons, I'd seen him slowly start to uncoil with me and some others. But this was the first new friend for him in quite a long time.

"Can't argue with that. Well, now that I do know, if you want my help, you've got it," I offered. "Can I take a look at the ritual?"

Gretchen held up the wet paper. "This copy's a bust, but it's in your grimoire."

Our grimoire, despite having been lying open on the coffee table as well, wasn't damp in the slightest. The page was blank, however, until I picked it up and the ink returned to the pages, shifting and forming into the ritual circle they'd used to make the potion. My eyes grew wide as I looked it over, and I yanked open my bag to pull out Bastien's taped-together ritual.

"What's that?" Cameron asked. "How did you already have a copy of my spell?"

"I didn't. Bastien did." They weren't identical, but they were very similar. I knew Bastien hadn't been in my grimoire, of course. But he was a smart, well-studied witch. "Of course. It's metamagic!" That was the term for magic that manipulated magic itself—moving it, containing it, redirecting it. Even severing itself was a form of metamagic. "He isn't trying to bind and banish a demon, he's trying to separate and contain demonic *power*."

Remi snorted. "He's on a fool's errand, then."

"What do you mean?" I asked.

"Death is the only way to part a demon from its power," Remi said, looking at me.

My brow furrowed. "Demons dole out their power all the time. Thralls, Bargains, other workings."

"That's different. That's *borrowed* power, it still belongs to the demon. We can use it to accomplish impossible things, yes, including empowering others, but the power itself is a part of us," Remi said.

My mouth felt dry, my fingertips tingling. "So once that power is in someone—in a demon—" I amended, "it's theirs for good? Until they die?" *How did this not come up in our conversation earlier, Remi?*

"Yes, it's—oh." He seemed to finally understand my line of questioning. "No, it's like that, I mean...well, it is, but..." He floundered trying to talk around it.

"The power in the ring?" I asked.

"You're fine. That's not your power," Remi said.

"Why didn't you mention—?"

"I thought you knew! And…I didn't want to add any further cause for concern for something that was only theoretical."

Gretchen nudged Cameron with her elbow. "Are they speaking in some kind of code?"

"Definitely. Anytime you wanna clue us in here, guys," Cameron said.

I hesitated; Remi spread his hands, leaving it up to me; I sighed. "I found Mari's engagement ring in Bastien's room. It had Lemaire magic in it, but demonic power as well. Like the magic is…tainted or demon-touched or something." I held out my hands. "I had to take it into myself, since we needed the diamond for something else."

Cameron chanted under his breath and looked at my hands. "Whoa! Yeah, that's weird, all right. Even thralls' magic doesn't look like that. What was Bastien doing with it? And with this spell?"

"Great questions. If I find him, I'll be sure to ask," I said, and caught them up on the situation, though I left out some details about the clusterfuck and the strangeness in my magic. By the time I'd finished, Gretchen had fetched some pretzels from the kitchen to snack on.

"So, Bastien is missing, he's working on a metamagic ritual to banish a dead Archdemon's power, Mom's ex runs some kind of outcast witches support group that Bastien's been going to, and his dead Archdemon wife's engagement ring has tainted magic in it," Cameron recapped.

"Pretty much." The ring was in my hand, still safely in its paper towel wrapper. "But that's a good point. It's not his ring. It was *hers*."

Remi peered over at us; Gretchen had given him his own bowl of pretzels as well. "Say more?"

"It's Saranthiel's ring. She was the one wearing it, she had his magic at the end. This is *her* power. That's why the ritual here has her name in it." It finally made sense. "She must have stored some of it in the ring before she was killed, and before they erased her name from the grimoire to annul the marriage."

"I'm a little lost. There was a demon signed into a grimoire?" Gretchen asked.

"Yeah. Has Cam told you about Saranthiel and what happened last fall?" I asked. She shook her head. "Okay. Short version, the Archdemon Saranthiel was disguised as a witch and tricked Bastien into marrying her. She set up the entire relationship and marriage just to get the Lemaire portal magic and open a portal to the Pit to let her army walk through so they could physically exist in this world," I explained. "Saranthiel was killed and, obviously, the marriage was very much canceled. Names removed, and everyone pretends it never happened."

"Yours truly inherited her mantle," Remi said. "Which means all of her power became mine."

"But," I went on, "apparently, being bonded to a witch's magic changed the rules. A witch's stored magic doesn't go away when they die; that item, whatever it is, stays enchanted. If these two powers are bonded the way Remi said, then that's why it stayed the way it is inside the gem."

"What about the missing gem?" Gretchen asked, nodding at the empty spot on the ring.

"He had it made from their grandmothers' rings. The Perez family most likely took theirs back. Meaning they might be sitting on a demonic portal magic gemstone and don't even know it." *Toi et moi*—it was *about the ring. Nothing to do with me.*

"Or they do know. Either way, not loving that math," Cameron said. "We need to get that gem."

"I do love a good diamond heist," Remi said.

"We need to get that *magic*," I corrected them both. "But if they haven't noticed for this long, it'll keep. Bastien is still missing. Once I find him, we can get answers to all the rest of this, gems and metamagic spells and support groups and whatever else I haven't turned up yet." I carefully replaced the ring in my bag and got out a pen. "Meanwhile, we've got a new threat in town. Codex, do you have any information on this demon?" I flipped to an empty page in Codex and began drawing the demon that attacked me earlier. Beneath it, I wrote, *tentacles, pitch-black, can inject a truth venom.*

As the ink sank into the pages while Codex did whatever it does with such information, Gretchen pulled a book from a backpack hanging in the front hall. "That's not a demon. That's a monster." She stopped on a much more detailed drawing of the thing that had attacked me. The page was filled with German, only some of which I knew. "*Geheimnis-sucher.* Secret-seeker."

"A monster?" I exclaimed. "Well, that explains a few things." No wonder I couldn't detect it or banish it. There was no place to banish it *to*. Monsters were nonhuman creatures that belonged to this world, as opposed to Fae or demons, who came from their own realms. "What book is that?"

"My grandpa's bestiary from when he used to hunt monsters in the Black Forest," Gretchen explained. "Says they are strong, fast, and their venom forces unwilling truth until the afflicted willingly shares a personally important and unknown truth."

New words filled the page in Codex as well. *She is correct. As well, despite not being demons, the seekers were known to serve the Archdemon of Secrets when it was still active.*

"Your grimoire is so cool," Gretchen said as she watched it reply in real time. "Nothing here about the demon connection, though. I've gotta add that."

Codex continued. *One attacked you?*

"It did," I said. "It wanted to know where Bastien was."

The Archdemon of Secrets sought those with powerful secrets for its thralls. They are powerful motivators that can drive people to dangerous extremes and make them open to such dealings. If Bastien was keeping any, it would have good reason to seek him.

"But if it's been inactive, how would it know to look for him? How would it know anything about him?" I asked.

Unclear. If he did something to catch its attention and it truly has been merely staying quiet, it may have deemed him worth finding. I had a feeling that extensive field research on the various Archdemons and their minions might count.

"Remi, we need to ask Dara about her old boss," I said after reading the latest response aloud.

"I will. It's been a long time since she served Secrets, though," Remi reminded me.

"Sorry, who's Dara, exactly?" Cameron asked.

"I'll explain later," I said, closing Codex and slipping it into my bag.

"Hey, I'm still using that!" Cam protested.

My phone buzzed. "Right now, I need it more," I said,

pulling out my phone to find a text message from Preston Chang, curiously.

> *Hey M, your mom and a total zaddy*
> *just showed up to get him a glamour,*
> *have u seen this guy??*

Preston ran an event planning business downtown, mostly weddings. But as a half Fae, he could also construct glamours that would last until the next sundown.

> *Yeah some old boyfriend.*
> *You give him one? What's he*
> *look like now?*

> *A boring, balding white dude, but don't*
> *be deceived. They said something*
> *about "visiting old haunts," pretty sure*
> *thats hip elder code for "hitting up old*
> *makeout spots." Get it Wendy!*

> *That elder is my mother, pls don't!*
> *Thanks for the heads up tho.*
> *You heard from Bastien lately?*

> *Not in a while. Why?*

> *Just wondering.*

As I was texting with him, Leo sent a message as well:

Had to relieve dad from Griffin duty;
dropped ur mom & Cyrus downtown.
<3 you, keep me updated

Cyrus had said he'd left town because he knew he wasn't welcome. Maybe they didn't want to risk his being recognized while he was here. Fae glamours were harder to see through than magic-based illusions. I'd rather be certain of who I was looking at and talking to whenever I ran into him again, however. Luckily, this was nothing a quick stop at the bar couldn't fix.

I pocketed my phone. "We should get some glamour drops before we head out," I said. "Where's Dara?"

"She's been continuing her self-guided tour of Arcadia Commons," Remi said. "We had plans to meet up at the academy just before sunset."

"That'll work. I've got some other research I need to take care of in the meantime."

"I should probably clean up some more and dry out the couch before Tom gets home, too," Cameron admitted.

Glancing around, I saw that he and Gretchen had a decent amount of work to do on that front. "I'm sure he'd appreciate that. All right, the academy at sunset. See you all there."

———————————— • ————————————

I wasn't the only Council member scouring the library, as it turned out. I waved at George O'Brien on my way in as he flipped through some periodicals. Partway to the spiral staircase that led up to the Uncommon Collection (and not a closed-for-safety-reasons widow's walk, as the mundane patrons believed), I doubled back upon remembering he was only a few years older than my mother.

"Hey, George. This is kind of random, but did you know a guy named Cyrus in high school? He dated my mom?"

Recognition lit his eyes. "Cyrus Craig? Yeah, I remember him, we were friends of a sort. Flame and fire, it's been ages since I thought about him."

Craig. Craig…why does that sound familiar? "You were friends? My mom found an old yearbook and mentioned him. I was curious," I added as an excuse for my questions.

George nodded. "Yeah, he was one of my classmates. We grew up together. A lot of us olds did, you know—me, your mom, Doug, Armand and Claudia. Giovanni Luppino." Armand and Claudia were Bastien's parents. "The classes weren't as big back then, everyone knew everyone, even if we weren't in the same year." I'd known that, but I had never really imagined my mom and the others as classmates and friends. When I was growing up, Mom would sometimes make reference to knowing the other witches in town, but never as friends, past or present. George she'd mostly spoken well of—he'd been her boss at the paper when she worked there—and she had been friends with Lucca and Leo's dad, Giovanni, and his wife, Mariella. Mariella was human, but Gio had been the werewolf pack leader before Lucca took over that role. Based on what Mom said at the meeting, it didn't seem like that friendship had rekindled, though I had a hard time imagining the Luppinos turning her away. Hearing that the rest of them had been friends once upon a time was jarring. I couldn't picture my mom hanging out with any of them the way my friends and I had in high school.

George went on, "Cyrus and your mom were together for years. Well, sort of. They broke up a lot, it was all very dramatic. You know how it is."

"I can imagine," I said, trying very hard not to draw parallels with my own life. "What was he like?"

"Good guy. Really fair-minded, you know? An activist at heart. He was on the student council, even. VP, I think? Secretary? Anyway, he always had a cause, protecting the environment and civil justice, better treatment for hedgewitches, that kind of thing."

Interesting. Cyrus sounded…decent. Downright likable, even. If he'd been standing up for hedgewitches, especially, I could see why my mom would've liked him. "What happened to him? I know he moved away, but that's about it."

George's smile faded. "Did she tell you about his parents?" I shook my head. "When we were in high school, both his parents were severed. Something about conspiring against the Council, I think it was? Which was something, considering his dad was on the Council."

That's where I'd heard the name! The last severing trial before mine had been for one Curtis Craig, for "endangering witchkind."

"Cyrus never said much about it or why it happened. After that, he kept to himself a lot, we lost touch. I think he eventually left for school somewhere in New York."

Kept to himself, or was quietly cast out by everyone he knew? I knew which one I'd place money on. "And that was it?"

This time George outright frowned, looking troubled. "I wish it was. No, a few years later he came back when his mother died. His father got into an argument with Frank Milton, he was the head of the Council back then. Frank died—got pushed and hit a rock. Cyrus's father was injured and probably would've gone to jail, but he died a few days later. Cyrus left town for good after that."

A chill ran from my scalp down my spine at how similar that story was to my own. "You weren't kidding about dramatic."

"He did have a way of being in the middle of things," George said, and I didn't love how familiar that felt, either.

"Guess so. Thanks, George, I'll let you get back to what you were doing," I said, making a hasty exit. I hadn't expected getting answers on who Cyrus was to open up so many new questions. It made sense that he'd left town and that he wouldn't want to be recognized now, with a family history like that. It also made sense that he would run a support group for supernatural outcasts.

But what had his parents actually done to be severed? What had happened that his father and Frank Milton killed each other? What was more, the Miltons were a family of seers. Their methods varied: visions, palm reading, or others. One of my mom's ancestors had married one, which was why she was always good with Tarot cards. I didn't know what form Frank Milton's talents had taken, but I had to imagine he'd argued with Curtis Craig that night for a reason.

Unfortunately, the Uncommon Collection didn't have any answers for me. All the trial records had were their names and reasons for severing:

Irina Anna Craig, née Galowych. Endangering witchkind.
Curtis Bruce Craig. Endangering witchkind.
Super helpful.

Something else jumped out, however. Some of the witches at the meeting in addition to Karamhad mentioned being severed, and they were much too young to have gone through that decades ago. But their names weren't listed here. Had they been severed by some other Council? I supposed it had to be the case, but Bedlam Books & Games was located in Cambridge and all of them ending up in this area felt like too many to be a coincidence. They hadn't always had the portal stones, after all, so most of them must be from this general area.

Despite more research and scouring of records for the rest of the afternoon, I didn't find any of their names, or anything else on Cyrus beyond a mundane article about Frank's and Curtis's deaths.

Someone was hiding something. But who, and what, and why?

My phone buzzed to remind me that sunset was approaching. Sighing at my lack of progress, I gathered my things and headed out. It was time to go back to school.

Chapter 11
Old Haunts

Besides the leylines, Arcadia Commons Academy was what put our town on the proverbial map in the supernatural community. A magnet school for middle- and high-school-aged children from all supernatural walks of life, it was one of the first of its kind in America. To the rest of the town, it was merely a private school with an esteemed national reputation that boosted the town's reputation and tax income considerably. The Council as well as the school board made sure that the academy didn't take away from the funding of the public schools and only added to the community overall; the last thing they needed or wanted was for the general public to start complaining about the institution not being good for the town.

Filled with gorgeous brick buildings in the collegiate gothic style and well-maintained landscaping, it was eye-catching without a doubt. It looked more like a college campus than anything else. From dorms to classroom buildings to function halls and administrative buildings, it was built to be a beautiful testament to no expense spared, no moment of education wasted.

I loved it. Sure, my teen years were tumultuous, and there was plenty here to call out as part of a privileged system that favored riches and witches over others, but I couldn't help it. I grew up here, met my best friends and first loves here, discovered who I was here. I learned magic here. This place was a part of me, and even if I knew it wasn't perfect, I couldn't help but love it.

In the late-day sun, it was downright idyllic. Spring blooms splashed the campus with color, bright against the brick red of the buildings and the smooth white-gray stone of the pathways wandering between them. Wood and metal benches—not wrought iron, of course, so the Fae could safely matriculate—dotted the paths, and picturesque trees offered patches of shade on the stretches of green grass on the main quad.

The four buildings bordering the quad weren't the only ones, but they were the main ones, named for various donors. Antonelli Hall housed the gymnasiums, the pool, and other athletic department rooms and equipment; behind it were the sports fields. Across from that was LaCroix Hall, with standard classrooms that were used for mundane subjects, like English, math, history, and so forth. Milton Hall was at one end of the quad, home to more specialized rooms, labs used for science and magic alike. Milton Hall also boasted the second-tallest tower on campus, rising above the three-story building and featuring a fancy stained glass window of the academy's seal. And then there was Lease Hall, the jewel of the campus. Filled with function rooms and administrative offices, it was the scene of many a school dance, including proms, and other school events. At four stories, it was taller than the other three, especially with the clock tower rising up from the entryway. With an opaque glass clock face on each of its four sides and bells above those that rang out every quarter hour, no one could ever honestly say they didn't know what time it was. Both towers were, in theory, locked to anyone who wasn't staff, but kids had been breaking into both of them for bragging rights, on dares, to illicitly smoke something, or just to hook up since the place was built. Hell, I'd done it a few times myself.

Elsewhere on the campus, later additions included a greenhouse, an art and music building—including a nicely appointed theater—a smaller two-building mini-campus for the middle school, and four dorms. The school also had its own dock at the marina and an elementary school that was loosely associated with it but open to students both supernatural and not.

The group of us—myself, Cameron, Gretchen, and Remi, who was female again—headed for the compass rose, a circular one made of stone that all the paths crossed through in the center of the quad. The inlaid metal circle was, of course, magical in nature and enchanted to bring good fortune and promote intellectual growth for the campus. At least, that's what the popular rumor was. Whatever runes were part of this particular spell were underground. True or not, it was hard to get a spot on the compass rose to study when finals were coming up, as everyone was desperate for whatever extra boost of smarts or luck they could get.

Today being Sunday, and there still being some light left in the day, a smattering of students were on the quad, studying, hanging out, enjoying the weather. Some prospective students and families strolled about, taking in the campus. And sitting on a bench at the compass rose, stinking up the place, was a picture-perfect blond demon.

Dara sat with a notebook in her lap, scribbling notes and looking up now and then at the buildings and the people. She was still rocking the secretary look: cat-eye glasses perched on her cute little nose, blond hair down and perfectly styled with a gentle curl at the bottom, pencil skirt and silk blouse. She smiled as she saw us approaching. The curdle of corruption crept through my veins as we got closer. Not wanting to get distracted by that during the conversation, I quietly cast a spell to ward my automatic demon detection.

"Gotta give it to her, she sure doesn't look like a demon," Gretchen said as we approached. She was wearing her own clothing again, as well as the potion bandolier.

"Illusion," Cam replied. "Under that, she's a hideous hell-beast. *Don't* trust her."

"Hello everyone!" Dara greeted us brightly, standing up. "McKenna, it's so good to see you again. And you must be Cameron!" She took a few steps to close the gap we'd left, offering her hand to him. I hid a smirk as Cameron, just like me and Mom, did not shake her hand, merely grunting in response instead.

Remi, on the other hand, went right up to Dara and

exchanged cheek kisses with her. My gut grumbled unhappily at the sight. "Dara, this is Gretchen Grothmann. Gretchen, this is Dara, my assistant."

"Nice to meet you," Gretchen said, waving. Cameron must've warned her not to touch the demon.

"And you! Remi said you wanted to talk about my old boss," Dara said, addressing all of us. "I'm not sure what I can tell you about her that you don't already know, or that would matter since she's no longer with us."

"Not that old boss. The other one," I clarified.

"The other one is *also* dead," Dara said.

"The *other* other one," I said. "The one who might not be dead. Secrets."

Dara's soft doe-brown eyes went wide. Remi had really taken pains to make her look as gentle and unthreatening as possible, hadn't she? "That one's been gone for a very long time."

"Gone, yes, but not dead. Not that you know of," Remi said. "And maybe not so gone anymore. Some of their old buddies have been in town."

I showed her the picture of the seeker sketch. "One of these attacked me this morning. Clever of your old boss to use monsters instead of demons. But I suppose maybe they ran out of demons after taking such a long nap?"

"The seekers..." Dara pressed a hand to her mouth. "Are they really here?"

"They are. I've got the battle damage to prove it," I said, gesturing to my bloodstained sleeve. I really needed to change my shirt sometime soon. "As for the big boss, jury's still out. Would these things come here on their own for any reason?"

Dara went back to the bench and sat down, still looking shocked. Remi sat next to her. "Dara, please. We need to know what we're up against here," Remi said soothingly, setting a gentle hand on Dara's shoulder. Cam and I exchanged a dubious glance. Dara was seemingly too shaken to respond. But I suspected it was an act, and we needed to know whatever she knew.

"Dara," I said, crouching down at the end of the bench. "A friend of ours is missing, and we know these monsters are looking for him. They may already have him, they may not, but if we want to find him, we need to know more. Remi's your Archdemon now, remember? She can protect you."

Dara let out a little laugh of disbelief. "Can she?"

"Even if Secrets shows their face, it's two mantles against one. I'd ask who you wanna bet on in that fight, but you already made your pledge to Remi," I pointed out.

Dara nodded slowly, and even smiled, if weakly. "I suppose I did. I'm sorry, Remi, I didn't mean to imply you aren't up to it, it's just…you don't know them like I do."

"Then fill us in so we're prepared," Remi said.

Dara nodded again. "Of course. I doubt the seekers would come here for any other reason. Secrets quite literally made them. They were the heralds, the vanguard. When Secrets wanted to invade an area, the seekers went first."

"Why?" I asked. Cameron leaned against a short stone wall behind the bench and listened.

"A sure way to destabilize a place is to learn its secrets. Not just for your own arsenal, but then to leave the people there in a state where they not only cannot lie but must share their full and honest truths," Dara said. I could believe it. If I'd had to deal with the rest of the Council while under the influence of that truth venom, that would've been very bad indeed. "Then Secrets would move in, find a righteous, angry soul or two to enthrall with the promise of getting revenge. Or someone with an even bigger, more dangerous secret to hide and offering immunity. Through them, Secrets could gain control of a whole town, a castle, a kingdom. A king."

"Would people telling the truth really cause that much chaos? Fae can't lie at all, and they're not all killing each other," Gretchen asked.

"Tell that to the ghost of Thomas Cromwell," Dara said.

"The Archdemon of Secrets had a thrall in Henry VIII's court?" I asked. "Who?"

Dara smiled wryly. "Not all demons started their lives as such."

My brows went up at the suggestion. *Is she saying she was one of his wives . . . ?*

"That's great and all, but not the history lesson we're here for," Cameron said, interrupting my thought. "What happened to your old boss that they went off-grid?"

Dara shrugged. "I don't know. A few hundred years ago, they were just . . . gone. They were investigating the New World, but I don't know if they were actually here. They always operated quietly; periods of no contact weren't unusual. But years stretched into decades, no new thralls, no orders. Those of us who were sworn to them began to diminish, so we found new masters to swear ourselves to. That's how I first met Remi." She smiled prettily at Remi, who returned the smile.

"They're just gone? Missing in action? And there's no proof, just a lack of evidence of existence?" I said.

"If they had died while I was still sworn to them, I would have known. I can't speak to whether they've died since then," Dara said.

"Convenient," Cameron remarked.

I stood up from the crouch. "Can't argue that," I said.

Dara frowned. "It's the truth. I'm sworn to serve Remi now. I wouldn't lie about this—I literally couldn't."

"It's possible for a minion to lie to their Archdemon. Just ask Forneus," I replied. "Or, at the very least, to withhold information. And you've bounced around between masters an awful lot. You left Forneus's service for Saranthiel before he was dead."

Dara smoothed her skirt. "More like I was traded."

I raised an eyebrow, looking at Remi for confirmation, but she was likewise surprised. "I never knew that," she said.

"Of course not. He knew we were close. He made it look like I left by choice and with his permission in order to damage our relationship and your sense of trust," Dara said. "He traded me for a legion of hellhounds."

It was Remi's turn to frown. "Forneus and Saranthiel did both work with hellhounds..."

"I didn't realize minion types were proprietary," I said. "Don't they all work with hellhounds?"

"That's like saying all humans have dogs, or cats, and not being specific about the breed," Remi replied.

"Oh, give me a break," Cameron said, rolling his eyes. "We're gonna trust your new girlfriend based on what breed of hellhound Forneus was partial to?"

Remi narrowed her eyes at him. "You're the ones who seem to have trouble with trust. I believe Dara."

"Yeah, and I believe she might actually *be* the Archdemon of Secrets," Cameron countered, drawing shocked reactions from all of us. Even Gretchen was alarmed at the suggestion, and her hand drifted to her bandolier. Remi glared at him, while Dara herself gasped aloud. I blinked in surprise but began reviewing the facts in my mind.

"Bastien was researching Archdemons; he comes back to town, and you showed up that same night. The first seeker attack was after that, too," I murmured.

"McKenna, she isn't the Archdemon of Secrets. She isn't any Archdemon!" Remi protested. "Don't you think I'd know? That *you'd* know?"

"I would, but if her whole thing is *secrets*, Remi, how do we know she can't hide that? No one's seen this Archdemon in centuries, they've stayed hidden somehow. What better way to hide than being able to pass as a bog-standard minion?" I pointed out.

"Bog standard!" Dara exclaimed incredulously. "I am *not* bog standard! Or—I am, I suppose, but I do not appreciate that term." Our raised voices were starting to draw stares from people on the quad.

"Keep it down," I hissed. "And if you're not, then prove—"

"Seekers!" Gretchen exclaimed, pointing up.

We all whipped around to look at the clock tower, where, sure enough, two of the pitch-black tentacled monsters were slinking up the bricks at remarkable speed. Panicked screams filled the quad as students and visitors alike ran for safety.

I shot a hard look at Dara, who held up her hands. "I have nothing to do with this!"

"We'll see." I pulled my athame from my bag, nicking my finger to get my blood flowing, eyes back on the monsters as they tore off the slats around the bells and slipped inside. "We need to stop them before they get into the building," I said, just as another scream was heard, this one coming from the tower itself. "Shit. Remi, get me up there!"

"Get *us* up there!" Cameron corrected, grabbing my arm.

"On it." Remi clasped my hand and *bamf*! A split second of darkness and then the three of us appeared inside the tower, behind the clock faces and below the trapdoor that led to the bells. It was a small room, maybe twenty feet across and twice that in height, crowded with gears and other clock parts enchanted to keep perfect time. A tight spiral staircase wrapped around a central pillar, leading both up to the belfry and down to the floor below, with a platform halfway up to allow access to the gears and mechanisms that weren't otherwise reachable. It also had a cozy little workbench that was perfect for illicit make-outs.

Right now, however, the vibe was a lot more death-from-above, what with the trapdoor in splinters and the pitch-black seekers grappling their way to the platform with fangs bared. Another scream split the air as one of them reached it.

"*Repello!*" I threw the spell at the leading seeker as it reached for whatever unlucky student was up there. It flew backward, smashing into the stone wall next to one of the clock faces. The second one hissed and pushed in toward the platform. "Remi, get up there!"

With a blade of shadows coalescing in her hand, Remi *bamfed* to the platform to attack the second one. The first one, already recovered, grabbed an axle and swung way toward Cameron and me, tentacles reaching for us.

"*Lacera!*" Cameron slashed the air with his hand. A blade of pale-gold magic mirrored his gesture, slicing into one of the tentacles coming at him. He simultaneously dashed around the corner of the pillar, making himself a harder target. "Zig-zag, Sis!"

Good call. I belatedly ducked behind a support beam, but the seeker was faster. Its tentacle grabbed my right arm, yanking me back out into the open and nearly throwing me to the ground. It had my knife hand, but I quickly switched the athame to my left and stabbed its squirming limb. The seeker roared and released me with another shove; I stumbled backward, teetering at the edge of a hole in the floor where a large gear was turning. "Shit—*repello!*" I tried to put less force into the spell, using it to push myself back onto my feet rather than attack this time, but still ended up stumbling a few steps. I was not used to fighting in a place with quite so many hazards.

"*Lacera!*" Cameron yelled again; this time, I felt a splash of sickly warm ichor on my back. Spinning around, I saw another tentacle had been about to grab me from behind, but it now had a deep gash, spilling midnight-black ichor on the floor. "Cut it off!"

I lunged forward, grabbing the end of it with one hand and pinning it to the floor with my body weight. I slashed my athame across my forearm to slick it with my own blood and brought it down on the gash, casting a quick spell to sharpen my blade. "*Acuere in sanguine!*"

The blood on the edge lit up in gold, giving the knife a razor's edge that went through the tentacle like sashimi. The severed limb fell to the floor in a pool of black, flopping and twisting grotesquely. The seeker's roar was high pitched this time as its remaining limbs recoiled back up its body, away from my blade.

Above us, the second seeker let out a matching scream of pain; I heard Remi quipping, a male voice yelling, *"Incisura!"* and a *very* familiar woman's voice crying out, "Cyrus, watch out!"

"Mom?" Cameron and I both exclaimed.

"Wendy, go!" Cyrus yelled from the platform.

Sure enough, hurrying down the stairs was our mother, looking scared and angry at once as she ran. Her arm was bleeding; she looked up upon seeing us, startled. "We need to get out of here!" she yelled, reaching the floor. "Those things are too strong!"

"You need to get out of here, we'll handle it!" I replied as we hurried toward her.

The pillar shook as the seeker from above chased its quarry, swiftly stalking her down the outside of the staircase, a shadow descending upon us. "Get down!" I ordered; Mom dove to the ground as Cameron and I cast *"Repello!"* as one, throwing the seeker back and into a cluster of gears on the ground. It screamed over the sound of groaning metal and tearing flesh as some of its tentacles were caught up in the cogs.

Mom scrambled over to us. "Are you okay?"

"Are *you?*" I asked, seeing now that the bite on her arm matched my earlier wound.

"It's small, I'll be fine," Mom said, but she was clearly shaken.

"What are you even doing here?" Cameron asked.

"Cyrus and I were making out," Mom confessed, then covered her mouth. "Oh, goddess. I didn't want to tell you that."

"Seven hells, Preston was right," I groaned.

As if on cue, Cyrus thundered down the stairs, disheveled and full of fury, glaring at the seeker that was just now pulling itself free of the gears. "*Eviscerate!*" he bellowed in Latin, his body bending forward with the force of his yell. His very words became the spell, bronze tongues of magic erupting from his mouth like dragonfire, striking the seeker with a force that drove it backward into the clock face. The thick opaque glass spiderwebbed under the blow, but the monster took the brunt of it, its body bursting open, black blood and viscera coating the floor in front of it.

Holy shit! I'd been practicing combat spells for months alongside Cameron, and the closest we'd come to something like that was when we'd forcefully banished the three demons the other day. That attack had been so effective due to the two of us casting together and the demons being in rotted bodies to begin with. Individually, we couldn't come close to what Cyrus had just done.

Well. Not entirely true. I *had* torn apart Saranthiel on my own, after all. But that had only been possible with the surplus magic of the barrier.

When he turned to us, Cyrus's face was clear of fury and filled with concern. "Wendy, are you all right?"

"It's just a small bite!" Mom exclaimed awkwardly. I'd done

enough talking like that earlier to know she was giving easy but honest answers to avoid saying something else.

Remi *bamf*ed into being in front of us. She, too, had some black blood splatter on her by now. "Nicely done and all, but there's still one left." The second seeker, sure enough, was starting to unfurl again, hissing and focused on our little cluster.

I nodded agreement, readying my athame in my hand again. "Cyrus, get her out of here," I instructed him.

"You're injured, I'm not. You take her," he pointed out, turning to face the remaining one as well.

"Hey, Hero Dee and Hero Dum, how about we capitalize on the four-to-one odds instead, huh?" Cameron suggested.

"Littlest Ellerbeck makes a good point. Spread out and let's flank this thing," Remi said, gesturing with her sword. "Someone cover Wendy." She *bamf*ed across the room, and Cameron jogged out along the base of the stairs.

"Fine, I'll do it," Cyrus and I both said at once, then exchanged a bemused look. He gestured for me to go, and I started to step away.

Mom laughed. "I always knew she got that stubborn heroism from you."

My foot froze midstep. Along with every other part of me.

I turned back to her, wide-eyed. My limbs felt like they'd all gone cold, and my heart had stopped beating so it could drop into my stomach. "...What did you say?"

"Wendy...?" Cyrus, too, looked utterly stunned.

Mom's face had gone pale, her hand pressed to her lips as if to keep her from saying more. But that was not how the venom worked. "Cyrus is your father, McKenna." The words shook as they escaped her.

Cyrus and I stared at her; then, slowly, at each other, as though seeing each other for the first time. My mind reeled. "But—but Dad…my dad is…"

"I know. I'm sorry, I…I can explain…" Mom stammered.

Yet another scream cut her off; we all turned to see Cameron, seized by the leg by the remaining seeker, being hauled into the air.

"A little help here!" Remi hollered, stabbing at it, but the seeker pulled out of her blade's reach.

"Cameron!" I darted over, fleeing my mother's confession for a far more manageable crisis. I thrust my hand out to cast something but quickly saw I couldn't. The seeker had pulled in on itself once again, anchoring itself onto one of the many metal bars several feet above our heads, and there was no way I could hit it but not Cameron. It yanked my brother to its mouth and bit down on his side, fangs and teeth alike sinking in, bright-red blood rapidly blooming on his shirt. "*No!*" I screamed. "Remi! Help him!"

"Working on it!" She *bamf*ed again, reappearing on a horizontal gear next to it, but the seeker's tentacle lashed out as she did, sending her flying off her perch. She teleported again to avoid hitting the wall, instead tumbling hard over the floor when she reappeared.

The seeker's tentacle and jaws alike tightened around my brother, drawing another strangled, gurgling scream of pain from him. It dragged him out of its mouth, teeth ripping into him and leaving bleeding red lines behind.

"*Secretssss . . .*" The command came in a hiss that tugged even at the remnants of the venom in my blood. But unlike my brother, I was not compelled to answer.

"I knew I . . . should've moved . . . before this town killed me . . ." Cameron gasped, blood on his lips, his words strangled and wet, ending in a weak laugh.

Surprisingly, there was still room for me to be shocked by revelations after what my mother had said—*Cyrus is my father?!*—but now was *not* the time. If Cam wanted to move, all I cared about right now was making sure he lived to do it.

This thing wanted secrets? Then I'd give it a target it couldn't refuse. "Hey!" I circled around to get its attention, waving my arms. "Hey, you want some secrets? I'm fucking full of them! Come and get me!"

A hissing laughter came out of it, and another tentacle lashed out at me. This time I was ready. I dove aside at the last second and the appendage went right into the gears behind me, crunching between the cogs with a burst of black blood. I dashed to where it held Cameron. "*Resera!*" It was the spell I usually used to open my tattoo wards, but the idea was similar enough—*release him, you fucking bastard!*

My magic hit the limb holding him, sending a shudder through it as the coils went slack and Cameron slumped out of its grip. I caught him, barely, falling to the ground under his weight. He was gasping for breath, covered in blood, and I was no expert, but I knew he had to have a broken rib or, worse, a punctured lung, judging by the horrible wet sounds coming out of him. I could stop his bleeding, and I cast a quick spell to do so, but fixing this was well beyond me.

"*Remi!*" I screamed. "Cameron needs the hospital, *now!*"

She was at my side in an instant, bloodied, battered, but hale enough to evacuate him—until the bells rang out.

There weren't many bells in the tower, but they were big enough and loud enough to be clearly heard across the campus. Being inside the tower as they rang was downright deafening. Every one of us clapped our hands over our ears, vibrating down to our teeth. Cam made a pained expression, cringing in my lap, and Remi and I bent forward to use our arms to cover his ears for him. Even the seeker howled and cringed, its remaining tentacles flailing around what I assume must have been its ears.

It couldn't have been more than a few seconds, but it felt like so much longer. Even after the bells stopped ringing, the vertigo remained, and we were all too stunned to move. "Remi," I finally croaked. "Get him to the ER. Now."

Remi nodded, shaking her head as though trying to clear it. She started to shift position so she could hold him more carefully before teleporting, but a black mass of movement pulled my eyes away. The seeker, recovered or not, was diving for us.

"Suck on this, beastie!" The unlikely battle cry came from the center of the room as the hatch door flew open and Gretchen burst out, tossing several bottles at the seeker. They shattered and the contents sizzled as they spread over the thing's face, eating away at its flesh. Coming up behind her was Dara, wielding a shadow weapon of her own, this one taking the form of a spear that she flung through the skull of the seeker. It slumped on the ground, dead.

Well, shit.

"Believe me now, demon's witch?" Dara said as she walked over.

"Sorry it took us so long. Oh, hells!" Gretchen's expression fell as she saw Cameron. "Cameron!"

I stood so Remi could get a grasp on him. "Go with them, Remi's taking him to the ER."

A shadow passed over us as Gretchen and I began to trade positions. I looked up to see a third seeker swoop into the tower, moving rapidly toward us, bigger and faster than the other two. I started to run out into the open, intent on keeping it away from my injured brother. But even as I ran, it was upon us, tentacles lashing out to grab both Gretchen and me. I was yanked off my feet, trying in vain to struggle against it. Another tentacle rushed past me to Gretchen, shoving her into the center pillar with a sickening crack. She slumped to the ground, but I had no idea if she was dead or just badly injured and unconscious.

Cameron bellowed in absolute fury, injuries be damned, blood flying from his lips. He smeared his hand through the blood on his shirt and thrust it out at the seeker, screaming with everything he had left. "*Eviscerate!*"

Just like when Cyrus had cast it, the spell hit the seeker like a missile, flinging it backward and violently tearing it open. This time, when it hit the already-damaged clock face, the glass gave way.

This time, when it hit, it took me with it.

The moments came in snapshots. The crack of the glass as it shattered. The sudden brightness of the sun as we left the tower. The black blood of the monster as it exploded around me. The screams that came from behind, above, below, within. The green, green grass of the quad rushing toward me. The absolute certainty that I was about to die. The sudden clarity that I had one way out of this.

The brilliant blue of Bastien's borrowed magic around my hands as I wordlessly ripped open a portal and fell through it.

Chapter 12
Friends in Low Places

The water was dark and deep and much too warm to be the Atlantic.

Even with the body of the seeker breaking the surface first, the water slapped my face hard enough to sting. With no time to get a breath before going under, I ended up with a mouthful of water that tasted unpleasantly like minerals. Fighting against panic, I kicked for the surface, but the tentacle was still wrapped around my waist. If I didn't get free, the monster's weight was going to drag me down with it.

I slashed with my hand, summoning magic to slice the limb off, same as I'd done the other night at the beach—and nothing happened. At all.

Panic came back for round two.

No! Panic means dying, and I am NOT going to die here. Keep your shit together, Ellerbeck! Hells, I'm not even an actual Ellerbeck— fuck that, not now, just cut this thing loose!

I slashed with the athame still in my other hand, hacking at the limb. Black blood blossomed in the water, then the tentacle suddenly jerked and the seeker surged upward, dragging me with it. *How is this thing still alive!?*

We broke the surface, me gasping and coughing up rancid water from several feet in the air. The monster below me was in a bad way—Cameron's spell had ripped it open, and so had the glass of the clock face. Though the sky and the water were already dark, the inky black blood filled the water around us, darkening it even further.

The seeker roared and hauled me toward it. I stabbed the athame into the tentacle again, determined to get free before it chomped on me as its buddy had done to Cameron. *Seven hells, Cameron, please be okay!*

Its pitch-black jaws cracked open, stained teeth glinting, but then an oversize crab claw snapped out of the water and into its side. The seeker roared again and slapped away the new attacker with another tentacle before buckling as another claw bit into its side. A third claw snapped at the tentacle holding me; I nearly dropped back into the drink, but my feet hit an uneven but solid surface. Looking down, I found myself standing on the back of a crab the size of a Great Dane with an enormous circular mouth full of tiny teeth on its back. And it was trying to eat my shoe.

"Fuck!" I screamed, and kicked at it, trying to pull my foot out while also not falling into the water again, holding on to the seeker's tentacle of all things for balance. Finally, my foot came free, sans sneaker, and I braced myself on either side of the thing's mouth. I looked around wildly, trying desperately to see a way out of this.

The sky was dark and red and starless. The landscape was utterly unfamiliar. The crabs were quickly overwhelming the seeker, and the shore was at least thirty yards away.

The only good thing was that the crabs were focused on the seeker right now and not me, but I couldn't count on that for long. I could hopscotch my way to the edge of the group and then swim for it. They were distracted, and I had years of swimming lessons and growing up in a seaside town on my side. Plan made, I cut through the last of the tentacle holding me, pulling it off and tossing it into the mouth of the crab I was on, and jumped for the next one—

—only to immediately slip on it and end up right back in the drink.

I slashed with my knife and kicked hard with my feet. I couldn't give these things any chance to grab me. If they did, I was done for. My knife hit something, my feet found enough purchase to push off something else, and I was off. The water stank and it stung my eyes and every single cut and scrape on my body. I didn't care, I didn't stop. I swam and held nothing back, still clutching my one and only weapon.

The shore was coming closer when a claw snapped in the air a few feet to my right. I slashed at it but hit nothing and kept swimming. Lucky for me, my feet hit the bottom a moment later and I stood, trying to run through the last few yards. I looked to my right, only for something on my other side to bump me hard enough to send me sprawling. One of the crabs' mouths loomed up at me and I wheeled my arms, desperate to not pitch face-first into it. "Fuck, fuck, fuck!"

A rock slammed into the mouth instead, crunching against the exoskeleton. It withdrew, and I caught my balance and looked to the shore. A man-shaped figure stood there, hoisting another rock and launching it at the second crab. "Keep going!" he yelled.

Good plan. Great plan. I was excited to be a part of it. I ran the last several yards while he kept up the rock throwing, bursting free of the water at last. I was about to collapse on the sand, but the man grabbed me under the arms and hauled me back up before I could.

"They'll come ashore, it's safer further up—*McKenna*?"

I looked up into a pair of familiar and startled storm-blue eyes. "*Bastien?*"

Behind us, claws snapped and far too many legs scuttled. Two of the crabs had made it to shore, and from the ripples behind them, they were not the only ones.

"*Repello!*" I yelled on instinct, but again, nothing happened.

"Run! I'll explain later!" Bastien grabbed my hand. We ran.

The rocky shore became an even rockier landscape. Bastien clearly knew where he was going; I didn't ask questions and just tried to keep up. Climbing one of the boulders, I slipped, catching my foot on a crevice just above a snapping claw. Bastien reached down from the top to pull me up. Finally, we took refuge in a tucked-away cave where a small fire burned. I bent over double in exhaustion, hands on my knees as I panted.

"We're safe enough here. The crabs can't make it up all the rocks. Or maybe just don't care to get too far from the water, I'm not sure," Bastien explained, catching his breath.

Firelight flicked over his disheveled blond hair, and I could pick out scratches in his glasses. He wasn't as winded as me, but then he'd only been in the final third of my hellish fight-swim-climb triathlon. The button-down shirt and slacks that had been so crisp yesterday were now wrinkled and dirt stained, torn at the knees and elbows, fraying in other places. Scrapes were scattered around his arms and face, including a large cut across his cheekbone.

"You look almost as bad as I did the other night," I panted.

He smiled wryly. "So do you."

I smiled back and threw my arms around him. "I've never been so happy to see you in my life." My voice rasped, suddenly thick with emotion.

"Me neither." His arms closed around me, warm against the chill of my soaked clothes and the adrenaline rush. His cheek rested against my head, his breath falling in sync with mine, and I actually felt *safe* for the first time in days. Maybe longer. No crabs, no seekers, no—

"Cameron!" I exclaimed.

"What? Oh, god, don't tell me he came through with you?" Bastien asked, pulling back to arm's length.

"No, but he was badly hurt—he needs a hospital—fuck, how do we get out of here?" My put-off panic roared back in full, now that my own life-or-death situation was past.

"McKenna, if I knew that, do you think I'd still be here?" Bastien replied. His eyes searched my face and he frowned. "Hey, it's okay. Just breathe, we'll figure it out."

"No, you don't understand, the seekers attacked us, and they—one bit him, *really* bit him, he could barely breathe—"

"Was he alone?"

"No—no, Remi was there, and Gretchen and Mom and Cyrus—oh, fuck me, Cyrus—"

Bastien's brows went up. "Cyrus? You met him?" I just barked with humorless laughter. "McKenna, slow down. Breathe. Cameron's got people with him to help, okay? We can't do anything for him from here. They'll take care of him."

"No, I need to help him, I—" My throat felt too thick, my heart was too fast. I couldn't breathe. My hands shook and I slipped in his grasp.

Bastien caught me, slowly lowering me to the ground. "Easy. I've got you." His hands hovered, then grabbed mine, and he stared into my eyes. "McKenna. I need you to slow your breathing. Biggest inhale you can, okay? I'll do it with you." I watched his mouth as he took an exaggerated breath, but mine caught in my throat. "Okay, try breathing with your nose. Like this. Breathe in. This is temporary. Breathe out. This is temporary."

He repeated it slowly, over and over, until the words swam around in my brain: *Breathe in. This is temporary. Breathe out. This is temporary. This is temporary. Temporary.*

When I could finally take a few breaths without him, he nodded. "Good. Keep doing that, okay? God, you're shivering. You need to get out of these," he said, taking in the rest of me. He pulled off his shirt and set it aside—he had a white tank top underneath—and caught my eyes again. "I need to take these clothes off you. You're soaked and you're too cold. We'll dry them by the fire and you can have my shirt for now. Okay? Can you nod or say yes if that's okay?"

As he said it, I felt it. My whole body was shaking, not just my hands. I slowly nodded. "Y-yes," I stammered.

"Okay. If anything hurts, let me know."

With gentle, mindful fingers, Bastien peeled my wet blouse off me. The air hit my skin, setting off goose bumps and more shivering. He left my bra alone but rubbed my arms with his warm hands, soothing some of the chill, and then wrapped his shirt around me. It wasn't much, but it held the warmth of his body and the fire and that was enough. With similar care, he pulled off my remaining shoe and my socks, then had me lift my hips to get my jeans. Once again, he rubbed my limbs to warm them. Then he moved me closer to the fire while he wrung the excess water from my things and laid them as flat as he could near the flames to dry.

He came and sat close to me. "Is it okay if I hold you? I want to make sure you warm up," he asked.

I nodded, my body shaking so much I stammered. "Y-yeah."

He put an arm around me, pulling me onto his lap while rubbing my arms and sometimes my legs. I curled up there, sighed out a breath, and rested my head against his shoulder. He started wringing out my hair, one small section at a time, somehow keeping most of the water from getting onto the borrowed shirt. When that was done, he combed his fingers through it.

My eyes slid closed at the soothing sensation. My breathing slowed. I stopped shivering. Warmth and calm overtook everything.

Safe crept back into my body, and my heavy eyes closed.

———————————•———————————

I didn't realize I'd fallen asleep until my eyes fluttered open sometime later. I felt almost hollow, wrung out and exhausted in the wake of the panic and adrenaline. But I held it together, even if only just. Thanks in no small part to the man holding me, the man I had thought rightly hated me. Bastien was leaning back against the cave wall, chest rising and falling slowly but steadily under my head. I thought maybe he was asleep, too, but as soon as I moved, he looked down at me, storm-blue eyes alert and concerned.

"Hey. How are you feeling?" he asked quietly.

"I'm…better." I started to feel foolish, sitting on his lap, so I shifted to the cave floor next to him instead. But only just, and he kept an arm around my back. "How long was I out?"

"Maybe an hour? Who knows. There's no sun and my watch is broken," he said. "How do you feel?"

"Sore. Strung out. Like I've had the day from hell."

"Not shocking. Do you have any idea how many bruises and scrapes you have right now?"

"I'll pass on taking a guess. But I'm not about to have another panic attack, if that's what you mean," I said, smiling ruefully. "…Thank you, by the way."

"You're welcome. I'm just glad you're all right. And, selfishly, here," he said, returning the smile and brushing some hair from my face. "Speaking of, are you ready to talk about *how* you got here?"

"I'm getting there. Give me a few minutes. You're good at that, the panic attack stuff," I said. It was the second time he'd helped get me through one since I'd come home.

"No teacher quite like firsthand experience."

"There sure isn't. What makes you...?" I didn't quite ask.

"What do you think?" He didn't quite answer.

We were quiet for a moment, perhaps both remembering his disastrous wedding. My brain and my body were too spent from the panic attack and the insane day I'd had for me to offer anything else. But the companionable silence and physical closeness, it seemed, were comfort enough for us both. The feel of his arm around me was a welcome warmth both physically and emotionally. Though as I recovered, I became more keenly aware of the fact that I was wearing only my underwear and his shirt. I gently pulled away to check on my drying clothes, adjusting them to get the damper sides closer to the fire.

"Okay...I think I'm as ready as I'm going to be. What happened to you?" I asked. "I got to your house, and it looked like there was a break-in, then a seeker attacked me, and... well, it was a fucked-up start to a fucked-up day."

"The *Geheimnissucher*? Wait, day—was it still Sunday when you came here?" he asked.

"Yes..." I replied, concerned. "It was Sunday evening when I...well, before I was here." I raised an eyebrow. "Did you think it was longer?"

He nodded. "Like I said, it's hard to tell time here. I've slept a few times, but I don't really know for how long or how far apart." He held up his smartwatch; the screen was cracked and blank.

"Yeah, about that. Bastien, where *are* we?" I asked.

"You really don't know?" he asked. I shook my head, shrugging my shoulders. "Then how did you..." He trailed off, letting out a heavy breath. "Seven hells."

"Yeah, it's complicated, believe me, I know."

"No, I mean…McKenna, *that's* where we are. The seven hells. We're in the Pit."

I stared at him. My brain wanted to deny it, it was impossible, and yet the pieces suddenly fell into place: the dark and sunless sky, the sulfuric water, the monstrous crabs, the complete absence of magic. It made perfect, terrifying sense.

And none at all. "The…Pit. As in the actual seven hells, the realm of demons, *that* Pit?"

"That Pit."

My legs felt weak again, another shiver running over my skin. The fire flickered, casting moving shadows on the wall. The Pit. We couldn't be in the Pit. Any fire would have to burn bigger, brighter, hotter if we were in the Pit. Right?

He gestured at the flames. "You'd think that, and yet." Had I said that out loud?

"But…but that's impossible, how could I portal…" I knew exactly how. "The corrupted magic."

He sat up straighter. "You know about that?"

I nodded. "I found the ring at your house. I took the magic from it so I could put another spell there—"

His eyes sharpened. "You took the ring? You took the *magic* in the ring?"

"One, you were missing, and it was one of very few clues I had to go on," I retorted. "And two, believe me, I didn't have much choice about taking it. But considering having that saved my life, not sorry."

Bastien's irritation lessened upon hearing that. "Saved your life? How?"

"I was thrown from the Lease clock tower and used it to open a portal."

"*Thrown* from the *clock tower*?" Bastien exclaimed. "What— why were you—hells, you never get in trouble by halves, do you?"

I shrugged with a self-deprecating smile. "What would be the fun in that?"

Bastien chuckled, shaking his head. "Okay, putting a pin in *that* for the moment, it sounds like you opened it on instinct, no planning or destination in mind?" I nodded. "Yeah. Same thing happened to me, it looks like that's part of how it works. I was in my living room, then a seeker crashed through the sliding door and I just reacted."

"And since magic clearly doesn't work here, we're stuck?"

"Essentially. I've yet to determine another way out."

I reviewed what I knew about the comings and goings of demons from the Pit. "Only Archdemons can come and go physically as they please, others need to be summoned or leave their physical bodies behind. Or go through a portal. Your ex couldn't have left us a little more juice to work with, huh?" Bastien gave me a confused look. "The corrupted magic Saranthiel put in the ring?"

"Oh . . . right. I . . . I don't think it would matter if we had more. Magic still doesn't work here."

"I suppose so. And we've got no way to contact Remi. Fantastic." A humorless laugh escaped me. "Suppose it was pretty inevitable I'd end up here one day."

"No, it's not. Your soul is your own, McKenna," Bastien reminded me.

"And yours isn't?" I shot back. My knee-jerk snark, however, was met with him avoiding eye contact. "Shit, please do *not* tell me you of all people made a Bargain."

"No! No, of course not," he replied quickly. "But I . . . dammit." He rubbed his face. "It's complicated."

I gave him a wry look. "Then to quote you: Start at the beginning. Let's uncomplicate it."

———————————————•———————————————

Eleven years ago

Bastien found me in the stacks at the library while I was reshelving books in the Uncommon Collection. "We need to talk."

A week had passed since the Homecoming Harbor Cruise, and after dancing with him three times that night, I'd basically ghosted him since. I didn't want to give any more of a false impression than I had already been forced to. *Deep breath, get it over with.* "I appreciate your help at Homecoming, but—"

"You're a thrall." It wasn't a question.

I stared at him. "I . . . what?"

"You're a thrall, aren't you?"

I pushed the cart down the aisle, even though I wasn't done in this area. "I don't know what you're talking about."

He followed. "It's the only thing that makes sense. You were seasick, which you don't get, then you were suddenly fine."

"You're the one who cast a spell to fix that," I said.

"Yeah, but there was this…resistance. Just for a second, before I felt it take, like there was something preventing it, or thinking about preventing it. And your magic got better out of nowhere last year."

"Some people are late bloomers," I said, stopping and shoving a book onto its shelf. I had to shake him. Convince him he was being an idiot. Except of all people who might suspect me, Bastien Lemaire was very much not an idiot.

"Not that much. And Remi, she's a demon, isn't she? How is she even in Arcadia?"

I scoffed. "Do you hear yourself? Demons can't get in here, Bastien. End of story."

"And yet, somehow, she is one. I saw her shapeshift," he insisted.

Where and when had he seen that? *No, don't ask, that would be admitting he's right.* "Half our classmates shapeshift," I pointed out instead.

"She's not Fae or a werewolf. She says she's a witch. But there's no record of a Blake family of witches," he went on.

This one I was ready for. "New witches happen. Not all of us come from a long line of perfect adepts and masters, you know." Book, shelved.

"You're deflecting."

"And you're tilting at windmills," I countered more aggressively. *Don't deflect, redirect.* "Look, if this is about Homecoming, I'm sorry if you got the wrong idea."

He was thrown by that and adjusted his glasses on his nose, not looking right at me. "It—no, it's not about that. It has nothing to do with that."

Wait, did it? I'd been bluffing, but did he actually...? *Not the time. Push the advantage while you can.* "I'm grateful for your help that night. I am. And it was nice hanging out... as friends. Which I would like to be, but...but not if you're going to go accusing me and my girlfriend of shit like this." There. Calm. Collected. Honest, even. I shelved a third book and pushed the cart along.

"I heard you talking about Forneus."

I stopped.

"About being sick of him. About wanting to get free. And I heard her say she's done being his minion."

My heart thudded in my chest. We'd said all those things last week. When she picked me up after the harbor cruise, in her car. How? How had he heard us?

"Your window was down, in the parking lot," he answered my unspoken question. "I was coming over to ask if you were feeling better off the boat, and then I heard you talking."

Shit! Shit, shit, shit! I was so fucked. We both were.

"Took some research to figure out who he is, exactly. There's a book in my family's library that mentions him. And...there's also one that talks about a sword. It might not even exist, but if it does...it says it can kill any true evil."

This time, my heart stopped for a second. I slowly turned around. Bastien was holding a book in his hand. The title was in French, and it promised tales of legendary heroes and true magic.

I couldn't stop myself from reaching for it. He pulled it back. "Are you?"

"I—" The words stuck in my throat. Literally. "—I can't tell you."

"Why not?"

"It's complicated."

Bastien nodded slowly. "Okay. Then start at the beginning. Let's uncomplicate it."

<hr/>

Now

Bastien let out a breath. "Right. After we left the hospital, I—"

I made a T with my hands. "Hold up, time-out. That's not the beginning."

"It isn't?"

"No. The beginning is what have you been up to since you told me to stay the hell away from you and blocked my number back in December, Mr. I Have a Secret Demon Murderboard in My Office," I informed him.

"You found that?" I nodded, unsure if the red in his face was from anger, embarrassment, or just the fire. Either way, his next words were stiff. "Well. You conducted an awfully thorough search, didn't you?"

"Of course I did! Shattered glass door, table sliced in half, and you were missing and magically untrackable! Guess now I know why. What was I supposed to do? Call the cops?" I asked sarcastically. "We went room to room through that place."

" 'We'?"

"Leo searched with me. I called her when I started having a

panic attack," I explained when he looked surprised. "Talked me down and stayed to help."

"You had a panic attack? Over me being missing?"

"Yeah. I…" I looked down at the rough, rocky ground, words sticking in my throat. *I was worried. Scared. I didn't know what to do, and I knew I was getting a taste of my own medicine.* Why was it so hard to say? "Anyway, in my defense, I didn't see the murderboard until after the seeker threw me into the wall."

"Exactly how many things have you been thrown into or out of today?" he asked in alarm.

I waved it off. "I'm fine. Your wall's seen better days, might wanna patch that up before your Realtor does any more showings."

"Uh…yes. I suppose so." He nudged his glasses back up on his nose.

Are you really leaving? For good? Those words, too, got stuck, but this time I knew it was because I feared the answer being yes. I cleared my throat. "Anyway. What happened after the Solstice Ball?"

Bastien took a moment to collect his thoughts before speaking. "I was angry. Not just at you, and if I'm honest, much of that was misplaced anger. I'd been used, made a fool, had my heart broken and my back stabbed, and my grandfather decided to kick me while I was down. Arcadia Commons was the last place I wanted to be at that point. The Arcadia Grand was about to be under construction for a few months, so I turned it into an excuse to visit other branches and get out of town."

"That explains your absence. What about the demon research?" I asked.

"After I found the support group," Bastien said.

"Proud member of the cabal of the covenless, huh?"

"Something like that. I was at a supernatural-friendly bar in Boston in February and got to talking to a fellow patron. Seems like you've already met Cyrus, though."

"*Cyrus is your father, McKenna.*" Mom's confession rushed back to me. "You just happened to tell a stranger your deepest, darkest secrets?"

"I may have been a little loose-lipped and in my cups," Bastien admitted. "It was Valentine's Day. I...I'd proposed on Valentine's."

"Oh...okay, yeah, understandable."

"I didn't jump right to it, even so. But the subject of having less-than-favorable encounters with demons came up, and he knew my family name since he used to live in Arcadia. Much like you, he's not terribly fond of my grandfather, or the Council."

"Heh, yeah, so I hear." My mouth felt dry. "Is there anything to drink?"

"No, sorry. But eating and drinking don't seem to be necessary here. I haven't had anything since I arrived, and I'm not only not dying from it, I haven't felt a need for it, either."

"Huh. Remi's told me she doesn't age when she's in the Pit, I guess time really *isn't* a thing here," I said.

"Not precisely, no. Your body will process anything in it, but there's no real need for more." I raised an eyebrow, curious how he knew that, and he looked slightly embarrassed.

"I...may have been a little in my cups when I portaled here, too." He picked up a branch and stirred the fire.

That explained the broken glass and the half-empty bottle of bourbon in his house. I gestured for him to go on. "So you met Cyrus."

"Yes. He invited me to the group, and it was...surprisingly helpful. Cathartic. I kept other people's names out of anything I said, but getting things off my chest, I felt...well, unburdened. I realized a lot of who and what I was actually mad at and about." Bastien broke off a piece of the branch and tossed it in. The flames crackled higher, and I felt his gaze on me.

"What is it?" I asked when he didn't continue, finally looking back at him.

"I'm sorry, McKenna," he said. "I should never have taken all that out on you."

His straightforward words caught me off guard. "I...I mean, you weren't wrong."

"No. I *was* wrong," Bastien said. "You're not a coward."

"I have done some pretty cowardly things," I replied. "You were right. I ran. I kept what happened to myself. And people got badly hurt because of it. Including you."

"That's true, but it's not the whole truth. You didn't hurt us on purpose, or by choice. The group—I'd already told Wendy about it. It sounds like you both ended up there?"

"Yeah. She showed up while Leo and I were searching the house, and we thought maybe we'd find you there, or at least some information that would help," I said.

"Then you've heard some of their stories," Bastien went on. "Well, the more I heard from them, the clearer it was just how insidious and destructive Archdemons are. They don't just lie, manipulate, and gaslight, they ruin people. Ruin who they are, who they want to be, their dreams, their relationships."

"Didn't you know all that before?" I asked. "Not trying to be a jerk, but you know how it was for me. You know what they did to my brother and mom."

"I did and I didn't. When I first started going, I was too wrapped up in my own pain to think that far beyond it," Bastien said. "Arcadia has been so sheltered from demons that what happened with you and Forneus felt more like a terrible exception to the norm. But outside Arcadia, people are completely vulnerable to them. What happened to you wasn't an exception, it was simply the first time I'd ever encountered it. As for what Saranthiel did…suffice to say I was still trying to process and unpack all of that. Still am, if I'm being honest."

"Then what made you feel ready to come back to town, if you're still processing all of that?" I asked. I was glad for him, for the healing and the insight he'd gained, but even hearing about his personal growth journey, I still had a lot of questions.

"Being part of that group has helped immensely, even if I've still got some work to do. I hoped it might help Wendy in the same way." Despite his words, he wore a guilty look.

"Because you knew she was struggling," I filled in. "Because even though you blocked my number, you were still in touch with her, and had even seen her recently, and invited her along, and neither of you told me this."

"For what it's worth, I was going to tell you when you came over," he said. "I wanted to bring you there, too."

"That's why you asked me to talk? That and not the demon research or the ritual you're working on?" I asked.

He did a double take. "You found that, too? How?"

"You still hide your weed in the same place," I replied, grinning. He laughed. "Why you're hiding it in your own house is a whole other question!"

"Habit?" He shrugged. "It wasn't just the support group I wanted to talk to you about. The ritual, too. Which probably would've led to the research, sooner or later."

"Good, 'cause I didn't peg you as the suicide mission type," I replied. "You know better than most how near impossible it is to kill Archdemons. You probably figured out real quick how hard it is to even research anything real about them. Judging by the contents of your board and the seekers on your trail, you also know asking demon questions lands you with demon problems."

"That it does," he confirmed.

"So why did you ignore the two biggest experts you know on the subject?" I asked, tapping my chest. "Remi and I were both right there! I know Remi's not exactly your favorite person, and you were pissed at me. But hell, I can name two more Archdemons for you right now. Was talking to me honestly worse than, oh, I don't know, ending up in the fucking *Pit*?" I gestured widely around us.

Bastien stared at the fire. "It wasn't that."

"Okay, then what was it?" I asked. "It doesn't sound like you're mad anymore. Thank you for the apology, speaking of. I think you know I'm sorry, too, but if you need me to say it again: I'm sorry, Bastien. I hurt you in a lot of ways, and I'm sorry for all of them, and I swear, I am trying to do better."

"Thank you. I know that…maybe too well, now." Bastien cleared his throat. "Because…I was trying to do the same thing. It started off as shutting you out because I was angry, but it turned into doing it to try and protect you. And myself."

Maybe I should not have been surprised at how familiar his story sounded to my own. Manipulated by demons, isolated from friends and family, directionless anger channeled into a pointless task, and even hunted by demons in the end. Maybe this was why I had a bad feeling about where this was going, because my tale had certainly ended explosively. Or maybe it was the feeling I couldn't shake that there was still something he wasn't telling me. "What do you mean?"

"You're probably wondering why I'm the Perez family's advocate, I imagine?" he asked.

"I am. I know you're justifiably mad at Brooke, too, but you know how awful severing is," I replied. "What's that got to do with it?"

"I didn't initiate this trial. But it's happening, it was always going to, and I need the Council to vote against Brooke if I'm going to co-opt that ritual for my own," Bastien told me. He met my eyes again, determined as I'd ever seen him. "It's the only way to restore Wendy's magic to her. And to get rid of the demonic power in mine."

Chapter 13
Like Calls to Like

"You're gonna *what*?" I sputtered. "None of what you just said is possible! You can't unsever someone, and you can't have—oh. Oh, *shit*. Yes, you can."

Bastien nodded, letting a breath out through his nose. "Yes. My ever-so-fleeting marriage didn't merely give Saranthiel my magic, it seems to have given me her power as well. Removing her name from my family's grimoire did nothing to correct that. Every time I open a portal, no matter where to, it opens one between our world and the Pit as well. It's one of the reasons I've encountered more demons in the last few months." He glanced at me. "That's also why I avoided you. I thought you might've been able to sense it."

I started to shake my head but stopped as I reviewed the last few days. "I think I did, yeah, I just didn't realize it was you. Right before you showed up at the meeting, and then before I saw you at the hospital, I felt something. I thought it was demons crossing the barrier," I said.

"Thankfully, none did those times. That would have been rather difficult to explain," Bastien said.

"Knowing your grandfather, I'm sure he would've found a way to blame me," I said, and we shared a knowing look. "Does anyone else know?"

"Only Cyrus," Bastien said. "And only because I was bitten by a seeker once on my way to a group meeting. Confessing that proved enough to clear the venom's effects."

"One of those things found you in the game shop basement?"

"No, this was before I set up the portal circle there. It's one of the reasons I did, so I could safely portal into a place warded against demons," Bastien explained.

I frowned. "Hate to break it to you, but in that case you've just been lucky. The seekers aren't demons. They're monsters created by the Archdemon of Secrets."

Bastien was surprised, but looked keenly interested. "Secrets? I haven't heard of that one."

"Neither had I until the other day." I recounted my encounter with the seeker at his house and my inability to detect or banish them, as well as what Gretchen and my grimoire had to say about them. Which led to a longer explanation about the Archdemon of Secrets, Remi's suspicious assistant Dara, and the clock tower incident that had ended in my defenestration. I left out my mother's confession about Cyrus.

"How did you find me when I got here, anyway?" I asked, tugging at a tangle in my hair. It wasn't a total disaster, thanks to his earlier attentions, but there were still some pins stuck in there along with a few tangles. My hair elastic was long gone, lost to the depths.

"I was looking for more fuel for the fire, and I felt a kind of tug in that direction. I'm guessing it was some sort of like calling to like, since you used my magic to get here. I followed it, and there you were." He gave me a wry smile. "Getting into scuffles with demons, as per usual."

"It's a living," I joked in return. "…Actually, it's not; no one pays me to do this shit, though I would really appreciate it if they did."

"They ought to. Wendy says you and Cameron have been having to deal with them more often lately?"

I nodded, grimacing as I pulled at a particularly stubborn knot. "The barrier's getting weaker. More of them are getting in. And now it looks like a new Archdemon is taking an interest."

"Do you want help with that?" he asked.

"The Archdemon? Obviously—oh, you mean my hair?" He nodded. "Unless you've got a comb, some deep conditioner, or a pair of shears, I don't really know how you can."

"I could use your athame," he offered.

The ritual knife was on the rocks near my drying pants. The edge was sharp enough to do the job, though this wasn't exactly the sort of thing it was intended for. Then again, neither was a lot of the hacking and slashing I ended up doing with it. I ran my fingers along the ends of my hair, both the ones that came partway down my back and the ones that now ended somewhere near my shoulder. When *had* my last haircut been, anyway? I'd taken to trimming my own ends in the last few years. Finding a good salon and stylist was always an ordeal, which made it a luxury I had neither the time nor money for while I was on the run, so I'd opted for the practical, affordable solution. In the last few days, I hadn't even given much thought to my hair beyond getting it pulled up so I didn't have to deal with it or questions about it.

"I know I'm no hairstylist, but I figured I could at least even it out for you," he elaborated when I didn't reply.

"It's not that, I was just…thinking. But yeah, thank you. I'd like that." I handed him the knife.

"It's no…you're welcome," he said, changing his response halfway through.

I sat with my back to him, legs crossed, hands in my lap and idly fiddling with one of the buttons on his shirt. He settled behind me, unhurriedly brushing my hair behind my shoulders, and I felt some of the tension of the last few days dissipate. "Do you want to talk about what happened?"

"Who says something happened?" I replied, a little too airily.

Bastien chuckled. "I suppose I'm not up to date on women's styles of late," he said, "but I did notice you don't seem to love the current state of it."

I smiled ruefully. "True enough." As he carefully worked at it with the knife, strands falling to the cave floor by my side, I filled him in on what had happened on the beach before the Council meeting.

"That sounds harrowing," he said, tone carefully mild.

"You could call it that," I agreed, my gaze drifting to my lap.

His hand came around, gently nudging my chin up. "Trying to keep it even," he explained. "And then you were thrown into the water again here, barely two days later?"

"I really need to stop before it becomes a habit," I joked. I kept my chin up, body still, and watched from the corner of my eye as the strands continued falling, firelight reflecting off them.

He brushed some strands with his hands, collecting them into a new section to work on. "I'm surprised the demon's body didn't let go when you banished it, though. They usually fall apart at that point."

"I...hadn't actually banished it yet." My chin started to dip again, but I caught myself.

"But you said you took care of it?"

Breathe in. Breathe out. This might not be temporary. This... this might be a problem. But given the situation with his magic, maybe one he would understand? Or, at least, not judge me for? "I...I pulled it out. The demon. I pulled it out of the body it made. Because..." *Breathe out.* "Because...that's a thing I can do, for some reason."

He was quiet for a moment while he worked it out. "You can manipulate demonic power."

My head turned, slightly, at the way he said it. "You don't sound surprised."

"I am, a little. But last fall...Saranthiel threw her power at us, but you were able to throw it back at her," he recalled. "And when she died..." He sounded like he was searching for the rest of the sentence, trying to remember what had happened.

I turned around to look at him, watching him realize the answer but struggle to make sense of it. "When she died, Remi wasn't there. I was alone with her. Because...I'm the one who killed her. Just me."

"Just you . . ." His eyes widened. "But then Remi came and claimed the mantle?"

I shook my head. "No. Remi came and *I gave* her the mantle. Because I didn't want to claim it for myself, and I didn't dare let it just go free."

Now he looked truly shocked. "*You* could've claimed it?"

"I don't really know what it would've looked like if I had, but yeah. I know I was capable of it. Even though it should be impossible."

"*All* of that should be impossible," Bastien agreed. "But . . . I'm sitting here with demonic power all over my magic that I didn't want. So it *is* possible."

"Yes, but I never married a demon," I pointed out, then winced. "Sorry, I didn't mean to sound like that."

"It's all right," Bastien said. "It's how I ended up with it. Face front for a moment? I'm almost done."

I did so, quietly sitting as he cut away the last of the longer locks. The athame clinked as he set it down and then ran his hands through the shortened ends. "Better?"

I shook my hair out lightly, pushing my fingers through it as well. It did feel better; lighter, as if for once I actually had *less* to deal with instead of more. "It is. Thanks," I said, turning more fully back to him. "And thanks for not freaking out about what I just told you."

"Thanks for not doing the same with what I told you," he replied. "I already intended to tell you about the ritual Cyrus and I are planning. But now it makes more sense than ever."

"Yeah, what's that all about?" I asked. I unbent my legs, stretching them, and checked my clothes. Still too wet to comfortably wear, aside from my socks, so I pulled those on. "Even with everything I just said, those still sound like two impossible tasks."

"They might turn out to be, but I have reason to hope they aren't. Cyrus specializes in metamagic. He's been working on a way to reverse severing for years, but he lacked a way to properly power the ritual. I was interested in helping him as soon as I knew that, but the only real chance came up when Sofia asked me to be their advocate."

"How does that change things?" I asked.

"Several ways. Severing trials in Arcadia Commons take place at the actual center of the leyline crossroads, the nexus. The ritual for doing so taps directly into the leylines. Cyrus believes, and I find myself agreeing, that the best chance for unsevering a person is having access to a power source like that."

I knew severing trials had a specific location, having survived one myself as a teen. The location of that trial, however, had always been a mystery to me. I'd been portaled to and from it but hadn't seen much of the place while there. I remembered it was made of stone and smelled of ocean and earth. Everything else was a blank; they'd probably used an illusion spell to further mask it, or possibly even meddled with my memory of it.

"Okay, powering it, that makes sense. But that doesn't explain why you volunteered to lead the charge against Brooke," I said.

"Because the accusing party's representative is the executioner, the third party used to channel the actual severing spell," Bastien told me. "The ritual itself uses me as its instrument."

If the spell hinged on him, then he was in fact the *only* one who could do this. "How is it you know this and I don't, even though I'm on the Council?" I asked. "I'm not trying to brag, believe me. Just trying to make sense of this."

"I only know because Cyrus told me."

"And how does *he* know?"

"Because his ancestors created severing. His parents were severed, and he himself was almost severed by the Arcadia Council thirty years ago."

Cyrus was? *That* hadn't been in any of the records I'd looked at. My trial had been, so I knew they didn't only list trials where severing happened, either. Unless his had been the one that was blacked out? If he had almost been severed, it was starting to sound like a genetic problem. I found myself suddenly needing to do something with my hands, so I started gathering the locks of hair on the ground. "What did he do?"

"Ironically, tried to undo another severing by tapping into the leylines. He was interrupted, it went wrong, and his dad and one of the Council members at the time died," Bastien told me.

"Frank Milton. I read about it, but nothing mentioned Cyrus being there. George O'Brien said Cyrus's father was the one who killed Milton," I said.

"Cyrus said it was an accident. They struggled, Milton was pushed, fell, and hit his head on a rock," Bastien said.

I raised a dubious eyebrow. "You do realize how incredibly sketchy all that sounds."

"I'm aware," he assured me. "But I looked up the incident, and the details lined up."

"I did, too, but they also leave a lot out. There's no record of Cyrus's trial, either."

"He wasn't severed, but he was essentially banished. It might be filed differently because of the outcome."

"Maybe." My hands full of hair clippings, I sat back on my heels. "When exactly did all this happen?" I didn't recall the dates from my research, but I had a feeling I knew the answer.

"Thirty years ago this past December."

My birthday was in September; I would be twenty-nine this year. My parents—my mom and her ex-husband, that is—had gotten married on New Year's Day. The timing worked out all too well. I always thought I'd been a honeymoon baby who came a few weeks early. Turns out I'd actually been born right on time.

"Solomon's fucking bones," I muttered.

Bastien tilted his head at me. "What is it?"

"At the clock tower, my mom got truth-venomed. And she said...she told Cyrus and me..." I closed my eyes, taking a moment. *Just say it. It's no more or less real if you don't.* "Cyrus is my biological father."

Bastien looked more surprised by that than anything else since I'd gotten here. "He...he and Wendy...?"

"Yep. Turns out they used to date. Including, apparently, when she was mere weeks away from marrying my dad!" My jaw tightened, anger building now that I'd finally said it. "Make that my stepdad, I guess. All this time I spent hating him for cheating on her and hey, turns out *she* did it *first*!"

I threw the pile of hair into the flames, watching it flare up with satisfaction.

It was significantly less satisfying when, seconds later, a horrible, sulfurous smell filled the cave as a result. Bastien and I both gagged and fled for the cave opening.

"What did you do that for?" he said when we got outside, coughing and sucking in the comparatively fresh air.

"I was thinking I didn't want to leave my hair sitting around where any old demon could find it and use it for who knows what!" I replied, fanning the smell away from my face. "I forgot that burning hair smells awful."

"Demons don't use tokens like witches do," Bastien pointed out.

"Yeah, but they deal with enough witches they could still use it for something," I said. "Not taking that chance. Also, it's not like I can get mad *at* my mom here, and burning something felt like a decent facsimile. Blegh."

"I can relate to that part, at least. We still need some more wood, or whatever else we can find to burn, may as well go look now while the cave airs out." I nodded but ducked back in to grab my athame, not willing to go entirely unarmed out here.

We started to walk, and I took a better look at the landscape. Out on the horizon, everywhere I looked, were mountains so tall and imposing that they seemed to be the sky itself. At the same time, it was impossible to tell how far away they were. Directly above us, impossibly far but still visible, was a distant patch of dark-red sky. The Pit was an *actual* pit.

Yet for all that Remi always described it as a dangerous and cutthroat place, it was strangely desolate. My neck prickled as though sensing eyes on us, but I couldn't see any signs of life or activity. Where *was* everyone?

All the same, I kept my grip on my athame tight.

"Cyrus is your father…did he know?" Bastien asked.

"I don't think so. He looked as shocked as me," I said. "Explains why she was acting so weird around him, though. She seemed happy to see him, but she asked me to use the name Kendra and not call her Mom in front of him. It was really pissing me off."

"For what it's worth, he's been a good friend to me. I never told him whose magic I wanted to restore specifically, but he didn't hesitate to agree to help. And he helped start that support group," Bastien said.

"That's something," I said, slightly mollified, but my resentment at my mother remained. "But it doesn't change the fact that my mom's been lying to me for my entire life."

"I'm sure she knew he wasn't welcome back in Arcadia," Bastien said.

"Not an excuse."

He made a noise of agreement. "It does explain why you can manipulate demonic power." I raised an eyebrow. "Not the demonic part, the manipulation part. It's metamagic."

"I guess so," I grudgingly admitted. "Maybe the demonic part is just a leftover from being a thrall. Speaking of…the ritual?" I prompted, wanting to get off the topic.

"The primary goal is to restore Wendy, which more metamagic can only help accomplish. But the other goal is to remove the corruption of Saranthiel's power from my magic."

The enmeshed magic in the ring had been impossible to

separate, however. "That's why the ritual had her rune in it. Have you had any luck with that?"

"Not yet. I've been trying to pull hers out and into that ring for weeks with no luck. I was beginning to think…but between the three of us, with the leyline nexus to power it? I'm certain we can," Bastien said, determined and optimistic. "I can finally be free of the last of that nightmare."

Oh, no. I was his new hope it could be done, and I knew it couldn't.

Maybe…maybe it can, though. Remi doesn't know everything, I've barely explored my abilities there. He'd been so kind to me, reassuring me, keeping me safe and caring for me. What kind of friend, what kind of person, would I be if I thanked him by crushing his last hope?

But I remembered too well what he'd said months ago. *"When have you ever told me bad news?"*

I had to tell him.

I stopped walking, touching his arm so he would as well. He turned to face me. "Bastien, I…I have some bad news," I said. "Demonic power doesn't work like that."

His blond brow furrowed. "What do you mean?"

"Remi and I tried to separate out the power and magic in the ring when we found it, but we couldn't. We assumed it must have been Saranthiel's since she had the ring last. Remi told me that demonic power, once it's claimed, that's where it stays." I said it as gently as I could, looking him in the eyes. I owed him that. "The only way to remove it is when the person holding it dies. I'm sorry, but I don't think we can separate hers from yours because…it's just yours now."

His face twitched through a few expressions. "No, that's . . . no. I didn't *claim* anything, this wasn't my choice. This was . . . forced on me."

"I'm not sure that matters. I didn't give Remi a choice," I admitted.

"But that . . . that bitch *forced* this on me!" Bastien said through gritted teeth, volume rising. "Till death do us part, well, she *died*!"

"But you haven't," I said. I reached for his arms to try to calm him, but he spun away, pacing out of my reach.

"What about you?" he asked, running a hand through his hair, pivoting back around. "Your magic isn't tainted like this, but you've used plenty of demonic power. You were a thrall, twice!"

"I never claimed any of it for myself, though. It was all borrowed power, or power I pushed away but never took for my own," I explained.

"No. No, *dammit*!" Bastien roared, his face red with anger. I nervously looked around, still feeling that prickle on my neck. I saw nothing, but if anything *was* nearby, it would know exactly where to find us.

"Bastien, I'm sorry. Look, maybe there is a way, but I had to at least tell you what I knew," I said, moving to him and grabbing his arm.

"You don't understand, this—I don't want this! I don't want any shred of that thing left in my life or my magic!" Bastien said, his eyes filled with fury and desperation. "I want it gone!"

He tore his arm from my grasp, and my veins lit up in alarm

as power burst from him, the path of his hand ripping through the air beside us. We both jumped back, looking through a ragged, uneven portal leading to a much more actively hellish landscape. It was similar to this place in some ways, but the air wavered with heat, and the rocky terrain glowed red with fire and rivers of lava. What little we could see of it, that is, beyond the two enormous hellhounds that growled at us as they stepped through.

"What…what the hell…?" Bastien stammered.

I grabbed his hand. "Run!"

We bolted away, the hellhounds fast on our heels. They were bigger than any hounds I'd seen before—taller, broader, stronger. Red shadowy tendrils encircled them, and their very skin seemed to be burning from within. One of them howled and the other answered, a deep sound that sank into me and burned there.

"What the fuck were you thinking?" I snapped at Bastien as we ran. My feet, protected only by socks, stung with every step, but I pushed on.

"Me? You're the one who basically told me I was stuck being part demon for the rest of my life! How did you think I was going to react?" he retorted.

"You wanted me to stop hiding the bad news from you, so I did!"

"And you just *had* to start with the worst possible example?"

Irritation flared. "Mixed signals much, Lemaire?"

He scoffed. "You want to talk mixed signals? Gods, Ellerbeck, you're infuriating! You—" Whatever else he would've said was lost as a hellhound tackled him from behind.

"Bastien!" I skidded to a stop, then saw the approaching

red-black beast from the corner of my eye. I pivoted, bringing up my blade. It was next to nothing compared with the bulk of the thing slamming me to the ground, but I stuck it to the hilt in its chest. My pivot kept my head from banging on the rocks directly, but a shock wave of pain blossomed in my left shoulder, and my bare legs scraped along the ground. The hound threw its head back in a roar of pain. I yanked the athame out and slashed under its throat, shutting my eyes as dark ichor poured from the wound. It slumped to the side and I rolled out from under it, looking for Bastien.

He was under his attacker, his right arm shoved in its mouth as it gnashed at him, red blood pouring from its attack. I hurried over and sank my athame into its back; it released him long enough to snap at me, though it didn't manage to land a blow. *Two witches in hell with one blade and no magic between us! What I wouldn't give for Remi's—*

"Bastien! Use your power, make a weapon!" I yelled. "Like Remi does!"

For a moment, nothing happened, and panic that he either couldn't or had no idea what I meant took hold of me. But then dark-blue shadows swirled loosely around his left hand before solidifying into a short, serrated folding blade: a rigging knife. With a yell, he slashed viciously at the hound, fighting back with a rage I'd never seen in him.

Rage! Of course! How angry he'd been when making that portal; how angry we had suddenly been with each other at the stupidest possible time; how Bastien was screaming with it as he hacked at the hound that had been on him, even though it was no longer moving.

"Bastien! Stop, it's dead!" I called out, staying far enough away that I wouldn't accidentally get hit.

He did stop, finally, sitting back on his heels and panting. His arm had a nasty bite mark, still oozing blood, and the rest of him was spattered with black ichor. Cursing, I wiped my knife on the hide of one of the hounds and then used it to carefully cut away the left sleeve of the shirt I was wearing. It was awkward at best, as every movement of my left arm set off a burst of pain in my shoulder. "Give me your arm," I instructed, kneeling next to him. My shins protested, already scraped and bruised, but between us we got his arm wrapped up. "That'll have to do for now. Are you okay otherwise?"

"Yeah, I…fuck. No, no, I am not at *all* okay," Bastien said, uttering a rare actual swear word. He looked at the shadow-knife in his hand, half-amazed, half-disgusted. It disappeared into a puff of blue shadows. "How did you know…?"

"This place is starting to make sense to me. Your magic doesn't work here, but your *power* does. I'm pretty sure you opened a portal into the part of this place that belongs to the Archdemon of Rage. It's what you said earlier, how you found me: like calls to like here. You were angry when you opened the portal, and those hounds made us both angry when they howled."

Bastien slowly nodded. "Makes a certain sense. Rage has hellhounds, too?"

"Turns out every demon loves dogs," I said.

"I thought you said my magic and the power were insep-arable? How can one work here but not the other, then?" he asked, getting to his feet and then helping me up.

"I don't know. Maybe there *is* a way to separate them. Or maybe it's like working with one hand tied behind your back." I said, shrugging, then crying out in pain. "Which is an apt analogy right now. I think I dislocated my shoulder."

"Hang on, I remember Brooke going on about how to do this properly…" He guided me through reaching my arm up and then over and across my body, and sure enough it popped back into place. It was still plenty sore, though, so he cut the other sleeve off and made a makeshift sling out of it for me.

"You need to close that portal before anything else comes after us," I said after my arm was settled. "I don't think we can survive another pair of hellhounds." Bastien agreed, and we made our way back. Thankfully, nothing else had come through yet.

Bastien made a few gestures, but aside from the dark-blue shadows swirling around his hands, nothing happened. I could see his frustration growing. "Some sorcerer I am," he muttered.

My brow went up. "Sorcerer?"

"What I have isn't magic and it isn't power. *Sorcery* seems as good a word as any," he explained, making another attempt that likewise failed. "*Ferme la porte.* Dammit!"

"It's a portal to Rage, Bastien. You're gonna have to let go of yours to close it," I pointed out.

"That's going to be a little difficult," he admitted, his brow lined with anger and irritation.

"Since when are you incapable of difficult things?" I said, forcing a lighthearted tone.

His answering smile was more like a grimace. "Be that as it may…"

He took a few deep breaths before trying again, but it made no difference. He'd played his answer off as a joke, but I was starting to see that it wasn't. I'd always known there was more to him under his society mask, even back when we were teens, but I'd never seen him like this.

But why shouldn't he be angry? Everything in his life had been taken from him, right down to his sense of self. His grandfather had used me to shame him. His magic had been forever altered by the demon who used him and broke his heart. His hotel had been nearly destroyed, and his own home wasn't his own. He was living in his own guest bedroom, and now monsters were breaking into the place.

And his one plan for trying to put some of it right had landed him in the Pit itself and then tossed his hot mess of an ex at him for good measure.

It was a wonder he hadn't burned something to the ground already.

Probably because even under all that, at his core, he was someone who cared deeply about the people around him. Which in turn made me finally contemplate just how much trouble he was bringing down on himself with this ritual he was planning, because it was absolutely the kind of trouble I knew well. Now I knew what he hadn't been telling me earlier, possibly because he hadn't realized it yet himself.

"Stop, stop," I said aloud. "This isn't gonna work."

"No kidding," he agreed, panting. "Maybe this only works one way. It's not like I've been able to get us out of here."

"It's not that, it's you," I replied. "You're still too angry."

"I'm doing the best I can," Bastien replied evenly. "If anger were so easy to let go of, there wouldn't be an Archdemon thriving off of it."

"Bullshit."

His attention sharply snapped to me. "Excuse me?"

"Own your anger, Bastien. Don't let it own you."

His eyes narrowed. "What exactly do you think I'm trying to do?"

I walked a few paces to stand in front of him. The heat from the burning landscape through the portal hit, and I could feel myself sweating already. "I think you're trying to ignore it, and that isn't the same thing."

Bastien let out a breath through his nose. "I have it under control."

I gestured at the portal. "Be that as it may?"

He rolled his eyes. "Fine. If you're the expert, how should I master my ill-gotten power?"

It could be his own anger making him snippy, or the proximity to Rage's land. Either way, I tried to treat it as valid. "Be honest about what you're really mad about." He gestured for me to go on. "I believe you've got most of it under control. Anger at Saranthiel, Brooke, your grandfather—hell, maybe your parents for staying out of Arcadia politics so much. Me."

"You've compiled quite a list."

"Yet it's incomplete, because the person you're the most mad at is you." His jaw tightened. "*You* fell in love with a demon. *You* married her. She used you and it—" Flashes of Jackie Harwell's lifeless body filled my mind. "—and it destroyed your life. You're furious and you're ashamed and you want to bury everything that reminds you of how you failed."

The storm had filled his eyes again, but this time the anger behind them wasn't cold, it was burning. "What makes you think that?"

"Because—" I tapped his chest, and then mine. "—like calls to like."

The anger dimmed, its form shifting. "What happened to us was very, very different, McKenna."

"It was, yeah. But that doesn't mean I don't know what that feels like. Bastien, why do you think I ran for ten years? To protect everyone, yeah, but also to run the hell away from what I'd done. From how much I fucked up and that it cost someone's *life*. Hells, at least you got over the running-away phase a lot faster than I did, I'll give you that!"

He shook his head. "I'm not trying to run, I'm trying to make things right, as much as I can."

"I know. You're putting everything you have into this and barely asking anyone for help," I replied, and pointed at myself. "Remind you of anyone?"

"I'm working with Cyrus—"

"You've got way more to lose in this than he does."

"It's for Wendy—"

"Who would tell you to forget it because she doesn't blame you for what happened to her," I said with confidence.

He scowled. "And wanting my magic to go back to normal? Is that me hating myself, too?"

I had to give him that one. "No. But no one likes to be reminded of the worst things that ever happened to them." I held up my left hand, with the self-inflicted scar in the middle of the palm, where I'd stabbed myself to banish Saranthiel after she made me kill Jackie. "Unfortunately, we don't get to choose our scars."

Bastien looked at me with another grim and rueful smile. His eyes were tearing up, though they didn't spill over. I reached for his hand with my good arm. "So instead of being so angry at yourself, may I point out how this is not all your fault? And suggest that you not take it all on yourself?" I asked, using words he'd once said to me.

A strangled laugh escaped him, and his hand gripped mine like a vise. His jaw clenched a few times, and he breathed like he was trying to leash some unruly beast. "Does it get any easier?"

"We're both stuck in the Pit, you tell me," I said, earning myself another bark of humorless laughter. "It does and it doesn't. You learn to live with the scars. Some fade, some you can't even see. They're part of you now, but you get to decide what that means."

Bastien took in a longer breath, one that seemed to steady him more than the others. "That's…reassuring, I suppose. Thank you."

"Anytime," I replied. "So, how about you close this thing?" I looked at the portal and saw motion in the distance. "Now would be good!"

Bastien faced the portal again, almost glaring at it. He gestured with one hand—his other was still holding mine—and spoke no words. I'd seen his grandfather cast without words, it was the mark of a master-level witch, but rarely did Bastien do so, and never with the ease he showed now. Dark-blue shadows swirled, and the ripped edges of the portal knit themselves back together, like a wound healing over, until there was no sign of it having been there at all. This close, with my hand in his, I could feel his power at work. It was a cool sensation in my blood, a comforting sort of coolness, especially in the wake of the heat of Rage's domain.

He blinked, staring in disbelief at the space where the portal had been. "I did it." His voice was hard to read—emotionless, but not in the forced way he often resorted to.

"You did," I confirmed gently; the moment felt fragile somehow.

Bastien stepped forward, moving his hand through the air where the portal had been. "There's not even a trace of it. And nothing needed, no words, no runes, no circle." His hand dropped. "The best portal closure I've ever done…and it wasn't even with magic."

His breath hitched once before a cry tore from him and he staggered, sobbing. I rushed forward, catching him in my one good arm. "I'm here. I've got you."

We sank to the ground, and I held him as he collapsed onto my shoulder and his world collapsed around him.

Chapter 14
There's Only One Cave

This time, when we made it back to the cave, it was Bastien who fell asleep on my lap, my fingers idly stroking his hair as he rested. With my left hand, of course; with my right hand I still held my athame, just in case. I didn't feel a need to sleep. Maybe because I'd done so earlier, or maybe it was part of the weird timelessness of the Pit.

Bastien hadn't said much throughout his breakdown, but he hadn't needed to. I understood too well what it was to realize there was no escaping what you'd been forced to become. If anything, I'd been putting off examining my latest iteration of that realization.

Knowing Cyrus was my father, knowing he specialized in metamagic, did finally give context to aspects of my magic. I wasn't sure what to make of the man himself. He seemed decent, but I'd known him less than a day. Bastien and my mom vouching for him helped. Cyrus hadn't held back in protecting Mom when the seekers attacked, and he didn't like the

Council, so he had that going for him. He not only wanted to reverse her severing, he also had a plan for doing so. If it actually worked, the ramifications would be immense. It would absolutely change how we doled out justice among ourselves, and with that ground broken, what else might come crumbling down with it?

And would that be such a bad thing?

On the other hand, the story about why Cyrus had been nearly severed but ultimately banished was concerning. Had Frank Milton's death really been an accident? I also didn't love how much risk Bastien was taking on with this ritual they were crafting. Bastien would do it. The crushing weight of guilt and the free fall of your life being in ruins were a perfect mixture for making needlessly self-destructive decisions. (Ask me how I knew!) Even if it worked—scratch that, *especially* if it worked, there was no chance the rest of the Council would just let that slide, family or not. What if they severed him? If he no longer had sorcery, to use his word for it, what place would he have among witches? What if they banished him from Arcadia, too?

The thought carved a pit in my stomach. He'd already lost so much. *I've already lost him twice. I don't want to do it a third time.* I looked down at his sleeping form.

Arcadia Commons without Bastien wasn't right.

It wasn't the same without him there. It wasn't home. *I miss him. I want him there. I want . . .*

What did I want?

My eyes slowly traveled down to Bastien's body, my hand going still on his hair. My long-absent friend whom I had missed. My long-ago love whom I had abandoned. The man who'd held me through that awful panic attack, given me the literal shirt off his back, even cut my hair for me. The person who'd visited my mother for years when she was institutionalized, and the only one who'd not hesitated to tell me the truth about what had happened to her when I came back to Arcadia Commons. The person whom I had thrown myself into finding the moment I knew he was missing.

I want . . . Bastien.

The thought bloomed through my body in a wave of heat. It was like a veil had lifted, and I finally let myself really look at him. He'd always been good looking, but he'd become an incredibly handsome man while I was gone. Even bloodstained and battle-damaged . . . actually, those were kinda doing it for me, too. Whether he was wearing one of his expensive and well-tailored suits or this, he looked damn good doing it. But it was the person underneath all that who truly had my admiration. My affection. *Oh, my god, am I blushing?*

He shifted in his sleep, one hand moving to rest on my thigh.

Well. I was definitely blushing now.

Whoa, whoa, slow down. He just had a total emotional breakdown in front of you, and his life is kind of in a complete shambles! This is not the time to go suggesting . . . whatever it is I might potentially be thinking about suggesting, I reprimanded myself. Maybe after we got out of here, or after we got through this trial. Maybe then we could talk.

And, of course, there was the Remi of it all. I hadn't made her any promises, but after the last few days, I knew I still felt something for her, too. At the very least, I owed her some answers.

Remi...holy shit. Remi!

I had a truly terrible idea. But it was crazy enough that it just might work.

I must have moved or made a noise at my revelation, because Bastien stirred, blinking awake. He looked up at me, storm-blue eyes calm again at last. "Hey. Everything okay?"

"Yeah, everything's fine," I said, my hand still resting against his hair. He smiled at me, unguarded, and my heart thumped again. "No one here but us humans. How are you feeling?"

"That's a relief. I'm...how'd you put it? I'm better." He sat up, sitting next to me, his knee bumping mine. "Thank you for getting us here and keeping watch."

"Of course." I set the athame down, finally, though I kept it close.

"And for helping me get that portal closed," he added after a pause. "I...I probably should've tried to get a handle on how to use this..."

"...sorcery?" I suggested. "It was a good word."

"Not one with a great history," he remarked, though he nodded. "But sure. I should've figured out how to use this sorcery a while ago."

"From who?" I asked. "It's not like this has ever happened before. Or if it has, how in the world would you find out?"

"True. Hopefully, it won't even be an issue for much longer, though," Bastien replied.

"Right. If your ritual works."

He hung his head, eyes on the fire. "You still don't think it will."

I shrugged one shoulder. "I have some doubts, yes. But it's not like we haven't done impossible shit before." He nodded again, but I could feel the shakiness to it. I reached over with my good hand to grasp his. "Hey. Whether it does or doesn't, you're not in this alone. I promise."

He looked up at me, and I could see the assurance meant as much to him as it had to me when I came back home. He believed me, which was good, because I meant it. He clasped his other hand on top of mine. My fingers tingled at the contact. "That helps to know. Though if it doesn't...I expect this won't be the last time I have an episode like this."

"Yeah, wish I could tell you these things are one and done, but as you've already seen from me, not so much," I said, scrunching my face apologetically.

"Few things are," he said, smiling in a what-can-you-do kind of way. Or...not? Was it my imagination, or was he looking at me like I might be included in that statement?

Get a grip, Ellerbeck! I cleared my throat, glad that the dimming fire likely hid the color on my cheeks. "Okay. Situation check-in. We're both injured, we've got one knife and a smattering of sorcery between us, a fire that's nearly burned out, and nothing new to throw on it. Unless we wanna start burning clothing."

"I think that would only make our situation worse in the long run," he said, letting out a breath. "We need light, at least, but if you're going to point out we're not in a good position to go out and get more, I agree. Unfortunately, we need to do something."

"We do," I agreed. "And I have an idea that might get us out of here."

His brows lifted. "Oh? What's that?"

"It's, uh . . . it's out there, but . . . hear me out. This place runs on like calling to like, right? We both portaled with or near one of the few things still loyal to the Archdemon of Secrets, so I'm pretty sure we're in the section of the Pit that belongs to Secrets. Whether or not that's Dara—Remi's new assistant, long story—consensus seems to be that the Archdemon of Secrets has been MIA for centuries and all their minions ditched them. That's why this place is so empty."

Bastien nodded. "With you so far."

"Same logic, you opened a portal to Rage because you were angry." He nodded again. "So, we have two options: one, figure out a way to get you to portal us home—"

"I'm happy to try, but believe me, I had some very strong thoughts and feelings about wanting to get back there when I first portaled here. Nothing happened," he said.

"I figured. Which leaves us with option two. We portal into Remi's part of the Pit," I said, looking anywhere but at him. "From there, finding her or getting a message to her should be much easier."

"How do we—*oh*." His eyes went wide as the light bulb went on. "Remi. Archdemon of Desire."

"And Madness, but, uh, I'm both less clear on and less inclined to try and make that connection." I tucked my hair behind my ear, keenly missing the longer locks. Twisting my fingers in it to expend my nervous energy felt excessively twee when they were that close to my face.

A silence the approximate length of an extended edition ensued until I pressed my hands to my face and shook my head. "Sorry. Forget it. We'll work on the home angle. Now that you've opened something once, maybe we can—"

"McKenna." Bastien took my hands in his, slowly pulling them down. "It's okay." His eyes on mine, unguarded, somehow only made me feel more twisted up.

"You sure? 'Cause, uh, asking one ex to make out with you so you effectively break into your other ex's house seems pretty freaking weird to me," I jested nervously.

He laughed lightly. "Weird, yes. But I can think of worse things than kissing you," he assured me, his voice soft. A fluttering feeling filled my chest, and I risked a smile.

"Likewise. For the record," I told him, and he smiled in return.

"And needs must and all." The fluttering wilted before he made a face. "I'm sorry, that's not—please forget I said that."

"No, it's . . . it is what it is," I said, quashing my own butterflies. This was just to get us out of here. Could be worse, like he said. "Straightforward, not complicated. Like riding a bike, right?" He gave me a bemused look, and I rolled my eyes at myself. "Okay, if this is the plan, please make me shut up before I sound like more of an idiotic teenager."

He smiled, chuckling again, a pleasant quiet rumble of a sound. We moved so we faced each other, still holding hands. With one of his, he reached over and tucked my hair behind my other ear. His gaze was soft, his eyes tracing over my face as his thumb brushed my cheek and his fingers moved along my jaw. But instead of feeling examined, I felt admired. And

invited to admire him in return. I licked my lips, my eyes falling on his, then catching him looking at my mouth as well.
Our eyes met again, and we both blushed. "McKenna," he
asked quietly, pulling his glasses off and setting them aside,
"can I kiss you?"

*First date. Sitting at the docks. His hand in mine was an anchor,
a lifeline, a solid thing that made me feel safe. "Can I kiss you?" he
whispered.*

"Yes," I said. Then and now.

Last fall, Saranthiel had kissed me while pretending to be
him. That kiss had been sudden, hard, and empty.

How I'd ever thought that was him baffled me.

Bastien's lips met mine slowly, softly, and filled with such
care that it stole my breath. The same care that had already
begun to pull my heart toward him, lighting up every mote
in me that still knew how to hope. Once, twice, again and
again our lips met, each of us unhurriedly mapping the other's
mouth until they finally parted and his tongue slid against
mine. Electricity ran through me, my good arm sliding
around his neck as one of his went around me, the other tangling in my hair as the kiss deepened.

We parted for a moment, both of us breathless, eyes bright
and wordlessly staring at each other before coming together
again. He pulled me closer and I readily went, sitting astride
his lap. His lips left mine, making their way across my jaw,
somehow still maddeningly slow yet perfectly paced, finding
the pulse point there and teasing it with his tongue. I groaned,
needing to taste him again, turning my head to find and kiss
his ear, lightly grazing his lobe with my teeth until I heard

him gasp aloud. His hand found my bare leg, sending a jolt of desire straight to my core. He captured my mouth with his again as the same hand skated up my side, under the shirt, alighting every nerve along the way. "*Toi, toi . . .*" he murmured against my lips. "*Toi et moi . . .*" He kissed me again, his fingers caressing the side of my breast.

Toi et moi. You and me. Words we'd said long ago, planning a future that had never come. Words he'd written on the ritual— and then scratched out.

Words that had become the engagement ring he'd given another woman.

My brain battled with my libido. One wanting more, wanting his hands and his mouth everywhere, wanting my lips tasting every inch of him, one reminding me why we were doing this and asking if those words were for me or just for whoever filled the space next to him. *Does it matter?* I asked myself . . . and found that yes, actually. It did.

I pulled back from the latest kiss; his lips made their way down my neck. "Bast. The portal," I reminded him breathlessly.

"The . . . fuck." *Oh, I wish.* "The portal. Right." Breathing heavily, keeping me right where I was but pulling his hand out from under the shirt, he gestured in the air, and another portal opened. Not as ragged as last time, either.

I smiled. "You did it!"

He smiled. "This one's definitely more of a *we*-did-it."

I laughed and then we were kissing again, the high of success fueling our desire anew. Or maybe it was the influence of the portal he'd opened and where it led. Either way, my niggling worries vanished and all I wanted was him, his lips, his skin on mine. One of his arms grabbed me under my ass and lifted me closer to him, pressing my hips against his hardness. I groaned again, running my hand down his chest, seeking the edge of his shirt to pull it off him—

"My, my, my. Aren't *we* cozy," purred a familiar voice.

Bastien and I froze. My lips left his, and I turned my head to find none other than Remi herself standing in the portal in a little black dress, arms crossed, hips canted, smirk firmly in place.

"One of the most unique invitations to a threesome I've ever gotten, though, I'll give you that," she went on. Her voice was teasing and flirtatious as usual, her expression, too, but I knew her smirk better than anyone. This one didn't quite reach her eyes.

"Remi!" I disentangled myself. "That's not—this isn't—"

"It most certainly isn't," Bastien agreed grimly, retrieving his glasses.

Remi pouted. "No? Shame, I came all this way."

I got to my feet, absently brushing my hair back in order. "We were—we needed to get a portal to your part of the Pit open," I finally explained.

Her grin widened. "Not the only Pit that was op—"

"Don't you even," I cut her off, glowering.

She gave me one of her I'll-humor-you sighs.

"How did you get here so quickly?" Bastien asked. He passed me my pants, which were finally dry enough to wear again. I went about pulling them on, accepting Bastien's help in staying steady while doing so one-handed.

"When McKenna disappeared halfway to the ground, I knew something was up. Once everyone was in a state to discuss it—"

"Is Cameron okay?" I interrupted. "And Mom? And Gretchen?"

"For varying definitions of *okay*, but yes, they're all recovering, no one's dead or dying," Remi assured me. I felt a huge weight lift from me just knowing that. "I got an inkling that maybe the tainted magic in that ring had something to do with it. Bastien's dear departed wife—"

"*Never* call her that," Bastien growled, throwing a dark look her way.

Remi shrugged. "Saranthiel had used that magic to open a portal to the Pit, so it stood to reason you might've done the same. I spent quite a while searching her old stomping grounds, with no luck. And you should be glad for that, that place makes an animatronic arcade gone wrong look downright pedestrian, ugh." She shook her shoulders out. "I really need to remodel. Anyway, then, just as I get into my usual demesne, what should I feel but the alluring sensation of someone trying to get it on and get into my territory. I wander over and voilà, here we all are, some of us more dressed than others." Her eyes looked me up and down as I finally finished doing up my jeans. "So that's me. What exactly has been going on with you two and this darling little cave you've moved into?"

"It's . . . a long story," I said, exchanging a look with Bastien. I wasn't about to go spilling his secrets for him; he didn't trust her the way I did. "I panicked on the fall and used the magic from the ring. It landed me here, which is where Bastien had portaled to when the seeker attacked him the other day. We're pretty sure this is part of the Pit that belongs to Secrets."

"Oo, the plot thickens! No one's been here in a while. Is there even anyone left?"

"Some nasty crab demons in the water, but that's about it."

Remi looked us over. "Looks like they put up quite the fight," she observed.

"They do, though the worst of this is from a pair of Rage hellhounds," Bastien put in. "Her things needed to dry out," he added as he handed me my shirt and remaining sneaker, though there seemed little point in putting either of them on.

"The good old let-me-get-out-of-these-wet-things ploy, eh? A classic never goes out of style," Remi teased, though once again I could see she was compensating.

"How long have I been gone?" I asked, changing the subject. "And can you take us back home?"

"About two days—and what a two days it's been! You've missed quite the drama—and yes, technically," Remi said.

"Drama?" I asked.

"Technically?" Bastien asked.

"Put a pin in the drama bit. Passage out of the Pit is a considerable favor. Not one I can just hand out for free. But tell me everything that actually happened while you were here and I think we can call it even," Remi offered, then smirked. "And I do mean *everything*."

Bastien scowled. "Never miss a chance to take advantage, do you?"

"I can't stop being a demon any more than you can stop

being human, Lemaire," Remi replied flatly. "This is literally how I function."

He looked about to retort, so I thrust my hands up to stop him. "Deal. Information for transport, healing, and comfort. And new clothes. Now can we go, please?"

She shook Bastien's hand and then mine, and an uncomfortably hot sensation settled on my skin as she did. "Yeah, you've taken your postapocalyptic chic a few steps too far. Ooh, but I see someone got a significant haircut! Intriguing." Remi walked through the portal to her domain, waving for us to follow. "Come on, let's get you back to civilization."

I was relieved to be going back home finally, but as I turned to share that sentiment with Bastien, leaving took on a bittersweet note. This cave had turned into a small sanctuary, a safe haven in a dangerous place, where we'd held each other, shared secrets, and shared a downright earth-shattering kiss. He, too, looked uncertain for a moment, until I took his hand.

"Let's go home," I said.

His expression stabilized some and he nodded.

We stepped through the portal together, and with his other hand he closed it behind us.

The lusty ambience of Remi's domain hit us, bringing that intimate and interrupted moment rushing back to mind. My hand tightened on his as I sucked in a breath.

He squeezed back, but then he looked at our hands. "Maybe we…shouldn't…" he said, suddenly awkward.

"Oh, yeah. Probably not a good idea here," I agreed, and reluctantly let go. He lingered a moment, but his expression had become more closed off again. His mask was slipping back into place.

He followed Remi, and I followed him, and somehow it was only then that I wondered if the reason we'd both been so open was that we'd been in the realm of the Archdemon of Secrets.

Remi looped an arm around each of us, making some flirty quip I only half heard, and teleported us all back to her condo in Arcadia Commons. Every sensation that had been dulled or erased by the Pit came back in full force—I was starving and thirsty and everything hurt. Bastien was in a similar state, and for once Remi put aside smirking to get us taken care of. She used her power to heal our cuts and bruises and then filled us with a not-unpleasant combo of sports drinks and bread. She shooed me to the master bathroom and Bastien to the guest room, promising that clean clothes would be available for us both by the time we'd washed up.

I was so exhausted that the mere idea of standing up for an entire shower was too much to deal with. Instead, I filled the tub and threw in a bath bomb I found in the cabinet and sank into wonderfully warm, purple-tinted, lavender-scented water. I gave myself permission to let go of everything else and zone out. By the time I had cleaned off the grime of the Pit, the water had turned cool and gray. I dried off and found Remi had retrieved some comfortable clothes from my home, including some pajamas (I decided to be grateful instead of bothered). As I was curling up on her extremely soft king-size bed, her black cat, Mr. Mephistopheles, pounced up onto the comforter, circled, and lay down next to me, a warm pile of purrs that instantly lulled me to sleep.

It was a wonder I didn't dream of hellhounds.

A gentle knock woke me some time later. Remi poked her head through the door, scanning my body for signs of alertness. "You awake? No is an acceptable answer."

I stretched out, feeling decently rested. Mr. M stretched with me, having shifted in the night to tuck himself up next to my face. I scratched his chin after. "I'm awake. But please tell me there's coffee."

"Obviously," Remi replied, opening the door farther and carrying in a mug of hot, precious caffeine. The cat trotted out into the rest of the condo to inspect his kingdom. "Feeling better?"

"Still sore, but yeah." I sat up and sipped the brew, glancing at the window. It had been around sunset when I'd lain down, but it looked like morning now. "I slept the whole night?"

"You both did. Spending a lot of time in the Pit is disorienting when you come back to the mortal world. Moreso, it seems, if you're not a demon," Remi said, sitting on the bed.

My eyes flicked to the door. "Is Bastien still here?"

"Crashed in the guest bedroom. I assume you two were okay with separate rooms," she said far too casually, studying her nails.

Sigh. "Can we not do this? I'm barely recovered, and you haven't even heard the whole story yet."

"Do what?" Remi said, with a faux innocence that neither of us believed. She saw my dubious look and gave up the pretense. "All right, all right. But can I say just two things and assure you that you need not react to either?"

"Okay..." I agreed warily.

"One, do us all a favor and don't pretend that little moment I interrupted wasn't real. I heard you say it was something about connecting with my domain, and maybe it was. But I'm the Archdemon of Desire, and I know real desire when I see it," she told me. She was surprisingly straightforward about it.

I opted for a simple nod, despite knowing my face was tellingly flushed. "Noted," I said. "And the second thing?"

"Two..." Remi leaned closer, her eyes dark and intense, her fiery scent filling my senses. A warmth emanated from her, sinking into my skin like a promise unspoken, though she didn't actually lay a finger on me. "As I told you, whatever you want this to be, I'm happy to have it, to give you. Including you not having to make a choice."

The suggestion slowly percolated, though it was utterly unexpected. This was not a place for vagueness. "What do you mean, exactly?"

"I mean, I'm okay with sharing. Maybe even being shared," she added with a smirk, but then she was serious again. "We have been open before, after all."

With Forneus being the Archdemon of Desire, he had tried to encourage me to act accordingly. I'd never been comfortable with it and almost never acted upon it. Not as much as he'd have liked me to, certainly. But understanding the position I was in, Remi had been clear when we dated back then that she was not the jealous type.

But that had been out of necessity. This was another thing entirely. "That was different," I said, the unwelcome memory making me glower.

"I know. And I'm by no means interested in forcing you—either of you—into something you don't truly want," Remi said. "But desire comes in many forms. I'm just letting you know you have options." She ran a finger through a lock of my hair and smiled. "I like the hair, by the way."

I was suddenly vibrating from much more than the coffee, my nerves and my imagination threatening to explode. I had barely started to come to terms with having feelings for Bastien again, and to now have Remi suggesting I could be with them both and she, at least, was completely fine with that? *That is . . . that is* not *something I have the capacity to unpack right now.*

Remi had said something while I was busy attempting to process. "What?" I asked.

She smirked. "Sorry, didn't mean to break your brain. I said, your brother is at the hospital, but in stable condition now, and so is Gretchen."

That was a lot better than how I'd last seen both of them. "That's good."

"I figured you'd want to know they're okay. Same for your mom and her boy toy," Remi said. "Who, by the by, is shacking up with her at your place. I overheard the two of them while retrieving your things."

"Too much information!"

She laughed. "Believe it or not, I just meant I heard them talking, but I do assume they're doing some non-talking as well."

"I am begging you to stop. What was the drama in town you mentioned?" I asked, desperate to change the subject.

"That, yeah…let's go group up with Golden Boy and I'll fill you both in," Remi said. "You get dressed. I'll get breakfast." She kissed my cheek, lingering just enough to remind me of her earlier suggestions. I finished my coffee and got dressed—Remi had brought a pair of jeans, a simple but comfortable T-shirt, and my favorite pair of everyday boots. I also finally took the time to properly look at myself and my new haircut. It wasn't perfect, but Bastien's work was a significant improvement. It now fell to an inch or so above my shoulders, and to be honest, I didn't hate it. It was wavy from air-drying the night before and swished in a fun sort of way. I'd worn it long for years, but maybe I had been overdue for a change after all.

Satisfied, I took my empty mug and headed into the main room of the condo to face whatever fresh hell the day was going to bring me.

Chapter 15
Tarnished Gold

Remi's condo was largely taken up by an open-concept room designed to let you feel the space. The living room was two stories tall, with big windows looking out at the ocean, and, come evening, offered a gorgeous view of the sunset. The kitchen was open to the living area, with a wraparound U-shaped marble counter that only took breaks for stainless steel appliances. One end served as a counter, with a few stools tucked under on the other side. A small dining table that did not see much use, as far as I knew, sat just outside the kitchen area, and between that and the plush couches and widescreen TV in the sitting area was a well-stocked bar that saw a lot more use. Her decor leaned heavily into lush gem tones, primarily dark reds, purples, and blues. It resulted in a space that felt both expansive and intimate at once.

Bastien was in the kitchen, pouring himself some coffee, with Mr. M rubbing against his legs for attention. He was clean and dressed as well, and I nearly did a double take when

I saw his outfit—a pair of dark slacks and a white T-shirt that were both far more fitted than anything I'd seen him wear before, but damn if he didn't look good in them. He wore an unbuttoned vest over the T-shirt in what might have been an attempt at modesty, to combat the clinging of the shirt to his chest. The morning sun lit his hair almost like a halo, gold and glinting, and his glasses were now free of scratches and other damage. He turned as he heard me approach and smiled in greeting, offering the coffeepot.

"Yes, please," I replied, holding out my mug. "So … this is a new look for you," I remarked, looking him over.

Bastien looked slightly embarrassed. "I didn't want Remi poking around in my house, so she offered some of her menswear for me to borrow. It's better than what I had, at least."

I couldn't hide my grin. "That explains it, this is definitely more her vibe than yours." It also explained why the pants were barely covering his ankles; Bastien was a few inches taller than Remi's male form. "But for what it's worth, not a bad look."

The color in his cheeks warmed me in turn. "Ah, thanks, I think. Have you had anything to eat yet? I haven't been able to find much outside of alcohol and coffee around here."

"Somehow I'm not surprised," I started to say.

"Fear not, hot pants, I've got breakfast," Remi interrupted, appearing from a room she referred to as her office and setting a bag from Rocket Café on the counter.

"Hot pants, really?" I repeated, raising an eyebrow at her.

"Who said I was talking to you? He's filling those out almost as well as I do," Remi replied with a saucy grin, throwing a wink at Bastien, who nearly choked on his coffee.

"I appreciate the loan, but don't ever call me that again," he said between coughs.

"Would you prefer sweetcheeks?" He glared at her. "Fine, fine. We'll workshop it. Now, since we're all awake and fully patched up, let's eat, and you two tell me what the hell you were doing in Hell?"

I distributed the breakfast sandwiches—the ones with meat to Bastien and Remi, vegetarian sausage to myself. "I thought it *wasn't* actually Hell?" Bastien said.

Remi shrugged. "Not in the religious sense. Or maybe it is, I don't know, but it certainly has the vibe. Stop stalling."

Bastien and I sat on the stools and recounted everything to Remi. I braced myself for her to get either flirtatious or nosy about how we'd opened the portal to her region of the Pit, but for once she ceded to better sense so we could focus on the rest. Bastien needed an occasional prompt to share the information on the state of his magic when we got to that, and we divulged the plan he and Cyrus had been making for co-opting the severing ritual.

"McKenna told me what you said about demonic power being only removable by death," Bastien said. Mr. M had joined us after eating his own breakfast, leaping up onto Bastien's lap, circling, and lying down with a plaintive meow. The cat was now receiving the requested attention and pets while we talked. "But if there's any chance, surely having access to the leylines' power will do it."

"If anything. I wouldn't hold my breath if I were you, Lemaire," Remi replied. "And I think you're forgetting an important factor. How do you expect to remove the very same power that you're using to cast this spell?"

"My understanding of how this affects my magic has shifted since we first planned the spell, but that's why there are two casters. As the accusing side's advocate, if and when the vote to sever is made, the spell to open the nexus goes through me. In the ritual we've designed, that is still my role. I open and close, Cyrus does the actual surgery, if you will," Bastien replied. "It's a complicated spell that we need to make simple. Which is also why I want to bring McKenna in on it."

"As a third caster?" Remi asked.

"If we had more time, maybe. We're too close to the trial to change the spell that much. But I'd rather have her checking our work and be aware of what's going on since she'll be there, too."

"Smart idea," Remi agreed.

"I'd rather be involved in casting. Especially with how my magic interacts with power," I pointed out.

Bastien was less convinced. "You're not a metamagic witch on the same level Cyrus is. Even if he is—" He brought himself up short, as we had not yet told Remi this part.

Remi looked between us. "If he's…what?" Neither of us spoke. "Come on, spill. You made the deal."

I sighed. "My father."

Remi blinked. "Wait, what? He's your…but what about that other asshole?"

I shrugged. "Apparently not actually a biological relation. While we were in the clock tower, mom told Cyrus and me that he's my actual father. I don't know more than that, aside from knowing they used to date. Magically speaking, it explains certain things I'm good at that aren't part of the

Younger side, like manipulating other kinds of magic. Doesn't fully explain why I can manipulate demonic power, but it does cover part of it."

"I guess so. That's got to be a bit of a mind fuck," Remi said. Her warm fingers brushed mine on the table. "How are you handling it?"

I smiled weakly. "Mostly avoiding thinking about it too much."

She chuckled ruefully, her fingertips squeezing mine. "That's my girl."

Bastien cleared his throat, and I self-consciously tugged my hand away from Remi's, picking up my coffee mug as he went on. "Anyway, even with that being the case, Cyrus has more experience using metamagic, particularly with how severing works. Given our time constraints, and with no offense meant for your own abilities, I think it's best we stick with that plan."

"Fair enough," I conceded.

Remi clapped her hands together with a pleased smile. "Well! This is downright diabolical, Lemaire. I'm impressed, I didn't think you had it in you." The cat turned over in Bastien's lap, showing his belly and purring loudly. "Looks like Mr. M agrees. I've still got questions, however. How does Cyrus even get in there? How does Wendy? How do you disrupt the spell everyone thinks they're casting?"

"We're still working some of it out, but Cyrus planned to use an illusion or glamour to get himself and Wendy where they need to be," Bastien replied.

"Mm-hm. And how do you stop the Council from interfering?" Remi asked.

"Once the severing spell begins, it must be concluded," Bastien said. "There's no stopping midspell."

"And afterward? What happens to everyone then?" Remi asked.

I'd been wondering this myself. "There *are* going to be repercussions, Bastien. They might try to sever you, or banish you along with Cyrus this time."

"So what? If it works, this demonic magic in me is gone and I could restore my magic through the same spell." Bastien shrugged, but he didn't look at either of us directly. He'd yet to say anything about his plans once this was done, in fact, even when we were in the Pit.

This time, I wasn't going to let it go. "No, no 'so what.' This is much more serious than that, Bastien. Maybe we'll have proven magic can be restored, but also maybe not. And even if we have, we need access to one or more leylines to do it. That's not exactly easy to come by. You need to think about what comes after this. Or," I added, realizing maybe he had, "you need to tell me why you aren't talking about it."

"This *is* starting to sound like one of those fall-on-your-sword scenarios," Remi agreed. "Or are you relying on granddaddy to bail you out from the big scary consequences again?"

Bastien's eyes flashed at her, a sudden furious storm brewing in them. "What makes you think he did last time?"

Remi's smile was all sly lines and secrets. "Didn't he?"

"I've been persona non grata in my family since the wedding," Bastien said, his voice short and sharp. "My grandfather has handed me nothing but busywork for the great sin of falling for a demon and her schemes. My aunt openly scoffs at me, along with most of the rest."

"But…your parents would never…" I said, unable to picture it.

He smiled without joy. "No. No, they don't, and they wouldn't, nor my sisters. But their pity is nearly as intolerable."

"You want their respect," Remi said, her dark eyes rapt upon him.

"Yes." Bastien's answer was immediate.

"You had it. You lost it."

"Yes." His eyes were fixed on her as well, in a way that was slightly unnerving. "My immediate family chose to remove themselves from the politics of this town and of our family. I chose otherwise. I thought I was building to something, to being someone. To being—to being on the Council." He didn't look at me, but I felt the weight of his attention all the same. "Now I see that was nothing but being made into my grandfather's tool. Once the truth about Saranthiel came out, I was reduced to nothing but a fool in his eyes."

I wanted to argue. But when I'd asked Laurent why the open spot on the Council wasn't being offered to Bastien, he'd admitted he didn't trust Bastien's judgment after what had happened. Fairness mattered almost as little as empathy to him.

"He told me…that he still intended for you to be on the Council one day. To lead it, even," I said.

Bastien raised one brow, but only just, and in the end didn't look surprised at all. "I'm sure he does. Once he's shaped me into a satisfactory vessel for all his opinions and intentions."

He shook his head. "Whether it's my family or Saranthiel, I've spent far too many years being someone's patsy. And I am *done* with it. I'm done being someone else's instrument." He spat the words. "If I'm to be severed or banished or disowned, so be it. At least it will be for my choices. I'll take that over being pitied and mocked any more."

His fervor echoed his anger at the Solstice Ball. This time, however, the wild storm in his gaze was not meant for me but for the people who had manipulated him and made him feel lesser. It was this strength, this potential, that I'd seen in him years ago, that I'd found so compelling. That I'd always wanted to see more of. It stirred the desire I'd had, months ago, years ago even, to change the Council and this town. To make it better, and if I was going to be damned for that, so be it. I'd go down on my terms and standing firm for my choices.

Something I was not so sure I'd been living up to of late.

I had the impulse to kiss him but was keenly aware we weren't alone. Instead, I slowly smiled as a new understanding unfurled. "You're really going full mask off with this."

"So he is," Remi said. Her eyes flickered with heat and power as she took him in; I wasn't sure if she was turned on physically, demonically, or both. "The Golden Boy's got some tarnish after all. Rebellious looks good on you, Lemaire."

Bastien actually gave her a mild smile this time. "Thanks."

"Okay, then," I said, looking at my co-conspirators. "Let's be rebels."

"I'll drink to that," Remi said, and we all clinked our coffee mugs.

Bastien set his mug down first. "The sooner I can reconnect

with Cyrus to finish planning, the better. This would also be easier to explain with a copy of the ritual spell we made."

"I had the taped-up one in my bag," I said, then asked Remi, "Do you know what happened to it? My phone was in there, too." I was anxious to be in touch with my family. Not to mention talk with my mom about Cyrus.

"Your mother took it, I think. Should we move this brunch of dissidents to the Ellerbeck residence, then?" Remi suggested, despite that we'd finished eating a while ago.

I nodded, but Bastien held up a hand. "Before we go, you mentioned we'd missed out on some 'drama' while we were away. What's been going on?"

"I think I'll go with show-don't-tell on this one. We'll take the scenic route back to Chez Ellerbeck," Remi said cryptically. Bastien and I exchanged a curious look.

"Fine by me. I'm a little over portal travel at the moment. A drive sounds good." I gave Mr. M some goodbye pets before we headed out.

Outside, I paused to soak in the sun and the familiar salt-scented air. I didn't want to go near the beach right now, but the smell was part of home for me. And Remi's neighborhood was about as far from watery, monstery doom as you could get. Built sometime in the last twenty years, the houses here were sparkling new compared with the majority in our very historical New England town. Nearly identical duplexes with white siding filled the few streets. It admittedly lacked character, and it was one of the last places you'd expect to find an Archdemon in residence, but bland Zen suited me just fine for now.

The restorative moment was ruined, however, by a sudden screaming match a few doors down. A man was out on his front lawn, cowering from a barrage of items a sobbing pregnant woman at the door was throwing at him. "You bastard! Get out of here, get out of my house!" she screamed, red-faced.

"Kendall, baby, it was just one time, it was a mistake—"

"Like hell! You've been ogling her since they moved in!"

I grimaced. "Yikes. When did this place go all *Real Housewives*?"

"Very recently, though that one's been brewing for a while. I was wondering if Kendall was ever going to figure it out," Remi said, twirling her car keys on her finger.

"You knew two of your neighbors were having an affair?" Bastien asked.

"Obviously." The *duh* was heavily implied. "The other one's pregnant, too. Hey, looks like there'll be a vacancy soon, Lemaire. Wanna be neighbors?" Remi flashed him a grin.

"Pass."

We got into Remi's bright-red Maserati, and I couldn't help but notice a few more expectant parents out taking strolls as we drove by "This place is really having a baby boom, huh?"

"People have to pass the time in those cold winter months somehow," Remi said, shrugging.

A shriek followed by a spray of water against the car pulled our attention to the other side of the car, where a woman was spraying her hose at a man who was yelling and slapping at his arms in a panic. "Get them off, get them off!" he cried.

"I'm trying!" the woman yelled back, casting a repulsed

look at the bushes in front of their house. "God, they're everywhere!"

Bastien was the first to say it. "What the hell?"

"Hornet's nest maybe? My neighbor did exactly that once when her husband tried to knock one down. He thought it was empty, it was not," I said, shuddering. "Poor Mr. Clement."

"I didn't see anything flying around him," Bastien said, craning his neck to look at the house, now behind us.

"The landscapers are good about getting on those before they're a problem, but maybe they missed one," Remi remarked.

"Paying an HOA fee and they still screw it up? Think I'll stick with non-condo living," I said.

"Which reminds me, rent is due," Remi said. Technically, she owned my house, but I was slowly buying it back via rent payments toward the mortgage. "You're good for this month?"

"Yeah, it's all set." Only just, though, given I'd missed a few days of work this week. I'd need to pick up some extra shifts.

"If this is what you were referring to, I fail to see how your neighborhood drama is worth filling us in on," Bastien said.

"Oh, we're just getting started. I predict some singularly unique people watching this morning," Remi said.

She was not wrong. Driving through downtown, we saw:

A woman throwing a full coffee cup at a man.

Two women screaming at a man and chasing him down the street.

A group of teenage girls in a full-on catfight, each with a

full handful of the other's hair, and a group surrounding them, half cheering them on and half trying to pull them apart.

Another teenager ranting at his phone, either on a video call or possibly streaming live online.

A man openly and very dramatically sobbing on a park bench.

A couple not-so-subtly tearing each other's clothes off as they ducked behind some shrubs that didn't provide nearly enough cover for that sort of thing. As evidenced by a woman on the street yelling at them to get a room.

A younger twenty-something hauling ass down the sidewalk as a Jeep tried to drive up on the sidewalk after him.

Two men arguing outside a convenience store, which ended with one of them ripping his name-tag pin from his shirt and throwing it on the ground before storming off.

And finally, police tape over the smashed windows and door of the bank, with tellers being interviewed outside by the police.

"Was there a *bank robbery*? In *Arcadia Commons*?" I asked, incredulous.

"What is going on?" Bastien asked. "I've never seen this many people arguing or acting out in public."

"Excellent question. It's been like this for the last few days, and word is that a number of Council members have been shut up in their homes as well," Remi told us.

"Not all of them—that's George O'Brien. Pull over," I requested, spotting my fellow Council member on the scene at the bank. I rolled down the window and called out to him. "George!" He looked around, squinting in the sunlight as he saw me.

"I didn't expect to see you until the meeting later," George said as he approached.

"There's a meeting today?" I asked. "When and where? My phone's been acting up."

"In about an hour, at the Lemaire mansion. Good thing I caught you."

"Definitely is, thanks. What's going on at the bank?"

"Some customers took umbrage with one of the tellers and started throwing rocks through the windows and the door," George told us.

"Relatable," Remi remarked. We all gave her a look. "Come on, have you *seen* bank fees lately?"

"Those are hardly the teller's fault," Bastien said.

"Bastien?" George noticed him. "In…Remi Blake's car, with your opposing advocate? What in the world are the three of you doing together?"

Remi smirked. "We had ourselves a little sleepover, and the least I could do was give them a ride home."

George was immediately flustered, and my face was once again aflame. "Oh, my god—that is not what happened!" I sputtered.

"I beg to differ," Remi said.

"Please ignore her, George," Bastien said, better composed than I, though I did notice his cheeks were pink. "What's going on in town? Everyone's acting…odd, to put it mildly. Surely you know something?"

George nodded, scanning the town square. "Sudden onset of brutal honesty, if you can believe it. I've had more calls and leads about local scandals in the last few days than the last ten years combined. For some reason, everyone decided to start confessing their darkest secrets all at once."

The three of us in the car shared a wary look.

"Like what?" Remi asked.

"Let's see—the police chief resigned after confessing to corruption, and a third of the force have been put on paid leave from fallout from that. That laundromat on the south side of town, Kyle's? Confirmed to be a front for laundering money. That one wasn't a shock, really. A ring of teens stealing packages from front steps confessed, estimates are that they've got a few thousand dollars' worth of merchandise on hand. Oh, and get this: Abby Bellerieve is suing Sofia Perez for harassment."

"What?" Bastien and I both said at once.

George nodded. "Abby claims that Sofia has been screwing with her sleep for months, making it impossible for her to sleep well, *and* that she cursed the beach, *and* that she fed false claims to the Better Business Bureau to try and get her B&B shut down. Supposedly Sofia admitted to all of it to her in person."

My jaw dropped. Abby had mentioned not sleeping well and business being slow the other day, but I'd had no idea it was that bad. Seeing as she was Brooke's aunt and guardian, it wasn't hard to imagine Sofia taking out her anger at Brooke on Abby, either. "What did Sofia say about it?"

"Nothing yet. She isn't answering my calls or emails," George said, checking his phone for good measure. "I'm surprised you didn't know about it," he added, to Bastien.

"Ah—yeah, I need to check in with her," Bastien said. "We

should let you get back to your work, though. Good talking to you, George."

"Of course. Stay safe, kids," George said. From him, I knew the "kids" was more reflex than anything else, given his children were our age.

Remi's eyes flicked between the two of us. "We all agree this is the Archdemon of Secrets at work, yes?"

"It's exactly what Dara said would happen," I said. "Secrets uses the seekers as a vanguard to destabilize a place before moving in on it. This place is *definitely* getting unstable."

"True, but this many people making sudden confessions and no public emergency about enormous squid monsters on the loose doesn't add up," Remi said. "Whatever's causing this, it can't be the seekers."

"Does Secrets have other minions? Or monsters, like the seekers, but more subtle?" Bastien asked.

"I don't know, but I'll ask Dara," Remi said.

"This is the same Dara who used to serve Secrets? And might actually be them?" Bastien asked.

"She is *not* the Archdemon of Secrets," Remi replied, rolling her eyes in my direction. "Would you stop telling people that?"

"She might be!"

"She's sworn to me, remember?"

"And the fact that these things showed up after she did?" I pointed out.

"Correlation is not causation, and she *did* help us, remember?," Remi replied. "She's the one who got Gretchen up to the clock tower, before she killed that second seeker, might

I remind you. She even killed another one that was outside before it could get in, too."

I had, admittedly, forgotten that. "That…might change things. I guess."

Remi smirked. "But you still don't like her?"

I made a grumpy noise, crossing my arms and looking out the window.

"Jealousy's not your best look, you know," Remi said smugly. I could feel my cheeks burning as surely as I could feel Bastien's eyes on the back of my head, though I didn't dare turn to look for the rest of the short drive.

My car wasn't in the driveway at the house; my mother not having her license didn't stop her from borrowing it sometimes. I punched in the garage code to get the spare key.

"I'll find my phone and call Mom. There's a copy of your ritual in my bag, too, Bast, but you'll want to make a clean one," I said as I unlocked the door leading from the garage to the kitchen. "Remi, can you check in with—Cyrus?"

Remi tilted her head in confusion, but there at the kitchen island with a mug of coffee, in a T-shirt and a pair of jeans, was Cyrus. I'd run into some of my mom's flings the morning after before, but none had been making themselves at home quite like this.

Nor had any of them been my biological father.

My brain buzzed for that first frozen moment. From the way his gaze fixed on me, maybe his was doing the same thing. Both of us trying to pick out anything that linked us to each other, any physical trait or sign. And I was also comparing him to the absentee father who'd left us years ago, searching for something, anything that I must've missed. How could I not have realized that man wasn't my father? How could Mom not have told me?

A further, unwelcome thought: Had she told *him*? Was *this* why my dad—her husband—had left and never bothered with us again?

Cyrus recovered first. "McKenna, Bastien! You're all right!"

"What are you doing here?" I bluntly asked in response.

Remi smirked. "I think we can all guess the answer to that one."

I gave her a look, and she held up her hands in surrender. I turned back to Cyrus, who had the decency to look embarrassed. "Where's my mom?"

"She's visiting Cameron," Cyrus replied. "He's going to be okay, he's at the hospital."

"I know. Why are you here without her?" I replied.

"I'm not sure what you've heard, but I'm not exactly a welcome face in this town. Given that, we figured it was better that I stay here, out of sight," Cyrus explained.

"Didn't stop you from being out and about the other day," I pointed out.

"I had a glamour then. It only lasted a day, and there hasn't been a chance to get another," he said. "But you two, what happened to you? Where have you been?"

"It's a long story," Bastien said, coming forward and shaking Cyrus's hand. "We can catch you up."

"Of course. Do you want some coffee? There's a fresh pot," he said.

You sure made yourself at home, didn't you? "It's my house. I can get my own coffee," I grumbled in reply, and went to do just that. I spotted my bag at the kitchen table and pulled out my phone, my grimoire, and the taped-together ritual from Bastien's house. Plugging in my phone to charge, I handed the ritual to Bastien. "I've got some blank sheets and pencils in my bag."

I busied myself with grabbing mugs for the coffee, even though I really didn't need a third cup, only to feel the gentle rest of Bastien's hand on my shoulder. Without words, I knew what it was saying: *Slow down, take a moment, it's okay.* Something in me shook at the very idea. Slowing down would mean...well, it would mean talking to Cyrus. Would mean dealing with this whole thing.

"You don't have to do it alone," Bastien murmured. His presence next to me was warm, comforting. My hand lifted to his and he squeezed my fingers.

"What if I don't want to do it at all?"

"That's your call, but avoiding it isn't much of an option right now," he pointed out.

"No kidding. Dude practically moved in already," I muttered, looking through the doorway to the living room, where Cyrus was typing on his phone. Remi was walking our way.

"Is this where the line to convince McKenna to talk to her bio-dad starts?" Remi quipped.

"Ha ha."

"You jest, but I see no lies," she said, gesturing at me and Bastien. "I won't pretend I know what this is like. Forneus was the closest thing I had to any kind of father figure, and we all know how healthy *that* relationship was. Cyrus seems to be a decent person. Cares about your mom, wants to get her magic back, helped Golden Boy here conquer his demons, doesn't like the Council, likes to make risky, dramatic plans. And you love all that shit," she listed, counting items off on her fingers. "Hell, he even throws down well in a fight."

"In short, he's actually a lot like you," Bastien concluded for her.

Remi grinned. "And now he's got the two of us agreeing."

"First time for everything," Bastien replied grudgingly.

I peered at Remi suspiciously, wondering what she was up to. "You're being awfully obliging."

"I contain multitudes," she said airily.

"Right..." Was this about her open-relationship suggestion again? *One complicated relationship at a time.* "Okay, okay. I'll talk to him. It might not be horrible, I guess. But I also need to get to that Council meeting soon. Remi, can you get an update from Lucca on any monster or demon attacks in the last few days?"

She saluted acknowledgement, Bastien retrieved fresh paper for the spell, and I went to talk to Cyrus.

He looked up from texting when I came in, with a look I could only describe as tentatively hopeful. Like someone approaching an animal, 90 percent sure it wouldn't bite. "Hi—uh. I texted Wendy to let her know you were back. She said she'll be back as soon as she can."

"Thanks," I replied. An awkward silence stretched out; I had no idea what to say, and apparently, he didn't, either, though a few times it seemed like he was about to say something. A few times I almost did as well.

Okay, just say SOMEthing! "This is…" Only for further words to fail me again.

"Ridiculous?" Cyrus suggested, smiling crookedly.

"Heh. Yeah. That." I ran a hand through my hair, still not used to how short it was. "I've saved up plenty of words for if my dad ever showed up again, but this isn't exactly what I pictured when I was scripting those."

"I can imagine," Cyrus said. "I can't say I had anything in mind at all; this is entirely unexpected. If there's anything I can answer, though, just ask."

I certainly had questions, but most of them were for my mom. But there were a few that only he could answer. "Why didn't you ever come back? Or get in touch with my mom again?"

"Like I've said, I'm not exactly welcome around here," Cyrus said. "And by 'not welcome' I mean more like 'on the wanted list.' Your mother was much safer without me, and besides, at that point, she was married to another man. I thought it was best not to get in the way of that, and let us both move on with our lives."

My brows rose. I opted not to remark on the fact he hadn't let her being engaged stop him. "I wasn't aware we had a wanted list, and I'm on the Council."

"So I've heard. Yet weren't you commiserating with me about them the other day?" Cyrus asked.

"Yeah, well…hard to change the system if I refuse to be a part of it," I replied, shrugging.

Cyrus grinned. "I wish you luck in that. It would take a miracle to change most of those people. Especially Laurent. Unless the latest members are better than the ones I knew?"

"Some of them probably are, but he's still at the head of it. But you were saying?" I prompted. "Wanted list?"

"Yes—have you heard about why I left? About my father?" he asked; I nodded. "The Council had me in jail, essentially, after Frank and my father died. They wanted to sever me. They needed to bring in a seventh Council member before they could do so, however. I had a few days to spare, and in that time some friends of mine, including your mother and Bastien's father, broke me out. I knew I had to leave town and stay away; I wouldn't be so lucky as to escape that fate twice."

My jaw dropped. What the hell sort of misspent youth had my mom been hiding from me? "They broke you out of *jail*?"

The floor creaked as Bastien stepped to the doorway upon hearing this. "My father did *what*?"

Cyrus's smile was nostalgic now. "Well, not jail so much as the warded basement of the Lemaire mansion, but yeah, they sure did. Gio Luppino helped, too. She was really remarkable, your mother. Still is." His smile turned affectionate for a moment. "Gio and Armand, they were good friends. I hated leaving all of them behind, but it was for their good as much as mine."

"I...I need to sit down," I said numbly, plunking onto the couch. Bastien leaned against the doorframe, his mind almost visibly struggling to process this. "I can't...I mean...how? Why? Okay, I guess I know why. But how? And how did they get away with it?"

"I'm still stuck on that my grandfather has a holding cell in the basement," Bastien added.

"Criminal past? Secret sex dungeon? You Lemaires get

more interesting all the time," Remi remarked, coming to the other side of the wide doorframe. Bastien, predictably, glared at her.

"Used to, at least, I'm not sure they still do. We broke a lot of wards getting out," Cyrus replied. "Armand told the others where I was, got them inside, and probably he's the one who covered our tracks at the house. Your mother put every drop of magic she had into breaking the binding. I'd never seen her like that; she was damn near glowing with magic. It strained her so much she passed out."

Remi, Bastien, and I shared a significant look. Cyrus could just as well be describing what I'd done at Bastien's wedding, when I'd pulled on my family's stored magic in the barrier to defeat Saranthiel.

"Gio's pack helped obscure the trail from there, while I hid out here," Cyrus continued, gesturing at the house. "The house belonged to your mom by then, and she was living here alone at the time. A few days later, Armand helped me portal out of town, and that was that. I didn't think I'd ever see any of them again."

A few days during which I was conceived, I thought, though I kept it to myself.

"Why didn't you tell me any of this before?" Bastien asked. "You knew who I was."

"I knew you were a Lemaire. I didn't know Armand was your dad," Cyrus replied. Bastien's dad had three siblings, including Adele. "I was surprised to meet you, but I didn't plan for any of this. I never planned to come back here, but once I did get to know you, what you'd been through, I couldn't get the plans my father and I had out of my mind. When you told me your friend had been severed, it felt like a sign. I've wanted to try this ritual for years, for the others in the cabal, but we'd only ever learn about the severings after they happened, but this time is different. And now, knowing that someone is Wendy? There's no turning back for me. She risked everything for me once. I'm not going to do any less for her."

Dammit. He really was my dad, wasn't he?

Chapter 16
Emergency Meeting

Bzzt bzzt! Bzzt bzzt! Bzzt bzzt!

"Okay, well, I'm glad you're ride-or-die for my mom, but I need to get that," I said, darting out of the room to check my phone, grateful for the excuse to escape.

With just enough charge to turn on, my phone was now catching up to several days' worth of missed calls and messages. There was one about the Council meeting and a few other messages from people attempting to locate me, my friends and Trevan among them.

"Everything okay?" Remi asked, coming into the kitchen.

"Yeah, but I need to get to that Council meeting." I sent off messages to my mom, Leo, and Trevan to let them know I was back.

"I was more asking about the part where you ran away from the emotional moment there," Remi said.

Of course. I pocketed my phone and grabbed my bag. "Look, I won't pretend this isn't a lot, but I don't think we've got time for a big heart-to-heart right now. The town's under some kind of quiet siege, those two need to pull off a magical heist under the noses of the most powerful witches on the Eastern Seaboard, plus Bastien probably has his own heap of unread messages and duties to catch up on, and the last thing I need is to be late to yet another Council meeting."

My phone buzzed again with a new message from Trevan.

Glad you're okay. We need to talk about your schedule this week.

        Sorry Trev, but I can't work until after the trial.
        I'll make up the shifts next week.

...

...

Talk to you when that's done.
Stay safe out there. Town's weird lately.

"That's an understatement." I turned to Remi. "Can I borrow your car?"

"If you top off the tank." She held out her hand to shake.

I raised a brow. "Really? You're making deals for gas money now?" She shrugged. "Sure, fine." We shook on it. The weight of the agreement was less than the last one we'd made, in the Pit. She handed me the keys. "You'll check in with Lucca?"

"Now that it's less interesting around here, yes. I'm certainly not about to hang out while those two geek out over magic theory," Remi replied, rolling her eyes. "Good luck with the old guard."

"I'm sure I'll need it."

I poked my head back into the living room. Bastien and Cyrus were already seated at the couch, poring over the sketch of the restoration spell that Bastien was redrawing, discussing adjustments to the runes. "Hey. I need to get to the Council meeting and whatever fresh hell that's gonna bring down. Are you staying here?"

"I kind of have to," Cyrus replied.

"For now. I want to get this clean copy made, but I'll need to get back to my house soon," Bastien said. "No doubt I've got a few missed messages as well."

"What are you going to tell anyone asking where you were?"

Bastien puffed out a breath. "Good question. I'll come up with something. What are you going to tell the Council?"

"Also a good question. I can't imagine that clock tower thing went unnoticed—"

"It didn't!" Remi called from the kitchen.

"Awesome. No doubt they've found a way to blame me for that already." I rolled my eyes. "I'll see what else they already know and take it from there. I'll keep you and all this out of it, obviously." I gestured at the two of them and the spell. "Text me when you get your phone back," I added before turning to go.

"McKenna, wait." Cyrus stood from the couch. I wildly hoped he wasn't about to try to hug me, half turning back toward him. "Why did you really join the Council? I can tell there's more to it. You seem to dislike them almost as much as I do. Given what they did to your mother, how your family's been treated, and what I understand they almost did to you once, what made you decide to join?"

I didn't love Cyrus accurately calling out my evasive answer earlier. But then, he did run a support group and had no doubt heard plenty of half truths before. There were many other answers I could give, and had given in the past. Because what else was I going to do, because they'd probably kick me out of town if I didn't, because you keep your enemies closer. But there was a deeper truth, and for some reason, I felt compelled to give it to him.

"Last fall, at Bastien's wedding, Saranthiel offered to let me choose someone else's soul for her to take in place of mine. She reminded me how they all felt about me, said that they owed me, that they'd sell me out without a second thought." I could see the room full of beaten, bloodied, and terrified wedding guests again now. "Part of me wanted to. But... that was their way of thinking. Not mine. I wasn't going to choose for someone else, and I wasn't only going to look out for myself. That's never made anything better. But getting my hands dirty, working with others? That has." Two faces in the crowd had stood out to me—Remi's and Brooke's. And now, in this room, Bastien's joined theirs. Someone working against what he'd been taught, who he might've been, to make things better. "Being better is harder. I had a chance to make things better for the rest of this town, so I took it."

"That's a choice not many would make," Cyrus said, his voice ruminative at first. "They're very lucky to have you."

His smile reminded me of the look he'd worn at the support meeting when my mother was talking. When I answered her. A look, I realized, of pride.

Naturally, my reflexive reaction was a self-deprecating joke. "Heh. Yeah, try telling them that." A pause, and I added, "Thanks. I'll, uh... I'll see you later."

I started to head for the door, then turned back. "The others in your group who were severed—did other Councils do those?"

"One or two, but most were done by the Arcadia Commons Council," he said.

Then why weren't there any records? Or were they making it up? It seemed highly unlikely, but I hadn't been able to check any of their auras myself at the meeting.

In the hallway en route to the front door, Bastien caught up to me, grabbing my hand. "McKenna." I turned, and he took my hand. "This town *is* lucky to have you... I'm lucky to have you." He leaned over to kiss my cheek, his lips soft and sparking a warmth that spread deeper within me. He smiled at me, squeezing my hand once before leaving me.

With my heart buzzing, I went outside and found Remi standing on the front steps, looking oddly self-conscious.

"You're right. Better is harder," she said. "But... it is worth it. I know you get frustrated with all my quid pro quo, but I am trying."

"I know. Honestly, Remi, you're one of the reasons I know it is," I told her.

Her face lifted, lighting up with a rare moment of genuine and unguarded delight. "Really? Me? Are we talking about the same Remi?"

I laughed. "We are."

"If I had another way to do it, I would," she said. "But it's how I'm built."

"I know." Did I, though? It occurred to me that she was uniquely built, in no small part thanks to me, and also uniquely on her own to figure all that out. "Or maybe I don't. Maybe when this latest crisis is done, we can try to figure something out."

Remi smirked dubiously. "Not sure that's possible, but I appreciate the sentiment."

This time, I smirked right back at her. "Hey, it's me. I do impossible shit all the time."

Remi laughed, tossing her head back, the dark waves of her hair shaking with mirth. "Now *there's* my black knight. That you do. You even make me believe it."

She cupped my face and kissed me. Her mouth was fierce and hot on mine, the sneaky swipe of her tongue igniting a fire that readily burned in me. Her other hand gripped my hip, pressing me against her for a moment before she released me. Her smirk this time was wicked. "We'll give it a try. But I can't be good *all* the time."

With a puff of shadow, she vanished, leaving me in a tumble of emotions and desires that took the entire drive across town to shake.

———————————— • ————————————

I wasn't late to the meeting, though I was the last one there. This time, however, no one even noticed when I came in.

They were all too busy yelling at one another about everything from harassment lawsuits to town laws to whose wife or husband was cheating, possibly with other people present in that very room.

It was worse than a high school lunchroom. I stared at the bickering adults incredulously before slowly turning my gaze on the one person in the room who wasn't saying a damned thing. Laurent sat in his usual chair at one end of the coffee table, taking it in, silent as a spider in his web watching the flies.

"Glad you could join us, Miss Ellerbeck," he said without looking at me.

"Are you going to do anything about this?" I asked.

"They'll tire themselves out eventually," he replied. "And where exactly have you been in the last few days?" He cocked an eye at me as he asked, watchful in a way that put me on edge.

"Busy."

He grunted in reply. "Keeping it short. Smart."

What is he talking about? I was about to ask when Sofia spotted me. "Stars and spells, not her."

"What did I do?" I asked.

"Your very presence is nothing but a reminder of everything I've lost, and I can't stand your attitude! Everything that's gone wrong in this town is because of you, and the fact you volunteered to represent that traitor is appalling!" Sofia snapped, so sudden and blunt that even she looked taken aback. The whole room did, in fact, as everyone had stopped talking when she started going off on me.

Something in me snapped as well. I opened my mouth to lash out in return, but suddenly heard Cyrus in my mind, something he'd said to his cabal.

"We're healing from things we've done as much as things done to us."

My ire softened into pity. "Sofia, I'm sorry for your loss. I really am. But it isn't my fault, and you need to stop blaming me," I said in a firm but not unkind tone. "You need to stop blaming Abby and Brooke, too."

"I—I'm not taking back my petition for the trial. She betrayed all of us!" Sofia replied after a brief falter.

"I didn't think you would, but what you're doing isn't helping anyone, least of all you," I replied. Something about her choice of words rattled in my head, the fact of what she'd said just now compared with what she usually said about Brooke. "Sofia, do you actually believe Brooke killed your daughter?"

Sofia Perez, always immaculately styled and holding herself with confident, lofty poise, bit her lips so hard they bled before the word burst out. "No!"

Adele gasped and grabbed several tissues from the box on the table, handing them to Sofia to dab at her mouth. The blood seeping down her chin stained the tissues red. The younger Lemaire glared at me. "Was that really necessary?"

"You're asking me that? She's the one needlessly accusing a woman of murder."

"Sofia, let me heal—" Douglas started to reach toward her, but she stopped him.

"No. Not this one."

"All right, well . . . I'll get you some ice, then," he said, hurrying out of the room.

"Looks like that's one charge we can drop from this trial," I remarked, and held up a hand before some of them could comment. "Yeah, yeah, I know, it's still happening, she still worked for a demon, I remember. Hey, show of hands, how many people here are incapable of saying anything but the truth right now?"

Everyone's hand went up, with Douglas calling an affirmative from the other room. Everyone's, that is, except for Adele's and Laurent's. *Of* course *they somehow avoided it.* "Follow-up, does anyone know how this happened to them?" A grumbled chorus of noes. "None of you got attacked by a huge black spider-squid monster lately, I take it."

"Those things in the clock tower? There's more of them?" Hilary asked.

"Probably. They're called *Geheimnissuchers.* Secret-seekers. Their bite injects a truth venom," I explained. "We killed the ones in the tower, but obviously the effect is spreading around town regardless."

"Only thing that's bitten me lately was a spider," George said as Douglas came back with ice for Sofia.

"Spider bites? We've had a huge rise in those the last few days," Douglas said. "The ER nurses were talking about it."

Hilary looked thoughtful. "There were spiders in the garden when I was planting. It's possible one bit me and I didn't notice."

This had to be it—these seekers could change their size, or maybe Secrets could make them in whatever size was needed for their plans. Tiny seekers were the perfect way to infect a town without attracting notice. Why send man-size seekers at all when you could send something as small as a spider? "Any of you remember what they looked like? George, can you make a drawing of yours?"

He started drawing, passing a sheet each to Hilary and Douglas, and they all made sketches. They were all listening to me. Without mocking or questioning or scoffing, they were actually *listening* to me. Even Sofia was paying attention and watching what they drew with interest. Laurent and Adele remained still, but Adele had no snipes for me, and I could feel a certain weight in Laurent's gaze that wasn't often there.

Was this what it felt like to be respected?

George held up his notebook, showing a dime-size black spider, without any identifying features otherwise. "Small, black. It was gone before I could swat it." Douglas and Hilary nodded agreement.

"There was one in my house. It was bigger than that, but also black," Sofia said from behind the ice. "What sort of demon is this, then?"

"It's not. It's a monster. How about you two?" I turned to look at the Lemaires.

Adele shook her head, while Laurent dryly informed us, "I don't garden. I take it you experienced the bite of this first-hand, then? Are you similarly afflicted?"

"Not anymore. Good news, there's a way to cure it." They all looked relieved. "You have to willingly tell the truth about something meaningful. Share a secret no one else knows."

A heavy silence ensued.

I cleared my throat. "I mean, you don't *have* to do it right n—"

"I was an exotic dancer in college!" Hilary exclaimed. Hilary, the terribly proper sixty-something grandmother whom I'd never seen in anything less than a shirt buttoned to her neck. "For extra money. My parents paid tuition and room and board, but everything else was on me because they didn't like that I majored in business instead of agriculture. I used the name Poppy. And I...I liked it. It was fun. The other girls were great, some of them are still some of my best friends today." She slumped back against the couch, then said, "...None of that was true. Oh! It worked! Seven hells, none of you better ever repeat that."

"Wow. Did Steve know?" Douglas ventured.

"Of course not!" Hilary turned as red as her stage name. "Well, one of you go, come on now."

"Helen and I are getting divorced," Douglas said quietly.

"Oh, no, Doug. I'm so sorry," George said, a hand going to the other man's shoulder.

"Thank you. I'm...it's a mutual decision, it's for the best," Douglas said, then looked a bit startled. "Oh—it did work."

"I had a child out of wedlock." Sofia's voice was muffled by the ice pack, and her eyes were riveted on the wall, looking at no one. "When I was eighteen, with a boy in Mexico. I put her up for adoption and I know nothing about what became of her. But I wish her a happy birthday every year."

Holy shit. The Perez family was as Catholic as one could get while still being a witch. That was no small confession for her.

It also meant there were two daughters effectively lost to her.

The room was still, dispirited in the wake of these admissions, and eventually our gazes all went to George.

He tugged on his collar. "I, uh…I fired an intern I didn't like for photocopying his butt. I knew it wasn't him. It was me."

A beat of silence was broken by Sofia Perez throwing her head back and outright *cackling*, and thank the gods, because it broke the seal on the rest of us cracking up at the ridiculous confession.

For the first time, I actually felt connected to these people.

Naturally, Laurent Lemaire had to step in and ruin it.

The old man leaned forward, speaking loudly over our mirth as it began to peter out. "If that's all, let's move on to addressing the cause of this infestation." With one statement, it was his court again. "Cyrus Craig is back. And he's laid a curse on Arcadia Commons."

Lucky for me, I was surprised enough at Laurent knowing Cyrus was around at all to blend in with the rest of the surprised and shocked people around me.

"Cyrus? I thought he was dead!"

"I thought he was magically banned."

"*Dios mío.*"

"McKenna, is that why you were asking me about him?"

I winced at George's question, which got everyone casting suspicious eyes my way. "No, my…my mom mentioned she used to date him. I realized you might've known him in school, that was all." I turned to Laurent. "What do you mean he cursed the town?"

"These monsters that are suddenly everywhere. Part of his long-delayed revenge. The Council severed his parents and would've severed him, too, if he hadn't escaped our custody somehow."

"Severed him? For what?" Hilary asked.

"Murder." Laurent's eyes bored into me as he said it. Jackie Harwell's pale face and slashed throat jumped into my mind's eye.

George asked the question for me. "Murder? I know he was there, Laurent, but his father is the one who killed Frank Milton, and that was by accident."

"That's just the story we told everyone after Cyrus escaped," Laurent replied. "I was there that night with Frank. The two of them were tampering with the leylines, trying to drain their power for themselves. Frank attacked Curtis, Cyrus's father, but Cyrus was the one who bashed Frank with a rock and killed him. We took him into custody, but he escaped before we could sever him."

"You let a murderer just go free?" Douglas asked. "At that point, why not get the mundane authorities involved?"

"Too much risk, given what he could do." What did that mean? Cyrus seemed mild mannered overall. The man had founded a support group, for goodness' sake. Although...I had seen what he could do when motivated. The spell I'd seen him cast in the tower had absolutely destroyed that seeker. "We worked a ban into the barrier that would prevent him from being able to cross back in," Laurent told us. "But with the barrier now faltering, it seems he's gotten back in."

"How do you know it's him?" I asked.

"Because I saw him with my own eyes," Laurent said, those same eyes boring into me once again. "Walking around town with your mother. Didn't have the good sense to just stay gone."

All at once, something Laurent had said to me months ago, when he'd found me handcuffed in a wine room in the midst of Saranthiel's chaos, came flying back to my mind: *"At least your father had the sense to stay gone when he left."*

I thought he'd been talking about John Ellerbeck. But no.

Somehow, Laurent Lemaire, the spider in the center of the web that was Arcadia Commons, knew Cyrus Craig was my father. He'd known all along.

If he knew that…what else did he know?

Chapter 17
Webs of Conspiracy

The rest of the meeting was a blur—plans for apprehending Cyrus and giving the mundane population a warning about an "invasive species of spider" to try to warn them off while we dealt with it. I barely listened, my mind in a whirl of trying to discern how Laurent knew about Cyrus and which version of the story was true. Was Cyrus a murderer, or a bystander and victim of slander? What had he and his father truly been doing with the leylines? On top of everything else I already had on my mind…

"McKenna?"

I was standing in the driveway when a voice startled me out of my thoughts. To my surprise, Sofia Perez was the one addressing me. "Sofia?"

An angry red line across her lip remained from her earlier outburst, the pink of her lipstick mostly wiped away, but a few traces of it remained in the creases. "Is that your car?" She sounded surprised. I followed her gaze to Remi's sports car; I'd forgotten I was borrowing that.

"No, just a loaner," I said. "But I doubt you wanted to talk about cars...?"

She tipped her head in acknowledgement. "No. I...as you are Mrs. Luppino's advocate, I am officially informing you that the charge of murder will be dropped," she said in a formal tone.

"Thank you, Sofia," I replied, with genuine gratitude. That, I knew, could not have been an easy one to let go of. The burden of proving it was always going to be an uphill battle, but that hadn't stopped her insistence before. While there were spells to recreate Brooke's memory of the events, unedited by any force, demonic or otherwise, they required being in the precise location where the events took place, and whatever happened to Mari was too dispersed. From the bluff they had gone cliff diving from to the beach where Brooke had been found later with an unconscious Mari, who had actually been Saranthiel, those were only the book ends of the story. And anything that had happened in the water, where Mari's real body had been lost to the depths, never recovered, was impossible to recreate even via magic. We could question Brooke under the truth spell of the trial for more details, but she'd so far maintained that she hadn't hurt the other woman.

Sofia went on, "We shall see if she was an accessory to such, and she *is* still guilty of conspiracy, of course. But...perhaps you had a point earlier." Her hand brushed her lip, the red line where she'd bitten it.

"I hope it helps," I offered, feeling compelled to say something. I wasn't remotely in a position to offer true comfort, but I *did* wish her solace for what she'd lost.

"So do I. I…hope it no longer weighs on your dreams, what happened to her." It was as close to an admission of sending me nightmares as I was going to get from her. "Also, have you seen or talked with Bastien? I've been trying to reach him," she asked before I could respond.

"Uh…" *Remember, you're his opposing advocate and not on good terms last she knew.* "Wouldn't Adele or Laurent be better people to ask that?"

"I have. They haven't talked with him, either."

Have they been to his house? If so, they surely would've seen the shattered glass door, the mess inside. "Maybe he's out of town again. I'm sure he'll be back for the trial." Sofia nodded again and adjusted her purse to retrieve her keys, in that getting-ready-to-excuse-herself sort of way, but another question jumped to my mind. "Sofia, what do you know about Cyrus Craig?"

Her face shifted into a look of distaste and alarm. "That he's a murderer and enemy of this town."

"But were you on the Council when all that went down?" She was older than most of the others, though not as old as Laurent.

"No. My father was. But I remember the fuss. Curtis Craig used to be on the Council as well, but he was of course removed when he was severed along with his wife. He and Frank argued all the time. My father would talk about them being at it again after every meeting," Sofia said.

"Why were they severed? And what would they argue about?"

Sofia waved a hand. "Who knows. The trial records are in the Collection, if you're so curious."

"The records are somewhere between unhelpfully succinct and intentionally obscured." I spun the keys on my finger. "I'm fairly certain there's outright missing information."

"Even the ones from other towns?"

"What do you mean? Since the nexus is here, this is where the severings happen."

Sofia shook her head. "The records are kept by where the charges are filed."

I caught the keys midspin. "...I need to go. Thanks, Sofia."

Remi's sports car hugged all the curves as I drove into town, making a few calls along the way. My mom didn't pick up, Bastien didn't pick up, Remi didn't pick up. Dammit. I at least had a text from Bastien saying Remi was going to bring him back to his house. Remi had also messaged to report that the wolves had not seen any seekers around but that some were also afflicted with the truth venom, that she'd told them how to alleviate it and was "taking care of other business" now, whatever that meant.

The one I most wanted and needed to talk to was my mom. She might know what had really happened that night with Cyrus, Curtis, and Frank.

She might also be sleeping with a killer.

Jogging up the spiral staircase to the invisible-to-mundanes fourth floor, I headed to the desk this time instead of the archives, and was happily surprised to see a familiar face.

"McKenna! It's been so long!" Kavya Oberoi, head librarian, greeted me with a ready smile and a hug. An older Indian woman with a kind smile and hair that was now more gray than black, she'd been my boss when I worked here in high school. She wore a bright-blue sari with yellow accents; I'd always loved how she embraced bright, bold colors every day. Her family was gifted in telekinetic magics, which, as most witches could easily do them, didn't exactly carry much prestige. But it sure made accessing books on the upper shelves easier—she'd never once had to climb a rolling ladder to get or reshelve one of those. "I heard you've been lurking about here again, I'm so glad I ran into you! How have you been?"

"It's good to see you, Kavya," I said. "I've…been busy. Yourself? I heard you were on leave?"

Her smile sobered some. "Yes. I took some time to go back to India. My mother passed away a few months ago."

"I'm so sorry."

"Thank you, dear. It's sad, but I was able to say goodbye and be with my family," she said. "It was good to be back there, even for such a reason, and it's good to be back here. Now, I hear you're doing advocate work?"

"I am, yeah, I'm defending Brooke Luppino. Actually, I was hoping to look at some severing trial records from other towns?" There were two ways to access records from other branches of the Uncommon Collection, both of which required librarian assistance: physically using the permanent portals to other branches or going to the Interlibrary Room. It was a unique space connected to all the branches at once. You could request a record and it would come straight to you there, so long as you had the right approvals for access. The IR was the faster of the two but required a higher access level.

"Certainly. Did you want to travel there or use the IR?" she asked, not even hesitating.

"I'd love to use the IR, if that's okay. Are you sure?" I asked.

"Of course! Why wouldn't I be?" Kavya started walking that way, motioning for me to follow.

"Because you demoted me to the mundane library for using restricted materials to summon an Archdemon?"

Kavya laughed. "I'm fairly certain you've learned your lesson since then, yes?"

"I, uh—yes. Definitely yes," I confirmed.

Kavya looked at me with kind eyes. "McKenna, you were a teenager back then. Of course I demoted you, but I didn't fire you, did I? It was ages ago. Now you're an adult, on the Council, an advocate."

"No, and I was always grateful for that," I assured her. "Thank you. I guess I've gotten used to people thinking I haven't changed at all."

"Oftentimes those are the people who haven't changed, I've found."

I smiled. "I missed you, Kavya."

Using a talisman, the witch equivalent of a key card, she opened a door to the Interlibrary Room. Though I knew about it, I'd never actually been inside before. The floor was stone, with a large decorative area rug on it. A table with comfortable chairs sat in the middle. On the wall was a large circular mirror with runes etched into its frame. Below it was a slim table and a large wooden box that was also enchanted with runes.

"The mirror is for scrying to find the records or books you're after and requesting them. They'll be sent to this box." She tapped the top of it. "When you're done, place the items inside and knock three times. They'll be sent back to the branch they came from. Make sure you're only sending them back to one branch at a time, or we'll have a whole mess on our hands, and you—"

"—know how you hate a mess," I said along with her, smiling. "I'll be careful with it. Thanks again, Kavya."

Her kind smile returned. "You're welcome. It really is good to see you back here."

"It's nice being here," I said. "It's still one of my favorite places in this town."

"You know, we have a part-time opening. It's not much, shelving and circulation. But if you're looking, you should put in an application," Kavya told me.

A rush of hope went through me at the idea. "Really? I'd love to. Are you sure?"

"Like I said, that was ages ago," Kavya said.

"Maybe, but I'm still kind of a disaster magnet," I told her.

"Well, don't write that down on the application," she teased me. "Just think about it, hm?"

I promised her that I would, and she left me to it. It took me a few minutes to get the hang of using the mirror as a catalog, but once I did, the requested records were sent over without delay. And what a story they told.

Though the Council was based in Arcadia Commons, it had jurisdiction over the northeastern part of the United States. Few towns, or even cities, had witches living in the same density as Arcadia, and some had smaller, local groups to handle minor issues. But when it came to larger matters or petitions, the Arcadia Commons Witches Council was the authority. Like I'd told Sofia, I had assumed that meant any severing records would be filed here. But it turned out that there had indeed been more severings and trials than our town records accounted for. When I put together a final timeline, I saw that there had been almost a severing a year for the last thirty years. I saw Karam's name from a few years prior; my guess was he'd ended up a thrall after being severed for "illicit alchemical practices and distribution." Magic legalese for "making magical party drugs." Another name I recognized from the cabal, Trina, had been severed just last year for "extreme violation of magical secrecy," with a note about requesting mental magic assistance to rectify the situation. They'd tampered with people's memories just to cover up that one.

It went on like that. Some charges were serious: murder, endangerment, conspiring with demons. But others were far less so, at least from what I could tell. Yet they'd ended in severing, and they were rarely from the same town twice in a decade, if not longer. Once I added some genealogical research, I confirmed that almost none of the families involved were powerful ones. Anytime those names were among the severed, their crimes were only the most serious ones.

There was no doubt in my mind about it: The Council was regularly severing witches from lower-powered families, and they were making sure the records were spread around so as to obscure this fact.

How could they do this? Laurent and Adele, I didn't even question their motives, but the others? Even Douglas Harwell, who I was sure had had a hand in the memory wiping they'd done on the mundane witnesses to Trina's magic?

They were using their power to decide who got to be a witch

and who didn't. But why? Why would they want fewer witches in the world? It wasn't like their existence alone harmed anyone. I couldn't help but feel that there was more going on, but the records weren't going to give me those answers.

Whatever the reason, it wasn't right. It had to stop.

I couldn't stop Brooke's severing trial from happening; we needed it to follow through on the plan. But damned if I wasn't going to bring all of this to the fore and try to make sure it was the last.

No one had gotten back to me by the time I returned to the car, and I was unsure about going back to my house just yet. I didn't want to be there alone while Cyrus was around, and as far as I knew, my mom was still with Cameron, and while I wanted to see my brother, too, I needed to share this information with Bastien. I decided to just drive to Bastien's house. He and Remi still weren't answering my texts, but the last text I had from Bastien said they were headed there not long ago.

As I drove up the private road to the house, it struck me that it was a perfect spring sailing day. Warm and sunny, enough wind to sail with and a cloudless blue sky. It was easy to imagine myself coming here to do exactly that, taking out the boat docked by his house to spend the day on the water with Bastien, something akin to a normal date, instead of talking and planning conspiracies and fighting monsters. With a bonus of him shirtless in a swimsuit.

In my mind's eye, Remi appeared on the boat with us, wearing a skimpy suit and a smirk.

Maybe before we got to that boat, if we ever did, I should figure out exactly who and what *I* wanted.

Bastien's car was still parked out front when I pulled up, as was an unfamiliar tan SUV. The hood was cool when I checked it; whoever it was hadn't arrived recently. Surely, he would've contacted me if there was trouble, right? Bastien had messaged to let me know he had his phone, so I knew he'd gotten at least as far as his office, but there'd been nothing since then.

I knocked on the front door, expecting, hoping, that Bastien would answer…but there was no response. Just like the other day.

A bad feeling started in my gut. I pulled out my athame and crept quietly around toward the back door, and almost immediately walked into a spiderweb face-first.

"Ugh!" I fumbled back, creeped out and startled, my skin jittery at the sensation of the invisible strands across my face even as I wiped them away. My eyes darted around, looking for a spider. There wasn't one on me, but when I looked again down the stretch of porch running to the back of the house, that bad feeling got worse. Webs ran all the way down to the back deck. Sunlight glinted off the gossamer lines and cobweb spreads of white, with dozens of black dots on them, some tiny, some less so.

"Seven hells," I hissed, stepping back and nearly falling down the front stairs before catching myself. I instinctively checked myself again for unwelcome arachnids, phantom sensations crawling over my skin.

But the line of webs was unbroken. No one had been through there. Had Bastien gone inside without seeing them? Had he gone around? And what about the other car?

"Bastien!" I leapt up to the front door again, banging on

it, ringing the bell and trying the knob. "Bastien, are you in there?"

No answer. The lights were off inside, and the curtains on the door still obscured my view. I skipped the porch and went the long way around to the back door, blasting magical wind in front of me to clear any webs, but they were concentrated on the porch rather than out in the open. The driveway turned to dirt and sand as I came around the corner.

The entire doorway was covered in webs. At least a dozen seeker-spiders, bigger than the ones on the porch, were perched on it. They were more spiderlike than the full-size seekers, with most of their long spindly legs ending in sharp delicate points, but a few of those legs were more tentacle-like, undulating in the air as if they sensed me. Some were still, predators in wait, while others moved, spinning and weaving, reinforcing the barrier to the inside.

Fuck.

Even if Bastien had gone in through the front door, there was no way he could have missed this.

Something was very, *very* wrong.

"Think, think, think." I ran my hand through my hair, going back to the front. I pulled out my phone and called him again. There! I could hear it in the house, faintly. Following the noise, I came around to the far side of the house from the driveway, to the window that led to his home office. On this side, it was higher than I could see into. I drew a quick circle in the dirt with my athame, scratched a rune for portaling, and cast. "*Ianuam aperi ad* Bastien's office."

Gold light filled the circle, and the vague impression of a

door appeared in it. It was a short distance, so the portal was not too difficult for me to cast, thankfully. I opened the door and stepped into his office.

There were surprisingly few signs of spiders or webs. A few in the windows, but their webs were still small, as though this room had only recently been breached.

Just past the partially open door into the hall, I saw the outline of a limp body on the ground.

Alarm shot through my veins. On instinct, I pressed my finger to the edge of my knife, letting both my blood and my magic flow. With my knife in one hand and a spell at the ready, I kicked the door open fully, ready for anything.

Shadows and webs hung over the hallway, their thick and dangerous finery draping every surface. They muffled both light and sound, swallowing even the white noise of the ocean. It was almost worse than total darkness; I could make out just enough to know there were things and they were moving, but not enough to know what or where. I pressed my bloody fingertip to my thumb, whispering, "*Lux.*" A mote of light appeared and grew into a floating ball above my palm.

The walls and floors were thickly dusted with glitter, shiny bits of silver reflecting the light back at me. Why and how had glitter gotten all over the webs? Whatever the reason, I'd take that over—

Oh. *Oh, no.* That wasn't glitter.

Those were *eyes.*

Hundreds of them. Thousands. Seekers waiting with bared fangs.

And *every single one of them* was staring at me.

Horror crept up my skin on imagined chitinous legs, and my eyes slowly dropped to the ground. Spiders the size of cats, several of them, had halted in wrapping the prone, unconscious bodies of Remi and Bastien. *No! Bastien—Remi—how the fuck did they get Remi, too?* I whipped my left hand toward their assailants. "*Repel*—ah!"

Another spider dropped onto me from above and sank its fangs into my arm, interrupting the spell. "Fuck!" I violently shoved it off my arm, only to feel the very real sensation of more of them on my back, on my legs, in my hair. Their creepy fucking legs all over me, their fangs finding exposed skin and sinking in. "Fuck, fuck, fuck!" I swatted and flailed, trying to shake them off, eyes squeezed shut, heart racing, I couldn't breathe, I couldn't—

No! If I panic now, we are all DEAD! I gritted my teeth, forced out a breath. *You're a goddamn badass witch, Ellerbeck, now act like it! This. Is. Temporary!*

Eyes open.

"*Repello!*" I screamed, thrusting my hand out, just in time to hit the cat-size ones leaping at me. Three of them were caught in the blast, flying back across the room, and a fourth was thrown off its path, smacking into the wall with a heavy thud. That one's legs went from stiff and spindly to flexible, fluid things as it hit the wall, and it opened a mouth of fangs hidden in its black head to hiss at me.

I dropped down, slicing into the webbing on Bastien. Multiple spider bites decorated his skin, but he had a steady pulse, thank the stars and spells. "*Sana*," I cast, pressing my bloodied hand to his chest and my magic into his body, hoping it was enough to rouse him. My left arm was going tingly and numb from the spider bite, and I had no idea how that might limit my casting.

I scrambled across the floor to reach Remi, pitching forward into yet more webs as I slipped on something. Looking down, I saw for the first time a gruesome streak of reddish-brown liquid on the floor. For a panicked moment, I thought Remi or Bastien was more gravely wounded, but the streak continued past them both, into the living room. There, a third body was wrapped in webs, but this one was stained with blood and who knew what other fluids.

His half-melted face was visible through a tear in the webbing.

I screamed.

From within the darkness beyond the body, something moved. Something *laughed*.

It was a low chuckle, a smug thing, that spread around the room, echoing from everywhere. Echoing from every spider big enough to have one of those creepy seeker mouths. The sound was a grating whisper made into a thunderous rumble when it spread to all of them.

And then they *spoke*.

"If we were Fear, such a feast would we be having." The words echoed, some voices lagging behind the others: *be having... having... having...* "But a feast we still have. This one, its secrets were few, but these new meals..." *meals... meals...*

A thousand mouths opened, hissing, tasting the air. "They have *so many*." *So many... many... many...*

The shadow behind the corpse came forward into the light.

A seeker, full size like the first one I'd met, its arachnid abdomen engorged. "Our next batch of young will be so well fed." ...*fed*...*fed*...*fed*...

Seven hells. That thing was full of *eggs*? Clearly not its first clutch, judging by the hostile takeover of Bastien's house.

I scrambled away from it, back toward Remi, slashing the webbing from her, slapping away spiders that tried to crawl over me. My left arm was practically dead weight at my side by now, and from some bite or another, my right arm was starting to join it. As I cleared her face and upper body, I uncovered a lot more bite marks on her than I'd seen on Bastien, especially around her neck. Whatever was numbing my limbs, they must've kept her pumped full of it to keep her down. Archdemon she might be, but her body was still human and vulnerable.

"And *that* one...that one will give its power to us. Bring it down, down to the depths...past the lines, through the bars, it shall give us *power*." *Power...power...power...*Its eyes locked on Remi, pure hunger in the voice and all its echoes. "Then we shall take *back* what was stolen!" These words ended in a hungry hiss that spread around the room.

"Not on my fucking watch," I snapped, forcing some bravado into my voice, working through the strands on Remi with my knife. "*Sana*," I hissed, sending my magic into her body as well.

Bastien groaned, starting to come around but not there yet.

Remi stirred; her demonic healing worked fast once it had a kick start. "Son of a bitch, my head...McKenna?"

The smug laughter echoing around the room again.

"Hard pass, I did *not* sign up for the creepiest ASMR ever," Remi muttered. In a flash, fire burned through the webbing on her, leaving her body untouched and free.

The larger seeker was prowling toward us. So were the smaller ones. Just about everything, really. "There is no escape. We will not be denied our prey, our power."

"I don't think so. No taking me by surprise this time," Remi replied, flames flickering in her eyes, her shadow blade coming to life in her hand. I looked back—some of the mid-size spiders were dragging Bastien farther from us, redoing the webs I'd slashed apart already.

I grabbed Remi's arm. "There's no time! We need to get Bastien and get out of here!"

Remi's eyes took in the rest of the room and the state I was in. "Shit. Yeah, make a path."

I needed two hands and more magic for that, and I couldn't get them with one knife and a numb hand. "Slice my hands," I told her, before grasping my athame in my teeth.

Remi didn't hesitate; she slashed a quick line down each palm with her blade. My blood flowed out and brought my magic with it in force, and I swept my hands in a circle around us. "*Repello!*" A wave of golden magic burst out from where I stood, blasting back the seekers, even the big one, and we raced forward to Bastien. Remi ripped into the webbing with her blade, pulling him free.

"Unh…Remi…?" he groaned, finally coming to.

"Yeah, sorry, sweetcheeks, not the rescue you wanted, I know. Deal." She pulled the last of the webbing off him. "Hope you've got good home insurance. Where to?"

My mind raced. What would get these things off of us? "My house. The pool."

"Coming right up." Remi grabbed Bastien's freed hand and mine.

"Wait." Bastien reached across us both to stop her. "We can't leave these things here."

"He's right. The town is fucked if all these grow to full size," I agreed, still blasting back the seekers.

"Well, whatever you're gonna do, do it now!" Remi said.

I could only think of one option, but it was his house. I looked at Bastien, knowing he must have thought of it, too. He gave me a curt nod. "Burn it down."

Remi grinned. "Now we're talking."

"On three?" Bastien held out his hand. With Remi's help holding them together, I got my left hand into his. "*Un . . . deux . . .*" Bastien counted in French.

"*Trois!*"

"*Boule de feu!*" Bastien threw his flames down the hallway behind us.

"*Sphaeram ignis!*" Fire exploded from my hand into the living room, right into the mother seeker, sending her flying back into the kitchen.

Into the stove.

The *gas* stove.

Heat and flame exploded back toward us; I screamed—"*Remi!*"

We plunged into the shadows.

Chapter 18
Coming Clean

One second my world was scorching fireballs and monster spiders, the next it was the jarring chill of shadows, followed by a plummet into my backyard pool.

At least it wasn't a hellish ocean filled with demon crabs this time.

The chlorinated water stung my nose as I was plunged into the deep end. My left arm was fully numb by now, my right nearly the same, but I shoved off the bottom and kicked upward. I came up coughing and bobbing awkwardly until someone grabbed me and pulled me into the shallow end. Once I could stand, I saw that it had been Remi. She went back to help Bastien as well.

"The spiders!" Bastien warned, just as I felt some of them still scurrying across me.

"I can't get them," I grunted, trying and failing to slap them off of me.

Remi grabbed each of us; a pulse of her power rippled

through me, and the heavy numbness left my limbs. "Best I can do. If I scorch them, I'll scorch you, too," she said.

"This is plenty, thanks." Now able to move, I slapped and shook them off, dunking my head back underwater to get them out of my hair. Some were gone, but there were still too many. Finally, I yanked my T-shirt off and tossed it in the deep end.

"Your clothes, get rid of your clothes!" I said, struggling to get my boots and jeans off while still in the water.

Remi tried to shake out her hair, then finally just shifted into a male form. Robbed of their perch, several spiders were dumped into the water from that alone. "Isn't getting people naked supposed to be my job?" he quipped.

His clothing did not change with him, and the low-cut panties left very little to the imagination. "You *are* practically naked!" I pointed out, the words blurting out of me. Apparently, Remi's quick fix for the paralytic did not extend to the truth venom. "Just grab Bastien and get out of the pool!" I sloshed out of the water and threw open the shed with the pool supplies, grabbing a bottle of shock treatment.

By the time I got the childproof cap open, Bastien, too, was down to his boxer briefs and out of the pool. The water was speckled with dozens of spiders. I made a lap of the deep end, pouring as much of the chemical powder as we had into the water, and tossed the empty bottle in for good measure. "Let's see you fuckers survive that!"

Bastien and Remi had collapsed onto pool chairs while they caught their breath. I slumped face-first onto a third one, breathing heavily, heart hammering in panic that had not quite subsided. I could still feel spindly phantom legs all over my skin, and I slapped at creepy-crawlies that were no longer there.

The three of us sat there recovering for several silent minutes, soaking wet, in our underwear, covered in spider bites.

"We just burned my house down," Bastien said dazedly, staring at nothing.

"Uh-huh," I grunted.

"And I'm pretty sure those things ate my real estate agent."

"Uh-huh."

"And this was not remotely how I planned on getting you two naked," Remi added.

Bastien and I both jerked our heads up at that. Remi, impossibly, actually *blushed*. "I mean—*plan* is a strong word, it's really more of a general intention—fuck! What the hell is going on?" Remi exclaimed.

Giddy laughter bubbled out of me. "You're cute when you're flustered."

"I am not *cute*!" the Archdemon retorted.

"No, she's right," Bastien said, starting to chuckle, "it's kind of endearing."

"Endearing!" Remi exclaimed. "Did you seriously just describe me, the Archdemon of Desire and Madness, as endearing?"

Bastien and I laughed even harder, and behind his sputtering, Remi began to snicker despite himself, and in moments all three of us were cry-laughing on our pool chairs. Salt and chalk, it felt good to let go for just a minute, to let all the life-and-death shit be as ridiculous and insane as it really was, because how was this my life?

I looked at the two men on the chairs next to me, a warmth born of laughter and affection inside me. "If this kind of insanity is going to be my life, I'm glad I've got you two in it with me." I'd meant to keep that thought to myself, but it was one I didn't mind sharing, at least.

"Always good to be in good company," Bastien agreed.

"And good eye candy," Remi added, and rolled his eyes at us when we looked at him. "Whatever, we all know we're hot."

"Sorry about your house," I told Bastien.

Bastien shrugged. "I hated that house. I thought it was perfect when we bought it, but since the wedding, I've hated even looking at it, never mind setting foot in there. I *am* sorry about Bernard, though. He didn't deserve that."

"The Realtor?" I asked; he nodded.

"Now we know those things are carnivorous, too. Arcadia's got a lot worse than honesty coming for it," Remi said. "My neighborhood collateral damage is downright quaint compared to those things."

Bastien and I once again both craned our necks to look at Remi, who winced and cursed under his breath. "Fucking truth venom!"

"What's this about neighborhood collateral damage?" I asked.

Remi visibly struggled to keep his mouth shut, not unlike me a few days ago and Sofia just earlier today, but the words burst forth. "I don't have full control of these mantles, and it's affecting everyone who lives near me. I'm the reason for the affairs, the fights, and the randomly destroyed yards. Most of them, anyway. I didn't exactly take a poll."

"Holy shit—Remi, that's—how long have you known this?" I swung my legs around, sitting up on the edge of the lounge chair.

"Suspected it for a few months now..." he said, trying to be contrite.

Memories of my mother and brother in the throes of Saranthiel's madness, even my own temporary madness from when she'd tricked me into killing Jackie, jumped to my mind. "And you never told anyone? You're just—Remi, you're destroying their lives, their marriages, maybe even their minds! You can't just *do* that and not tell anyone!"

"And what was anyone, which we all know means *you*, going to do about it?" Remi snapped, standing up. "You can't control demonic power, McKenna. At least not once it's *in* someone."

"What do you mean?" An uneasy feeling stirred. "Wait. Are you mad at me for giving Saranthiel's mantle to you?"

"Yes! No. Both? Ugh!" Remi clenched his hands in frustration, then ran them through his damp hair.

"What do you think I should have done, take it for myself?" I bristled.

"Kind of, maybe!"

The admission hit in an almost physical way. He *wanted* me to have taken it? Even after I'd told him how I felt about claiming demonic power?

"McKenna—I didn't mean—"

"Stop trying to make her more like you." Bastien got to his feet between the two of us.

"I'm not," Remi insisted.

"What do you call wanting her to have taken an Archdemon's mantle, then? After how hard she fought to stay human?"

"I call it wishing I *didn't* have it. And it's not like I got a choice in the matter." I flinched at Remi's words, because that part definitely *was* on me. "I would've thought you could relate, *sorcerer*."

Bastien's back tensed. "When I realized what happened to me, I started taking steps to fix it. I didn't hide in a crowded neighborhood and put everyone there in danger."

"Did you? Or did you run away, even when people here needed you?" Remi countered, leaning into Bastien's personal space. "I've been redirecting and helping McKenna handle most of the demons that have tried to get into Arcadia for the last six months. Without me, this town would've been overrun a long time ago. But you, hey, you went and found yourself a dangerous revolutionary to ally with! Bang-up job, Lemaire!"

"Dangerous? To the Council, maybe!"

"Actually, according to your grandfather, he might be a murderer," I said. "He claims Cyrus killed Frank and that the seekers are him getting revenge on the town."

"What? No—no, that's—we don't know if that's true." Bastien stumbled over the assertion he knew was unverifiable.

"And yet you're already in too deep to get out," Remi said. "Oh! And let's not forget you took the time to make sure McKenna blamed herself for all of it and thought you hated her before you ran away."

"He was mad, and he had a right to be," I countered.

"He hurt you for something you had no control over," Remi said, giving him a sharp glare.

"I hurt him!" I exclaimed. "Either way, that's between us, and Bastien and I already talked about it!"

"In your little Pit love nest?"

"I would've thought jealousy was beneath you," Bastien put in.

Remi smirked. "It is. Envy, on the other hand…"

I rolled my eyes. "Not now, Remi."

Bastien looked between us. "Not what now?"

It was my turn to try to hold back, but as Remi started to speak—"Oh, did she not mention?"—I had to jump in.

"Remi suggested a triad," I blurted out.

Bastien was baffled. "What?"

"A triad, it's a three-person relationship," Remi helpfully provided.

"I know what it *is*," Bastien snapped. "When did this happen?"

"This morning," I told him.

"And you said…?"

I shrugged my hands in the air. "I didn't say anything! Remi didn't want an answer, he was just…putting it out there. And you're probably going to ask, so no, no, I don't know what I think. It's been kind of a busy day!" I gestured widely around us, then between Bastien and myself. "And it's not like we've even had time to talk about us, just us, either."

"No, we haven't, and do you really think that needs the added complication of whether I want a relationship with Remi as well?" Bastien replied.

"You don't have to." Remi's voice and form shifted back to her female form again, and she sidled up alongside him. Her wet hair was long enough to just cover her breasts, which were otherwise bare, her skin damp and dewy, and despite myself, I couldn't stop my eyes from tracing her curves; even Bastien's eyes dropped downward for a quick moment before flicking back up. "Unless you'd like to, of course. Even if it's just on occasion. Maybe a little hate-fuck to get it out of your system." She made a clawlike gesture with her hand, her nails coming just shy of touching his bare chest.

"Remi. What are you doing?" I asked. This was too far, even for her.

"Just finding out what appeals to our boy here," she purred, her flickering eyes not leaving Bastien's.

Bastien was clearly unamused. "Stop it."

"Ooh, why don't you make me?"

"Remi, this is crazy—" And it hit me—*of course* this was crazy. She'd literally just said she was having trouble controlling her powers.

Bastien wasn't rising to her bait, just glaring at her stonily, so she began circling him. "You know what I think? I think you've always been worried you're a little *too human* for her tastes. But now look at you, tainted with just a little more danger. It is compelling, you know, knowing the Golden Boy got a little tarnish on him. What's another taste of a demon lover at this poi—ahh!"

A blast of water from the garden hose in my hands knocked her back a few feet. She nearly toppled into the overchlorinated and spider-infested pool, but Bastien grabbed her arm and hauled her back to the pavement.

"*Refrigera*," I cast, making the water on her go from cold to icy. "You very much needed a cold shower."

Remi wrapped her arms around herself, teeth chattering. "F-f-fuck...th-this..." She gave a frustrated grunt, and a puff of fire emanated from her body. The water and ice flash-evaporated, and she sank back down onto one of the pool chairs, head in her hands.

"Are you good?" I asked, keeping a distance.

Remi laughed mirthlessly. "Hardly. But it'll have to do." She lifted her head enough for me to see her eyes were dark brown again, the fires of the Pit hidden once more. "I...I didn't mean to..."

"And yet, given the circumstances, you did." If Bastien had been wearing anything other than his boxer briefs, the statement would've come with a stiff straightening of lapels.

"All that means is it wasn't a lie. There are a few miles between that and actual honesty," Remi replied.

"Clearly, we all need to find some unprompted truth to tell before we bite each other's heads off," I said. Remi started to speak, but I held up a finger, stopping her. "No. No asking questions, just say something that no one here knows that's actually meaningful and vulnerable in some way. And I'm talking, so I may as well go first, so—" *Deep breath. Eye contact. If I'm gonna say this, I'm gonna make sure they hear it.* "—I care about you. I have feelings for you. *Both* of you. I...don't know what I want or what I'm ready for, I just know I...I want you both in my life in some way. I lost so much time with everyone I care about, and no matter what I do, I can't fix the damage that did. I'm trying so hard to make up for it, to—to make amends, but it's impossible. Those ten years are on me, and I'm going to regret them for the rest of my life, but what I really want is to stop having that hang over me all the time and actually *enjoy* having my life back and being with those people now. Including both of you. Because…you're two of the only people who make me feel like it's enough to just be me." The words poured out, not unlike in the support group. Just like then, I wasn't sure if it was purely the truth venom urging me onward or the deep need I hadn't been fully aware of to say these things aloud. What I had thought was going to be just a statement of how I felt about them had become something else altogether in the middle there.

My hands itched to take theirs while I spoke, but I clenched them tight, nails pressing into my palms. "This isn't a plea or an ask. I'm not asking either of you for any kind of response. In fact, please don't. I'm just…I'm saying how I feel. That's all."

Remi softened as I spoke, her frustration and anger replaced with a gentle, affectionate smile that was somehow still a smirk, too. "You already know my answer."

"Yeah. But you know it's not as simple as that," I replied. She shrugged and nodded in acknowledgment.

Bastien, on the other hand, was struggling to keep on his neutral mask but failing thanks to the truth venom. His features riffled among confusion, affection, and a few other things that were hard to pick out. "How can you say I make you feel like that? After what I said to you at the Solstice Ball?" he finally asked.

"We've already talked about that. And even when you were

mad at me, you didn't lurk around lording it over me like some people have. I'm not saying I want to forget the damage I did. I can't and I'm not going to. But one moment that we've both moved beyond doesn't define our entire past, or our future," I told him.

A smile flickered into place on his face—one of those genuine ones that I held so dear—and he reached to take my hand. "I'm glad to hear you say that. I want there to be some kind of future for us, too."

His fingers were cool and comforting in mine, but neither of us missed how Remi looked elsewhere, frowning and looking like she was holding something in. Bastien and I exchanged a glance, and he released my hand along with a heavy breath. "This isn't a story I particularly want to tell, I've barely ever told anyone, but…needs must, and the situation calls for it. I…I dated a couple in college."

Remi's head whipped back around so fast her hair nearly caused a wardrobe malfunction. "*You?*" She was speaking for the both of us, really, but my jaw hadn't recovered from dropping enough for me to join in.

Bastien sighed again. "Yes, me. During my semester abroad."

I gasped. "Is *that* why you said it was so 'unforgettable'?"

His cheeks colored. "Part of the reason. Anyway, it didn't last long and was a terrible idea from the start. Two friends of mine, both women, had been dating for a few months. They were both queer, one of them I'd drunkenly made out with a few times before the relationship. One night we were all inebriated and…" He cleared his throat, the pink on his cheeks deepening. "One thing led to another."

"Oho, I bet it did," Remi said lasciviously. She was eating this up.

"*Anyway*," Bastien went on, ignoring her. "We ended up deciding we should date. The three of us. For a few weeks, I was riding that high, but it quickly became apparent I wasn't really an equal partner, just a bedmate. I told myself I could live with that, but I couldn't. I felt...used. By people I had thought were my friends. I broke it off before they could, they stayed together, and by the end of the semester, we weren't more than acquaintances." He spoke with the dull pain of an old wound, yet blinked several times as though keeping back something deeper. "No one stays. No one ever..." The sentence ended in a puff of breath as he tried to expel the emotions.

Even in high school, I'd suspected Bastien was more demi-sexual than not, someone who needed a strong emotional bond before romance or sexual attraction came into the picture. Our relationship had taken a slow burn from friendship to romance, after all, and from what I'd heard, "Mari" had been his only serious relationship since then. I couldn't speak to all his relationships, but I remembered how he'd been stifling his sadness at breaking up with that mundane girl in high school; I knew how things had been between us; and I'd seen his hurt and anger in the wake of Saranthiel's deception. When he fell, he fell hard, and when his heart broke, it shattered.

It wasn't hard to see how this current situation, or potential situation, would be dragging up old pains for him.

While I was mired in thought and halfway to guilt about it, Remi scoffed loudly. "What a couple of bitches!" Bastien blinked at her in surprise. "Let me guess, you thought I was going to say you were being too uptight or something?"

"Well…"

She rolled her eyes. "I'll be the first—well, one of the first—to admit my communication skills aren't always top tier, but even I make sure everyone knows what they're getting into if they're getting into bed with me. Maybe they had good intentions, maybe not, but stringing someone along to be a live-action sex toy? Poor form, ladies."

Bastien started laughing again, and I caught a gleam of satisfaction on Remi's face. She went on to say, "I get this isn't the time for *that* discussion. Before that, there is something you should both know anyway, relating to my control of my powers and why I had Dara move in."

I raised a brow, curious about both those things. "Go on."

"For starters, McKenna, no, I don't wish you had this mantle instead of me. I don't know what that would do to a human, even one like you, and I'm not interested in you being how we all find out. I…" She paused, visibly struggling with what words came out next. "I wish there'd been another option. I don't mind a little chaos, but I don't like being unable to control my own power. One thing that I think has been helping is making more deals. Even small ones."

"Is that why you made one with me for filling up your gas tank?" It had struck me as somewhat petty at the time.

"Yep. Little deals that don't cost people much give me a better handle on it."

"That's helpful, but why is it something *we* should know, specifically?" Bastien asked.

"Because typically relationships involve a lot of...favors for free," Remi said, putting it as delicately as one could. "Things you do for someone just because you can, or want to, or because they need it or it makes them happy, without expecting recompense. But the more of those I let sneak by, the more my power sneaks out of me."

"Meaning you basically have to keep score?" I extrapolated.

"Bingo."

There was a pause as this set in, the potential scenarios lining themselves up in my mind. Judging by Bastien's slightly furrowed but otherwise carefully neutral face, he was doing something similar.

I turned back to Remi. "What does Dara have to do with this?"

"I know you don't trust her, but Dara is one of my oldest... well, the closest thing I've had to a friend in the Pit. She's shrewd, she's smart, she's as loyal as one can expect, and she's also very interested in climbing the demon corporate ladder, as it were," Remi said.

"Yeah, she's an ambitious hottie, we get it," I said, gesturing for her to go on.

Remi smirked. "Well said. Dara has agreed to take on the mantle of Madness from me and maintain a truce of nonaggression between us when she does."

My jaw dropped. "What? *How?*"

"I thought demonic power could only be removed or transferred by death of the owner," Bastien added.

Remi shrugged. "That we know of. This is contingent on finding a way to do so that doesn't mean me dying or losing my host body. Hey, they said restoring severed magic was impossible, but you and Cyrus have come up with a way to make it work."

Bastien tilted his head, acknowledging the point. "In theory."

"But what if you can't? What if it's impossible?" I asked.

Remi grinned. "Please, in this town, we do six impossible things before breakfast. Especially you, my black knight. If it's impossible, then Dara stays my right-hand demon and that's that." She paused, then added, "Also I hate your face. Ha! It worked! I can lie again. Thank hells that's over. Also, your face is great."

"Thanks," I said, albeit without much enthusiasm. There was too much whirling around in my mind. We'd all shared our truths, cured ourselves of the truth venom...but somehow, I felt heavier knowing all these things. Judging by the silent pause, I wasn't the only one.

Now that we could all lie again, it seemed like a good time to use a little white one. "I don't know about you two, but the pool fumes are starting to get to me. Let's get inside and clean up before we do anything else."

They both murmured agreement. Using the spare key once again, we went inside the thankfully empty house. I probably should've been wondering where Cyrus had disappeared to, but I decided to put creature comforts first.

———————————•———————————

It wasn't long before I was alone in the house. Remi opted to retrieve her car and erase any evidence of our presence at

Bastien's house, and she said she'd clean up at her place. Bastien took a quick shower, borrowed some clothes from Cameron's room before deciding he was done wearing clothes that weren't his, and excused himself to correct that state of affairs and, in his words, "practice looking shocked that my house burned down with my Realtor inside."

I took a very, very long shower, scrubbing my hair several times to do what I could to get rid of any lingering arachnids. I spread antibiotic ointment on the slashes on my hands and wrapped them in gauze, too spent just now to put the effort into a healing spell. And then I wrapped myself in my most comfortable sweats and flopped onto my bed.

I knew I should be focusing on the seekers, on the supposedly missing but clearly active Archdemon of Secrets, on whether my mom was dating a murderer, on the upcoming trial, but my mind refused to focus on any of those. Instead, it kept returning to Remi and Bastien, to the moments I'd shared in the last week with them both, to the confessions made mere hours ago. Some part of me, I realized, had hoped for some kind of resolution after I told them how I felt, but their own confessions had only made the whole thing even messier.

As if I have any idea what the hell a resolution would look like, or what I even want. I'd never entertained the idea of seriously dating more than one person at a time, not really. But now that Remi had put the notion in my head...I found myself coming back to it more and more. What did that say about me? Was I indecisive? Selfish? Insatiable? Primed to hurt and be hurt yet again?

Or was I just falling for two different people at the same time?

And if I was, was it going to cost me one or both of them?

"You look like you're in desperate need of a girls' night." My mom was standing at the door.

"Mom?" I sat up. "When did you get home?"

"Just now. I called up, I guess you didn't hear me. You were pretty lost in thought there." She came into my room and sat on the bed next to me.

"How's Cameron?"

"He'll be okay. He's stable, he's got good doctors. It'll be a long recovery, but he'll be fine," she told me. "You should come with me to see him tomorrow."

"I'd like that," I said. "I want to see him. Plus, it'd be a nice break from everything else."

"Oh? What's going on?"

"What isn't?" I shrugged my hands into the air. "I've been to the Pit and back, monster spiders are invading the town, there's another Archdemon out there somewhere plotting against us, don't even get me started on Remi and Bastien, and oh, yeah, my dad isn't who I thought he was, and also might be a murderer!"

Mom blinked in surprise, but only a little. "I take it you've heard some of the worst rumors about Cyrus, then."

"You think?" I sighed. I leaned my face into my hands, elbows resting on my knees. "But you know who I didn't hear any of it from? You."

Mom looked down. "In my defense, you kind of disappeared right after I told you about him being your father."

"Sure, and how about the twenty-eight years prior to that? Eighteen if we skip the ones I wasn't here, sure. Six if we're only counting from when dad left us. Let's go with that, then, what's your excuse for those six years?" I pressed, anger building. "Why didn't you tell me, Mom?"

She spread her hands, searching for words. "I…I don't know."

"Seriously? That's the best you can come up with?" Shaking my head, I got up from the bed.

"No. No, it's not. I'm sorry. I've imagined this conversation a million times, but I've never known what to say," she said. "I was scared what would happen if I did. For a long time, I told myself you weren't his, but…I think I always knew that wasn't true. When our magic came back and I saw what you could do, how strong your magic was, that erased any doubt. Then I told myself I was never going to see him again anyway, so why hurt you by giving you another absent father figure? Just another person in your life to feel abandoned by and disappointed in?"

"At least I would've known the truth!" I rounded back to face her. "At least I could've made that choice of whether or not I wanted to find him. Or finally known the real reason Dad left."

"What? What are you talking about?"

"It had to be that. He found out, didn't he? That you're the one who cheated first, that I wasn't even his?"

"McKenna. Your father—John leaving had nothing to do with you, or with Cyrus." Mom stood, level with me when she spoke this time. "He never knew what happened that night. I gave him a choice, that he could either be there for his family and stop stepping out on us, or he could leave. He made his choice."

"But you were in love with someone else the entire time!" I yelled. "That doesn't strike you as being even a little bit your fault?"

She glowered. "No. It does not. For one thing, I did not spend my life pining after Cyrus. I mourned for a while, yes. But he was gone, and I *did* love your dad. I did everything I could to make our marriage work, keep our family together. He's the one who made the choice to leave. That bastard didn't deserve any of us."

I knew these things. I knew them even if I hadn't heard them in so many words, hadn't ever had this conversation. Yet the act of hearing them set off some kind of whirlwind in me. I wiped my eyes before I realized I was crying. Why? Why now? My dad had been gone for nearly two decades, what right did he have to get any more tears from me?

"Oh, sweetie." Mom pulled me into a hug, and I found myself wrapping my arms around her, grateful for the warmth and welcome of it. I couldn't remember the last time we'd hugged. When had it been? Since we'd both come home, yes, but not in a while. She stroked my hair, and I felt like a kid again. In a good way. "None of what happened was your fault or Cameron's. You know that, right?"

"I know. It was practically the first thing you told us," I said, words muffled by her shoulder. "Do you regret it? Choosing him and not Cyrus?"

"That's a complicated question." She sat us both back

down on the bed. "The choices I made gave me you and your brother, and I could never regret that. Do I wish John had treated us all better? Of course. Do I wonder what life would've been like with Cyrus? Of course. But there's no guarantee that would've been any better."

"I guess a guy who was the Council's enemy number one, a possible murderer, freshly escaped from jail, and about to go on the run wasn't exactly a compelling option."

Mom snorted. "Something like that." I grabbed a tissue from my nightstand and blew my nose. "Is this actually about Cyrus, or is something else on your mind?"

. . . Oh, crap, it is, isn't it? "It's . . . not *not* about him."

"Fair enough. How about we get some wine, some pizza, and go talk downstairs?"

There were at least a dozen things I should be doing right now. Plans I had to make, cryptic clues I needed to comb through, people I should probably be contacting. But in that moment, having a night in with my mom was my only priority.

"That sounds perfect, Mom."

We settled in on the couches with a veggie pizza, a bottle of red wine, and two glasses.

"Where *is* Cyrus, anyway? I thought he was crashing here?" I asked as I grabbed a slice.

"He has been, and he'll be back later. He wanted to visit a few other old friends. He has a glamour, don't worry." Mom poured for both of us.

"He'd better. The Council knows he's in town. I don't know how, but Laurent brought it up at the meeting today,"

I told her. "Said he saw him walking around town with you."

"He did? But…Cyrus had a glamour the whole time we were in town," Mom replied.

"Not before you went to see Preston. He messaged me about it."

Mom still frowned. "He had an illusion on before that. And it's been thirty years, it's not like he looks exactly the same as the last time he was in town. Also, since when does Laurent Lemaire randomly go walking around downtown?"

These were all good points. Laurent had spoken with total confidence, though; he wouldn't have brought it up at all if he weren't certain. But why say he'd seen them with his own eyes if he hadn't?

I put a pin in that for now. "Either way, he knows. Also, I'm pretty sure Laurent also knows that he's my biological father."

"What?" Mom was clearly far more surprised by this. "How the hell does he know that?"

"No idea, and granted I'm just guessing, but…" I explained my suspicions to her.

"Okay, that's hardly a smoking gun, but considering the source, you might be onto something," she admitted.

"Speaking of smoking guns—Mom, *did* Cyrus kill Frank Milton? What happened that night?" I asked.

Mom sighed, setting down her glass. "I…I don't know. No one was there except for Cyrus, his father, and Frank."

"Laurent said *he* was. That he saw Frank attack Curtis for trying to do something to the leylines, and that Cyrus is the one who killed Frank."

Her brows lifted. "If he was, Cyrus never mentioned it, and I can't see why he wouldn't. He said Laurent and the others showed up after his father and Frank had it out."

"Someone's lying. The question is who and why." I washed down the thought with a gulp of wine.

"Whatever happened, Cyrus was being held at the Lemaire mansion afterward. Armand came to Gio and me to tell us what happened, that they were going to sever him, and we decided to get him out. Cyrus told us his father and Frank attacked each other, but they wanted to punish someone for it, so they were going to blame him," Mom explained. "He stayed here for a night and... when Armand portaled him out of town in the morning, that was the last time I saw him. Until the other day."

"Do you believe him? About Frank and his father?" I asked. "Do you know what they were trying to do at the leylines?"

"I believe him. They were trying to restore Curtis and his wife's magic."

I dipped my crust in the cup of marinara sauce on the table, nodding. "The same thing Cyrus wants to do for you now."

Mom nodded, lips pressed together in thought. "Yes, he told me the plan he and Bastien have."

I waited for her to say more, eventually prompting her, "What do you think about it?"

"I think... hells, McKenna, I would love to have my magic back. You know that," she replied, yearning in her voice for her lost abilities. "But there's no way this doesn't get danger-ous. Last time, two people died. Goddess knows I don't want anything like that happening again."

It was, more or less, what I had thought she would say; I'd told Bastien as much in the Pit. But it was a relief to hear it all the same. "If it works or if it doesn't, they're taking a huge risk."

"They are." She sighed again. "But it's their choice to make. I could tell them not to until the barrier comes down, but neither of them is going to change their mind if they don't want to. And Cyrus, he's always wanted to change the super-natural world for the better. Even the playing field, especially for hedgewitches." A dreamy smile spread on her face.

"And that's what you always liked about him. I get it." I tucked one leg under me on the couch.

She laughed. "Yeah. I was a spunky hedger teen witch with an attitude problem—yes, you come by it honestly—and he was this powerful, popular older boy, rebelling against the old guard, saying things like the system was broken, but if enough of us teamed up, we could change the way things were." Mom shook her head, though her affectionate smile remained. "Of course I was head over heels for him."

"So what happened?"

"We were overdramatic teens, that's what. We fought, we broke up, we got back together, rinse, repeat. My friends used to joke that whatever our status was, by the next week it would change, and they were usually right. It only really changed when I left for college and he stayed here in town," she said. "I told myself it was the clean break we needed. I met John there, he came back here with me, we got engaged and…" She let out a heavy breath. "And then one night Armand shows up telling me Cyrus is in trouble."

I chewed a second slice while turning that over. It was relatable. Hell, it was downright familiar. Even before our own "clean break" after she became an Archdemon, Remi and I had had our share of melodrama and micro-breakups. Thank goodness Bastien wasn't anything like my dad, though.

"Cyrus said you were glowing with magic when you broke their wards," I said.

"Yep. Down in the subbasement of the Lemaire mansion."

I laughed. "A subbasement. Of *course* the Lemaire mansion has a dungeon *and* a subbasement."

"Like all the best villain lairs," Mom replied, smirking. "And yeah, that's what they tell me. Probably the most magic I've ever used at once. It knocked me out for a few hours, and I couldn't cast anything else for at least a week."

"That happened to me at Bastien's wedding. When I tapped into the barrier magic."

Mom's brows went up. "I didn't know that. Do you think that's what I was doing that night?"

"Maybe. We were never *not* connected to it, it was just a one-way street for a long time. But if you were as desperate to save him as I was to face Saranthiel, then, yeah, I think maybe you did," I told her.

"Wow." She smiled, a quiet, melancholy expression. "Solomon's bones, I miss that feeling. I miss *magic*." The ache in her voice set off an ache in me. I remembered how it felt to be cut off from magic; I'd spent the majority of ten years that way by choice, and every second of it had just plain sucked. But I'd always had the option to have it back; Mom was not that lucky.

Unless, of course, the plan worked. Unless Cyrus and Bastien could really pull this off.

"I hate that I can't help them do this," I said aloud. "Help you get your magic back."

Mom reached over to pat me on the knee. "Sweetie, you are helping. You're making sure they can try."

"Yeah, I know, but I don't want to just be on the sidelines. Not for something like this."

She smiled knowingly. "You can't be integral to *every* major life-changing spell in this town, you know. Leave some room for everyone else."

It got a laugh out of me. "Okay, that might be *part* of it. But mostly, I *want* to be. It doesn't feel right relying on other people to fix my fuckup."

Mom stopped in the middle of reaching for the wine bottle. "Your fuckup? What are you talking about?"

"The fact that this never would've happened to you if I hadn't run away."

Her face went from confusion to comprehension. "Solomon's bones—is *that* why you've been doing all this? Paying the rent and the bills, giving me free drinks?"

"Yeah, you...wait, why did you think I was doing it?" I cocked my head at her.

"Putting up with me being an inept middle-aged burden you got saddled with!" Mom exclaimed, flopping back on the couch. "That you thought I was completely useless, unemployable, and irresponsible. I know at least that last one is true."

"I think you've been *acting* irresponsibly, but I don't think you're an irresponsible person," I told her. "But yeah, I thought there was this whole silent agreement to not talk about how I ran away and you paid the price and I owed you something I could never possibly repay."

"Goddess, sweetie, no. Never." Mom sat up, leaning over and grabbing my hand. "You don't owe me anything! Without you, I'd still be in the Harwell Institute and so would your brother. I had no idea that's what you thought was going on."

I half laughed, feeling a phantom weight start to lift. "I had no idea, either! I don't think you're inept or useless. I mean, I'd love it if you got a job and I wasn't the only one paying for everything, yeah, but I didn't think you were incapable of it. Just kind of refusing to? Up until you talked about it at the support group, anyway. I hadn't thought much about how hard it is for you to get another job now. I probably should have, considering how it's been for me."

"I *have* leaned a little hard on partying away my worries," Mom admitted. "I'm sorry. I admit I was annoyed that you thought... well, that I *thought* you thought that poorly of me. Not that thinking I'd be that selfish is a lot better."

"More like you'd earned a break from needing to be responsible," I said. "But I'm sorry for assuming."

"Me, too." Mom smiled kindly at me. "Starting over's hard, huh?"

I barked out a mirthless laugh. "You can say that again." I squeezed her hand. "Finding a new normal at home has been, too. Sometimes you act like I'm still a teenager, and sometimes like I'm a stranger. It hurts, kind of."

"It is hard. We didn't have years of you going from a teen

who acts like an adult to an actual adult for us both to adjust," Mom said, and we both laughed. "How about we both do better starting now, then?"

"Agreed." We clinked our wineglasses and drank to that, and the rest of the invisible weight slid away.

We spent the next hour or so finishing the pizza and the wine alike, talking about everything from how much job hunting sucked to things that had happened in our years apart. I filled her in about the Pit and the events of the day, including that our pool was going to need some serious cleaning before it was safe to use again.

"You're telling me that you, Remi, and Bastien all had to strip down in the pool? The three of you?" Mom asked, smirking. "How *interesting*."

"Mom!"

"That's not a wine blush! There is something going on. But with who?" Mom asked, eager for the gossip. "Come on, fill me in!"

"What, so you can taunt me about it like the other night?" I asked. "Or tell me how Remi's a bad idea again?"

Mom grimaced. "Sorry about that. That was the drinks and some passive-aggressive annoyance coming out. I shouldn't have said those things."

"But you did. Do you still think Remi's a bad idea?" And if she did, did I agree?

Mom let out a breath, thinking as she spun the stem of her glass in her hand. "I don't know. She has done a lot of good. I do think she's complicated, that's for certain, and it sounds like you've maybe got a less complicated option? Or is Bastien off the table?"

"He's not, but that's complicated, too. And might I point out you're already having overnights with your complicated ex, you know, the one wanted for murder?" I added.

"Fair enough. Maybe it's genetic," Mom said, shaking her head. "But who are you interested in?"

I stared at my glass, not looking at her. "I might be interested in both of them, actually. Which Remi has been clear she's okay with."

Mom's brows went up. "I see. Are *you* okay with it? Is Bastien?"

At her nonjudgmental response, I risked looking at her. "I don't know, on either account. It's been hard to figure it out."

"I can imagine." Mom sipped her wine, quiet for a moment. "Whatever you decide—all of you—I just want to know you're happy, McKenna. That's the most important thing to me, that you and Cameron are happy, healthy, and hopefully safe."

I grinned wryly. "Hopefully?"

"I know you both too well to think that one's a given," she replied.

I chuckled. "Thanks, Mom." It was reassuring to have ventured the idea to one person and not felt judged for it. I was still unsure, but it helped to know my mom had my back. I didn't expect us to never disagree again by any means, but salt and chalk, I felt so much better about us now than I had in the last six months.

And maybe I couldn't give Mom her magic back directly, but there was one thing I could do.

"Mom, I want you to be my proxy vote at the trial."

"Your proxy?"

"Since I'm Brooke's advocate and part of the trial, I can't take part in the vote. I can name any witch as my proxy, and I'm choosing you," I explained. "Cyrus won't need to sneak you in this way. You'll be there for completely legitimate reasons."

Mom was pensive. "That would probably help. But for the plan to work, I'd need to vote to sever her, wouldn't I?"

"You would. I don't think anyone will question you wanting to see Brooke punished, though," I said.

"No doubt. Between us, though? I don't," she told me.

"Really? Why not?"

"Because I don't think the Council or anyone else has a right to take magic away from someone," she said. "Bind it if they need to, sure. But to remove it entirely is cruel, and it's hurt too many people. What it did to Cyrus's parents, to me, and those are just a few examples. Plus, being a new mom and postpartum is hard enough as it is."

"So I hear," I said.

"If we're going to do all this, though, we should tell Brooke beforehand," she said.

I nodded. "Yeah, that's on my to-do list for tomorrow. After I go visit Cameron, that is."

"We'll go first thing in the morning," Mom agreed, then covered a yawn. "After some sleep."

"Sounds good."

We cleaned up; Mom said she was going to stay up to wait for Cyrus to come back. I headed up to my room and, to my surprise, found a new phone in a box on my bed, along with a note from Remi:

Thank you for saving my ass from the spiders. Love, Remi
P.S.—Yes, I got one for Golden Boy, too, he attempted to be stupidly heroic before we both got knocked out. I'm only telling you so no one accuses me of playing favorites.
P.P.S—You already know you're my favorite, obviously.

Chuckling, I opened the phone. It was starting to become a habit. This was the second time she'd gotten me a new one since I'd moved back to town. I texted her to say thank you.

Thanks for the phone. And for not
interrupting me and my mom.

It seemed the polite thing to do :)
Things all good in the Ellerbeck house?

Definitely better than they've been
I need to crash. Night Remi. Sweet dreams.

Nighty night my knight <3

As I settled into bed, I sent another text, this time to Bastien—Remi had already programmed his new number into the phone.

Bast, it's McKenna. New number.

Hello, McKenna. Yes, Remi added
your information to this phone already.

A surprisingly helpful gift.

           It is, yeah. Where are you staying?

The hotel for now, Room 1210.

           Whoa, not the penthouse?:P

No, that was already booked.
Hopefully it's just for a few days.

Because he was moving? Or some other reason? Once again, I didn't want to ask.

        Comfortable enough for now, no doubt
        I know things have been crazy, but we've got
        a few days before the trial. We'll get this
        figured out.

I hope so. We've certainly got plenty on our plates.

        We will.:)
        I'm heading to bed, just wanted to
        text so you had my number

As am I.
Good night, McKenna. Sweet dreams.

        Sweet dreams, Bast

He'd never been a very effusive texter, but I smiled all the same. Making a mental checklist for the next day was exhausting in and of itself—visit Cameron, talk with Brooke and Lucca, discuss plans with Cyrus and Bastien, address this spider problem—and sleep eventually overcame my obsessive need for practicality, and I drifted off.

Chapter 19
One Crisis at a Time

This time, when Laurent Lemaire showed up at my house, he didn't ring the bell.

He portaled right into the kitchen.

Mom and I nearly dropped our coffees when the bright-blue portal appeared and the old man himself stepped out, with Adele on his heels.

"What the hells, Laurent?" I exclaimed, feeling not at all intimidating in my pajamas and slippers. "It's called a doorbell!"

"A nicety I don't reserve for traitors," Laurent said in his gravelly voice.

That raised my hackles. "What are you talking about?"

"Wendy Ellerbeck"—he turned to face my mother, ignoring me—"you've been accused of aiding and harboring the murderer Cyrus Craig. You're coming with us pending your trial for these crimes against your fellow witches."

Mom stood up, aghast. "What? No, that's—look around the house, Cyrus isn't here!"

"No, but he was thirty years ago when he was meant to be standing trial for his crimes. And you were seen with him yesterday in town," Laurent replied.

"You didn't say anything about this yesterday," I argued. "Where is this coming from?"

"From us confirming that it was in fact Cyrus when we took him into custody last night," Adele said. "And his admitting that Wendy is the one who helped him escape before."

"*What?*" Mom and I both exclaimed.

"Are you going to come willingly, Wendy?" Laurent said.

"Whoa, slow down. Why is she going anywhere?" I cut in, getting between Laurent and my mom.

"Because she's being tried tonight, and I don't intend to give her a chance to run," he said. "As your family is so very fond of doing."

"*Tonight?* Okay, hold up a minute! This is crazy, not to mention rushed as fuck. What happened to a week's notice? We aren't even rushing Brooke's trial!" I protested.

"We are now," Adele replied. "Brooke, Cyrus, and Wendy are all being tried tonight. Emergency circumstances."

"What emergency?"

"The apprehension of a murderer who's thirty years overdue for his sentencing," Laurent replied. "He got away from us once. It won't happen again."

"But—my mom—what are you going to do to her? She's already severed!" I exclaimed.

"We can relieve her of the memory of what she's lost," Adele said.

Mom's eyes went wide with panic. "No! No! You can't do

that—you can't take that from me!" She backed away rapidly, about to flee the room.

"Unwillingly it is, then." Laurent gestured toward her, and a portal opened on the floor beneath my mom; she screamed as she plunged through, and it snapped shut before I could get there or even see where it led.

"What the fuck, Laurent?" I rounded on him, fury tightening every muscle in my body. "Bring her back, *now*!"

Laurent fixed me with steely eyes, not intimidated in the least. "Your mother is a criminal. She's where she belongs."

"Bullshit!"

"Your family doesn't get special treatment just because you're a Council member," Adele said, her voice thick with condescension.

I glared at her. "Oh, yeah? Hope you're ready to round up your big brother and take on the wolves, then, cause Armand and Gio helped Cyrus escape, too!"

For the first time ever, Laurent Lemaire was stunned.

After her own shocked pause, Adele stammered. "Wh-what? No. Armand would never."

"No? You think my mom, nothing more than a hedger without even a grimoire at the time, somehow found Cyrus in your house and got him out all on her own?" I pointed out. "How do you think she knew where he was in the first place?"

"You're lying," Adele hissed.

"Only one way to find out."

"Adele!" Laurent snapped. "We're leaving." Adele looked like she might protest, but seeing her father's expression, she slunk back to him. He opened a portal behind them, back to their mansion. Laurent turned his gaze once more to me. "If you're making this up just to try and save your parents…"

I lifted my chin. "I'm not. And how do you know who my father is?"

"Unlike John Ellerbeck, I can read a calendar." He and Adele stepped back through the portal. "The trial starts at sundown. Bring your proxy with you."

"Where?"

"Be here. We'll open a portal."

With that, his current portal snapped shut. The bright blue of the magic danced on my eyelids as I closed them. I forced myself to take several slow, deep breaths, but it was no match for the tidal wave of panic. My mother was on trial, *again*, and this time they might erase her memory; my newly found father might lose the magic he'd barely escaped with before, and my mom's only chance at getting hers back with it; and I'd just ratted out Bastien's dad and Leo and Lucca's dad to boot. And it was all going down in a matter of hours.

The slow breaths turned into shallow gasps; my head felt light and unmoored to the rest of me, to the rest of the world, and I was on the floor, when had I gotten on the floor? Where was the rest of the room, where was my mom, seven hells what was going to happen to my mom, I had to help her, had to fix this, had to fix all of this—

Stars glittered in the corners of my vision, and the room was growing dark around me; I was going to pass out, I knew I was, and I didn't have the time to spare for that, but I had to do something. *Passing out isn't going to help her! Neither is panicking, she needs a plan, I need a plan!*

"I need to help her, I need to help her," I gasped. My heart raced. I shut my eyes.

I felt the ghost of Bastien's hands on mine, heard his calm, steady voice: *Breathe through your nose. Like this. Breathe in. This is temporary. Breathe out. This is temporary.*

But this isn't temporary, not if I don't do something about it!

Then Remi's voice joined in. *You're McKenna Ellerbeck. There's nothing you can't handle.*

I held the image of them both in my mind, repeating their words, and eventually my breathing slowed. The panic wasn't gone, not by a long shot, but it was manageable.

I'd faced hellhounds and Archdemons and even the Council before. I could do this. I *had* to do this. My mom needed me, and this time, I was going to be there for her.

But I couldn't do it alone. Lucky for me, I didn't need to.

I hadn't done many Zoom meetings, but this one started with about the expected amount of chaos, judging from what I'd heard.

Baby Josie was bawling loudly, and nothing Lucca or Brooke did was getting her to quiet down. Cameron's nurses came in to check his vitals and change his IV right after Gretchen got her phone set up in his room. Remi and Dara called in from the condo, so naturally Mr. M was walking on the keyboard and showing us all his butt. Leo, who was at work at her day job doing graphic design, and Bastien, who was in his car, were the only ones who had considerately put in earbuds and muted themselves, and they were waiting patiently for the rest of us to get ourselves in order so we could start. Finally, I let out a sharp whistle.

"Okay. Everyone, hope you're listening. If you missed it, here's the deal: Cyrus Craig, aka my bio-dad—"

"Your *what*?" Lucca, Brooke, and Leo all exclaimed, coming off mute. Cameron, to my relief, didn't look shocked, just disgruntled—Mom must have told him already.

"Long story for another time. He supposedly killed a witch thirty years ago, and they caught him last night. He told them my mom is the one who sprang him last time, so Laurent and Adele portaled her somewhere this morning, no idea where. I, uh, might've been the one to tell them Armand Lemaire and Gio Luppino were in on that, too—"

"Yeah, thanks for that, by the way," Lucca said, briefly coming off mute.

"Sorry, but I was pissed off and making a point. I take it someone stopped by for your dad, then?"

"Laurent came to my house to tell me Dad was on their shit list for helping Cyrus, and apparently witches don't believe in a statute of limitations," Lucca said, a growl in his voice. Josie had settled down; in the background, we could see Brooke rocking her in a wide arc. "At least he was smart enough to come to me about it." Lucca had taken over as alpha of the pack for his dad when he turned eighteen.

"What did you tell him?"

"That we'd talk about it. I want to tell him to get fucked, but he's obviously super serious about this whole thing if he's bringing it up at all," Lucca said, continuing to forget to not swear in front of the baby. "I'm gonna talk to my dad, but my plan is I'll agree to bring him but only *if* I'm there, too, and any punishments are my call."

"The jackass should've already been letting you go to it with Brooke," Leo said.

"Damn right he should've," Lucca growled.

"What about you, Bastien?" I asked.

Bastien's camera was off, but he unmuted to reply. "My mom called me just after Grandfather came to see them. She's worried, though it sounds like he received better treatment than Wendy. He wasn't taken into custody, but I assume Wendy and Cyrus are in my grandfather's home."

"Is this about to turn into a raid on the Lemaire mansion?" Cameron asked. "'Cause no way I'm missing that."

"Yes, you damn well are, dude with two broken ribs and a recently reinflated lung," Gretchen cut in.

"What she said," I agreed. "And no. Busting people out of there is what got our parents into this in the first place. I hate to say it, but I think we need to do this the witch way and go through with the trial."

I could hear Cameron rolling his eyes. "Yeah, *that'll* go well. Totally fair and unbiased."

"There are conflicting reports on whether Cyrus killed anyone, and the rest of our parents certainly didn't," I replied.

"If you can prove them innocent or get this crap dropped through official channels, it'll be gone for good," Leo pointed out. "But do you think you can really sway enough people to vote with you?"

"I can always help with that," Remi offered, smirking.

"Kinda doubt that's gonna help," Lucca said. "Plus Lemaire's clearly out for blood."

"*One* Lemaire," Bastien corrected him. "Well, two."

"Right, yeah, sorry, man. Hey, did I hear your house burned down?" Lucca asked, causing a whole commotion as this was news to most people on the call.

"Yes, it did, but it was a little more, ah, intentional than not. The seeker monsters had completely overtaken the place. We had no other choice."

Leo gaped at the screen. "You committed arson on your own house?"

Remi piped up, "Did he ever, and it was glorious, Leo. I've never been prouder of the boy. Actually, I don't think I've ever been proud of him at all, but still."

"Let me rephrase—you committed arson on your own house and *Remi was there?*"

Bastien's voice belied the embarrassed flush of his face. "It was . . . complicated."

"McKenna was there, too," Remi helpfully added.

"Remi!"

"Mickey! You have been holding out on me," Leo said.

"Yeah, what she said!" Brooke agreed, leaning in to get on camera, unintentionally nearly flashing us all, as she was now breastfeeding Josie.

"Brooke! Wardrobe malfunction!" Leo said, thrusting a hand out to cover her phone screen. "You're gonna get me in trouble at work!"

"I don't think they can if it's breastfeeding related," Remi mused.

"They can if it's not *my* breast!"

"Breastfeeding is natural and not sexual," Brooke replied, though she did adjust her angle.

"Is it safe?" Cam asked, keeping his eyes distinctly elsewhere.

"Yes, Cam, the big scary boob is gone," Gretchen teased him.

"If we could focus, please. My question is, How does this new wrinkle affect Bastien and Cyrus's original plan?" Dara said, finally speaking up. Much as I was still unsure about her, I appreciated someone getting us back on track.

"What original plan was this?" Lucca asked.

"Cyrus and I were planning to use the severing ritual to instead reverse Wendy's severing and restore her magic," Bastien said.

"You can do that?"

"In the middle of Brooke's trial? When were you gonna tell us?" Lucca said.

"Today, actually," I told him. "They worked out a two-part ritual to reverse the spell and, instead of pulling magic out of a person, put it back into a designated person. But half of it was Cyrus's job to cast."

"Some good news on that front. I've got photos of an older copy of his half. With your help, we can finish it, and I'll be able to cast both halves," Bastien said.

"That sounds like a lot for one person to do at once," Gretchen said.

I chewed my lip. "It is. I'll do Cyrus's half. I've got better metamagic, and you can catch me up on whatever else I need to know."

Remi frowned. "Are you sure about this? There were some very specific reasons for you not getting involved in casting."

"I hate agreeing with Remi, but yeah. What if they decide to sever you for it next?" Cameron asked.

"If it works, it won't matter," I replied. "And we're out of other options. Gretchen, I want you to be my voting proxy tonight."

She did a double take. "Me? Uh—you sure?"

"Positive. If you're willing to, and cleared by the doctors?"

"Yeah, I've been cleared for a few days now. Sure, I guess so."

"Thanks. Cam, if you weren't bedbound, I'd ask you. Now, while I don't think anyone should be, we need to make sure at least one person is sentenced to severing to pull this off. But that doesn't need to be Brooke anymore since they've got Cyrus now."

"Actually…" Brooke and Lucca exchanged a significant look. "I'm going to plead guilty. I'm going to ask them to sever me."

Just about all of us exclaimed in shock at that one.

"What?"

"Why?"

"Are you serious?"

"Are you *crazy*?"

"Mrow!" Even Mr. M was getting in on it.

"Quiet down! Yeah, she's serious, no, she's not crazy. We talked about it," Lucca said.

Brooke nodded. "We did. I don't want to be a witch. There's no joy left in magic for me. I lost my family, I've been teased and mocked for being a hedgewitch, I sold my soul, I nearly lost Lucca. The pack is my real family. They're the ones who made me feel welcome, like I had a home and a family again. That's where I belong, and once I'm severed, hopefully, I can be one of them."

There were few ways for a supernatural being to become something else. Witches couldn't become werewolves, even if they were bitten. But maybe a severed one could?

"What if it doesn't work?" Leo finally said. She'd tried every way to become a wolf that she could, even if she'd never admit to all of the attempts. "If it doesn't, you'll just be, you know, human. Normal."

"Then I'll be human, and that's fine, too. I know some pretty great humans," Brooke said. She smiled, a smile clearly meant for Leo, who returned it after a moment.

"Hell yeah you do," she said.

Dara cleared her throat. "This is all terribly fascinating, cheers on your self-empowerment, rah-rah, and no offense meant, but I assume you have something on that agenda that you needed the rest of us on this call for?"

Right. "I do. We still have a monster problem. We took out all the seekers in Bastien's house, but those things are all over town and range from crumb size to werewolf size. Remi and Dara, we need you two to work with the wolfpack on hunting down as many of them as you can find, plus any other minions that Secrets tries to sneak into town, while we're busy with the trial. I still don't know what Secrets is up to exactly, but I've got a feeling it's coming to a head soon."

"You know we're good for it," Lucca said, speaking for the pack.

In the chat window, I messaged Remi privately: *Play nice*

with the wolves and protect the town from those things and I'll owe you. Deal?

A smirk lifted her lips as she read it. "As are we." *Deal,* she wrote back. *You'll owe me one dinner date.*

The subtle weight of a deal settling on me didn't feel unnerving this time. I could live with a dinner date, and it would help keep her power in check.

"I've got an anti-seeker potion recipe, I can brew up some extras for you," Gretchen offered. Remi and Dara agreed to meet up with her, and Lucca said he'd get her in touch with Chris and the rest of the pack.

"Anything the token human can do?" Leo asked. She hated being sidelined as much as Cameron.

"There is. You and Cam are on watchtower duty," I said.

I saw Cameron's and Leo's eyes both flick to particular parts of their screens as each looked at the image of the other. "We are?" Cameron said hesitantly.

I knew they were exes, and it had to be awkward, but neither of them was able to go in the field, so to speak. But together they had the skills needed for this.

"You are. Cam, you can still cast and locate any demons on a map, maybe figure out how to track seekers, too—"

"I have a spell for that, too!" Gretchen said. "It just needs a sample subject."

"Perfect, show it to him before you leave. And Leo, you can keep tabs on everyone and make sure any sightings are covered," I concluded.

"Sure, I guess. I'll tell the boss I gotta leave early today," Leo replied. Even through the screen, her face had a look of *you owe me for this one*. "What about you? You're getting whisked off to some supersecret location, any way we can keep tabs on you?"

"Bastien and I will work on that if we can," I promised.

"Speaking of, I'm almost at your house," Bastien said.

"Good. I think that's everything. Any questions?" Half of them immediately started talking, so I raised my voice to speak over them. "Any questions that are absolutely necessary?" Quiet grumbling answered me. "Good. Then we'll all be in touch as needed. And...thanks, everyone."

They started logging off, but Leo and Remi lingered.

"Mickey? I'm really proud of you," Leo said.

"For what?"

"For not trying to do it all yourself for once," she said. "I know that wasn't easy, but it was the right call. The *smart* call."

"You know, it actually wasn't as hard as you might think," I told her, smiling fondly.

She smiled back. "Well, isn't that surprising?" We both laughed. "We got this. I'll talk to you later." She signed off.

I turned my gaze to Remi. Dara had walked off somewhere, and Remi was now alone on her camera, with Mr. M curled up in her lap. "I take it you had something to add as well?"

"A few things. Leo's right, so there's that. Two, think about where you want to go on our date. I'm thinking somewhere outside of town for once," Remi mused. "Happy to spring for a hotel, of course, if you want to make another deal."

My face warmed and I cleared my throat. "Noted, but that's going on the to-do list for after this is all done."

"Naturally. And three, have fun making magic together with Bastien," she said, winking at me through the screen. "You can tell me all about it at dinner."

Now my face was really flushing. "Anything else? That isn't more flirting?"

Remi chuckled but then looked a shade more serious. "Yes. The...offer to make a deal there. Thanks for that."

"You're welcome. We need you clearheaded, after all," I said.

"We do, and that helps. Maybe I mean more, thank you for understanding."

I smiled at her. "You're welcome for that, too." The doorbell rang. "That'll be Bastien. I'll talk to you later, Remi." She waggled her fingers at me and disconnected.

Bastien came in with a briefcase and a garment bag, dressed in a pair of khakis and a button-down shirt that both looked fresh off the rack, complete with packaging crease marks on the shirt. "I assume you have spell supplies, because all of mine are cinder and ash."

"I do, and hello to you, too," I replied. "You brought a change of clothes?"

He hung the garment bag in the hall closet. "I did, as I also assume I may not have time to go back to the hotel to change before it's time for the trial. It's lucky I kept some spare suits in my office."

"You don't think it'll look strange if your grandfather finds you here when he comes to portal me to wherever it is we're going?" I asked.

Bastien shrugged. "It will, but I don't particularly care at this point. He's gone too far."

"Now that I like to hear," I replied. "Although I hadn't thought about what to wear, but I'll figure that out later."

"Anything will be an improvement on the BEACH BUM shorts," Bastien said, some humor lighting his eyes despite the seriousness of the situation. I shook my head, smiling, and waved for him to follow me to the basement.

The basement level of my house was finished, and in my youth it had served as a playroom and then a second living room when I was a teen. Those furnishings had been claimed by my brother for his apartment some time ago, though, so since moving back in, I'd turned it into my very own witchy workshop. Mismatched furniture that had been Freecycled or scrounged from yard sales filled it now: a bookcase that was missing a middle shelf, making it perfect for some of the larger volumes I owned; an old desk-turned-workbench, its surface scuffed and scratched and stained from its past life as well as some of the work I'd done on it; jars of spell implements and ingredients. But this was modern witchcraft, so I also had a desk chair, a laptop stand, a printer, and a small couch for more comfortable seating. The middle of the room was clear of any furniture, however, for that was where I did my rituals, inside the circle I'd drawn in chalk on the hardwood floor. Codex sat inside that circle now, in fact—keeping it there made for an added measure of protection against anyone getting ideas of making off with it.

"This changed since high school," Bastien remarked.

"I needed a proper workspace," I said, setting my computer on the stand and collecting the grimoire from the floor. "Not quite designer, but it gets the job done."

"I like it," he said. "Efficient, comfortable . . . it's very you."

I snorted. "Ah, yes, 'efficient and comfortable,' exactly how I've always longed to be described."

"I mean it's the kind of space I know you prefer. Clean, organized, adaptable—but with some creature comforts," he clarified. He set the papers on the desk. "Believe me, if I were asked to describe you, I'd be using very different words," he added. His eyes rested on me in a way I could almost feel on my skin.

The statement begged for a follow-up. "Maybe you can tell them to me . . . sometime," I replied, my face warming, deeply curious about what those words were. But the efficient part of me knew now was not the time. I crossed to the desk, grabbing some clean paper and pencils. "But right now, we need to figure out these rituals."

For the next hour, we went over both ritual circle designs. The one that Bastien had already recreated from Leo's patch-up job didn't need any work, but he did need to walk me through it so I could understand what his part was and what Cyrus's had been intended to be.

Bastien's ritual was mainly focused on reversing the severing spell. Cyrus had seen the original severing spell when it was used on his parents, so they'd adapted it from there. The spell was designed to open access to the power source—in this case, the leyline nexus—and direct magic into it. Instead, this version would reverse that direction. Additionally, Bastien had worked in runes to try to separate the demonic power in his magic and banish it. I still had my doubts about the feasibility of that, but the runes all checked out. And maybe with the leylines' power, it would be possible.

While Bastien was essentially turning the spigot, Cyrus was the one controlling the hose. His portion of the spell focused on his metamagic specialty. With access to the source secured, his spell would direct the power to the intended target. Since they needed to differentiate my mom from the supposed target, Brooke, they had created a unique rune that the target needed to carry.

"Mom didn't say anything about that, so I'm guessing he didn't give it to her yet," I said.

He nodded. "We can place it on a stone or something small. I can't imagine they'll refuse to let you see or speak to her at all when we get there, and you can slip it to her."

"Here's hoping." I flipped open my grimoire. "That should be easy enough. But what about the ritual spells for you and Cyrus? How were you going to put those into action?"

"As an advocate, I was going to see the trial grounds before-hand, to be familiar with it ahead of the trial—"

"Gee, so nice of anyone to offer me that chance, too."

"—and I'd make the changes needed to the circle then. Since that's obviously not going to happen, I'm open to ideas. Cyrus never said what his plan was, but said he had it covered."

My eyes narrowed. "Cyrus kept an awful lot to himself about this."

"It didn't seem like much at the time, but adding it all together now, it *is* a concerning pattern," Bastien agreed, brows pinching together. "I'm not sure why. Maybe to protect me from backlash if we were found out or things went awry."

I spread my hands. "I'd say things have officially gone awry! On a scale of one to ten, how protected would you say you feel?"

His grin was wry and humorless. "Somewhere around a one."

"Same. In other words, the supposed wise elders are useless, and it's up to us to save the day." With a sigh, I rubbed my scarred palm, thumb smoothing over the old wound as I stared at the sketches.

"I'm all for it, but how do we pull it off?"

My thumb stilled, and I looked down at my hand. "That's it." I held up my wrist, pointing to the inactive wards on it. "We wear them!"

Bastien reached up, taking my wrist, his fingers tracing the lines on my skin. "That would work. And it would be dormant and undetectable until we activated them. But neither of us is a tattoo artist, nor do we have time to find one who could do an enchanted tattoo."

"We don't need to. It only needs to last through the trial. All we need is a marker or some smudge-free body paint or something," I said. I turned back to my grimoire. "Codex, what do you have for enchanted ink or paint?" Golden light flared over the page and faded into black ink as spells appeared. "Good... okay, eliminate any that might smudge on skin." A few of them disappeared.

Bastien watched me curiously. "It's almost like you're having a conversation with it."

"Well, yeah, I basically am."

His head cocked in thought. "Interesting."

He'd seen me call it forth and command it firsthand when experiencing my memory of the night Jackie died, but that was the closest I'd come to using my grimoire in front of another witch other than Cameron. We were all so unreasonably paranoid about sharing them. But what good had that done me? As a result, I knew very little about how grimoires other than mine worked. Living ones, that is; the Uncommon Collection had some dead grimoires, ones without any living owners, families who'd died off. But those books were inert and fixed. Living grimoires were more malleable, but the particulars were private to each family.

Bastien's reaction told me maybe my grimoire was entirely alone in its interactivity. Interesting, indeed.

How much more might I know—might we all know—if we stopped holding back and holding ourselves apart? Stopped letting the witch community, even the supernatural community, be so separated? Knowledge is power. Why shouldn't we share it?

I angled the book so he could see it, ignoring the anxious feeling that old habits and beliefs stirred in me as I did so. "What do you think?" Bastien was surprised as I openly shared the book with him, but leaned over to take a look.

"Some of these will take too long to set," he noted. A few of them disappeared from the page. "Oh—thanks. This one would work, do you have the ingredients?"

I did a quick inventory. "Got it all, even the pixie dust. Let's make Grothmann proud."

The act of making the ink was straightforward—mix the ingredients, chant the incantation, let it mix, boil, and cool. More difficult was figuring out where to draw the runes so they were both big enough to be distinct and required neither working backward in a mirror nor risking a broken line from bending awkwardly. Soon enough, there was only one clear solution: drawing them on each other.

"These will both need to be either back or stomach to make sure there's enough room," I said, reviewing the sketches as the ink finished cooling. "What's your preference?"

Bastien stretched one hand behind him, frowned, then instead slid it under his shirt to his stomach. The button-down lifted, revealing a sliver of his sculpted abdomen. "Stomach. Easier to reach with my hand to activate. You?" His gaze moved over me in a way that made something coil and curl pleasantly in me.

"Same. I can pinprick my finger and do the same to cast mine without it being too obvious." I checked the ink. "This is cooled off and ready to go. I'll get you first. Set up the circle and I'll get the ink ready," I instructed, passing my grimoire to him. He cradled the spine gently in his hand. I could swear I almost felt the light pressure on my own, a whisper of his magic moving over my skin at the contact with the book. He carefully drew the lines needed to enchant the application of the ink, lit some candles around the edge of the circle, and tossed down a couch pillow for comfort, all while murmuring the words for the spell.

Meanwhile I got the ink and a thin paintbrush, wafting incense over the silver liquid. I spoke my own spell over it, adding to the growing feel of magic in the air. Picking up the jar of ink and the brush, I turned, waiting for Bastien to finish with the preparations. Once he had, our eyes met and we spoke the final part of the spell together as we both walked to the center of the circle.

When we were both there, we knelt on the floor, the ink between us. Using a small pin, I pricked a finger and added a single drop of blood, turning the mixture gold as it hit the surface. "By my blood, I bind this spell with my magic." The connection between myself and the mixture was forged, a line between me and it that I could feel thrumming within me.

"By my touch, I bind this spell with my magic." Bastien dragged the tip of his finger across the surface, stirring it and leaving a trail of blue that spilled into the gold. I felt the pulse of his magic, his sorcery, in my blood as it mixed with my own, the two swirling around each other, the ink becoming a marbling of blue and gold.

My blood, my body, felt warm with it, my breath coming heavier than I'd expected, but then, we were loading a lot of firepower into this. Looking at Bastien as I set the jar down, I could see it hitting him, too, his storm-blue eyes fixed on me. Without words, I reached forward and undid the buttons on his shirt, working my way down and revealing his leanly muscled chest and abdomen as I went. He didn't speak, either, just watched me as I slid the garment from his shoulders, my fingers trailing over his arms, and set it aside. Only then did he move, gently taking the hem of my shirt in his hands, pausing with a silent request for consent. I nodded, lifting my arms, and he peeled the shirt from me, fingertips somehow still cool as they brushed my skin in passing, and set the shirt down with his.

For a moment we stayed there, kneeling and shirtless—my bra remained on—taking each other in, the intoxicating mix of our magic heavy in the air. Seven hells, I wanted to touch him. To kiss him. To pick up where we'd left off in that cave.

But there was work still left to do.

I put my hand to his shoulder. My hand felt like a fire compared with his coolness. "Lay back," I instructed, gently pushing him to recline. He nodded, eyes never leaving me as he did so.

Taking a breath to steady the rushing inside me, I laid out the grimoire, open to the runes for the ritual spell. Dipping the brush into the ink, I picked my starting point and began to paint, drawing the bristles in a slow, steady curve across his stomach. He flinched, breath catching, and I paused, not lifting the brush. "Are you all right?"

"Sorry—that tickled. I'm fine," he replied, taking a breath. "The ink sort of tingles, but it's good. It's working. Keep going."

I did so, focusing totally on my task. The more lines I painted, the more natural it started to feel, as though my connection to the ink, and through that, to him, were leading the brush as much as my eyes. The rune took shape on the hard planes of his abdomen, the ink and the magic sinking into his skin. At some point, he closed his eyes, and I could feel him steadying his breath so as not to disturb my work.

"Just one more. I'm almost done." I leaned over him to finish the last rune on the far side of his stomach. As I finished and lifted the brush, the entire thing glowed with gold and blue light, flaring and sealing itself to him. Bastien let out a shuddering breath, grabbing my arm tightly for a moment before his grip went slack. "Ha, you need a minute?"

He laughed breathlessly, his hand sliding down to squeeze mine. "You'll see." He moved aside, making space for me to lie down while he knelt where I had a moment before. Rewetting the brush, he started as I had, drawing the brush in a slow circle around my abdomen. Despite my trying to steel myself for some kind of jolt, it still took me by surprise as the magic sank into my skin, leaving my veins and hands tingling. I gasped and he smiled knowingly, saying nothing else as he continued painting. His hands moved with unrushed confidence, every stroke stirring the magic in me further, until I was nearly dizzy with it. I was used to being overfull of magic—it had become a constant problem when I locked mine up for the better part of ten years. But instead of my feeling ill, poisoned, and overwhelmed, this feeling was euphoric, bursting with possibility and energy. A spell just before being cast, teetering on the edge of unleashing, all the potential on the verge of becoming kinetic. It came close to how I'd felt when I'd used the energy of the barrier to kill Saranthiel, though that feeling had been much more intense and had quickly turned toxic. Maybe it was the control and purpose the runes gave the magic, maybe it was engaging in it with a partner this time, but this was different. This was better.

Knowledge, power, magic . . . they're meant to be shared, I found myself thinking, my eyes lingering on Bastien. He leaned over me, one arm tensed to support his weight while the other traced the lines onto my body. His eyes flicked to my face and, finding my gaze on him as well, held there for a moment.

"Last one," he finally said, dipping the brush into the last of the ink. Without his eyes leaving mine, he swept the brush over my ribs, and magic blazed through my body, lighting every nerve, head to toe. The runes flared, and I sucked in a breath, my back arching as the sensation swept through me.

"Seven hells," I panted, my body still tingling from the completion of it.

He set the brush in the empty jar, sliding it aside. "Thankfully not literally this time," he said with a soft chuckle. "Now to test it…"

"Test? I'm about one hundred and ten percent sure the magic worked just fine," I replied, pushing up on my elbows.

Bastien smiled. "As am I. But will the lines keep?" He lifted his hand, his fingers settling down on my abdomen just below my bra. My skin felt hyperaware of the pad of each fingertip as he drew them down my stomach toward my waist, his eyes once again never leaving mine, not until they reached the waistband of my jeans. Only then did they flick down, and he nodded. "Perfect. Not a one out of place."

He started to move his hand away, but I grabbed it, holding it in place. "Don't stop."

Bastien's eyes met mine again, pretense gone, echoing the desire in me. "McKenna…"

I knew this question. I knew my answer. "You don't have to ask."

He smiled, coming closer, the lean muscle of one arm tensed as he held himself above me. "Yes, I do." He tilted his head and kissed my jaw, featherlight and setting off sparks. As he reached my ear, he whispered, "Will you tell me what you want?" His hand tightened on my hip. "And how?"

His words, his breath on me, his touch, were all so gentle, and yet they pounded through me. "Kiss me. Touch me. Everywhere. The way you do. Like time is short but you have to savor it," I answered, kissing just under his jaw, tasting his skin with a quick flick of my tongue and feeling him shudder from it. "If this all goes to hell and yours is the last magic I'm going to feel, I want to feel all of it." My hand slid down his stomach, his side, grabbing his hip and pulling him against me. "All of *you*."

With a groan, his lips finally found mine, sweet and hot, unhurried but eager, forcing patience on my more aggressive kiss. He lowered me back onto the pillow as his hand moved from my hip to my ass, and I hooked my leg over his to pull myself closer. In a matter of moments, my bra was tossed aside and he cupped my breasts, teasing the hard peaks until I moaned. "Kiss me," I urged in a breathless moment.

"I *am* kissing you," he laughed, his lips and tongue finding mine again.

"Everywhere," I clarified when I could.

He hummed in acknowledgement and began moving his way down my body, long fingers trailing paths that his lips followed. He moved from one breast to the other, licking and sucking at each until I dug my nails into his shoulders. "More. More, Bastien, please, touch me," I begged.

"I was hoping you'd say that," he replied, sliding my jeans and underwear alike off my hips. His hand slipped between my legs, stroking my center with a perfect, maddening lightness. I must have growled or said something, because the next thing I knew, he was laughing throatily and pulling the clothing off entirely. Settling between my legs, he murmured something indistinct in French.

"Are you casting something?" I asked, lifting my head. "And if yes, why? Why now?"

"You're the one who said to savor," he reminded me, placing a lingering kiss on the inside of my thigh. "And that you wanted to feel my magic."

"I was being metaphorical."

He chuckled. "Yes, I know. But why be metaphorical when you can be literal? Relax, and reach out with your magic."

Cocking an eyebrow, I lay back, taking a breath and trying to do so. Not so easy when the hot guy you've been wanting is inches from tasting you. He grasped one of my hands, fingers twining with mine. "*Un cadeau de ma magie pour toi*," he whispered, his breath tickling my most sensitive spot, and waves of blue magic splashed on me, into me, through me. Usually demonic power felt vile to me, corruption trying to seep into my blood. But his unique mixture, his sorcery, wasn't like that at all—it had a certain sharpness, yes, but one I liked, followed by a coolness that was like a balm. Mine responded almost on its own, racing through my veins, threads extending outward to meet him, to weave around him.

Like the last time I'd taken his magic into me, from the diamond, my hands suddenly became supersensitive, almost tingling. But this time, so did other parts of me, and as Bastien's tongue lapped at me at last, I gasped aloud at the heightened sensation. "Fuck!"

"Too much?" he asked.

"Hell no," I panted. "Do that again."

He grinned and did exactly that, employing his hands and mouth alike, teasing me at a pace both maddening and intoxicating, not stopping until I came on his tongue, back arching and extremely glad no one else was in the house. He held me as I came down from the near-dizzying orgasm and caught my breath. "Just…gimme a minute…"

"No rush. You don't have to do anything," he told me, kissing my shoulder as he spooned me from behind.

"There's no 'have to' about it, I absolutely want to," I assured him.

"Far be it from me to deny the lady what she wants, then," Bastien replied, the smile in his voice again.

"That spell was…holy shit. I mean, I can still feel it," I said, flexing my fingers, running them along his arm. "What does it feel like to you?"

"I'm much more aware of the magic around me. And much of it feels like I could shape it, use it if I wanted to," he said. "It's interesting. Different."

"Different from what?"

He hesitated enough that I was about to say he didn't need to answer, but then he spoke. "I created that spell for Mari. Because I believed she had lost her magic, and it was a way for her to feel some, even if only for a little while," he told me. "I've never cast it with a partner who actually had magic before."

A fire roared in me at hearing this, anger that made me wish I could kill her a second time. "…The ways that wretched bitch could've ruined you just keep stacking up." I twisted my neck to look at him, reaching up to cup his face. "I hope you know how strong you are. Coming through all that, and you're still . . . you."

His eyes glanced aside. "I don't know about that."

"I'm not saying you're not changed by it. You are, but . . . salt and chalk, Bastien, the things you've had to go through, and you're still looking out for other people, trying to do right by them. That part of you hasn't changed."

He looked back up, kissing my palm. "Maybe it's not me. Maybe it's just what you bring out in me."

I grinned. "*Toi et moi?*"

"Something like that." He smiled against my hand. "*Nous.*"

"*Us.*" *Is there an "us"? I want there to be.* But that was a topic to tackle another time. "So would you say the experience compares favorably, then?"

"Very much so," Bastien replied. "Vastly improved experience. Ten out of ten, would cast again."

"Excellent." I turned in his arms, moving so I was atop him this time. "Is now a good time?"

"Now is a perfect time," he replied. "Though I wouldn't mind something softer than the floor."

I pouted. "Yeah, but my bed is two floors up—whoa!" Without warning, a portal opened under us and we fell a few feet to land on my bed. Looking up, I saw a blue portal lined with gold threads close above us.

"Did you just—?"

"How did you—?"

We looked at each other midquestion. ". . . Did we just open that portal together?" I asked.

"I think we may have," Bastien said slowly, thinking it over. "That's the first time my portals haven't been corrupted since the wedding. Your magic kept it controlled. McKenna!" He sat up under me, excitedly grabbing my shoulders. "We might actually have a solution to my sorcery problem!" He beamed at me, and then we were kissing, again, which led to other things, again. "Shouldn't we... write this down or something?" he panted as I pulled his pants and boxer briefs off at long last.

"One crisis at a time," I replied, pressing my finger to his lips and sitting astride his lap. My other hand slid down his chest, his stomach, until I found and grasped his cock and began stroking him. "And that one can definitely wait."

Bastien moaned, kissing me deeply, desperately as I worked my hand over him. He was already worked up from before, but I delighted in feeling him grow harder, pressing into my touch, moaning as he steadily came undone with desire. Every sound he made heightened my own craving to make him feel every bit as good as I did, to kiss him breathless until he cried out my name and came beneath me.

But first, it was my turn to ask. My lips found his ear, and I whispered, "Tell me what you want."

"You. I want *you*, McKenna." The growl in his voice only turned me on more.

"In what way?"

"*This* way." He grabbed my ass to lift me up and over him; my pulse pounded, body tingling in anticipation. "Guide me." The instruction sent another delicious chill through me. We each murmured a quick contraceptive spell, then

I did just that, each of us positioning the other, working in concert until we were joined. As he slid inside, sensation rolled through me, a smoldering heat building with every touch, every movement, and I wanted, I needed, more. My face buried in his shoulder, kissing and nipping at a sensitive spot, thrilled at the sounds he made. He swept my hair aside and found a place beneath my ear that did the same for me, driving out any thoughts that weren't here, now, this moment with him.

"Hells, McKenna, you feel amazing," he murmured against my lips when he came back to them. "*You're* amazing." My eyes, half-lidded, found his and he smiled.

Stars and spells, I loved his smile. His real smile, the one that brightened his whole face, brought out the clear skies in his storm-blue eyes. The look he gave me held not just lust and desire and satisfaction but *joy*. A joy that echoed in me, I realized, and I found myself smiling back just as widely.

"So are you, Bastien," I told him, cradling his face to mine. "I hope you know that. I hope you always know that."

He answered with a groan and another deep kiss, his arms tightening around me. One wrapped around my hips, his hand gripping my ass as he thrust deeper, faster, hitting the perfect spot and making me groan aloud again. My legs wrapped around him more tightly, anchoring me against him. Every feeling echoed through my veins and along my nerves until I truly did lose track of where his pleasure ended and mine began.

"Bastien...fuck, don't stop," I begged, breathless at the pleasure building in me.

"Not a damn chance." His kisses grew harder and messier, his hand tangling in my hair as we both came closer to the brink. His forehead pressed to mine and our eyes locked together. No hiding, no chance for it, but hells, I didn't want to. I wanted to see his pleasure, his want, his joy, his moment of release. Wanted him to see mine, which was both thrilling and terrifying. It felt like lightning was building in my body, burning, striking, turning me to glass in his arms: strong and sharp and delicate, transparent and bound to shatter.

"McKenna...I'm...I'm close..."

"Yes, yes," I gasped, breathless, rolling my hips against his. "Bastien, come for me, please."

At my urging, Bastien's whole body shuddered with release, and he crushed me to him, crying out my name—"McKenna...*McKenna*!" One last rush of his magic pulsed through me, pushing me over the edge, my pleasure spilling over in a climax that left me gasping his name and clinging to him. We moved together again, slowly, riding out the waves and aftershocks with whimpers and light kisses. Finally, we collapsed down onto the mattress in a warm, sated tangle. Bastien's arms cradled me against him, his legs still twined with mine. I soaked in that moment, his chest rising and falling under my cheek, my fingers splayed on his stomach, tracing the still-crisp lines of the runes painted there.

I hadn't shattered after all. If anything, I felt stronger and more aligned than I had been in a long time.

His fingers brushed through my hair. "I hate to ask...but how long do we have until that next crisis?" he asked, kissing the side of my head.

"It'll keep at least a few minutes more," I murmured.

Whatever else this day would bring, it had brought this. Brought us here, brought us together. And despite the instincts each of us often had to go it alone, it felt so, so good to know that this time, we'd chosen each other.

Chapter 20
Trial and Punishment

Having thoroughly tested the smudge-proof aspect of the ink, Bastien and I showered (which also didn't affect the ink) and got dressed just in time for Gretchen's arrival. She was wearing what I highly suspected was repurposed steampunk cosplay, based on the number of pockets and the slight Victorian flair of some of the details. Taking one look at my hair, she insisted on cleaning it up for me and gave me a quick trim to fully even it out and even add some sideswept bangs that I had to admit I rather liked.

As I finished my makeup, I spotted my black knight necklace on my bureau, the one Remi had given me in high school. I'd told her it hadn't felt like it fit for a while now—since killing Saranthiel, she was right about that. Maybe because I'd tried to play the part of the diplomat instead, or because I'd made myself a team player for the wrong team. Maybe because I'd been afraid of what my magic really was and what else it could do. But with subversive plans in play, a secret restoration spell painted on my body, fully intending to rebel against the Council? Today, it fit. Today, I felt like the black knight again. I felt like *me* again. As I fastened it around my neck, the charm was comfortingly familiar against my chest.

At sundown on the dot, a portal opened in the living room with Laurent on the other side, and he was indeed surprised to find his grandson. "Bastien? What are you doing here?"

"One less portal for you to spend time on, and McKenna and I had some trial matters to discuss beforehand." Bastien's prepared answer was as smooth as his lapels.

Laurent gave one of his noncommittal grunts. "I take it Miss Grothmann is your proxy?"

"Yes, she is," I replied. "Gretchen, this is Laurent Lemaire."

"Nice to meet you, Mr. Lemaire," Gretchen replied.

"You as well," Laurent said, with a minimal amount of politeness. "This way, then, all of you."

We stepped through, and for a moment, I was a scared sixteen-year-old again, being pushed through a portal to an uncertain fate. Then, I'd been blindfolded, with no idea what to expect. This time, I walked through with my eyes open, though the ramifications of tonight were just as up in the air.

The stone chamber was a heptagon, a seven-sided room, that had no doors and no windows but somehow still smelled of earth and salt. Far above us, in the ceiling, were openings that let in light and air but were impossible to reach without magic. The feeling of being underground was pervasive, and I remembered how, the first time I'd been here, it had felt like being buried alive in a way, and I'd wondered if that's what might happen to me. There was very little decoration to the place—each of the seven walls had a rune carved into it, and on the walls were sconces lit by magic. A series of seven concentric circles were set into the floor, the largest about seven feet from the wall, with equal spacing between the circles. Each was made of a different material, clearly enchanted against the wear and tear of time, declaring without words that this was a place meant for witches only. The innermost was silver, followed by iron, gold, black tourmaline, solid rock salt, diamond, and then—

"Seven hells, is that orichalcum?"

Laurent nodded. "That's right, you've seen orichalcum before. Yes, this is the largest singular piece that exists."

I hadn't seen the outermost circle up close before, but now I saw the brassy golden color, the subtle rainbow sheen. An extremely rare metal that was as bad for demons as iron for Fae or silver for werewolves. The only other orichalcum I'd ever seen had been the sword that killed Forneus. Getting our hands on it had been an extremely difficult ordeal, and it had been made truly fatal to demons through a process that was now impossible to repeat. The act of using it had destroyed it along with the Archdemon it killed. I hadn't thought I'd ever see the metal again anywhere. Yet here it was, probably enough to make seven swords, right beneath our feet.

My first time here, I'd thought the Council just had a real hard-on for the number seven. It was a mystical number, not uncommon in magic. There had been seven founding witch families, and thus there were always seven Council members. Now that I knew this place was where the leyline nexus was, I knew the seven circles weren't just here for the aesthetic. They were here to protect that nexus and the very tempting power it offered.

I reached out with my magic, curious about what it felt like, and promptly tripped over my own feet before pulling back my awareness. Bastien caught me before I could fall on my face, thankfully.

"Are you all right?" he asked.

"Yeah. Word of advice, do *not* look directly into the leylines," I said, blinking and rubbing my head. "Oof."

"Direct experience always was your favorite teacher," he teased mildly.

Until now, the barrier was the most powerful thing I'd interacted with. I'd been able to use it to kill an Archdemon with some left over. Doing so had also nearly killed *me*, of course. There was enough left in it even now that if I tried claiming and using it all at once, it would still be potentially lethal. And that paled in comparison to what lightly tapping on the leylines had felt like just now. If regular magic was a static shock, we were standing on top of a lightning storm. Neither magic nor power, it was pure mystical energy without shape or specification, nothing but immense potential.

No wonder so many demons were eager to get their hands on it.

The other Council members were there, minus Adele, and Sofia had Isabella Martinez with her, whom I hadn't seen since the Solstice Ball.

"Where are we?" I asked Laurent.

"Beneath the town," the old man answered.

I rolled my eyes. "Yeah, I figured that part out, thanks. I meant where specifically."

Laurent turned an eye toward Gretchen. "The location of the leyline nexus isn't something we share with non–Council members."

Seven hells, this was getting old. "Salt and chalk. Why not? If this place were accessible by anything other than portaling, someone would've found it by now. I'm sure the place is more warded than your mansion. Plus, I *am* on the Council and I still don't know, and I don't see you including Bastien in that statement."

Laurent looked annoyed, big shocker there, but then he tapped his temple and murmured under his breath. I silently opened my mental ward for a moment and heard his gravelly voice in my mind. *Beneath the library. The leyline nexus chamber is connected to the Uncommon Collection's network.*

That's how the Council had been doing so many severings that weren't technically in Arcadia Commons, but still managed to have the power to do them. It was probably how the Uncommon Collection had the magical mojo to maintain itself, come to that—Arcadia Commons was the original branch, after all. It was all connected to and powered by the leylines.

That, and the magic they were taking away from witches.

Our biggest source of shared knowledge, and it's being used for this? It's being powered by this? All the things we could use the leylines for, use the Collection for, and this is what they're doing? Seven hells, this is so wrong!

Cyrus was right. We really did have to claim our own power. Not only was no one else going to do it for us, they'd take it from us if they could. And trial or not, with cause or not, I refused to be part of that any longer. My hand tightened around the brooch in my pocket meant for my mom. It was only a matter of minutes now.

A moment later a portal appeared and Adele stepped through, leading first my mother and then Cyrus behind her. Both were blindfolded, and Cyrus's hands were bound with rope enchanted to prevent him from using magic.

"Mom!" I ran over to her. Each circle I crossed sent another flare of sensation through me.

"Miss Ellerbeck, no fraternizing with the accused," Laurent warned.

"She's my *mother*," I snapped. I pulled off her blindfold and hugged her. "Are you okay?"

"McKenna!" She held me tightly. "I'm managing. They let me get dressed, if you can call this an outfit." She was wearing slacks and a blouse that were all beige and white and screamed Adele and left her looking washed out, her bright-red hair a stark contrast. "Honestly, I'd rather have come in my robe," she whispered, winking at me.

I laughed, glad to see her spirits were up despite the situation. At least Adele's boring fashion sense gave me an excuse for what I needed to give her. "I had a feeling they might do something like that, so I brought you this." I pulled out the sparkling yellow topaz brooch, shaped like a butterfly in profile, wings flung back in flight. It was one of her favorites and had a very small rune drawn on its backside.

"Oh, sweetie! Thank you, this is perfect." She pinned it on and then hugged me again.

"You're welcome. Make sure you keep it on for luck, okay?" I whispered. I wanted to tell her why, but she was about to step into the truth circle. I couldn't risk our plan being exposed.

"McKenna." It was Cyrus, who'd already taken off his own blindfold. He was wearing what I'd last seen him in, jeans and a plain maroon shirt with a few buttons at the top. "I . . . I'm sorry for your mother getting pulled into this mess. This isn't exactly how I hoped our first few days of knowing each other would go."

"Me neither," I said. "But everything's going to be fine. I've got it all covered."

He gave me an appraising look. "Oh?"

Mom squeezed my arm. "She always has something up her sleeve."

Cyrus smiled then, at both of us, affection in his eyes. "Sounds a lot like her mother."

It had been so long since I'd felt any sense of family with two parents that I nearly didn't recognize it. I was still getting to know Cyrus, but for a brief moment, I felt it. It was unexpectedly nice.

"Council members, if you'll take your positions," Laurent said, gesturing to the various sides of the heptagon. "Proxies, go with your respective parties."

With a last squeeze of Mom's hand, Gretchen and I went to my spot across the room. "What about Brooke and Lucca?"

Laurent gestured. On the far side of the room, where the accused parties stood, a new portal opened, this one leading to the Luppinos' living room. On the other side, Brooke, Lucca, and Gio Luppino all stood together. Brooke looked nervous, and Lucca and his dad wore nearly matching serious-doggo faces.

Lucca and Brooke stepped through first, with Gio following in a cloud of cologne so strong I could smell it from across the room. Finally, one more portal was opened, adding Armand Lemaire to our collective. He had the same tall, lean build as Bastien, the same Lemaire blue eyes, though his blond hair had begun to turn to silver, and he favored a pair of tortoiseshell frames for his glasses. His clothing style also ran less formal, something of a Beach Vibes Lemaire look—khakis, a nice short-sleeved polo, and a blue cardigan.

Gio and Armand shook hands before they made their way over to join my mom and Cyrus, with Brooke and Lucca trailing behind them. "Looks like the band's back together," Gio said with dry humor and a smile much like his son's.

"It's good to see you both. Too bad about the circumstances," Cyrus said, shaking both their hands. My mom hugged both of the other men, then took Brooke's hands before hugging her, having some quiet conversation with her that ended in Brooke looking tearful but smiling and the two of them hugging.

"Now that the accused are all present, we call this trial to order," Laurent said. He made a gesture over the ground in front of him. A pillar rose from the stone floor, reaching waist height before the two panels on the top opened to either side, revealing a book—the Council grimoire. He flipped it open and pulled a quill from somewhere, the same one I had used to sign the book four months ago. "We're here to pass judgment upon Brooke Luppino, Cyrus Craig, Wendy Ellerbeck, and Armand Lemaire, who respectively are accused of—"

He was cut off by a sharp, loud laugh from Cyrus. "Really, Laurent? What's the use of standing on ceremony when the conclusion is foregone?" he asked, his voice echoing around the chamber. "We've all got lives to get back to, don't we? Allow me to save us all some time and cut to your inevitable conclusions: guilty, guilty, guilty"—he pointed to himself, Mom, and Brooke, then to Armand and Gio—"innocent, and the wolves' problem to take care of. Can't risk the ire of the pack, now can you?"

"Mr. Craig, I advise you to—"

Cyrus scoffed. "It's Cyrus, now, Laurent. I'm not a child you can badger and belittle with formality anymore. And if I'm interested in your advice, I'll…well. I'll never be interested in your advice."

I felt my heart race, shocked and thrilled at once at hearing him talk back to Laurent with absolutely no fear of what the old man might do in return. I'd never heard anyone talk to him like that. Not even me!

"Should I take this to mean you're pleading guilty, then, Cyrus?" Laurent replied.

Cyrus grinned widely. "Not a chance. And your circle doesn't scare me, either. I didn't kill Frank Milton, and I'm not conspiring against my fellow witches. I'd consider conspiring against you, specifically, but that's really neither here nor there," he replied cockily. "I'm just saying what we all already know, and that's that the Council's decision is already made."

"Not necessarily," said George. "The facts matter, and we hardly know all of them yet."

"He's right," Douglas agreed. "Besides, the facts aren't always black and white."

"For that matter, I wish to withdraw my accusation of murder," Sofia added, drawing surprised looks from just about everyone, Brooke most of all. "I do not believe Brooke had a hand in Mariposa's death."

Brooke clutched a hand to her chest, eyes shining. "You don't?"

Sofia shook her head, though she only briefly looked at Brooke herself. "No."

Uh-oh. As much as hearing them speak up was a triumph on its own—especially Sofia, despite what she and I had talked about yesterday—we needed this to stay at least a little on track with some of those foregone conclusions.

Sofia continued, "Though the accusations of conspiring with demons and treason against witchkind remain."

Phew.

Brooke wiped at her eyes and willingly stepped into the smallest circle, the truth circle. Her legs buckled and she would have fallen but for Lucca reaching over to steady her.

It had nearly driven me to my knees when I stepped in as well. The memory of that moment was visceral even now. The overwhelming wave of magic that stripped away every shred of privacy as they interrogated me. It was even worse than the truth venom, never letting up, never lessening. I wondered now if somehow the witches who'd created it had used seeker venom to create the thing, or did its strength merely come from its being on top of the leylines?

"Thank you, Sofia. I swear I never hurt Mari, or meant for her to get hurt. She really was my friend," Brooke said.

"I never meant to betray any witches, but I know my actions entailed doing so, and I can't deny that I conspired with a demon. I plead guilty to those charges."

"If you're hoping for mercy by admitting to your guilt, you'll be sorely disappointed," Adele said, a sneer in her voice.

"I don't. I welcome it. I want the Council to sever my magic," Brooke said. A ripple of surprise went through the other Council members.

"You *want* this?" Douglas was incredulous.

Brooke nodded. "I do. I wasn't meant to be a witch. I'm not that good at it, and it's rarely brought me anything but misery. The pack is my real family." She smiled at Lucca, her face full of melancholy and joy at once. "That's where I belong and what I was meant to be."

"You want to give up being a witch to become a *werewolf*?" Adele sneered.

"It won't work," Hilary added. "There's no record of a witch ever becoming a werewolf. His own sister couldn't even become one."

"Leo's case is unique. It might work for a severed witch," I said, refusing to let them take all hope from her. "If Brooke is severed, she'll have no existing connection to the supernatural. She knows the risk. If it's what she wants, then why shouldn't we do it?"

"This Council is not in the practice of giving traitors what they want," Laurent said imperiously.

"You want to sever her, and you'll get to! Unless you mean to tell me this Council *is* in the practice of tormenting witches, rather than protecting them or seeing justice done? I don't recall that being mentioned in the book I signed. Does anyone else?" I scanned the faces of the other members.

"Sidenote, if the Witches Council intends to torment my wife, they can expect to hear from me and mine," Lucca added in a growl. A few of the others looked distinctly uncomfortable with that. Even Adele, though she was clearly pissed off about it.

Laurent was about to speak, but Sofia got there first. "That won't be necessary. Indeed, it is *not* our practice or purpose to extend anyone's suffering. If our outcome happens to be one Brooke also finds preferable, there's no reason for that to sway our decision. Isabella?"

"Uh, yes. I vote in favor of severing," Isabella said when prompted. She lifted her right hand, and the rune on the wall behind them lit up.

I nudged Gretchen, and she did the same. "I vote in favor of severing." The votes went around the room: Douglas, George, and Hilary all voted in favor of severing. Adele hesitated, looking at her father first.

Laurent's face was steely and still. It was his version of Bastien's society mask, except his was hard edged instead of polite. He was angry. Angry at me, which was nothing new, but this time I was fairly certain some of it was for Sofia for agreeing and kicking off the vote.

Power was slipping from his hands, and he didn't like it one bit.

He raised his hand, though, his eyes on Brooke. "I vote in favor of severing." Adele quickly followed suit.

Brooke let out a little sigh, her shoulders sagging. Not from despair, but relief. She grabbed Lucca's hand, her eyes filling with hope and tears alike. Like everything was going to be okay. Here, somehow, in the midst of the doom and the schemes and the power plays, their future had become a little more clear, more certain.

Once, months ago, looking at Brooke had reminded me that it was time to stop letting others tell me what I deserved and who I was. Right there and then, she and Lucca reminded me that maybe it was time to stop letting them tell me what I owed them and what I was worth. That what made me stronger, what made any of us stronger, wasn't power or magic or debts owed and repaid.

It was love.

It didn't matter how hard or how long I worked, how many debts both mystical and financial I paid off, how much I scrapped and kowtowed, how many invisible and moving goalposts I met: People like Laurent would never care, never consider me an equal or my mistakes made up for. But the people who mattered, people like my mom, Cameron, Bastien, and Remi—they believed in me anyway. They loved me anyway. Hell, maybe even inclusive of it. And I loved them. *I loved them.* It was complicated, it was messy, it wasn't always straightforward, but it was there and it was real. It wasn't owed, expected, or demanded. It was freely given, and it was so much stronger.

I looked at my mom. *I just want to know you're happy, McKenna.* At Bastien. *Toi et moi.* I felt Remi in my heart. *Do what they don't expect. Be the black knight.*

Determination filled me.

It was time.

Laurent turned the pages of the Council grimoire. "Council members, channel your magic through Bastien. Bastien, prepare yourself to complete the spell. Brooke, join Bastien in his circle."

Brooke stepped into the next circle, where Bastien stood, and Laurent began to cast in Latin, to my surprise. The ancient language sounded strange on his tongue, since the Lemaires always cast in French. *Cyrus casts in Latin, though, and his family are the ones who created the spell*, I remembered. "*Arte magica coniunctum, te facimus instrumentum nostrum, te facimus gladium nostrum ut dividatur ars magica ab hac maga et cedatur origini,*" he chanted. As we had been instructed the day before, with each iteration of the words, one of us joined him, in order of seniority: Hilary, Sofia, Douglas, George, Adele, and me.

The magic flowed out from each of us—blue, green, gray, silver, red, blue again, and finally gold. The seven strands of magic twined together, losing their individual colors in favor of a brilliant iridescence. The strength of it thrummed and buzzed through the air, my fingers, my blood, as it grew in power and brilliance, steadily reaching toward Bastien.

Just as it reached him, I saw a flicker of nervousness in his eyes. Then the magic connected with him, filling him until he glowed. The circle he and Brooke stood in filled as well, as though the stone were peeling back to reveal a hidden layer of pure magic and light, so bright it turned the two figures atop into silhouetted figures in a shadow play. I realized the stone floor *was* gone, disappeared or dissolved or something, and I was looking at the leyline nexus itself. Mystical energy in its most raw form, dazzling and strong and full of every possibility. My mind spun at the magnitude of it as my magic, through Bastien, connected directly to it.

Then the possibility turned poisonous and my blood ran like acid in my veins at the unmistakable sensation of something demonic from within.

The fuck?! My instinct was to pull back, but I couldn't, not just because that would ruin our entire plan, but because I *couldn't*. We had connected our magic to the leylines for this ritual, and the leylines weren't letting go. *Once the severing begins, it must be concluded.* Laurent had warned us, but I hadn't realized he was being so literal. But something was in there. Something I couldn't see but could feel with every cell of my body, something demonic and powerful and angry was *inside* the nexus.

My body shuddered in pain, fever and weakness overcoming me. My legs gave out, and I crashed to my hands and knees. Gretchen jumped to my side but hesitated to help me up, not certain if she should touch me midspell. "McKenna? Are you all right?"

Her question barely registered; my eyes were fixed on Bastien as he moved his hand under his shirt to trigger the reversal spell. I had to stop him, warn him, but I couldn't speak, couldn't scream. I could barely even gasp for air. Whatever was locked inside the leylines wasn't magic, stolen or otherwise.

And Bastien was about to unleash it.

For a moment, my only relief was that at least it wouldn't end up attached to my mother, because I wasn't remotely capable of triggering my part of the ritual. But then my eyes fell on Cyrus.

Cyrus, who leaned forward eagerly, eyes fixed on Bastien and Brooke.

Cyrus, who had been here before.

Cyrus, whose family had created the severing ritual.

Cyrus, who had planned this entire thing.

"We reclaim our lives and our power, because we've all learned the hard way that no one's going to do it for us." How carefully chosen his words had been. *That bastard knew!*

A mass of power exploded from the ground under Bastien, rushing through him and into the air. The tendrils of power began to take form, coming together into—what else?—an immense tentacled monstrosity. Between that and the effect it had had on me, I was certain: This thing was an Archdemon. It wasn't fully formed, however. It seemed to be struggling to become so, as though part of it was still stuck in the nexus.

The innermost circle shattered, the metal and the carved line alike cracking with a resounding boom that made us all cringe. The Archdemon's form became more solid. *It's breaking the bindings!*

A half dozen blue circles, portals, opened up across the room, centered around Cyrus, and various members of his cabal stepped through, all of them armed. Brun, Karam, Trina, and others carrying various implements and weapons, including a few Tasers.

"Take out the Council!" Brun commanded.

"Nonviolently!" Cyrus stressed. Six of them headed for us, while Brun sliced through the ropes binding Cyrus, freeing him to use his magic. I saw my mother pull back from him in shock, no doubt demanding to know what was going on, but she was drowned out by the shriek of the half-formed Archdemon.

The sound grated on my ears and in my veins. Even so, I felt its power ripple through the air, and then the portals, the ones made with Bastien's corrupted magic, turned ragged and dark. Water began gushing into the chamber, knocking several people at the back off their feet and carrying with it minions of the Archdemon of Secrets. The horrifying crabs who had nearly devoured me in the Pit, and a host of walking squid-faced demons with a writhing nest of tentacles for mouths, like the ones Cameron and I had banished, now whole and hale in their own flesh.

Meaning *this* was the Archdemon of Secrets. This was where it had been. How, why, for how long, were all questions for another time. A time after we'd survived the absolute clusterfuck that had just exploded around us.

Someone screamed—it might've been me. It might've been Brooke. It might've been a lot of people. Someone roared, and that was definitely Lucca as he shifted into wolf form and lunged forward to attack the demons as they quickly spread across the room, attacking cabal members, witches, and everyone in sight.

A loud skittering pulled my attention to a pair of crabs, these coming right for Gretchen and me. I tried again to pull away from the spell that held me fast, but it was no use. *Shit! Please tell me you have potions, Gretch!*

Gretchen didn't disappoint. She pulled off her blazer,

revealing her bandolier of potions. Pulling out a bright-yellow one, she hurled it at the crab in the lead. The glass shattered on its face, and it screamed as its flesh began to burn, filling the air with an acrid smell. "Bull's-eye!" Losing no time, she pulled out another. This one held two liquids, the green floating atop some reddish-brown fluid, and as she threw it, she called out a spell in German. "*Knall!*"

The potion exploded on impact with the second one's back, blasting apart a chunk of its tough carapace. "Yes!" Her celebration was short-lived, however, as a squidface raced up from behind the second crab. "Oh, shit! Uh—*lashero!*" She tried casting one of our attack spells while she scrambled to grab another potion—Cameron must've taught it to her—but flubbed the pronunciation, and lacked the confidence, the magical strength, or both to pull it off, and it fizzled. Just as she got the next potion out, however, the demon's tentacles lashed out and grasped both of her hands. "*Help!*"

I watched, eyes wide, desperately fighting the spell, but it held me fast, unable to move or speak. I could do nothing but watch as this thing dragged a struggling Gretchen across the stone floor toward it.

Then, suddenly, I was free.

"*Lacera!*" I yelled, slumped on the ground and aiming my hand toward the demon's legs. The spell slashed open its flesh and it stumbled, freeing Gretchen even as it dragged her down with it.

Gretchen smashed her potion on its face. "*Ätz!*" The tentacles burned without flame, blackening as the potion spread. She scrambled back to me, and we helped each other up. "Thanks for the save!"

"Right back at you," I said, not sure how it had even been possible. Scanning the room answered the question—one of the cabal members had escaped the demons long enough to fire a Taser at Hilary. The older woman was on the ground, unconscious, and it looked like that had broken the hold the spell had on the rest of us. The painful burning in my veins lessened now that my direct connection to the Archdemon was gone. "Also, so glad you came armed."

Gretchen grinned. "Like Mom always says, never leave home without a few potions."

"Smart lady."

"You know it. Okay, what's the plan now?"

Drawing my athame from my belt, I scanned the room, trying to come up with one. Chaos had taken over at the far end, where the portals were. Demons, witches, and the cabal alike were trading blows and spells, while the sulfuric waters of the Pit continued to gush forth into the room. A thin layer of water already covered most of the chamber, and as big as this place was, it wouldn't be long before that was a serious problem.

Lucca was ripping the legs off of a crab demon while George O'Brien threw fire spells at a writhing tentacle. Meanwhile, Remi and Dara were both wielding shadowblades and— *Wait, what?! When did they get there? And why is Remi wearing Armand's cardigan? Why is Dara dressed like Gio?* Then it clicked that neither Gio nor Armand was here, and they never had been. Remi and Dara had snuck in pretending to be them. *Meaning Lucca and his dad and Armand all willingly worked with them? This day gets weirder and weirder.* I was deeply curious how they'd pulled that off. Meanwhile, I was glad they were here, especially since Remi was defending my mom from a cadre of demons. Cyrus, meanwhile, was fighting alongside them. That man and I had some *words* to exchange.

Words that would have to wait. Because while Mom was taken care of for now, Bastien was another story. The boom of the shattering second circle drew my attention back that way. Bastien and Brooke were protected, barely, by a vortex of water that Brooke was maintaining around them, but two squidface demons were lashing through it and trying to grab her. Between them and us were at least three more demons. Above them, the immense kraken-like form of the Archdemon became more discernible. It lashed at a wall, but the long tentacle passed through it. Insubstantial for now, but I had a feeling that wouldn't last much longer.

I slashed a line across my palm, letting my blood and magic flow. "The plan is we get past the demons, kill 'em if we can, close the portals, and protect our friends," I told Gretchen, and shrugged my shoulder. "Possibly not in that order."

"Works for me. I like a flexible plan." She drew out more potions, and we charged forward.

"*Eviscerate!*" The nearest crab demon was thrown back by my spell and torn apart, slamming into another one hard enough to knock it off-balance. Gretchen threw two more acid potions on the second one. It staggered erratically as its shell dissolved, making eerie screaming noises, clipping my arm with a flailing pincer, but we otherwise managed to slip past it without incident.

"Cam said you took out a whole ballroom full of demons once, why not just do that?" Gretchen asked.

"Not exactly what happened. Plus I was sitting on a lot more readily available magic that time." I might be able to take out a lot of them here, but only if I tapped into the barrier. But with the power I'd need, I didn't know if there would even *be* a barrier after. And with that Archdemon hovering and trying to re-form itself nearby, I wanted to keep that option in my pocket just in case.

"What about banishing them?"

I gestured at the portals at the back wall. "I could, but as long as those are open, these things can just keep coming back. Destroying their bodies won't kill them forever, but it'll take a lot longer for them to find or grow new ones than to swim back to those portals." I paused to send an evisceration spell at another squidface. The spells were powerful enough to take them out, but they were also getting harder to cast. I had to either start conserving my magic or tap into the barrier. "Sorry, Gretch, we gotta do this the hard way."

"Ugh. The worst." She rolled her eyes. "Is it just me, or are these things getting bigger?"

A quick survey of the room confirmed what she'd said—the demons coming out of the portals now were bigger than the first batch. The crabs were starting to rival Lucca's wolf form, the squidfaces his human form. The rising water level wasn't helping. It was up to my calves now, and soon the demons would be able to move through it far more easily than the rest of us.

"Incoming!" Gretchen yelled.

One of the bulkier squidfaces was barreling toward us with a blade of sharpened coral. I barely stopped in time to throw myself to the side as it lunged forward with it.

"*Repello!*" The demon backpedaled a few paces but wasn't knocked down. Gretchen tossed another exploding potion, setting it off inches from the thing's face, but it brought up an arm, blocking most of the damage. "This one's smarter than the average squid."

Gretchen jumped back to grab some more bottles. "Not how I like my sushi."

Behind the demon, I could see Brooke's vortex was starting to falter. "We don't have time for this wannabe Cthulhu. *Liga daemonium!*" This time when I thrust my hand out, golden threads shot out, wrapping around the squidface and binding it tightly. It struggled against the hold, which meant I had to keep funneling magic into the spell to keep it restrained. "Kill it, quickly!"

Gretchen dashed forward, this time smashing an acid potion onto its face directly, then making a slashing motion with her hand. "*Lacera!*" This time, the spell worked, and a line of her bright-green magic cut deep into its flesh, severing several tentacles and biting deep into its neck, black blood spraying out as it gargled and slumped to the ground.

"Ew!" Gretchen wiped the blood from her face. "But awesome teamwork!" She went for a high five, but another boom shook the room, this one making her stumble—three circles shattered. Brooke's hold on her vortex was broken, and it collapsed into the water around us as the squidface surged forward to grab her.

"Brooke!" I dashed forward, moving as fast as I could through the water, but it slowed my steps. "*Lacera!*" But I was too tapped out and too far away; even though the spell hit, it didn't do enough to deter the demon that had grabbed her, lifting her off the ground, one tentacle wrapping around her head to cover her mouth and muffle her scream. Another latched around her body, pinning her arms.

It began to twist.

No! I threw my hand out again, this time not hesitating to tap into the barrier for strength. *"Liga—"*

Another tentacle grabbed me from behind, yanking me off my feet and tossing me halfway across the room. I tumbled into the water and stone, barely covering my head and neck in time that it wasn't worse.

Panting and spitting water, I got up and looked back over at my friends, my heart leaping with hope for a moment when a snarling black wolf appeared. Lucca raced for Brooke, jumping into the air to attack the demon. *Yes!* He'd get there in time, he'd save her, he'd never let her die—

But then an immense pincer snapped him out of the air. I watched in terror as the biggest crab demon I'd seen yet held him fast around his midsection. He snarled, howled, scrabbling at the thing but unable to find purchase or damage the carapace enough to get free.

SNAP.

My brain struggled to tell me it was the next circle breaking, but the second crack of bones breaking did not allow it.

SNAP.

Brooke and Lucca both went limp and fell, unmoving, into the water.

Chapter 21
The Movement of Magic

Get up, get up, please get up!

I struggled to my feet, running back toward the second circle, eyes fixed on the spots where Lucca and Brooke had slumped into the water. The seconds felt like hours as I hoped, prayed for even one of them to get up, to move, to show any sign of life.

There was none.

And no help was coming.

Everyone was trying their damnedest just to survive, Bastien was still held fast by the energy pouring out of the nexus. Even Gretchen, who was closest, was trying to dodge the squidface who'd just killed Brooke—

My mind rebelled against the idea. *No! No, she—she might be alive, she just can't move, someone just needs to help before she IS dead!*

But I knew. I knew it would take a miracle for them to live, if they were even still alive now.

A miracle...or a Bargain.

"*REMI!*" My scream echoed through the chamber, and in the next second, the demoness was at my side.

"McKenna, what—"

"Lucca and Brooke! Heal them, save them! Now!" I said, not pausing as I ran, just pointing ahead to where they weren't.

Remi looked, brow furrowed, but then teleported there, reaching down and lifting Brooke's body from the water. A squidface tried to attack her, but she merely turned a fiery gaze at the thing and it fell to its knees, gabbling senselessly and grabbing at its own face with claws and tentacles alike.

A crab came at me, but I was done hamstringing myself. I pulled on the barrier's power and exploded the thing with nothing more than a gesture. As I reached Remi, I looked around, searching for Lucca's body, finally finding him a few feet away. He had shifted to human form, and as I hauled his upper body from the water, he gasped and coughed, spitting out water. It was readily apparent his lower body wasn't moving, and I wasn't strong enough to drag him far. "Brooke..."

"Is she alive?" I asked Remi.

She nodded. "Barely. McKenna, I can't without a deal—"

"Done, I'll owe you, just do it!" My choice was already made.

"Done." Her voice reverberated, her eyes aflame with the fires of the Pit as we made our deal. The weight of it was heavy on my shoulders before the sensation passed. Remi set her hand to the back of Brooke's neck and her shadows coiled around Brooke. There was another *snap!* and Brooke's head and neck realigned themselves. She gasped loudly before choking up water, and my entire body wanted to sag in relief, but we weren't done yet.

Remi left her to stand on her own and moved swiftly to Lucca's side.

"No—just her," he tried to protest, tears in his eyes as he saw Brooke moving and breathing again.

"Sorry, furball, the deal was a two-for-one," Remi said, setting her hands to his side as well. Not only was Lucca's back broken, but he was also bleeding from the sharp edges of the claw, but as soon as Remi's shadows passed over the wounds, they were gone, and another sharp crack signaled his spine had been helped as well. The shadows withdrew, and he fell onto his hands and knees before clambering forward to Brooke, wrapping her in his arms.

Finally, despite the battle raging around us, I collapsed in relief.

Remi helped me to my feet. "That wasn't a thrall deal, my knight, but it was a weighty one," she murmured to me. "The price will be high."

"Worth it," I replied.

"Figured you'd say that," she said, smirking with a glimmer of pride as the fires in her eyes faded out. "But first we all need to get out of here alive."

"Not gonna happen if we don't get those portals closed," I said. "Laurent and Adele haven't done so yet, so I'm guessing they can't. Since they open to the Pit, I'm betting Bastien has to be the one to close them."

"Why's that?" Brooke asked. She and Lucca joined us.

"Long story," I sighed. "You okay?"

She smiled weakly. "Completely, thanks to you. I…thank you, McKenna. And you, Remi, for saving us both."

"Even if I did tell you not to," Lucca grumbled.

"Charming," Brooke admonished him.

He sighed. "Okay, yes. Thank you for saving our lives. But please don't use a demon to save me again."

"No promises," I replied, smiling despite the chaos. "And I'm the one who owes her, not you. You feeling up to killing more demons?"

"Hell yeah I am," Lucca replied. "Be careful, babe." He kissed Brooke, then shifted back to wolf form.

"Gretchen, back him up, but keep your distance." Gretchen gave me a thumbs up and hurried off to follow him. I turned to Remi. "Where's my mom?"

"Behind your bio-dad's shield spell," Remi said, jerking a thumb over her shoulder. Sure enough, Cyrus was holding a shield over the two of them and a few of his cabal members at the back wall. Mom didn't look too happy about it, and was looking our way with a tense expression.

I raised a hand to wave at her and took a moment to examine Cyrus's magic for the first time. It was bronze, rich and deep and shimmering…and threaded through with a dark shadow of itself, a corruption that was stronger and more enmeshed than it was with Bastien's. Even if I'd looked at it before, I might've missed it, it was so much a part of his magic.

Not just magic. Somehow, Cyrus, my biological father, wielded demonic power. Wielded *sorcery*.

No wonder he didn't come back to Arcadia Commons for thirty years. I doubt he'd been able to get past the barrier. Not until we'd taken him with us, directly past it through a portal.

No wonder my magic interacted with power like it did. I didn't know how he'd ended up with sorcery, but he had, and some portion of it had been passed along to me.

Salt and chalk, this asshole's played every single one of us. My hands clenched in anger, nails biting into my palms. He'd made Bastien his patsy, he'd put everyone in this room at risk, and all signs pointed to him trying to push demonic power onto my mom to boot. *Not on my fucking watch, Cyrus.* My eyes flicked back to the portals, and then to Bastien. *One crisis at a time.*

"I have an idea. Guard me and Bastien," I told Remi. "Don't suppose you could summon some of your minions here?"

"This deep inside the barrier, not really. I think Secrets here only managed because it was piggybacking off Bastien's spell," Remi said, "But Dara's holding her own. Just work fast, would you?"

"I'll try. Brooke, think you've got another vortex in you?"

Brooke murmured a spell quietly, and one started spinning up from the now thigh-deep water around us, sealing Bastien and me off from the rest of the room.

Now that I could finally get a good look at him, my stomach twisted to see what he'd been going through. Through the glowing floor beneath us, energy streamed up through him. But instead of the pure energy of the leylines, it was the dark and shadowed power of the Archdemon that was slowly rebuilding itself in the air above us. The energy held him a few feet off the ground, back arched and tense, shadows pouring from his eyes, nose, and mouth. The runes on his stomach were glowing with magic through his shirt. Guilt stabbed at me for my part in putting them there.

I reached up and grabbed his hand. Usually, his hands were calmingly cool, but now his skin was feverish. This afternoon felt so far away. "Bastien, it's me, it's McKenna," I told him. His fingers gripped back tightly and he gave a pained groan. He was awake and aware. "I'm so sorry. Cyrus played us, he used us. I...I think this was his plan the whole time. I finally looked at his magic. It's demonic, he's a sorcerer, too. I should've looked sooner, it was stupid not to. I...I fucked up and you got hurt. Again. How the hell could I just *trust* him like that?" Bastien squeezed my hand again, his thumb rubbing my fingers as though to console me. I smiled weakly, a tear slipping down my cheek. "Stop trying to make me feel better."

A gross squelch came from outside the vortex, a splatter of black blood streaking into the rushing water. "Any chance you could hurry it up in there?" Remi called out.

Wincing, I turned back to Bastien. "Okay, if you don't already know, Secrets used your portals to bring its minions here from the Pit. They're all over the place, *and* it's filling with water. Since sorcery opened them, sorcery needs to close them, and Cyrus sure as hell isn't helping. We need to work together on this one—I need to use your magic. I opened a Pit portal with it before, so it's possible. I haven't done this directly from another witch before, but I know we can do this. Okay?" His fingers squeezed tightly again, nearly crushing mine. "I'll take that as a yes." I kissed his hand.

I let my magic fill me, looking at him, examining his aura. His bright blue was there, with its ever-present shadow, and the deep gray of the Archdemon of Secrets was, too, flowing through him. I tried to reach for the strands of his magic with mine, to twine them and pull them toward me, but I couldn't get a hold on them. Even the demonic aspects evaded me, no matter how much I pushed.

Cursing, I blinked away the auras, panting from the effort. The water was around my hips now. "I can't get it, it keeps slipping from me. I know you're trying, but it's..." I racked my brain for a solution. We were running out of time, and if I couldn't figure this out, people I loved were going to die.

Love. Something Saranthiel had said suddenly came back to me, about why she bothered getting Bastien to fall for her as Mari in her scheme to get his magic. *"Because it had to be real. Your human magic is influenced by your emotions."*

Of course it was. It was why Remi and I had accidentally made that hot spot at the bar; why I'd been able to use Bastien's sorcery to portal in the first place. Why we'd been able to call out to Remi with our mutual desire. Why we'd been able to portal together at my house this afternoon.

It had to be real.

Since kissing him wasn't an option, I'd need to make it real the hard way: admitting how I felt.

"Bastien, listen. I know this is hard, I know it hurts, I know... I know it probably feels hopeless. Cyrus used us both, he's putting our friends and family in danger, there's an Archdemon floating in the air above us—hells, I'm terrible at this. The point is... the point is I know we can do this. I know *you* can do this. I hate that you got hurt again, but I—I love that you can't help keeping your heart open. That you give people the benefit of the doubt, that you want to make the world better. You build houses for people, you visited my mom for years while I was gone, you…you even took a chance on me again. Not just letting me back in your life, but letting me back in your heart and…and I'm so glad you did because I love you." My voice shook as I said it, my heart hammering in my chest, but once the words left my lips, my doubts in saying them disappeared. I knew they were true, I'd known since making love to him, I'd probably known before then. "*I love you. And we can do this, together. You and me. Toi et moi. Nous. Us."*

His fingers squeezed again, and, slowly, as though moving against gravity itself, his head turned to me. For a moment, from under the shadows of Secrets' power, his storm-blue eyes shone through, soft despite the pain he was in, filled with yearning, with affection—with love. Maybe he would've said it back if he could've, maybe not, but it didn't matter. I knew. He knew.

I took a breath and reached out with my magic again.

His responded, twining with mine, flowing with it, wrapping around it until it was in me and I could wield it as surely as my own.

"Brooke, drop the vortex." I turned to look toward the back wall where the portals were, still holding Bastien's hand in mine. The whirl of water around us stopped, splashing down into the water that was now up to my waist. My eyes locked on the portals, water gushing out of seven of them at once, demons slithering through with the waves. Magic and power tingled along my skin as I lifted my free hand and drew a circle in the air that closed in on itself. "*Fermez les portes.*"

Bastien's sorcery shot out from my hand in a wave, and the portals all snapped closed at once.

I heard cheers of relief, but our work wasn't done—the room was still full of water and demons. "Get everyone out past the fourth circle," I told Brooke and Remi.

"What about you two?" Remi asked.

"We'll be fine. Go."

I knew she didn't like it, but she went, *bamf*ing around the room to make sure our allies were in the safe zone. Once they all were, I gestured at the ground, reaching for and tapping into the fourth circle, the smallest one still intact, and made a gesture in the opposite direction. "*Ouvre la porte à* the Pit," I cast, and then made a wave gesture away from myself. "*Inverser le courant.*"

The moment the spell was cast, I grabbed Bastien's arm with both hands and quite literally climbed him like a tree before a portal almost thirty feet in diameter opened up beneath us to the Pit. The water rushed back through, pulling the sea monster minions with it. Some were forcibly shoved in by the others, and I saw Douglas use a spell to grab Sofia and Isabella back from the edge when the water nearly swept them in with it.

In moments, the sea was back in its hellish home and nearly every demon was gone with it. "*Ferme la porte!*" I closed the portal and released Bastien's sorcery once I did, feeling empty and drained. I slid off Bastien's body and onto the floor just as the fourth circle shattered and a new rush of Archdemon energy flew through him and into the demon kraken above us. The flailing tentacles smashed into a wall and this time sent chunks of stone falling to the ground.

Shit.

The damage wasn't as bad as it should've been, given the size of the kraken, but there were only three circles left between us and a full-strength Archdemon. Even if we all portaled out of here, this thing would wreak havoc on Arcadia Commons, and maybe other towns, too, since this chamber was connected to the Uncommon Collection's network.

Suddenly, a tentacle seized me around the waist and yanked me into the air. A sharp pain erupted in my side, and my stomach dropped at the speed of the blurred room whizzing past me. Only when the Archdemon held me before its circular mouth, opening wide enough to swallow me whole and shred me with rows upon rows of sharp teeth, did things come back into focus.

"*Repello!*" I screamed. The spell shoved me back, away from the mouth, but only by a measure of inches. It was too strong, and the portal spells had drained me. It roared, which I was fairly certain a squid shouldn't be able to do, and began bringing me in again. I stabbed my athame into the tentacle holding me, piercing its limb again and again. Every movement felt like the knife was stabbing into my side as well, but I didn't stop until its black blood had coated my hands. Despite that, it was little more than an annoyance to the demon. Its tentacle coiled tighter, so tight I couldn't breathe, stars exploding along the shadowed edges of my darkening vision.

From those shadows, Remi burst into being, bringing her blade straight through the tentacle, severing it from the kraken—and dropping me full tilt at the stone floor. Before I could even scream, she appeared again, tackling me mid-air and teleporting us both to the ground. Her body, much taller and larger than usual, wrapped around me as we tumbled across the stone. I yet again heard the snap of breaking bone, but I had no idea whose bone it was. When we finally stopped, my whole body ached, the stabbing pain in my side still there as I gasped for breath.

"Sorry for the rough landing, but I wasn't about to let you plummet into nothingness again," she said, lifting her head and carefully unwrapping herself. Blood poured from a nasty gash on her head, along with several others all over her body. Her forearm, the one that had been wrapped around my neck, was clearly broken. Her eyes were slightly unfocused while the head wound healed over, and she grimaced as she snapped her bone back into place. As her eyes came back into focus, she looked at me. "You all right?"

"I'm fi—ugh, okay, not fine," I replied, wincing and holding my side.

"Here, let me." She put a hand over my side. I felt one more sharp pain in my ribs, but then I could finally breathe again.

"Thanks. Mind if we settle up for that one later?"

"Don't worry about it," Remi said, helping me to my feet.

"I don't want to contribute to you losing control," I said.

Remi waved a hand, then paused. "I…huh. I don't think I will," she said. My brows went up. "Possibly because you already currently owe me…?" Her eyes suddenly lit up with hope. "I think I just found a way around one of my relation-ship problems."

She was bloody, battered, she'd just saved my life twice… and now she was telling me there was a way to *not* owe her for that?

Remi had very nearly never been more attractive.

Not the time! I reminded myself, too keenly aware of both the danger and the fact that I'd just told Bastien I loved him. The room shook as the circle number five, the salt circle, shattered.

Two left.

I cleared my throat, refocusing. "What do we do about the kraken in the room?"

She reshaped into her usual female form. "I've got a feeling your go-to plan of becoming its thrall isn't going to work here, so let's cross that off the list."

"I was *not* going to suggest that!"

"Had to be said. Just in case. I know it's one of your favorite moves," she replied, humor glinting in the corner of her smirk.

"Whatever it is, we're gonna need help." But our options were slim: On one end of the chamber were the remaining Council members and witches, all battered and bruised; Adele and Hilary were nowhere to be seen; Laurent, Sofia, George, and Douglas were arguing about something, gesturing at Bastien, the Archdemon, the circles; Gretchen, Isabella, and Brooke were with Lucca, the wolf prowling in front of them protectively.

At the other end, Cyrus still held a protective shield spell

up to protect himself, his cabal, and my mom. They were…
silent. All of them, other than Mom, were watching the Archdemon. They were *waiting*. Waiting for the Archdemon to be
fully free.

What was his deal? He had demonic power, he had sorcery,
and he'd clearly set all this up to free Secrets. But why? Were
they working together? For as little as I could trust Cyrus at
this point, I found it hard to believe. The seekers had viciously
attacked all of us in the clock tower, he and my mom included,
and if nothing else, his affection for and desire to protect her
seemed to be genuine. Was it just that the Archdemon was in
the way? He'd designed a ritual to draw mystical energy from
a source, but was the source the demon or the leylines?

Mom, on the other hand, was at the edge of the shield,
eyes wide and stressed and fixed on me. I lifted my hand in
acknowledgement to let her know I was okay, and she started
gesturing. She tried to keep her movements low and hidden from the others near her, making it hard to know what
she was trying to say exactly. She pointed from Cyrus to the
Archdemon, made a downward knocking gesture, and then a
pulling gesture. I shrugged my hands, shaking my head. She
kept trying, but the kraken struck the wall above us, forcing
Remi and me to run farther away from her.

"Any idea what she's trying to say?" I asked Remi.

"No, but I'm certain there's a reason she's not being more
obvious about it," Remi said.

"I need some Harwell help here." I looked for Douglas. He
was stalking away from Laurent, looking pissed, and I waved
both arms to get his attention and tapped my head.

McKenna! You're all right? he asked in my mind a moment later.

Yeah, I'm fine, but we need a—

You need to stop Laurent. He's going to kill Bastien, Douglas said.

"*What!?*" I exclaimed aloud and in my head. My eyes darted to the old man, still arguing with Sofia and George. Adele reappeared through a portal next to him, holding a book—a grimoire. *No. No, even he can't be that fucking heartless!*

He thinks the only way to stop the spell is to remove the conduit. He suggested severing first, but we don't have the time or the witches for that. He even asked me what sort of injuries would kill him but that he could still be brought back from, Douglas told me, my horror growing as he spoke. *He thinks it's the only way to keep the Archdemon from getting free.*

"What is it?" Remi asked.

"They're . . . they're gonna kill Bastien to stop the spell," I said, my voice as hollow as my chest. "To keep the demon from getting free, he . . ."

"Put the needs of the many ahead of the few? Or in this case, the one?" Remi finished for me, her voice hard. "Wow. Even I didn't think the old bastard had it in him."

I stared at Bastien, still caught in the grip of the ritual, surrounded by the shadowy power, helpless to defend or even speak up for himself. His own family, his grandfather whom he'd obeyed and listened to and worked for his entire life, was going to sacrifice him.

I saw the logic. It was hard not to. "If the Archdemon of Secrets escapes, they're going to destroy Arcadia Commons.

Whether it's today or months from now, with tentacles or secrets and infighting, they're going to tear it apart. Have everyone at each other's throats, and thralls lining up to help them do the dirty work. What's happening now will only get worse."

"It will," Remi confirmed grimly.

"Even when they were active, they were slippery and hard to find, right?" I asked; I saw her nod out of the corner of my eye.

"They were."

My fingers rapped on the handle of the knife in my hand. "Stopping the ritual is the smart thing to do. It saves lives." Remi didn't reply, but I felt her eyes on me. My eyes stayed on Bastien, memories of his smile, his hands, his kiss, his voice filling my mind. *Toi et moi. Nous.* My hand gripped the black knight chess piece on my necklace.

"All but one," she replied, and wrapped her hand around mine on the necklace.

I looked at her and saw the flicker of flames in her eyes, anger held back. I knew that whatever my choice was, she'd be with me. But we both knew that choice had already been made. "Keep that book out of Adele's hands. Whatever it is, they need it for what they're doing."

"What are you going to do?"

"Get my hands dirty."

Remi grinned darkly. "By your command, my knight." She teleported away, and I ran toward Cyrus. *Douglas, we're on it. Tell Isabella I need her over here.*

Cyrus saw me and let down the shield enough to let me in. Mom ran over and grabbed me in a tight hug.

"McKenna, I—" Cyrus started to say.

"No. I'm talking now," I interrupted. "I don't trust you, Cyrus, I don't know what your end goal is, and I'm not on your side. But right now, Bastien's life depends on taking down those last two circles, fast." I looked at his followers, noticing a few had sledgehammers and pickaxes. "Those are for the final circle, aren't they?"

Cyrus only briefly hesitated before nodding. "Powerful as it is, the Archdemon can't break through orichalcum enchanted to bind it, not without more time or spending a great deal of power."

The fact that he'd considered how much power the Archdemon would lose to that did not escape me.

"What do you mean, about Bastien?" Mom asked.

"Laurent's going to kill him to stop the spell. It's the only way to do so without Secrets getting to full power and getting free," I explained.

"No!" Mom exclaimed, and even Cyrus looked disgusted and angry, to his credit.

"We have to stop him," Cyrus said.

"Agreed. That's why I'm here. But let's be clear, once Bastien is free, my priority is containing that thing again," I replied.

"McKenna, I'm only doing what I said I would—I'm giving your mother and these people their magic back," Cyrus said.

"By giving them demonic power? That's not magic!"

"It is! You don't see it yet. I didn't at first, either. But I've been living with this power for thirty years, McKenna, and

I've learned so much. Call it magic, or power, or even glamour. They're nothing more than names and forms of mystical energy, and it's the person using them who shapes what they are, not the other way around," Cyrus said. He spoke with a passion, a confident conviction, with the voice of someone who'd experienced this, who'd learned the lessons he spoke of. It was compelling, provoking, and just the right amount of rebellious.

It was remarkably similar to how Forneus had once spoken to me, when he promised the power to change my family's fortunes. Maybe Cyrus wasn't an actual demon, but I didn't doubt his particular brand of power made his words much easier to believe in.

"Hard pass. I've heard this pitch before," I said.

Reinforcements arrived in the form of Lucca, Brooke, Gretchen, and Isabella. Looking across the room, I saw that Remi and Dara were making themselves bothersome by "accidentally" drawing the kraken's attention to the area the Council witches were in.

"Dr. Harwell caught us up. How can we help?" Isabella asked.

"Isabella, you need to help us weaken the last two circles." Bastien was her friend, too, and her earth magic specialty would help immensely, if she was willing to go against the Council.

Isabella looked nervous and scared, chewing her lower lip, but then she nodded. "Yes. I'll do it. Um, as long as I can do it from here? Please?"

"Absolutely," I assured her. I turned to the whole group.

"That will help us get past the enchantments designed to protect them from normal wear and tear. I'll weaken the binding itself, and the rest of you, do your best *Minecraft* impressions. Cyrus, Brooke, Gretchen, protect Bastien and everyone else with magic as best you can. Lucca, I assume you can handle any physical attacks?"

"Let 'em try and get through this," he boasted, thumping his chest.

"Good. Any questions?"

Brun spoke up. "What about the power Cyrus promised us?"

Karam joined her. "Yeah, we still want our magic back. Whatever form it takes, I don't care, I just don't want to live like *this* anymore."

There was a grumble of agreement with the sentiment. As much as I wanted to tell them this wasn't the time, I needed them on my side, at least for now. Besides, it wasn't their fault Cyrus had lied to them, too. They'd been hurt, and someone had promised them power. I knew too well what that was like.

"When this is over and that Archdemon is taken care of, if the Council won't try and figure out how to get your actual magic back, then I will. You have my word," I told them.

The words came out before I could think twice about them and who was hearing them. It wasn't until I felt the weight of a Promise settle on me that I remembered Brun was part Fae.

"That'll do," she said with grim satisfaction.

"Salt and chalk," I cursed under my breath. I'd meant what I'd said, but now if I failed for any reason, she could revisit it upon me threefold. And thanks to my nonspecific wording, that might mean I was bound to actually restore their magic, regardless of whether it was impossible.

One crisis at a time, Ellerbeck, I reminded myself. *But maybe stop adding to the list, too.*

Without another ill-considered word, I turned to face the center of the room. *We're coming, Bastien. I'm coming.* "Let's save our friend."

"Now!" Cyrus yelled, and dropped the shield. We surged forward, half his cabal echoing his yell. They went to work on the last two circles: diamond and orichalcum. Despite that diamond was the tougher substance, most went to the orichal-cum circle since that would be the one that was harder for the Archdemon to get through. Cyrus, Brooke, and Gretchen posted up near Bastien, while Isabella hung back and put her hands to the ground, channeling some sort of spell at the circles.

I went to the last circle, slashing cuts on both hands and putting them to the rare metal. My magic extended into it, seeking out the binding spell. Can't undo a knot if you don't know which strand to start with. And this was one of the twistiest knots I'd ever encountered. Not one binding, but several, layered on top and through one another, the golden threads of my family's binding magic woven in among a myriad of other colors: red, white, bronze, green, silver, purple, blue, black, and more. A gorgeous tapestry of magic, threaded together, working together to create something that rivaled the barrier in strength. *They worked together to make this. Not just the seven founders—there's so much magic in here!* The beauty, the complexity…part of me hated that I had to destroy such an achievement, and without any time to truly study its construction.

As I searched for a way in, a way to unravel it, there was one thing I couldn't help but notice: This spell was still going, still moving, still shaping and reshaping itself. It was a living spell, constantly refreshing, adapting. It was a magical achievement beyond any I'd studied up close. But how? How could a spell like this still be active and changing and containing an Arch-demon when it had been cast hundreds of years ago?

I followed one of the golden threads, those being easier for me to trace. But it faded, ceasing to be my family's magic and instead becoming another color. Then another…and another…and another. Other magics, too, fell out of the spell as it went—no more blues, no more greens, or reds, or silvers. As the variation lessened, so too did the cohesion of the spell. Threads were easier to pick apart, the magic weaker. *Maybe it takes time for threads to come together? Maybe the newer aspects aren't as strong from the get-go?* I wondered.

Then I reached a section that was bronze. The color of the Craig family, of Cyrus.

Not too far from that, there was at last another gold section.

This was what was being done with the severed magic. It wasn't being channeled into the leylines to strengthen them. It was being used to reinforce the binding on the Archdemon.

The floor opened up under one of my knees, and I nearly fell through a portal. I grabbed at the stone floor and rolled to the side before I could fall into what looked like a dungeon. I whipped my head up to see Laurent Lemaire approaching me.

His hands closed the portal but were poised to open another. "Miss Ellerbeck, I strongly suggest you rethink your choice of allies."

I rose to my feet, my own magic tingling throughout my body and along my fingers as my blood dripped down them. "Big words coming from someone who's trying to kill his own grandson, Laurent."

There was the slightest wince in his expression, a blink-and-miss-it twitch of his mouth before it returned to assured and stony neutrality. "Only temporarily. Only to protect this town and the rest of witchkind by maintaining the binding on that Archdemon."

"Do you ever stop spouting bullshit justifications? How is making a binding out of *severed magic* going to protect all of witchkind?" I retorted, gesturing at the orichalcum circle. "You hid this, you hid all of this! You buried the severing records in different towns, you conducted trials and severings for trumped-up charges, you severed people who didn't deserve it, who could've been shown mercy or understanding or just plain been *helped*! And don't think I didn't notice whose magic *isn't* in there!"

"That magic came from those who betrayed their fellow witches or endangered themselves and others. They were always going to lose their magic—this way they lost it to a cause that benefitted us all," Laurent replied. "Why do you think they bound the Archdemon of Secrets? Why here, in a place where three leylines meet? To *keep us safe*."

BOOM!

The room shook again, rocking even harder than before,

as the sixth circle shattered. Debris fell from the gashes the kraken had smashed into the wall, and the cabal cheered as they focused their efforts on the final circle.

I looked at him, studying the constant quiet calculation in his face. I kept his hands in my periphery, knowing he could open a portal faster than anyone. "Safe from what? More demons? *My* family's the one that's been doing that."

"No. From the rest of humanity."

"What are you talking about?"

"How do you think we maintain our secrecy?" Laurent snapped, finally raising his voice. "That thing is what protects us from being maligned and hunted and killed by the rest of the world! Our forebears came here fleeing the witch trials of Europe and America alike, and they found a solution. Harnessing the ultimate power of secrecy to protect all of us."

I wanted to be shocked. But it made sense. It all made perfect sense. From the reasons to the solution, the way they'd continued to feed the spell to keep it going…and why it was no longer working as well.

"Fine. I get why they did it, even if I don't agree with it. But what you've been doing? The way you've decided to keep it up, sacrificing the magic of the ones you've judged to be less than perfect, or useful, or desirable? That's wrong in every way."

"Think what you like, Miss Ellerbeck, but it worked."

"My name is *McKenna*, Laurent. And it hasn't worked," I told him. "The spell is weak, and you know why? Because you stopped working together on it! The older parts, they're interwoven, they're strong, because those witches worked together and willingly gave their magic to it! Makes me wonder if the barrier started that way, too." I shook my head. "All you've done is lift yourself up by pushing everyone else down, and you're making us all weaker, more vulnerable, and worse off for it!"

His lips pressed into a line, his jaw tightening. His hands had lowered to waist level, deceptively posed to look non-threatening, but I caught the movement of his fingers. "You had promise. It's why we spared you the first time. A shame you never lived up to it."

My hands clenched into fists, pain jolting from the cuts on them, fresh blood oozing over my knuckles, and I lifted my heels. I was only going to have one shot at this.

"No, Laurent. It's a shame you didn't." To my surprise, I was genuinely sad about it. He could've done so much for us, made us stronger and brought us together rather than dividing us. But he hadn't. He'd used the power given to him selfishly.

His hands jerked, rapidly tracing the circle. The blue line began to tear through the ground below me. In the same moment, I leapt to the side, over the orichalcum circle I knew he wouldn't risk interrupting. Landing and then sprinting across the last few feet between us, I slid to the ground, grabbing his leg with one hand and slapping my other hand on the circle. "*Magiam transfer!*"

Why untangle a spell when you can move it?

The threads of woven magic moved through me, tearing away from the circle and wrapping themselves around Laurent, almost as if they knew he was the one responsible for them being there in the first place. He let out a strangled yell and collapsed to his hands and knees. The last of the immense binding spell passed through me to him, and I slumped to the ground, exhausted.

His portal snapped shut, and though he gestured at me, spat spells at me, even tried to curse me, nothing happened. He stared at his hands as they shook impotently before him, and there was nothing but hate in his eyes as they moved to me. "What have you done?"

I gave him a grim smile. "Welcome to being a bound witch, Laurent."

The last circle shattered.

Chapter 22
Bargaining

The room shook as if hit by an earthquake this time, and maybe it had been. A fissure cracked through the center, bisecting the chamber with a six-foot gap, from which poured both light and shadow—though not for long.

The shadows, blue tinged, rushed through Bastien and into the kraken. Suddenly, it was huge, larger and more solid than ever, with tentacles that could circle and crush a house. They lashed out, striking the walls and raining chunks of rock that were practically boulders at us. Screams filled the air, people ran; some didn't make it. My eyes rapidly moved around the room, checking for my friends and my mom—all were safe. Cyrus had thrown another shield over himself and Mom.

"You!" Laurent snarled, lunging at me, grabbing me with both hands and shaking me, too furious for more words than that. Righteous anger or no, I at least outmatched an octogenarian in physical strength and threw him off easily.

"You wanna live to get revenge, then work with me, not against me!" I snapped. "Come on!"

Not waiting to see if he was following, I hauled ass toward the center, where Bastien had collapsed once the spell released him on my side of the fissure. Bastien was slowly sitting up, and he looked like hell, but he was alive. I crouched at his side, my arm going around him to help him up. "Are you okay?"

"As you like to say, I've been better," he groaned, holding on to me. His storm-blue eyes were tired and bloodshot. "Given our ongoing crisis, I'll manage." The room shook again as we got him to standing, another crack appearing in the floor—and this one began gushing water into the room. "We need to get out of here."

"We need to deal with that thing," I corrected him, hurriedly getting us both away from the kraken.

"Please don't make a thrall deal with it," Bastien remarked.

"Why does everyone keep saying that? I'm not going to, that is not the plan!"

"Oh?" He grunted as we reached our friends. "Then what is?"

"Admittedly, I don't exactly have one."

At this point, the witches and our friends were on one side of the crevasse in the room with Cyrus and the four remaining cabal members on the other. My mother was still with them, but I knew that was for lack of a way to safely reach us. Dara was with us but couldn't teleport the way Remi could, and Remi, well…Remi was the only reason any of us were still alive.

Remi had shapeshifted herself into a twenty-foot demonic

titan and brought the fight directly to the Archdemon of Secrets. She was every inch the devil, her skin a tough red hide, with cloven hooves for feet. She had a pair of black curling horns sprouting from her head and shredded batlike wings on her back. Her eyes blazed, and shadows coiled around her, black and red and churning like a hellish thunderstorm as she wielded the power of both mantles with the same terrifying expertise as the immense shadowblade in her hand. She was as terrifying as she was magnificent to behold.

The kraken was no slouch, however, giving as good as it got, and for every tentacle Remi lopped off, another seemed to grow in its place. The chamber shook with their battle, and for all that Remi was defending us, this place was no safer for any of us.

I shook off my awe; Remi was fighting for us, and we had to make the most of it. "We need to get my mom away from Cyrus and get everyone out of here. Between us and Remi— maybe we can force Secrets back into the Pit?" I looked at Bastien. "Think you can do it, if we work together?"

Bastien puffed out a breath. "I can try."

"That'll have to do." I turned to inform the others, only to find the other Council witches, minus Laurent and Adele, already facing us.

"We'll help," Sofia said. "We may not be Lemaires, but we can help with the portal."

"We pledged to protect this town. We're not going to leave while that thing is still here," Douglas agreed.

George added, with a significant look at Adele, "Of course, it would go much easier if Adele helped, too."

Adele, who was standing by Laurent as though guarding him, glared icily. "*Help her?* She unleashed that thing, bound my father, and put us all in danger. Why in the seven hells would I help her?"

"Because you signed that book, too. You vowed to protect this town and all of witchkind. If you can't uphold that duty, then leave this chamber and the Council now," Sofia replied, mustering all her commanding poise.

Adele gave me a long look, hatefully saying loud as day, *This isn't over.*

No, Adele. It really isn't.

"Fine. I'll help."

As they began to circle up to join their magic with ours, I felt an itch along my veins, some new demonic power in the room being used. The kraken and Remi had become a sort of mystical background noise for me at this point; this was something else. But the source was easy enough to find—Cyrus. In a clear space on the other side of the room, a piece of chalk was dancing rapidly over a clear space, his bronze magic directing it, drawing a ritual faster than any human could manage. I didn't need to see the runes to know the spell—it was his half of the ritual, the spell that would let him control where the demon's power went. He watched the battle without fear but with a hungry expression, a starving man viewing a feast. With sudden horror, I realized why: He was about to get three Archdemon mantles for the price of one. He was going to drain Remi right along with Secrets.

"Cyrus, stop!" But the chalk finished its drawing and he stepped into the circle, breathing his bronze magic out over the runes and speaking the spell. His cabal took up spots around the edge of his circle. Brun's strong hands held my mother in place beside her, the brooch glinting in the light of the leylines. Cyrus's sorcerous magic lit up the circle and lanced toward the Archdemon of Secrets.

No!

There was only one way to stop him. I pushed up my shirt and slapped my still-bloody hand over the painted runes. *"Potestas, quae liberata est, in me sumo."*

Gold threads shot out from my body, latching onto the kraken along with his. The two magics spread over it as the thing let out an unearthly screech, writhing under our warring magics. The gray shadows of its power slipped and pulled back along the threads toward us both. I felt the power hit me, filling me with a new, strange, intoxicating sort of hunger.

More. I needed *more.*

But my father's sorcery was stronger than my magic. He'd let us all tire ourselves out, fighting the kraken, protecting one another. Breaking the circle. I didn't have enough to keep him from taking it all, even pulling it back out of me.

Not unless I did the two things I really didn't want to do.

I reached for the barrier, and this time, I took it *all.* *"Per magiam maiorum meorum, per sanguinem magiam tuam ego evoco."* It wasn't whole anymore, but it was enough. The magic of my ancestors funneled to me, filling me until I felt like I might burst, and even Cyrus finally looked shaken as he saw my glowing form from across the room. Then I reached for the demonic power I'd already beckoned to me, and every bit of power that rushed to me now.

"I claim thee. I claim thee. I claim thee."

Over and over, I claimed it all, I made it mine. It fused to my magic, turning the bright-gold threads to a deep, tarnished shade. The possibilities, the potential, unspoken promises of what could be done with it blossomed within me. The unspoken secrets of the people around me filled my senses like a drug. I wanted them, I had to have them, know them, and in return, I could offer them *power.*

If not for Cyrus. I sneered. He practically *glowed* with the secrets he was hiding. This *man*, this wannabe parent, was trying to take *my* newfound power from me. *How fucking dare he.*

I lifted my arm, only a moment before he did the same. The glowing, shadowy sorcery we both wielded struck at the same time. A bronze-and-gold tug-of-war in which neither of us could gain ground. *Some father figure you turned out to be!* With that thought, the shadowed magic became a weapon in my hands, a long chain with a weighted globe at the end. A meteor hammer.

Before I could begin to wield it, a hand grabbed mine. "McKenna, stop!" Bastien urged, stepping into my line of sight. "Don't let it control you. Just let it be part of you."

My glowing eyes flicked from him to Cyrus and back. I knew he was right. "I can't let him have it."

"He's claimed his half of the power. Unless you want to kill him, you don't have a choice," Bastien said.

Dammit. He was right.

I gritted my teeth against the truth of it, and how it conflicted with the undeniable drive for more within me. "I need to stop him. He'll drain Remi next," I said. "I *need* to know what he knows, I need…"

The Archdemon wasn't quite dead yet, which meant its mantle was still up for grabs.

That was what I needed.

My full attention went back to the dwindling Archdemon, pulling more power from it, racing to the end of its supply, certain whichever of us got there first would have it. The thing was shrinking by the moment, pinned in place by Remi's shadowblade, now the size of an adult human...a child...a dog...

There. I could feel it, the core of its power, of its very being, its mantle. I knew Cyrus felt it, too, both of us redoubling our efforts, pulling with everything we had to get there first...

A blond figure darted forward, falling to her knees before the shrinking squid. "Az'glieth—you promised me!" Though she was half the room away, I heard her perfectly.

"Daraxzos..." Az'glieth, the Archdemon of Secrets, spoke its final words. "*I crown thee.*"

"NO!"

The scream came from all corners of the chamber—me, Cyrus, Remi, probably others. But with a crack like lightning, the last of the power and the mantle that went with it hit Dara, blue shadows enveloping her.

That bitch! Anger boiled inside me, but Bastien once again grabbed my hand. "We have to portal them *now.* All of them!"

My gaze swept out. Dara, Cyrus, and his cabal. Now was our chance to get them out of Arcadia Commons, at least for now.

One problem. "My mom!" Brun still held her against her will.

Bastien gave a sharp whistle. "Remi! Get Wendy!"

Remi, who had been staring, mouth agape, at Dara, snapped to attention. Looking over, she teleported to them. Without so much as a clever quip, she slugged Brun in the face and grabbed my mom as the half Fae staggered back, reappearing at our sides a moment later.

"Now!" Bastien grabbed the hand of Adele, who was next to him—the other witches had all already linked up. "*Ouvre la porte à the Pit!*"

I channeled my magic into his spell, as did the rest of us. For the second time, a blue circle ripped open on the floor, and this time, everyone on the other side fell through it. Dara, Cyrus, and his remaining cabal members plummeted into the Pit. Before it closed, the last thing I saw were my father's eyes, boring into mine, and I knew this wasn't over.

But today's skirmish certainly was. The entire chamber shuddered seismically once again. Adele whipped open another portal, this one back to the Lemaire mansion, and we all rushed through before the entire place collapsed in on itself behind us.

The Council chamber and its direct access to the leyline nexus were gone.

So was the anti-demon barrier.

And I'd just claimed roughly half the power of an Archdemon.

Chapter 23
We Need to Talk

One week later

"Got everything you need?"

"Who's the mom here, me or you?" Mom laughed. "Yes, I've got everything. And I'm going to my sister's house in Hartford, not the deep wilderness."

"Tough to be loved," I joked. Despite her protests that she had it, I helped her get her suitcase into the luggage section of the bus before she got on. "Text when you get there. And give Aunt Louisa and Aunt Alice my love. Tell them next time, I'll come with you."

"Will do. How do I look? Do I look all right?" She fussed with her shirt.

"You look great, Mom, and Louisa's just plain going to be happy to see you at all after so long," I assured her.

"Probably, but I'm still nervous. It will be nice to finally get out of town for a while, though," she said. "How about you?

You going to be okay by yourself at the house?"

"Are you forgetting our new roommate already?"

"No, and I'm sure you aren't, either," she teased. "Speaking of, good luck and let me know how that talk goes, okay? Remember, whatever happens, I'm Team McKenna, and you should be, too."

"I will." I laughed, despite that I was about as nervous for that as my mom was for seeing her sister. But both were things we knew we needed to do.

"And let me know how it goes with the Council, too. *Especially* if they give you any trouble!"

"I'm pretty sure they're ghosting me and hoping I'll take the hint at this point," I replied. "No news from them is good news." I had another project in mind where that was concerned. Mom didn't know about it yet, but I hoped that when she returned it would be far enough along for me to fill her in.

The bus driver hollered a last call, and Mom hugged me tightly. "I love you. Talk to you soon!"

"Love you, too, Mom." I lingered in the embrace. I generally didn't think of myself much of a hugger, but I was starting to reconsider. At least where certain people were concerned.

Mom grabbed her carry-on bag and boarded the bus. I stayed until they pulled out, waving at her as she went on her way. I was glad she was going, but I was more glad she'd be coming back.

Getting in my car, I headed to stop number two for the day: the Veil and Horn.

————————•————————

Trevan handed me my last paycheck. "Sorry it had to come to this, McKenna. I liked having you here, but..."

"Hard to rely on an employee who keeps showing up late or not at all. I get it." I had been neither surprised nor disappointed when Trevan fired me. The lack of disappointment *had* been a surprise, but that job wasn't for me, not really. It had been a means of getting by, that was all. Now that Mom was truly looking for a job and we had a new, if temporary, roommate who was loaded, the financial pressure was lifting. "No hard feelings, don't worry."

Trevan gave me a friendly smile. "Glad to hear it. But hey, if you want one last free drink before you go, it's all yours."

I shook my head. "No thanks. I've got a few more stops to make. Maybe next time I'm in, as a customer." We shook hands, and despite that I was being fired, I felt a sort of warmth, a centering. Like things were finally settling to the way they were meant to be. "Meanwhile, you'll think about what I said?"

"I will. It's an interesting proposal, to be sure, but it's a lot to think about," he assured me. "We'll talk soon." As I left, he headed back to the bar to continue training my replacement. "Gretchen, here's where we keep the glamour drops..."

I gave Gretchen a thumbs-up on my way out, then hopped in the car and headed over to the Luppino household, my visit carefully planned to be during Josie's nap time. Lucca let me in and was quite happy to see the bag of enormous frozen pot pies I'd brought from the store.

"Ohmigod, I could eat three of these right now, like, without even heating it up," he said. "Thanks, Mickey."

"Seriously, dude? You're giving werewolves a bad rep," Leo teased him.

Brooke came into the room, looking tired but certainly better than she had a week ago after the trial fiasco. "Lucca, if you eat those frozen, I swear, no back scritches for a month!"

Lucca pouted and gave a canine whine. "I was joking!" He hustled to put them in the freezer.

Once we were all seated, I launched into my pitch. "I know we're running on Josie's good graces of napping, so I'll get right to it: I want to form a new Council. A *better* one."

"Kinda hard to do worse than the last one," Lucca said.

"Hard agree," Leo said. "Does that mean the last one is kaput? And why are you telling us?"

"I don't know if they are, but after much digging and finally finding a copy of the original charter between supernaturals, what I *do* know is the Witches Council has seriously dropped the ball on their end. I'm telling you because by 'better' I mean one that isn't just witches. This one will have representatives from all corners of our world—werewolves, witches, Fae, demons, and humans."

Leo's brows went up. "You had my curiosity, now you have my attention."

I grinned. "Good. I've talked with a few others about this, haven't said anything to the current Council yet—"

Lucca snorted. "Are you even, like, allowed to talk to them after what happened?"

I shrugged. "They didn't officially kick me out, but I'll worry about that later. Besides, if Laurent was telling the truth about the leylines and Az'glieth being why the supernatural has remained a secret, it's only a matter of time until we can't keep that cat in the bag. We need a united front when that happens, to have each other's backs. This is *our* town, all of ours. It's been witches first for way too long."

Leo smiled. "I think you know I'm all in, Mickey. It's about damn time someone included humans in on this stuff."

Lucca nodded. "Consider the pack in, too."

Brooke smiled, too, though she had some hesitation. "I'm supportive, though I don't exactly speak for any particular group."

"I wouldn't say that, Brooke. You've been in touch with demons, wolves, and witches in ways most haven't. You're the only witch I've heard of who wants to be severed so she can become a wolf. You've got a very unique perspective to offer," I told her.

Her smile grew more confident, her green eyes sparkling, and she threw her arms around me in a tight hug.

"Oof!"

"Thank you! Tides, you're right. I guess I do," she said, releasing me.

"You're one of a kind, babe," Lucca said, kissing her eyebrow. She giggled.

Leo and I exchanged an age-old half-amused, half-sarcastic *can you believe these two?* look, and for a moment, it really did feel like old times.

That moment lasted into the next, and the next. The awkward feeling of estrangement that had swooped back so often for the last six months just...didn't.

The warmth in my chest expanded.

"One more thing, Brooke. I'm sorry we haven't been able to sever you yet. With the nexus buried, I'm not sure when we will be able to," I said. "Honestly, I've got no idea what might happen when the Council does meet again with regard to you. Are you still sure that's what you want? You did some pretty handy work with water magic at the trial."

Brooke shrugged. "It came in handy, yeah, but I know being a wolf is what I want. Since we're delayed, though, I did have a thought about that."

I'd had a feeling that would be her answer, but it was good to hear anyway. "What's that?"

"Well," Brooke said, looking at Lucca. "We talked about it, and being a wolf will always be there. Maybe in the meantime, with your new, um, sorcery, you can find a way to give my magic to someone else. Specifically, to your mom."

My brows jumped up. "Seriously?"

"Seriously. She deserves it, and…I owe it to her. It is kind of my fault she lost hers," she said, a wash of guilt coming over her.

I reached over to touch her hand. "Hey. It's not your fault. You had some part in it, but you're far from the only one. Don't take on more guilt than you need to. Trust me, I know from experience."

Brooke smiled tentatively. "I'll try not to."

The four of us chatted a little longer until Leo and I both had to go. We walked out to our cars together.

"Is the big talk up next?" Leo asked, spinning her keys on her finger.

A puff of anxiety escaped me in a sigh. "Yep."

"Whew. Kinda can't believe you're really doing this," Leo replied.

"Honestly, me neither. But gotta follow my heart…right?" It was phrased rhetorically, but with her, it was an honest question.

Leo grinned. "You absolutely do. Good luck, Mickey. Let me know how it goes."

We hugged, and I headed back home. The sun was getting low, and Remi's sleek car was already parked outside when I arrived. Vainly, I checked my hair and makeup in the rearview before going in, but I knew I was just putting it off.

Deep breath. "You can do this, Ellerbeck."

Through the garage and into the kitchen I went. Savory, mouthwatering smells of cooking filled the air, and on the island, a bottle of red wine stood next to three filled glasses. Remi was seated there, female today, sexy as ever, her black hair in bouncy waves past her shoulders, smooth legs crossed, making her short skirt even shorter. Her lips, painted a tempting red, smiled as I walked in. "There you are. Running behind, are we?"

"It's my house. That means I'm on time and you were just early," I replied. "Bastien, whatever you're cooking smells amazing."

"Ratatouille." He was wearing an apron, which looked much hotter on him than it had any right to, over his button-down short-sleeved shirt. He also had on a new pair of glasses, these ones with darker rims than his last pair, which had been crushed in the Council chamber. "And no, no rodents assisted in the process," he added, directing his answer at Remi before she could ask.

"A home-cooked meal, a bottle of wine, and cracking wise? You're getting downright comfy in here, Lemaire," Remi replied, plucking up one of the glasses. "Now that we're all here, cheers."

"Cheers," I said, taking up a glass. Bastien did the same, and we clinked and sipped. I drank perhaps a bit more deeply, trying to let the warmth of the wine calm my nerves.

Since his house had burned down and he had been very much fired by the Arcadia Commons Grand Hotel, Bastien had taken up residence in our guest bedroom. We'd all been exhausted and slightly traumatized, my mom included, so things had remained on a platonic level between the two of us for the past week. Still, there had been some lingering glances and touches. Just like there had been some flirty texts with Remi. Which is why I had planned for this talk to happen now, while Mom was gone and before things went further on any front.

"You're probably all wondering why I called this meeting..." I joked, and set my glass down. "A few reasons, though. One, we're all officially carrying around our own share of demonic power, and we all need to work on controlling and using it. Stating the obvious, I think it's a good idea if we work on that together."

"It's a sensible plan," Bastien said. "My share may be the smallest, but even that has proven risky."

Remi stretched her arms showily. "I suppose I could show you kids a few tricks," she said with a show of arrogance.

I gave her a look. "Remi. This is as much for you as both of us. Your double mantle is a problem, and your backup plan absconded with her own mantle."

Remi frowned, dropping her arms. "Fucking Dara. Do you know what showed up in my mailbox today? An apology card. With a literal postmark from the Pit! 'Sorry Remi, but I had to go with the sure thing. You understand. Kisses, Dara.'" She did a perfect imitation of Dara's overly innocent ingenue voice.

"Told you I didn't trust her."

"Yeah, yeah, you told me so, et cetera," Remi said, her voice normal again. "This is why demons get a bad reputation!" Bastien and I both gave her a look this time. "It was a joke! I'm not *that* un-self-aware." She picked up her glass. "And how is your half mantle holding up?"

"I don't have a mantle," I reminded her. *Just a boatload of sorcery boiling in me and lighting up everyone who's holding a secret like a Christmas tree...* "It's...challenging. Bindings are helping for now, but those aren't a forever solution." I pulled up my sleeve, showing her a binding rune that I had painted around my arm, using the same ink Bastien and I used for the leyline ritual spells. A matching one was on my other arm. "Second reason, you both already know about the new Council idea. Are you in?"

"You know I am. For demonic power training and your Council 2.0," Remi said. "But only if I get to be head of the social committee."

I chuckled. "Sure, it's all yours. Bastien?"

He nodded. "We've made good strides together so far. Working together on mastering it completely makes the most sense. And you already know I support the new Council idea."

Anxiety is a funny thing, because why had I really expected their answers would be any different? Still, it was nice to feel one knot of it undo, replaced by that same warmth of everything starting to feel right with the world. "Great. Cheers to that, too, then."

Once again, we clinked and drank.

"So…" Remi ran her fingers along the stem of the glass, lips pouting just slightly. "Was that all you wanted to discuss? Those two particular things?"

Bastien cleared his throat, removing the apron and setting it on the counter, hands settling in his pockets. "I admit I was wondering the same."

No backing down now. "No, there was one more thing." I set down my glass, stepping back to be able to talk to them both. "Things have been…kind of intense, recently, between me and each of you."

They each smiled at me. Bastien's was slight, intimate, meant for just me. Remi's was, of course, her damned sexy smirk. So different, but they both set my heart racing.

"And I, um…I told you, at the pool that day, that I care about you both and I want you in my life, but I didn't know what else that meant, then." They each nodded, giving me space to talk. My thumb rubbed over the scar on my left hand nervously. "I've had some time to think since then, and…I do know now. Or at least, I have a better idea, I mean, I—"

"Just say it, McKenna," Remi said, her smirk fading a bit. "Rip off the Band-Aid."

"I'm trying, I just—I don't know how you're going to take this, I barely know how *I'm* taking it," I said.

Bastien glanced at Remi, then me. "It's all right. I think I know what you're going to say, if that helps."

"You do?" I really doubted that.

"Yes." He gave me a melancholy smile. "And it's fine. I understand, and I want you to be happy. I may need some time to myself, but I won't interfere or be upset, if that's what you're thinking."

"Wait a second, Golden Boy, what are you talking about?" Remi said. "She's clearly choosing you."

"I hardly think that's the case," Bastien replied.

"Um, duh, you're the sexy, smart, and most importantly *human* one she's still crazy about," Remi replied.

"Thank you, I think? And not that it's your business exactly, but McKenna's been clear this past week that we're just friends," Bastien said.

"Hello, Archdemon of Desire here, I think I know what I'm talking about," Remi countered.

I burst out laughing. "Salt and chalk. You're both wrong! It's both of you. I want to be with *both* of you."

They both looked at me with surprise this time. Remi smiled first, a catlike expression on her face. "You're serious?"

"I am." My anxious knot had become a giddy, nervous bubble, not quite ready to burst as I looked between them. "If that's okay. I don't really know what this would look like, this is a completely new idea to me, but I..." One more deep breath. "I love you. I love both of you. In ways that are different and the same, but just as strong, and... I don't know. Maybe I want too much, but like I said, I lost so much time and I've let myself feel guilty about too many things already, and with this, with both of you... I don't want to lose more time, and I don't want to feel guilty about how I feel. So... what do you think?"

I looked nervously between the two of them. Bastien's eyes were down, his face pensive as he processed this, while Remi just grinned widely. "I told you before, you know my answer," she said.

"Yes, but it would help to actually hear it," Bastien said.

"Oh? Then yes. Obviously yes, of course yes," Remi said. She hopped down from the stool and took my hand, her warmth spreading to my skin, her eyes dark and flickering, but not with hellfire this time. "I love you, McKenna. I always have. Whatever means being with you, I'm in. I'm all in." Her eyes flicked to Bastien. "And Lemaire's growing on me, what can I say."

My heart surged to hear it, but that was only half of the equation. "What about you, Bastien? It's okay if you need more time. I can wait."

"No, I..." He took in a breath and looked up. "I care about you a lot, McKenna. More than anyone else in my life, maybe. I'm... not quite ready to say those words back to you, though. It's not about you, it's what I've been through."

I nodded, disheartened, but it was okay. Truly. It had only been six months since his life fell apart at what should've been the start of his happily ever after. "It's okay, Bastien. You don't have to say it if you're not ready."

"Thank you. That said, I think—" He paused, as though doing one last check-in with himself first. "—I'm willing to try this. See if it can work. I do know I want to be with you, if nothing else. I want us to have a chance."

"You're sure?" I asked. "I don't want you to feel like you have to. Only if you want to."

"I appreciate the clarification, but yes, I'm sure that I want to try," Bastien said, taking my other hand. His gaze met mine, and there was no storm, no clouds. Just clear skies and the warmth of his affection.

"Even if it means I'm in the picture, too?" Remi asked.

"To be clear, I'm only interested in dating McKenna," Bastien said. "But yes."

The giddiness turned into a trembling sort of happiness, and I squeezed his hand. "I'm...I'm really glad to hear that. And we can take all this slow, one day at a time, because honestly, I have no idea what I'm doing, what we're doing, I just...I know how I feel."

And how I felt, holding the hands of the two people I loved, was *amazing*.

"I think this calls for another toast," Remi said, picking up her glass.

"I could certainly use a drink," Bastien agreed.

I had to let go of their hands to reach for my glass, but just then the doorbell rang. "What timing," I grumbled. "I'll be right back."

The bell kept ringing as I crossed the house to answer. "I'm coming! Mom, if that's you, I swear to—" I pulled open the door and the words died on my tongue.

Mariposa Perez stood on my doorstep, smiling smugly at me.

"Hey, hedgebitch," she said. "We need to talk."

The story continues in...

Book THREE of the McKenna Ellerbeck Series

ACKNOWLEDGMENTS

Writing a book is hard. Writing a second book, turns out, is an exercise in extreme frustration, self-doubt, and second-guessing the likes of which I've never before encountered. Whereas for book one I could leisurely take my time over the course of some five years to write, rewrite, workshop, edit, and fine-tune the story, this was my first experience writing under a deadline. What is the same, however, is that I could not have done this without the support and help of many wonderful people!

Brandon, thank you for your love and support, being there for me to bounce ideas and titles and more off of, and being a wonderful dad, especially whenever I had to escape the house to crank out more words. And for being the first person to write fanfic of my book! Truly, the greatest honor, for both of us! Sorry your choice of title didn't get picked, but maybe next time.

Mom and Dad, like the dedication says, you're the ones who showed me and taught me what love and support look like. There was never once a time you said I should give up writing or pursuing it. While my characters often have complicated, imperfect, or outright missing parents, trust me when I say you were the opposite of all of that!

Acknowledgments

Rowan, I continue to be amazed by how you're growing, how creative you are, how funny, how talented, not to mention how sweet, kind, and considerate. I hope you never lose any of that.

Mel, thank you for the many days of sitting and writing at Restoration Coffee, or in your kitchen, or over Zoom or Discord, for always being up for helping me brainstorm, providing delicious gluten-free food, being my general BFF all-star, making sure Remi's car could actually fit three people, and, of course, being the OG founding member of Team Bastien!

Speaking of which, thanks to Restoration Coffee and Tatte Bakery for your tasty lattes and gluten-free treats, which got me through many a writing session!

The Writer's Cabal—Eve, Greg, Cindy, Mel, Henry, and Ryan—thank you for once again providing me with feedback and suggestions and guidance for this book, and a special shout-out to Henry for brainstorming and giving feedback to help me find my way through some of the trouble spots in this one along the way.

Once again, thanks to the Loons, the best Slack out there, for always being supportive and having fantastic advice and generally being awesome people all around.

Thank you to the 2024 Debut Slack, another of the best groups out there! It's meant so much to have such a great community to debut with and get to know.

My fellow OWAs: Laura, Sophia, Jasmine, Juliet, Andy, and David—you rock, and I'm so gladthat we have one another. Here's to a long and successful road ahead for all of us!

My beta readers—Joy, Sandy, Josh, Michelle, John, Allyson,

Acknowledgments

TJ, Christian, and Lucy—thanks for your time and your feedback!

Amy, Alessandra, Amr—should I call you the A-Team?—thank you for helping me translate the spells into Latin, French, and German!

Thank you to Miranda Meeks, who created the gorgeous cover art for book one, I will always treasure my first cover, you absolutely nailed McKenna and Remi and the vibe I dreamed of for that cover. Elizabeth Perio, who took over for book two's cover, thank you as well for the amazing art and capturing McKenna and Bastien perfectly as well! I am so grateful and honored to have gotten to work with such talented artists! And to Emily Lawrence, who brought McKenna and everyone else to life in the audiobook, thank you for your amazing talent in giving my characters a voice! Thank you to my agent, Brenna English-Loeb, for your continued guidance and support on this journey. I'm excited for everything ahead of us!

Thank you to Stephanie Lippitt Clark once again for choosing me and McKenna, for your insights and suggestions and support, and for making my published-author dreams real. Thank you to everyone at Orbit who worked on this book—Brit Hvide, Nick Burnham, Bryn A. McDonald, Alexia E. Pereira, Steph Hess, Maggie Curley, Ellen Wright, Oliver Wehner, Xian Lee, S. B. Kleinman, and Jeanette Shaw.

And once again, thank you, readers of this book! I don't have a cocktail recipe for you this time, but I raise my glass to you with my deepest thanks all the same. Cheers!

MEET THE AUTHOR

KATIE HALLAHAN is a fantasy author who loves tabletop RPGs, vampire TV shows, corgis, dabbling in nail art, and pumpkin spice everything. She has designed award-winning narrative adventure games at Phoenix Online Studios, an indie game studio she cofounded. She lives with her husband and son in Boston, Massachusetts, where, shockingly, she actually uses her blinker when making turns.

Find out more about Katie Hallahan and other Orbit authors by registering for the free monthly newsletter at orbitbooks.net.

RAISING READERS
Books Build Bright Futures

Thank you for reading this book and for being a reader of books in general. We are so grateful to share being part of a community of readers with you, and we hope you will join us in passing our love of books on to the next generation of readers.

Did you know that reading for enjoyment is the single biggest predictor of a child's future happiness and success?

More than family circumstances, parents' educational background, or income, reading impacts a child's future academic performance, emotional well-being, communication skills, economic security, ambition, and happiness.

Studies show that kids reading for enjoyment in the US is in rapid decline:

- In 2012, 53% of 9-year-olds read almost every day. Just 10 years later, in 2022, the number had fallen to 39%.
- In 2012, 27% of 13-year-olds read for fun daily. By 2023, that number was just 14%.

Together, we can commit to **Raising Readers** and change this trend. How?

- Read to children in your life daily.
- Model reading as a fun activity.
- Reduce screen time.
- Start a family, school, or community book club.
- Visit bookstores and libraries regularly.
- Listen to audiobooks.
- Read the book before you see the movie.
- Encourage your child to read aloud to a pet or stuffed animal.
- Give books as gifts.
- Donate books to families and communities in need.

BOB1217

Books build bright futures, and **Raising Readers** is our shared responsibility.

For more information, visit **JoinRaisingReaders.com**

Sources: National Endowment for the Arts, National Assessment of Educational Progress, WorldBookDay.com, Nielsen BookData's 2023 "Understanding the Children's Book Consumer"

Follow us:

/orbitbooksUS

/orbitbooks

/orbitbooks

Join our mailing list
to receive alerts on our
latest releases and deals.

orbitbooks.net

Enter our monthly
giveaway for the chance
to win some epic prizes.

orbitloot.com